James Thomson

Sophonisba

James Thomson

Sophonisba

ISBN/EAN: 9783743389588

Manufactured in Europe, USA, Canada, Australia, Japa

Cover: Foto ©Andreas Hilbeck / pixelio.de

Manufactured and distributed by brebook publishing software (www.brebook.com)

James Thomson

Sophonisba

B E L L's

BRITISH THEATRE.

VOLUME the EIGHTEENTH.

LONDON.
Printed for John Bell near Exeter Exchange
Strand.

BRITISH THEATRE,

Confiſting of the moſt eſteemed

ENGLISH PLAYS.

VOLUME THE EIGHTEENTH.

Being the Ninth VOLUME of TRAGEDIES.

CONTAINING

SOPHONISBA, by Mr. THOMSON.
PHILASTER, altered from BEAUMONT & FLETCHER.
VIRGINIA, by Mr. CRISP.
GUSTAVUS VASA, by HENRY BROOKE, Eſq.
ULYSSES, by N. ROWE, Eſq.

LONDON:

Printed for JOHN BELL, at the Britiſh Library, Strand.

M DCC LXXX.

Mrs BARRY in the Character of SOPHONISBA.
Assure him that I drank it, drank it all.

(3)

TO THE

Q U E E N.

MADAM,

THE notice your Majesty has condescended to take of the following tragedy, emboldens me to lay it, in the humblest manner, at your Majesty's feet. And to whom can this illustrious Carthaginian so properly fly for protection, as to a Queen, who commands the hearts of a people, more powerful at sea than Carthage, more flourishing in commerce than those first merchants, more secure against conquest, and, under a monarchy more free than a common-wealth itself.

I dare not, nor indeed need I here attempt a character, where both the great and the amiable qualities shine forth in full perfection. All words are faint to speak what is universally felt and acknowledged by a happy people. Permit me therefore only to subscribe myself, with the truest zeal and veneration,

MADAM,

Your Majesty's

Most humble,

Most dutiful, and

Most devoted servant,

JAMES THOMSON.

PRE-

PREFACE.

IT is not my intention, in this preface, to defend any
faults that may be found in the following piece. I am
afraid there are too many : but thofe who are beft able
to difcover, will be moft ready to pardon them. They
alone know how difficult an undertaking the writing of a
tragedy is : and this is a firft attempt.

I beg leave only to mention the reafon that determined
me to make choice of this fubject. What pleafed me
particularly, tho' perhaps it will not be leaft liable to ob-
jection with ordinary readers, was the great fimplicity of
the ftory. It is one, regular, and uniform, not charged
with a multiplicity of incidents, and yet affording feveral
revolutions of fortune ; by which the paffions may be
excited, varied, and driven to their full tumult of emotion.

This unity of defign was always fought after, and ad-
mired by the antients : and the moft eminent among the
moderns, who underftood their writings, have chofen to
imitate them in this, from an intire conviction that the
reafon of it muft hold good in all ages. And here allow
me to tranflate a paffage from the celebrated Monfieur
Racine, which contains all that I have to fay on this
head.

‘ We muft not fancy that this rule has no other foun-
‘ dation but the caprice of thofe who made it. Nothing
‘ can touch us in tragedy, but what is probable. And
‘ what probability is there, that, in one day, fhould hap-
‘ pen a multitude of things, which could fcarce happen in
‘ feveral weeks ? There are fome who think that this
‘ fimplicity is a mark of barrennefs of invention. But
‘ they do not confider, that, on the contrary, invention
‘ confifts in making fomething out of nothing : and that
‘ this huddle of incidents has always been the refuge of
‘ poets, who did not find in their genius either richnefs

‘ or

' or force enough to engage their fpectators, for five acts
' together, by a fimple action, fupported by the violence
' of paffions, the beauty of fentiments, and the noblenefs
' of expreffion.'—I would not be underftood to mean that
all thefe things are to be found in my performance: I
only fhew the reader what I aimed at, and how I would
have pleafed him, had it been in my power.

As to the character of Sophonifba; in drawing it, I
have confined myfelf to the truth of hiftory. It were an
affront to the age, to fuppofe fuch a character out of nature; efpecially in a country which has produced fo
many great examples of public fpirit and heroic virtues,
even in the fofter fex: and I had deftroyed her character
intirely, had I not marked it with that ftrong love to her
country, difdain of fervitude, and inborn averfion to the
Romans, by which all hiftorians have diftinguifhed her.
Nor ought her marrying Mafiniffa, while her former hufband was ftill alive, to be reckoned a blemifh in her character. For, by the laws both of Rome and Carthage,
the captivity of the hufband diffolved the marriage of
courfe; as among us impotence, or adultery: not to
mention the reafons of a moral and public nature, which
I have put into her own mouth in the fcene between her
and Syphax.

This is all I have to fay of the play itfelf. But I cannot conclude without owning my obligations to thofe
concerned in the reprefentation. They have indeed done
me more than juftice. Whatever was defigned as amiable
and engaging in Mafiniffa fhines out in Mr. Wilks's
action. Mrs. Oldfield, in the character of Sophonifba,
has excelled what, even in the fondnefs of an author, I
could either wifh or imagine. The grace, dignity, and
happy variety of her action have been univerfally ap-
plauded, and are truly admirable.

P R O.

PROLOGUE.

By a FRIEND.

WHEN learning, after the long Gothic night,
   Fair, o'er the western world, renew'd his light,
With arts arising Sophonisba rose:
The tragic muse, returning, wept her woes.
With her th' Italian scene first learnt to glow:
And the first tears for her were taught to flow.
Her charms the Gallic muses next inspir'd:
Corneille himself saw, wonder'd, and was fir'd.
   What foreign theatres with pride have shewn,
Britain, by juster title, makes her own.
When freedom is the cause, 'tis hers to fight;
And hers, when freedom is the theme, to write.
For this, a British author bids again
The heroine rise, to grace the British scene.
Here, as in life, she breathes her genuine flame:
She asks what bosom has not felt the same?
Asks of the British youth——Is silence there?
She dares to ask it of the British fair.
   To—night, our home-spun author would be true,
At once, to nature, history, and you.
Well-pleas'd to give our neighbours due applause,
He owns their learning, but disdains their laws.
Not to his patient touch, or happy flame;
'Tis to his British heart he trusts for fame.
If France excel him in one free-born thought,
The man, as well as poet, is in fault.
   Nature! informer of the poet's art,
Whose force alone can raise or melt the heart,
Thou art his guide; each passion, every line,
Whate'er he draws to please, must all be thine.
Be thou his judge: in every candid breast,
Thy silent whisper is the sacred test.

D R A.

DRAMATIS PERSONÆ.

M E N.

Mafiniffa, King of *Maffylia*.
Syphax, King of *Mafæfylia*.
Narva, friend to *Mafiniffa*.
Scipio, the *Roman* General.
Lælius, his Lieutenant.

W O M E N.

Sophonifba, —————— Mrs. Barry.
Phænifa, her Friend.

Meffenger, Slave, Guards and Attendants.

S C E N E, The Palace of *C I R T H A*.

SOPHO.

SOPHONISBA.

ACT I.

Enter Sophonisba *and* Phœnissa.

SOPHONISBA.

THIS hour, Phœnissa, this important hour,
    Or fixes me a queen, or from a throne
Throws Sophonisba into Roman chains.
Detested thought! For now his utmost force
Collected, desperate, distress'd, and sore
From battles lost; with all the rage of war,
Ill-fated Syphax makes his last effort.
But say, thou partner of my hopes and fears,
Phœnissa, say; while, from the lofty tower,
Our straining eyes the field of battle fought,
Ah, thought you not that our Numidian troops
Gave up the broken field, and scattering fled,
Wild o'er the hills, from the rapacious sons
Of still triumphant Rome?
    Phœn. The dream of care!
And think not, Madam, Syphax can resign,
But with his ebbing life, in this last field,
A crown, a kingdom, and a queen he loves
Beyond ambition's brightest wish; for whom,
Nor mov'd by threats, nor bound by plighted faith,
He scorn'd the Roman friendship (that fair name
For slavery) and from th' engagements broke
Of Scipio, fam'd for every winning art,
The towering genius of recover'd Rome.
    Soph. Oh, name him not! These Romans stir my blood
To too much rage. I cannot bear the fortune
Of that proud people.——Said you not, Phœnissa,
That Syphax lov'd me; which would fire his battle,
And urge him on to death or conquest? True,

He

He loves me with the madness of desire ;
His every passion is a slave to love ;
Nor heeds he danger where I bid him go,
Nor leagues nor interest. Hence these endless wars,
These ravag'd countries, these successless fights,
Sustain'd for Carthage ; whose defence alone
Engag'd my loveless marriage-vows with his.
But know you not, that in the Roman camp
I have a lover too ; a gallant, brave,
And disappointed lover, full of wrath,
Returning to a kingdom whence the sword
Of Syphax drove him ?
   Phœn. Masinissa ?
   Soph. He :
Young Masinissa, the Massylian King,
The first addresser of my youth ; for whom
My bosom felt a fond beginning wish,
Extinguish'd soon : when once to Scipio's side
Won o'er, and dazzled by th' enchanting glare
Of that fair seeming hero, he became
A gay admiring slave, yet knew it not.
E'er since, my heart has held him in contempt ;
And thrown out each idea of his worth,
That there began to grow : nay had it been
As all-possest, and soft, as hers who sits
In secret shades, or by the falling stream,
And wastes her being in unutter'd pangs,
I would have broke, or cur'd it of its fondness.
   Phœn. Heroic Sophonisba !
   Soph. No, Phœnissa ;
It is not for the daughter of great Asdrubal,
Descended from a long illustrious line
Of Carthaginian heroes, who have oft
Fill'd Italy with terror and dismay,
And shook the walls of Rome, to pine in love,
Like a deluded maid ; to give her life,
And heart high-beating in her country's cause,
Meant not for common aims and houshold cares,
To give them up to vain presuming man ;
Much less to one who stoops the neck to Rome,
An enemy to Carthage, Masinissa.

                           Phœn.

Phœn. Think not I mean to check that glorious flame,
That juſt ambition which exalts your ſoul,
Fires on your cheek, and lightens in your eye.
Yet would he had been yours! this riſing prince;
For, truſt me, fame is fond of Maſiniſſa.
His various fortune, his reſplendent deeds,
His courage, conduct, deep-experienc'd youth,
And vaſt unbroken ſpirit in diſtreſs,
Still riſing ſtronger from the laſt defeat.
Are all the talk and terror too of Afric.
Who has not heard the ſtory of his woes!
How hard he came to his paternal reign;
Whence ſoon by Syphax' unrelenting hate,
And jealous Carthage driven, he with a few
Fled to the mountains. Then, I think, it was,
Hem'd in a circle of impending rocks,
That all his followers fell, ſave fifty horſe;
Who, thence eſcap'd, thro' ſecret paths abrupt,
Gain'd the Clupean plain. There overtook,
And urg'd by fierce ſurrounding foes, he burſt
With four alone, ſore-wounded, thro' their ranks,
And all amidſt a mighty torrent plung'd.
Seiz'd by the whirling gulph, two ſunk; and two,
With him, obliquely hurried down the ſtream,
Wrought to the farther ſhore. Th' aſtoniſh'd troops
Stood check'd, and ſhivering on the gloomy brink,
And deem'd him loſt in the devouring flood.
Mean time the dauntleſs, undeſpairing youth
Lay in a cave conceal'd; curing his wounds
With mountain-herbs, and on his horſes fed:
Nor here, even at the loweſt ebb of life,
Stoop'd his aſpiring mind. What need I ſay,
How once again reſtor'd, and once again
Expell'd, among the Garamantian hills
He ſince has wander'd, till the Roman arm
Reviv'd his cauſe? And who ſhall reign alone,
Syphax or he, this day decides.
    Soph. Enough.
Thou need'ſt not blazon thus his fame, Phœniſſa.
Were he as glorious as the pride of woman
Could wiſh, in all her wantonneſs of thought;
The joy of human kind: wiſe, valiant, good;

With every praife, with every laurel crown'_;
The warrior's wonder, and the virgin's figh:
Yet this would cloud him o'er, this blemifh all;
His mean fubmiffion to the Roman yoke;
That, falfe to Carthage, Afric, and himfelf,
With proffer'd hand and knee, he hither led
Thefe ravagers of earth.——But while we talk,
The work of fate goes on; even now perhaps
My dying country bleeds in every vein,
And the warm victor thunders at our gate.

Enter a Meffenger *from the battle.*

Soph. Ha! Whence art thou? Speak, tho' thy bleed-
Might well excufe thy tongue.   [ing wounds
    Meff. Madam, efcap'd,
With much ado, from yon wide death—
    Soph. No more.
At once thy meaning flafhes o'er my foul.
Oh, all my vanifh'd hopes! Repairlefs chance
Of undifcerning war!——And is all loft?
An univerfal havock?
    Meff. Madam, all.
For fcarce a Mafæfylian, fave myfelf,
But is or feiz'd, or bites the bloody plain.
The King——
    Soph. Ah! what of him?
    Meff. His fiery fteed,
By Mafiniffa, the Maffylian prince,
Pierc'd, threw him headlong to his cluftering foes;
And now he comes in chains.
    Soph. 'Tis wond'rous fit,
Abfolute gods! All Afric is in chains!
The weeping world in chains! Oh, is there not
A time, a righteous time, referv'd in fate,
When thefe oppreffors of mankind fhall feel
The miferies they give; and blindly fight
For their own fetters too?—The conquering troops,
How points their motion?
    Meff. At my heels they came,
Loud-fhouting, dreadful, in a cloud of duft,
By Mafiniffa headed.   [Shou'.

Soph. Hark! arrived.
The murm'ring crowd rolls frighted to the palace.
Thou bleed'ft to death, poor faithful wretch; away,
And drefs thy wounds, if life be worth thy care:
Though Rome, methinks, will lofe a flave in thee.
Would Sophonifba were as near the verge   [*Exit Meff.*
Of boundlefs, and immortal liberty!   [*Paufes.*
And wherefore not? When liberty is loft,
Let flaves and cowards live; but in the brave
It were a treachery to themfelves, enough
To merit chains.   And is it fit for me,
Who in my veins, from Afdrubal deriv'd,
Hold Carthaginian enmity to Rome;
On whom I've lavifh'd all my burning foul,
In everlafting hate; for whofe deftruction
I fold my joylefs youth to Syphax' arms,
And turn'd him fierce upon them; fit for fuch
A native, reftlefs, unrelenting foe,
To fit down foftly-penfive, and await
Th' approaching victor's rage; referv'd in chains
To grace his triumph, and become the fcorn
Of every Roman dame—Gods! how my foul
Difdains the thought! and this fhall fet it free.
                              [*Offers to ftab herfelf.*
Phœn. Hold, Sophonifba, hold! my friend! my queen!
For whom alone I live! hold your rafh point,
Nor through your guardian bofom ftab your country.
That is our laft refort, and always fure.
The gracious gods are liberal of death;
To that laft bleffing lend a thoufand ways.
Think not I'd have you live to drag a chain,
And walk the triumph of infulting Rome.
No, by thefe tears of loyalty and love,
Ere I beheld fo vile a fight, this hand
Should urge the faithful poniard to your heart,
And glory in the deed.   But, while hope lives,
Let not the generous die.   'Tis late before
The brave defpair.
    Soph. Thou copy of my foul!
And now my friend indeed! Shew me but hope,
One glimpfe of hope, and I'll renew my toils,
Call patience, labour, fortitude again,

B

The

The next unjoyous day, and sleepless night;
Nor shrink at danger, any shape of death,
Shew me the smallest hope! Alas, Phœnissa,
Too kindly confident! Hope lives not here,
Fled with her sister Liberty beyond
The Garamantian hills, to some steep wild, ,
Some undiscover'd country, where the foot
Of Roman cannot come.
    Phœn. Yes, there she liv'd
With Masinissa wounded, and forlorn,
Amidst the serpent's hiss, and tiger's yell.—
    Soph. Why nam'st thou him?
    Phœn. Madam, in this forgive
My forward zeal; from him proceeds our hope.
He lov'd you once; nor is your form impair'd,
Warm'd, and unfolded into stronger charms:
Ask his protection from the Roman power,
You must prevail; for Sophonisba sure
From Masinissa cannot ask in vain.
    Soph. Now, by the prompting genius of my country!
I thank thee for the thought. True, there is pain
Ev'n in descending thus to beg protection
From that degenerate youth. But, Oh, for thee,
My sinking country! and again to gaul
This hated Rome, what would I not endure?
It shall be done, Phœnissa; though disgust
Choak'd up my struggling meaning, shall be done.
                                        [*Kneels.*

But here I vow, propitious Juno, hear!
Could every pomp and every pleasure join'd,
Love, empire, glory, a whole kneeling world,
Unnerve my smallest purpose, and remit
That most inveterate enmity I bear
The Roman state; may Carthage smoak in ruins!
Rome rise the mistress of mankind! and I,
There an abandon'd slave, drag out a length
Of life, in loathsome baseness and contempt!
This way the trumpet sounds; let us retire.   [*Exeunt.*
    Enter Masinissa, Syphax *in chains,* Narva, *Guards,* &c.
    Syph. Is there no dungeon in this city, dark
- As is my troubled soul, that thus I'm brought
To my own palace, to those rooms of state,
            2   Wont

Wont in another manner to receive me,
With other signs of royalty than these?

[Looking on his chains.

   Maf. I will not wound thee, nor infult thee, Syphax,
With a recital of thy tyrant crimes.
A captive here I fee thee, fallen below
My moft revengeful wifh; and all the rage,
The noble fury that infpir'd this morn,
Is funk to foft compaffion.   In the field,
The flaming front of war, there is the fcene
Of brave revenge; and I have fought thee there,
Keen as the hunted lion feeks his foe.
But when a broken enemy, difarm'd,
And helplefs lies; a falling fword, an eye
With pity flowing, and an arm as weak
As infant foftnefs, then becomes the brave.
Now fleeps the fword; the paffions of the field
Subfide to peace; and my relenting foul
Melts at thy fate.
   Syph. This, this, is all I dread,
All I deteft, this infolence refin'd,
This barbarous pity, this affected goodnefs.
Pitied by thee!————Is there a form of death,
Of torture, and of infamy like that?
It kills my very foul!——Ye partial gods!
I feel your worft; why fhould I fear you more?
Hear me, vain youth! take notice——I abhor
Thy mercy, loath it.——Poifon to my thoughts!
Wouldft thou be merciful? One way alone
Thou canft oblige me.—Ufe me like a flave;
As I would thee, (delicious thought!) wert thou
Here crouching in my power.
   Maf. Outrageous man!
If that is mercy, I'll be cruel ftill.
Nor canft thou drive me, by thy bittereft rage,
To an unmanly deed; not all thy wrongs,
Nor this worfe triumph in them.
   Syph. Ha! ha! wrongs?
I cannot wrong thee.   When we lanch the fpear
Into the monfter's heart, or crufh the ferpent;
Deftroy what in antipathy we hold,

B 2

The

The common foe ; can that be call'd a wrong ?
Injurious that ? Abfurd ! it cannot be.
  Maf. I'm loth to hurt thee more.—The tyrant works
Too fierce already in thy rankled breaft.
But fince thou feem'ft to rank me with thyfelf,
With great deftroyers, with perfidious kings ; .
I muft reply to thy licentious tongue,
Bid thee remember, whofe accurfed fword
Began this work of death ; who broke the ties,
The holy ties, attefted by the gods,
Which bind the nations in the bond of peace ;
Who meanly took advantage of my youth,
Unfkill'd in arms, unfettled on my throne,
And drove me to the defart, there to dwell
With kinder monfters ; who my cities fack'd,
My country pillag'd, and my fubjects murder'd ;
Who ftill purfu'd me with inveterate hate,
When generous force prov'd vain, with ruffian arts,
The villain's dagger, bafe affaffination ;
And for no reafon all.   Brute violence
Alone thy plea.—What the leaft provocation,
Say, canft thou but pretend ?
  Syph. I needed none.
Nature has in my being fown the feeds
Of enmity to thine. ——Nay, mark me this ;
Couldft thou reftore me to my former ftate,
Strike off thefe chains, give me the fword again,
The fceptre, and the wide-obedient war :
Yet muft I ftill, implacable to thee,
Seek eagerly thy death, or die myfelf.
Life cannot hold us both !——Unequal gods ! ,
Who love to difappoint mankind, and take
All vengeance to yourfelves ; why to the point
Of my long-flatter'd wifhes did ye lift me,
Then fink me thus fo low ? Juft as I drew
The glorious ftroke that was to make me happy,
Why did you blaft my ftrong extended arm ?
Strike the dry fword unfated to the ground ?
But that to mock us is your cruel fport ?
What elfe is human life ?
  Maf. Thus always join'd
With an inhuman heart, and brutal manners,

Is irreligion to the ruling gods;
Whofe fchemes our peevifh ignorance arraigns,
Our thoughtlefs pride.——Thy loft condition, Syphax,
Is nothing to the tumult of thy breaft.
There lies the fting of evil, there the drop
That poifons nature.—Ye myfterious powers
Whofe ways are ever-gracious, ever-juft,
As ye think wifeft, beft, difpofe of me;
But, whether thro' your gloomy depths I wander,
Or on your mountains walk; give me the calm
The fteady, fmiling foul; where wifdom fheds,
Eternal funfhine and eternal joy.
Then, if misfortune comes, fhe brings along
The braveft virtues. And fo many great
Illuftrious fpirits have convers'd with woe,
(The pride of adverfe fate!) as are enough
To confecrate diftrefs, and make even death
Ambition.

Syph. Torture! Racks! The common trick
Of infolent fuccefs, unfuffering pride,
This prate of patience, and I know not what.
'Tis all a lie, impracticable rant;
And only tends to make me fcorn thee more.
But why this talk? In mercy fend me hence;
Yet—ere I go—Oh, fave me from diftraction!
I know, hot youth, thou burneft for my queen;
But, by the majefty of ruin'd kings,
And that commanding glory which furrounds her,
I charge thee, touch her not!

Maf. No, Syphax, no.
Thou need'ft not charge me. That were mean indeed,
A triumph that to thee. But could I ftoop
Again to love her; Thou, what right haft thou,
A captive to her bed? Nor life, nor queen,
Nor ought a captive has. All laws in this,
Roman and Carthaginian, all agree.

Syph. Here, here, begins the bitternefs of death!
Here my chains grind me firft!

Maf. Poor Sophonifba!
She too becomes the prize of conquering Rome;
What moft her heart abhors. Alas, how hard
Will flavery fit on her exalted foul!

 How

How piteous hard! But, if I know her well,
She never will endure it, she will die.
For not a Roman burns with nobler ardor,
A higher sense of liberty, than she;
And tho' she marry'd thee, her only stain,
False to my youth, and faithless to my vows;
Yet I must own it, from a worthy cause,
From public spirit, did her fault proceed.

   Syph. Blue plagues, and poison on thy meddling tongue!
Talk not of her; for every word of her
Is a keen dagger, grinding thro' my heart.
Oh, for a lonely dungeon! where I rather
Would talk with my own groans, and great revenge,
Than in the mansions of the blest with thee.
Hell! Whither must I go?

   Maf. Unhappy man!
And is thy breast determin'd against peace,
On comfort shut?

   Syph. On all, but death, from thee.

   Maf. Narva, be Syphax thy peculiar care;
And use him well with tenderness and honour.
This evening Lælius, and to morrow Scipio,
To Cirtha come.   Then let the Romans take
Their prisoner.

   Syph. There shines a gleam of hope
Acrofs the gloom—From thee deliver'd!—Ease [lighter!
Breathes in that thought—Lead on—My heart grows
          Mafinissa alone.   [*Exeunt.*

   Maf. What dreadful havoc in the human breast
The passions make, when unconfin'd, and mad,
They burst unguided by the mental eye,
The light of reason; which in various ways
Points them to good, or turns them back from ill.
O save me from the tumult of the soul!
From the wild beasts within!——For circling sands,
When the swift whirlwind whelms them o'er the lands;
The roaring deeps that to the clouds arise,
While thwarting thick the mingled lightning flies;
The monster-brood to which this land gives birth,
The blazing city, and the gaping earth;
All deaths, all tortures, in one pang combin'd,
Are gentle to the tempest of the mind.   [*Exit.*
      END of the FIRST ACT.

A C T II.

Enter Mafiniſſa *and* Narva.

MASINISSA.

'TIS true, my friend,   [form'd,
    Thou good old man, by whom my youth was
The firm companion of my various life,
I own, 'tis true, that Sophoniſba's image
Lives in my boſom ſtill ; and at each glance
I take in ſecret of the bright idea,
A ſtrange diſorder ſeizes on my ſoul,
Which burns with ſtronger glory.   Need I ſay,
How once ſhe had my vows ? 'Till Scipio came,
Reſiſtleſs man ! like a deſcending god,
And ſnatch'd me from the Carthaginian ſide
To nobler Rome; beneath whoſe laurel'd brow,
And ample eye, the nations grow polite,
Humane and happy.   Then thou may'ſt remember,
Such is this woman's high impetuous ſpirit,
That all-controuling love ſhe bears her country,
Her Carthage ; that at this ſhe ſacrific'd
To Syphax, unbelov'd, her blooming years,
And won him off from Rome.
   Nar. My generous prince !
Applauding Afric of thy choice approves.
Fame claps her wings, and virtue ſmiles on thee,
Of peace thou ſoft'ner, and thou ſoul of war !
But Oh, beware of that fair foe to glory,
Woman ! and moſt of Carthaginian woman !
Who has not heard of fatal Punic guile ?
Of their ſly conqueſts ? their inſidious leagues ?
Their Aſdrubals ? their Hannibals? with all
Their wily heroes ? And, if ſuch their men,
What muſt their women be ?
   Maſ. You make me ſmile.
I thank thy honeſt zeal.   But never dread
The firmneſs of my heart, my ſtrong attachment,

                          Severe

Severe to Rome, to Scipio, and to glory.
Indeed, I cannot, would not quite forget
The grace of Sophonisba; how she look'd,
And talk'd, and mov'd, a Pallas, or a Juno!
Accomplish'd even in trifles, when she stopp'd
'Ambition's flight, and with a soften'd eye
Gave her quick spirit into gayer life,
Then every word was liveliness, and wit;
We heard the Muses' song; and the dance swam
Thro' all the maze of harmony. I flatter not,
Believe me, Narva; yet my panting soul,
To Scipio taken in the fair pursuit
Of fame, and for my people's happiness,
Resign'd this Sophonisba; and tho' now
Constrain'd by soft necessity to see her,
And she a captive in my power, will still
Resign her.

   Nar. Let me not doubt thy fortitude,
My Masinissa, thy exalted purpose
Not to be lost in love; but, ah! we know not,
Oft, till experience sighs it to the soul,
The boundless witchcraft of ensnaring woman,
And our own slippery hearts. From Scipio learn
The temperance of heroes. I'll recount
Th' instructive story, what these eyes beheld;
Perhaps you've heard it; but 'tis pleasing still,
Tho' told a thousand times.

   Maf. I burn to hear it.
Lost by my late misfortunes in the desart,
I liv'd a stranger to the voice of fame,
To Scipio's last exploits. Exalt me now.
Great actions raise the mind. But when a friend,
A Scipio does them; then with more than wonder,
Even with a sort of vanity we listen.

   Nar. When to his glorious, first essay in war,
New Carthage fell; there all the flower of Spain
Were kept in hostage; a full field presenting
For Scipio's generosity to shine.
And then it was, that when the hero heard
How I to thee belong'd, he with large gifts,
And friendly words dismiss'd me.

Maf.

Maf. I remember.
And in his favour that imprefs'd me firft.
But to thy ftory.
      Nar. What with admiration
Struck every heart, was this—A noble virgin,
Confpicuous far o'er all the captive dames,
Was mark'd the General's prize. She wept, and blufh'd,
Young, frefh, and blooming like the morn.   An eye,
As when the blue fky trembles thro' a cloud
Of pureft white.   A fecret charm combin'd
Her features, and infus'd enchantment thro' them.
Her fhape was harmony.————But eloquence
Beneath her beauty fails ; which feem'd, on purpofe,
Pour'd out by lavifh nature, that mankind
Might fee this action in its higheft luftre.
Soft, as fhe pafs'd along, with downcaft eyes,
Where gentle forrow fwell'd, and now and then
Dropt o'er her modeft cheek a trickling tear ;
The Roman legions languifh'd ; and hard war
Felt more than pity.   Even Scipio's felf,
As on his high tribunal rais'd he fat,
Turn'd from the piercing fight, and chiding afk'd
His officers, if by this gift they meent
To cloud his glory in its very dawn.
      Maf. Oh, gods ! my fluttering heart ! On, ftop not, Narva.
      Nar. She queftion'd of her birth, in trembling accents,
With tears and blufhes broken, told her tale.
But when he found her royally defcended,
Of her old captive parents the fole joy ;
And that a haplefs Celtiberian prince,
Her lover and belov'd, forgot his chains,
His loft dominions, and for her alone
Wept out his tender foul ; fudden the heart
Of this young, conquering, loving, godlike Roman
Felt all the great divinity of virtue :
His wifhing youth ftood check'd, his tempting power,
By infinite humanity —————
      Maf. Well, well ;
And then !
      Nar. Difdaining guilty doubt, at once
He for her parents and her lover call'd.

The

The various scene imagine : how his troops
Look'd dubious on, and wonder'd what he meant ;
While stretch'd below the trembling suppliants lay,
Rack'd by a thousand mingling passions, fear,
Hope, jealousy, disdain, submission, grief,
Anxiety, and love in every shape.
To these as different sentiments succeeded,
As mixt emotions, when the man divine
Thus the dread silence to the lover broke.
We both are young, both charm'd. The right of war
Has put thy beauteous mistress in my power ;
With whom I could, in the most sacred ties,
Live out a happy life : but know that Romans
Their hearts as well as enemies can conquer.
Then take her to thy soul ; and with her take
Thy liberty and kingdom. In return
I ask but this.   When you behold these eyes,
These charms, with transport ; be a friend to Rome.
   Mas. There spoke the soul of Scipio—But the lovers—
   Nar. Joy and extatic wonder held them mute ;
While the loud camp, and all the clust'ring crowd,
That hung around, rang with repeated shouts.
Fame took th' alarm, and thro' resounding Spain
Blew fast the fair report : which, more than arms,
Admiring nations to the Romans gain'd.
   Mas. My friend in glory ! thy awaken'd prince
Springs at thy faithful tale.   It fires my soul,
And nerves each thought anew ; apt oft perhaps,
Too much, too much to slacken into love.
But now the soft oppression flies ; and all
My mounting powers expand to deeds like thine,
Thou pattern and inspirer of my fame,
Scipio, thou first of men, and best of friends !
What man of soul would live, my Narva, breathe
This idle-puffing element ; and run,
Day after day, the still-returning round
Of life's mean offices, and sickly joys;
But in compassion to mankind ? to be
A guardian god below? to dissipate
An ardent being in heroic aims ?
Do something vastly great like what you told ?
Something to raise him o'er the groveling herd.

And

And make him ſhine for ever ?——Oh, my friend !
Bleed every vein about me ; every nerve
With anguiſh tremble ; every ſinew ake ;
Be toil familiar to my limbs; ambition
Mix all my thoughts in an inceſſant whirl ;
The third time may I loſe my kingdom ; and again
Wander the falſe inhoſpitable Syrts ;
Yet Oh, ye liberal gods ! in rich award,
And ampleſt recompence——I aſk no more——
Share me the wreath of fame from Scipio's brow !
But ſee, ſhe comes ! mark her majeſtic port.
       Enter Sophoniſba *and* Phœniſſa.
    Soph. Behold, victorious prince ! the ſcene revers'd ;
And Sophoniſba kneeling here ; a captive,
O'er whom the gods, thy fortune, and thy virtue,
Have given unqueſtion'd power of life and death.
If ſuch a one may raiſe her ſuppliant voice,
Once muſic to thy ear ; if ſhe may touch
Thy knee, thy purple, and thy victor-hand ;
Oh, liſten, Maſiniſſa ! Let thy ſoul
Intenſely liſten ! While I fervent pray,
And ſtrong adjure thee, by that regal ſtate,
In which with equal pomp we lately ſhone !
By the Numidian name, our common boaſt !
And by thoſe houſhold gods ! who may, I wiſh,
With better omens take thee to this palace,
Than Syphax hence they ſent.   As is thy pleaſure,
In all beſide, determine of my fate.
This, this alone I beg.   Never, Oh, never !
Into the cruel, proud, and hated power
Of Romans let me fall.   Since angry heaven
Will have it ſo, that I muſt be a ſlave,
And that a galling chain muſt bind theſe hands ;
It were ſome little ſoftening in my doom,
To call a kindred ſon of the ſame clime,
A native of Numidia, my lord.
But if thou canſt not ſave me from the Romans,
If this ſad favour be beyond thy power ;
At leaſt to give me death is what thou canſt.
Here ſtrike——My naked boſom courts thy ſword ;
And my laſt breath ſhall bleſs thee, Maſiniſſa !

                                        Maſ.

Maſ. Riſe, Sophoniſba, riſe.   To ſee thee thus
Is a revenge I ſcorn; and all the man
Within me, though much injur'd by thy pride,
And ſpirit too tempeſtuous for thy ſex,
Yet bluſhes to behold thus at my feet,
Thus proſtrate low, her, for whom kings have kneel'd,
The faireſt, but the falſeſt of her ſex.

Soph. Spare thy reproach——'Tis cruel thus to loſe
In rankling diſcord, and ungenerous ſtrife,
The few remaining moments that divide me
From the laſt evil, bondage—Roman bondage!
Yes, ſhut thy heart againſt me; ſhut thy heart
Againſt compaſſion, every human thought,
Even recollected love: yet know, raſh youth!
That when thou ſeeſt me ſwell their lofty triumph,
Thou ſeeſt thyſelf in me.   This is my day;
To morrow may be thine.   But here, aſſur'd,
Here will I lie on this vile earth, forlorn,
Of hope abandon'd, ſince deſpis'd by thee;
Theſe locks all looſe and ſordid in the duſt;
This ſullied boſom growing to the ground,
Scorch'd up with anguiſh, and of every ſhape
Of miſery full: till comes the ſoldier fierce
From recent blood; and, in thy very eye,
Lays raging his rude ſanguinary graſp
On theſe weak limbs; and clinches them in chains.
Then if no friendly ſteel, no nectar'd draught
Of deadly poiſon, can enlarge my ſoul;
It will indignant burſt from a ſlave's body;
And, join'd to mighty Dido, ſcorn ye all.

Maſ. Oh, Sophoniſba! 'tis not ſafe to hear thee;
And I miſtook my heart, to truſt it thus.
Hence, let me fly.

Soph. You ſhall not, Maſiniſſa!
Here will I hold you, tremble here for ever;
Here unremitting grow, till you conſent.
And can'ſt thou think, Oh! canſt thou think to leave me?
Expos'd, defenceleſs, wretched, here alone?
A prey to Romans fluſh'd with blood and conqueſt?
The ſubject of their ſcorn or baſer love?
Sure Maſiniſſa cannot; and, tho' chang'd,
Tho' cold as that averted look he wears;

Sure

Sure love can ne'er in generous breafts be loft
To that degree, as not from fhame and outrage
To fave what once they lov'd.
    Maf. Enchantment! Madnefs!
What wouldft thou, Sophonifba?——Oh, my heart!
My treacherous heart!
    Soph. What would I, Mafiniffa?
My mean requeft fits blufhing on my cheek,
To be thy flave, young Prince, is what I beg;
Here Sophonifba kneels to be thy flave;
Yet kneels in vain.   But thou'rt a flave thyfelf,
And canft not from the Romans fave one woman;
Her, who was once the triumph of thy foul,
Ere they feduc'd it by their lying glory.
Immortal gods! and am I fallen fo low?
Scorn'd by a lover, by a flave to Rome?
Nought can be worth this bafenefs, life nor empire.
I loath me for it.   On this kinder earth,
Then leave me, leave me, to defpair and death.
    Maf. What means this conflict with almighty nature?
With the whole warring heart?—Rife, quickly rife,
In all the conquering majefty of charms;
O Sophonifba, rife! while here I fwear,
By the tremendous powers that rule mankind,
By heaven, and earth, and hell, by love and glory,
The Romans fhall not hurt you——Romans cannot;
For Rome is generous as the gods themfelves,
And honours, not infults, a generous foe.
Yet fince you dread them, take this facred pledge,
This hand of furety, by which kings are bound,
By which I hold you mine, and vow to treat you
With all the reverence due to ruin'd ftate,
With all the foftnefs of remember'd love,
All that can footh thy fate, and make thee happy.
    Soph. I thank thee, Mafiniffa.   Now the fame,
The fame warm youth, exalted, full of foul,
With whom, in happier days, I wont to pafs
The fighing hour; while dawning fair in love,
All fong and fweetnefs, life fet joyous out,
Ere the black tempeft of ambition rofe,
And drove us different ways.   Thus drefs'd in war,
In nodding plumes, o'ercaft with fullen thought,

C

With

With purpos'd vengeance dark, I knew thee not;
But now breaks out the beauteous fun anew,
The gay Numidian fhines who warm'd me once,
Whofe love was glory.   Vain ideas, hence!
Long fince, my heart, to nobler paffions known,
Has your acquaintance fcorn'd.

    Maf. Oh, while you talk,
Enchanting fair-one! my deluded thought
Runs back to days of love; when fancy ftill
Found worlds of beauty, ever rifing new
To the tranfported eye; when flattering hope
Form'd endlefs profpects of increafing blifs,
And ftill the credulous heart believ'd them all,
Even more than love could promife.   But the fcene
Is full of danger for a tainted eye;
I muft not, dare not, will not look that way.
Oh, hide it, wifdom, glory, from my view!
Or in fweet ruin I fhall fink again.
Difafter clouds thy cheek; thy colour goes.
Retire, and from the troubles of the day
Repofe thy weary foul, worn out with care,
And rough unhappy thought.

    Soph. May Mafiniffa
Ne'er want the goodnefs he has fhewn to me.   [*Exit.*

    Maf. The danger's o'er; I've heard the fyren's fong;
Yet ftill to glory hold my fteady courfe.
I mark'd thy kind concern, thy friendly fears,
And own them juft; for fhe has beauty, Narva,
So full, fo perfect, with fo great a foul
Inform'd, fo pointed high with fpirit,
As ftrikes like lightning from the hand of Jove,
And raifes love to glory.

    Narva. Ah, my Prince!
Too true, it is too true; her fatal charms
Are powerful, and to Mafiniffa's heart
But know the way too well.   And art thou fure,
That the foft poifon, which within thy veins
Lay unextinguifh'd, is not rouz'd anew?
Is not this moment working thro' thy foul?
Doft thou not love? Confefs.

    Maf. What faid my friend,

Of

Of poiſon, love, of loving Sophoniſba?
Yes, I admire her, wonder at her beauty;
And he who does not is as dull as earth,
The cold, unanimated form of man,
Ere lighted up with the celeſtial fire.
Where'er ſhe goes, ſtill admiration gazes,
And liſtens while ſhe talks. Even thou thyſelf,
Who ſaw'ſt her with the malice of a friend,
Even thou thyſelf admir'ſt her. Doſt thou not?
Say, ſpeak ſincerely.
   Narva. She has charms indeed;
But has ſhe charms like virtue? Tho' majeſtic,
Does ſhe command us? Is her force like glory?
   Maſ. All glory's in her eye; Perfection thence
Looks from his throne; and on her ample brow
Sits Majeſty Her features glow with life,
Warm with heroic ſoul. Her mien! ſhe walks,
As when a towering goddeſs treads this earth.
But when her language flows, when ſuch a one
Deſcends to ſooth, to ſigh, to weep, to graſp
The tottering knee, Oh, Narva! Narva, Oh!
Expreſſion here is dumb.
   Narva. Alas, my Lord!
Is this the talk of ſober admiration?
Are theſe the ſallies of a heart at eaſe?
Of Scipio's friend? And was it the calm ſenſe
Of fair perfection, that, while ſhe kneel'd
For what you raſhly promis'd, ſeiz'd your ſoul,
Stole out in ſecret tranſports from your eye,
That writh'd you groaning round, and ſhook your frame?
   Maſ. I tell thee once again, too cautious man,
That when a woman begs, a matchleſs woman,
A woman once belov'd, a fallen queen,
A Sophoniſba! when ſhe twines her charms
Around our ſoul, and all her power of looks,
Of tears, of ſighs, of ſoftneſs, plays upon us,
He's more or leſs than man who can reſiſt her.
For me, my ſtedfaſt ſoul approves, nay, more,
Exults in the protection it has promis'd:
And nought, tho' plighted honour did not bind me,
Shall ſhake the happy purpoſe of my heart;

C 2

Nought,

Nought, by th' avenging gods, who heard my vow,
And hear me now again.
    Narva. And was it then
For this you conquer'd ?
    Maf. Yes, and triumph in it.
This was my fondeſt wiſh, the very point,
The plume of glory, the delicious prize
Of bleeding years.   And I had been a brute,
A greater monſter than Numidia breeds,
A horror to myſelf, if, on the ground,
Caſt vilely from me, I th' illuſtrious fair one
Had left to bondage, bitterneſs, and death.
Nor is there ought in war worth what I feel,
In pomp and hollow ſtate, like this ſweet ſenſe
Of infelt bliſs, which the reflection gives me,
Of ſaving thus ſuch excellence and beauty
From her ſupreme abhorrence.
    Narva. Maſiniſſa,
My friend, my royal Lord ! alas, you ſlide,
You ſink from virtue ! On the giddy brink
Of fate you ſtand.   One ſtep, and all is loſt.
    Maf. No more, no more ! If this is being loſt,
If this, miſtaken ! is forſaking virtue,
And ruſhing down the precipice of fate,
Then down I go, far, far beyond the din
Of ſcrupulous, dull precaution.   Leave me, Narva ;
I want to be alone, to find ſome ſhade,
Some ſolitary gloom, there to ſhake off
This weight of life, this tumult of mankind,
This ſick ambition, on itſelf recoiling,
And there to liſten to the gentle voice,
The ſigh of peace, ſomething, I know not what,
That whiſpers tranſport to my heart.   Farewel.   [*Exit.*
    Narva. Struck, and he knows it not.   So when the
Elate in heart, the warrior ſcorns to yield,   [*field,*
The ſtreaming blood can ſcarce convince his eyes,
Nor will he feel the wound by which he dies.

                                        [*Exit.*

                 End of the Second Act.

                                        ACT

ACT III.

Mafiniffa *alone.*

IN vain I wander through the fhade for peace;
'Tis with the calm alone, the pure of heart,
That there the goddefs talks—But in my breaft
Some bufy thought, fome fecret-eating pang,
Throbs inexpreffible; and rowls from—What?
From charm to charm, on Sophonifba ftill
Earneft, intent, devoted all to her.
Oh, it muft out!—'Tis love, almighty love!
Returning on me with a ftronger tide.
I'll doubt no more, but give it up to love.
Come to my breaft, thou rofy-fmiling god!
Come unconfin'd! bring all thy joys along,
All thy foft cares, and mix them copious here.
But why invoke I thee? Thy power is weak,
To Sophonifba's eye; thy quiver poor,
To the refiftlefs lightning of her form;
And dull thy bare infinuating arts,
To the fweet mazes of her flowing tongue.
Quick, let me fly to her; and there forget
This tedious abfence, war, ambition, noife,
Even friendfhip's felf, the vanity of fame,
And all but love, for love is more than all!

Enter Narva.

Welcome again, my friend—Come nearer, Narva;
Lend me thine arm, and I will tell thee all,
Unfold my fecret heart, whofe every pulfe
With Sophonifba beats.—Nay, hear me out——
Swift, as I mus'd, the conflagration fpread;
At once too ftrong, too general, to be quench'd.
I love, and I approve it, doat upon her,
Even think thefe minutes loft I talk with thee.
Heavens! what emotions have poffefs'd my foul!
Snatch'd by a moment into years of paffion.

Nar. Ah, Mafiniffa!——

Maf. Argue not againſt me.
Talk down the circling winds that lift the deſart ;
And, touch'd by Heaven, when all the foreſts blaze,
Talk down the flame, but not my ſtronger love.
I have for love a thouſand thouſand reaſons,
Dear to the heart, and potent o'er the ſoul.
My ready thoughts all riſing, reſtleſs all,
Are a perpetual ſpring of tenderneſs ;
Oh, Sophoniſba ! Sophoniſba, Oh !
    Nar. Is this deceitful day then come to nought ?
This day, that ſet thee on a double throne ?
That gave thee Syphax chain'd, thy deadly foe ?
With perfect conqueſt crown'd thee, perfect glory ?
Is it ſo ſoon eclips'd ? and does yon ſun,
Yon ſetting ſun, who this fair morning ſaw thee
Ride through the ranks of long extended war,
As radiant as himſelf ; with every glance
Wheeling the pointed files ; and, when the ſtorm
Began, beheld thee tread the riſing ſurge
Of battle high, and drive it on the foe ;
Does he now, bluſhing, ſee thee ſunk ſo weak ?
Caught in a ſmile ? the captive of a look ?
I cannot name it without tears.
    Maf. Away !
I'm ſick of war, of the deſtroying trade,
Smooth'd o'er and gilded with the name of glory.
Thou need'ſt not ſpread the martial field to me ;
My happier eyes are turn'd another way,
Behold it not ; or, if they do, behold it
Shrunk up, far off, a viſionary ſcene ;
As to the waking man appears the dream.
    Nar. Or rather as realities appear,
The virtue, pomp, and dignities of life,
In ſick diſorder'd dreams.
    Maf. Think not I ſcorn
The taſk of heroes, when oppreſſion rages,
And lawleſs violence confounds the world.
Who would not bleed with tranſport for his country,
Tear ever dear relation from his heart,
And greatly die to make a people happy,
Ought not to taſte of happineſs himſelf,
And is low-ſoul'd indeed—But ſure, my friend,

There

There is a time for love, or life were vile!
A fickly circle of revolving days,
Led on by hope, with fenfelefs hurry fill'd,
And clos'd by difappointment.   Round and round,
Still hope for ever wheels the daily cheat;
Impudent hope! unjoyous madnefs all!
Till love comes ftealing in, with his kind hours,
His healing lips, his cordial fweets, his cares.
Infufing joy, his joys ineffable!
That make the poor account of life complete,
And juftify the gods.
    Nar. Miftaken prince,
I blame not love.   But——
    Maf. Slander not my paffion.
I've fuffer'd thee too far.—Take heed, old man.
Love will not bear an accufation, Narva.
    Nar. I'll fpeak the truth, when truth and friendfhip call,
Nor fear thy frown unkind.—Thou haft no right
To Sophonifba; fhe belongs to Rome.
    Maf. Ha! fhe belongs to Rome.——'Tis true—My.
Where have you wander'd, not to think of this? [thoughts,
Think e'er I promis'd? e'er I lov'd?—Confufion!
I know not what to fay—I fhould have lov'd,
Though Jove in muttering thunder had forbid it.
But Rome will not refufe fo fmall a boon,
Whofe gifts are kingdoms; Rome muft grant it fure,
One captive to my wifh, one poor requeft,
So fmall to them, but, Oh, fo dear to me!
Here let my heart confide.
    Nar. Delufive love!
Through what wild projects is the frantic mind
Beguil'd by thee!—And think'ft thou that the Romans,
The fenators of Rome, thefe gods on earth,
Wife, fteady to the right, feverely juft,
All incorrupt, and like eternal fate
Not to be mov'd, will liften to the figh
Of idle love? They, when their country calls,
Who know no pain, no tendernefs, no joy,
But bid their children bleed before their eyes;
That they'll regard the light fantaftic pangs
Of a fond heart? and with thy kingdom give thee
Their moft inveterate foe; from their firm fide,

Like

For whom my life fhould pay, if he met harm ;
So fhe does ufe me.

   Phi. Why, this is wondrous well :
But what kind language does fhe feed thee with ?

   Bel. Why, fhe does tell me, fhe will truft my youth
With all her loving fecrets ; and does call me
Her pretty fervant ; bids me weep no more
For leaving you ; fhe'll fee my fervices
Rewarded ; and fuch words of that foft ftrain,
That I am nearer weeping when fhe ends
Than 'ere fhe fpake.

   Phi. This is much better ftill.

   Bel. Are you not ill, my Lord ?

   Phi. Ill ! No, Bellario.

   Bel. Methinks your words
Fall not from off your tongue fo evenly,
Nor is there in your looks that quietnefs,
That I was wont to fee.

   Phi. Thou art deceiv'd, boy :
And fhe ftroaks thy head ?

   Bel. Yes.

   Phi. And does clap thy cheeks ?

   Bel. She does, my Lord.

   Phi. And fhe does kifs thee, boy ? ha !

   Bel. How, my Lord !

   Phi. She kiffes thee ?

   Bel. Not fo, my Lord.

   Phi. Come, come, I know fhe does.

   Bel. No, by my life.

   Phi. Why, then, fhe does not love me. Come, fhe does,
I bade her do it ; I charg'd her by all charms
Of love between us, by the hope of peace
We fhould enjoy, to yield thee all delights.
Tell me, gentle boy,
Is fhe not paft compare ? Is not her breath
Sweet as Arabian winds, when fruits are ripe ?
Is fhe not all a lafting mine of joy ?

   Bel. Ay, now I fee why my difturbed thoughts
Were fo perplex'd.   When firft I went to her,
My heart held augury ; you are abus'd ;
Some villain has abus'd you : I do fee
Whereto you tend.   Fall rocks upon his head,

        4

That

That put this to you ! 'tis some subtle train,
To bring that noble frame of yours to nought.
  Phi. Thou think'st I will be angry with thee ; come,
Thou shalt know all my drift : I hate her more
Than I love happiness ; and plac'd thee there,
To pry with narrow eyes into her deeds.
Hast thou discover'd ? Is she fall'n to lust,
As I would wish her ? Speak some comfort to me.
  Bel. My Lord, you did mistake the boy you sent :
Had she a sin that way, hid from the world,
Beyond the name of sin, I would not aid
Her base desires ; but what I came to know
As servant to her, I would not reveal,
To make my life last ages.
  Phi. Oh, my heart !
This is a salve worse than the main disease.
Tell me thy thoughts ; for I will know the least
That dwells within thee, or will rip thy heart
To know it ; I will see thy thoughts as plain
As I do now thy face.
  Bel. Why, so you do.
She is (for ought I know) by all the gods,
As chaste as ice ; but were she foul as hell,
And I did know it thus, the breath of kings,
The points of swords, tortures, nor bulls of brass,
Should draw it from me.
  Phi. Then it is no time
To dally with thee ; I will take thy life,
For I do hate thee ; I cou'd curse thee now.
  Bel. If you do hate, you could not curse me worse ;
The gods have not a punishment in store
Greater for me, than is your hate.
  Phi. Fie, fie !
So young and so dissembling ! Tell me when
And where thou didst possess her, or let plagues
Fall on me strait, if I destroy thee not !
  Bel. Heav'n knows, I never did : and when I lie
To save my life, may I live long and loath'd !
Hew me asunder, and, whilst I can think,
I'll love those pieces you have cut away
Better than those that grow ; and kiss those limbs,
Because you made them so.

Phi.

From regal pomp and luxury, to dwell
Among the foreſt beaſts; to bear the beam
Of red Numid.an ſuns, and the rank dew
Of cold unſhelter'd nights; to mix with wolves,
To hunt with hungry tygers for my prey,
And thirſt with Dipſas on the burning ſand;
I could have thank'd him for his angry leſſon;
The fair occaſion that his rage afforded
Of learning patience, fortitude, and hope,
Still riſing ſtronger on incumbent fate,
And all that try'd humanity can dictate.
But there is one curs'd bitterneſs behind,
One injury, the man can never pardon;
That ſcorches up the tear in pity's eye,
And even ſweet mercy's ſelf converts to gall.
I cannot—will not name it—Heart of anguiſh!
Down! down!

   Soph. Ah! whence this ſudden ſtorm? this madneſs,
That hurries all thy ſoul.

   Maſ. And doſt thou aſk?
Aſk thy own faithleſs heart; ſnatch'd from my vows,
From the warm wiſhes of my ſpringing youth,
And given to that old hated monſter, Syphax.
Perfidious Sophoniſba!

   Soph. Nay, no more.
With too much truth I can return thy charge.
Why didſt thou drive me to that cruel choice?
Why leave me, with my country, to deſtruction?
Why break thy love, thy faith, and join the Romans?

   Maſ. By heavens! the Romans were my better genius,
Sav'd me from fate, and form'd my youth to glory;
But for the Romans I had been a ſavage,
A wretch like Syphax, a forgotten thing,
The tool of Carthage.

   Soph. Meddle not with Carthage,
Impatient youth, for that I will not bear;
Though here I were a thouſand fold thy ſlave.
Not one baſe word of Carthage—on thy ſoul!

   Maſ. How vain thy phrenzy! Go, command thy ſlaves,
Thy fools, thy Syphaxes; but I will ſpeak,
Speak loud of Carthage, call it falſe, ungenerous,

                          —Yet

—Yet shall I check me, since it is thy country?
While the Romans are the light, the glory——
　　Soph. Romans!
Perdition to the Romans !—and almost
On thee too—Romans are the scourge
Of the red world, destroyers of mankind,
The ruffians, ravagers of earth ; and all
Beneath the smooth dissimulating mask
Of justice, and compassion ; as if slave
Was but another name for civiliz'd.
All vengeance on the Romans !—While fair Carthage
Unblemish'd rises on the base of commerce ;
And asks of heaven nought but the general winds,
And common tides, to carry plenty, joy,
Civility, and grandeur, round the world.
　　Maf. No more compare them ! for the gods themfelves
Declare for Rome.
　　Soph. It was not always so.
The gods declar'd for Hannibal ; when Italy
Blaz'd all around him, all her streams ran blood,
All her incarnate vales were vile with death ;
And when at Trebia, Thrasymene, and Cannæ,
The Carthaginian sword with Roman blood
Was drunk—Oh, that he then, on that dread day,
While lifeless consternation blacken'd Rome,
Had raz'd th' accursed city to the ground,
And sav'd the world !—When will it come again,
A day so glorious, and so big with vengeance,
On those my soul abhors?
　　Maf. Avert it, heaven !
The Romans not enslave, but save the world
From Carthaginian rage.
　　Soph. I'll bear no more !
Nor tenderness, nor life, nor liberty,
Nothing shall make me bear it.—Perish, Rome !
And all her menial friends !—Yes, rather, rather,
Detested as ye are, ye Romans, take me,
Oh, pitying take me to your nobler chains !
And save me from this abject youth, your slave !
——How canst thou kill me thus ?
　　Maf. I meant it not.
I only meant to tell thee, haughty fair one !

How

How this alone might bind me to the Romans;
That, in a frail and sliding hour, they snatch'd me
From the perdition of thy love; which fell,
Like baleful lightning, where I most could wish,
And prov'd destruction to my mortal foe.
Oh, pleasing! fortunate!

   Soph. I thank them too.
By heavens! for once, I love them; since they turn'd
My better thoughts from thee, thou——But I will not
Give thee the name, thy mean servility
From my just scorn deserves.

   Maf. Oh, freely call me
By every name thy fury can inspire;
Enrich me with contempt—I love no more—
It will not hurt me, Sophonisba.---Love,
Long since I gave it to the passing winds,
And would not be a lover for the world.
A lover is the very fool of nature;
Made sick by his own wantonnefs of thought,
His fever'd fancy: while to your own charms
Imputing all, you swell with boundless pride.
Shame on the wretch! who should be driven from men,
To live with Afian slaves, in one soft herd,
All wretched, all ridiculous together.
For me, this moment, here I mean to bid
Farewel, a glad farewel to love and thee.

   Soph. With all my soul, farewel!---Yet, ere you go;
Know that my spirit burns as high as thine,
As high to glory, and as low to love.
Thy promises are void; and I abfolve thee,
Here in the prefence of the lift'ning gods.
Take thy repented vows---To proud Cornelia
I'd rather be a slave, to Scipio's mother,
Than queen of all Numidia, by the favour
Of him, who dares infult the helpless thus.   [*Paufing.*
Still dost thou stay? Behold me then again,
Hopeless, and wild, a loft abandon'd slave.
And now thy brutal purpose must be gain'd.
Away, thou cruel, and ungenerous, go!

   Maf. No, not for worlds would I refume my vow!
Difhonour blaft me then! all kind of ills
Fill up my cup of bitternefs and fhame!

When I refign thee to triumphant Rome.
Oh, lean not thus dejected to the ground !
The fight is mifery——What roots me here ?   [*Afide.*
Alas ! I have urg'd my foolifh heart too far ;
And love deprefs'd recoils with greater force.
Oh, Sophonifba !
   Soph. By thy pride fhe dies.
Inhuman prince !
   Maf. Thine is the conqueft, nature !
By heaven and earth, I cannot hold it more.
Wretch that I was ! to crufh th' unhappy thus ;
The faireft too, the deareft of her fex !
For whom my foul could die !---Turn, quickly turn,
Oh, Sophonifba ! my belov'd ! my glory !
Turn and forgive the violence of love,
Of love that knows no bounds !
   Soph. And can it be ?
Can that foft paffion prove fo fierce of heart,
As on the tears of mifery, the fighs
Of death, to feaft ? to torture what it loves ?
   Maf. Yes, it can be, thou goddefs of my foul !
Whofe each emotion is but varied love,
All over love, its powers, its paffions, all :
Its anger, indignation, fury, love ;
Its pride, difdain, even deteftation, love ;
And when it, wild, refolves to love no more,
Then is the triumph of exceffive love.
Didft thou not mark me ? Mark the dubious rage,
That tore my heart with anguifh while I talk'd ?
Thou didft ; and muft forgive fo kind a fault.
What would thy trembling lips ?
   Soph. That I muft die.
For fuch another ftorm, fo much contempt
Thrown out on Carthage, fo much praife on Rome,
Were worfe than death.   Why fhould I longer tire
My weary fate ?   The moft relentlefs Roman
What could he more ?
   Maf. Oh, Sophonifba, hear !
See me thy fuppliant now.   Talk not of death.
I have no life but thee. Alas, alas !
Hadft thou a little tendernefs for me,
The fmalleft part of what I feel, thou wouldft——

D

What

What wouldſt thou not forgive? But how indeed
How can I hope it? Yet I from this moment,
Will ſo devote my being to thy pleaſure,
So live alone to gain thee; that thou muſt,
If there is human nature in thy breaſt,
Feel ſome relenting warmth.

   Soph. Well, well, 'tis paſt.
To be inexorable ſuits not ſlaves.

   Maſ. Spare, ſpare that word; it ſtabs me to the ſoul;
My crown, my life, and liberty are thine.
Oh, give my paſſion way! My heart is full,
Oppreſs'd by love; and I could number tears
With all the dews that ſprinkle o'er the morn;
While thus with thee converſing, thus with thee
Even happy to diſtreſs.—Enough, enough,
Have we been cheated by the trick of ſtate,
For Rome and Carthage ſuffer'd much too long;
And, led by gaudy phantoms, wander'd far,
Far from our bliſs: but now ſince met again,
Since here I hold thee, circle all perfection,
The prize of life! ſince fate too preſſes hard,
Since Rome and ſlavery drive thee to the brink;
Let this immediate night exchange our woes,
Secure my bliſs, our future fortunes blend,
Set thee, the queen of beauty, on my throne,
And make it doubly mine.—A wretched gift
To what my love could give!

   Soph. What! marry thee?
This night?

   Maſ. Thou dear one! yes, this very night,
Let injur'd Hymen have his rights reſtor'd,
And bind our broken vows.----Think, ſerious think
On what I plead. A thouſand reaſons urge.
Captivity diſſolves thy former marriage;
And if 'tis with the meaneſt vulgar ſo,
Can Sophoniſba to a ſlave, to Syphax,
The moſt exalted of her ſex, be bound?
Beſides it is the beſt, perhaps ſole way,
To ſave thee from the Romans; and muſt ſure
Bar their pretenſions: or, if ruin comes,
To periſh with thee is to periſh happy.

   Soph. Yet muſt I ſtill inſiſt——

Maſ. It ſhall be ſo.
I know thy purpoſe; it would plead for Syphax.
He ſhall have all, thou deareſt! ſhall have all,
Crowns, trifles, kingdoms, all again, but thee,
But thee, thou more than all!
  Soph. Bear witneſs, heaven!
This is alone for Carthage.
[*To him.*] Gain'd by goodneſs,
I may be thine. Expect no love, no ſighing.
Perhaps, hereafter, I may learn again
To hold thee dear. If on theſe terms thou canſt,
Here take me, take me, to thy wiſhes.
  Maſ. Yes,
Yes, Sophoniſba! as a wretch takes life
From off the bleeding rack.---All wild with joy,
Thus hold thee, preſs thee, to my bounding heart;
And bleſs the bounteous gods. Can Heaven give more?
Oh, happy! happy! happy! Come, my fair,
This ready minute ſees thy will perform'd;
From Syphax knocks his chains; and I myſelf,
Even in his favour, will requeſt the Romans.
Oh, thou haſt ſmil'd my paſſions into peace!
So, while conflicting winds embroil'd the ſeas,
In perfect bloom, warm with immortal blood,
Young Venus rear'd her o'er the raging flood;
She ſmil'd around, like thine her beauties glow'd;
When ſmooth, in gentle ſwells, the ſurges flow'd;
Sunk, by degrees, into a liquid plain;
And one bright calm ſat trembling on the main.

END of the THIRD ACT.

A C T   IV.

Sophoniſba *and* Phœniſſa.

PHOENISSA.

HAIL, queen of Maſæſylia once again!
  And fair Maſſylia join'd! This riſing day
Saw Sophoniſba, from the height of life,
Thrown to the very brink of ſlavery:

D 2

State

State, honours, armies vanquifh'd; nothing left
But her own great unconquerable mind.
And yet, ere evening comes, to larger power
Reftor'd, I fee my royal friend; and kneel
In greatful homage to the gods, and her.
Ye powers, what awful changes often mark
The fortunes of the great!
   Soph. Phœnifla, true;
'Tis awful all, the wonderous work of fate.
But, ah! this fudden marriage damps my foul;
I like it not, that wild precipitance
Of youth, that ardor, that impetuous ftream
In which his love return'd.   At firft, my friend,
He vainly rag'd with difappointed love;
And, as the hafty ftorm fubfided, then
To foftnefs varied, to returning fondnefs,
To fighs, to tears, to fupplicating vows;
But all his vows were idle, till at laft
He fhook my heart by Rome.   To be his queen
Could only fave me from their horrid power.
And there is madnefs in that thought, enough
In that ftrong thought alone, to make me run
From nature.
   Phœn. Was it not aufpicious, Madam?
Juft as we hop'd? juft as our wifhes plann'd?
Nor let your fpirit fink.   Your ferious hours,
When you behold the Roman ravage check'd,
From their enchantment Mafinifla freed,
And Carthage miftrefs of the world again,
This marriage will approve: then will it rife
In all its glory, virtuous, wife and great,
While happy nations, then deliver'd, join
Their loud acclaim.   And, had the white occafion
Neglected flown, where now had been your hopes?
Your liberty? your country? where your all?
Think well of this, think that, think every way,
And Sophonifba cannot but exult
In what is done.
   Soph. So may my hopes fucceed!
As love alone to Carthage, to the public,
Led me a marriage-victim to the temple,
And juftifies my vows.   Ha! Syphax here!

What

What would his rage with me ?   Phœniſſa, ſtay.
But this one trial more---Heroic truth,
Support me now !

Enter Syphax.

Syph. You ſeem to fly me, Madam,
To ſhun my gratulatious.   Here I come,
To join the general joy ; and I, ſure I,
Who have to dotage, have to ruin lov'd you,
Muſt take a tender part in your ſucceſs,
In your recover'd ſtate.

Soph. 'Tis very well.
I thank you, Sir.

Syph. And gentle Maſiniſſa,
Say, will he prove a very coming fool ?
All pliant, all devoted to your will ?
A glorious wretch, like Syphax ?   Ha ! not mov'd !
Speak, thou perfidious ! Canſt thou bear it thus ?
With ſuch a ſteady countenance ? Canſt thou
Here ſee the man thou haſt ſo groſly wrong'd,
And yet not ſink in ſhame ? And yet not ſhake
In every guilty nerve ?

Soph. What have I done,
That I ſhould tremble ? that I ſhould not dare
To bear thy preſence ? Was my heart to blame,
I'd tremble for myſelf, and not for thee,
Proud man ! Nor would I live to be aſham'd.
My ſoul itſelf would die, could the leaſt ſhame
On her unſpotted fame be juſtly caſt :
For of all evils, to the generous, ſhame
Is the laſt deadly pang.   But you behold
My late engagement with a jealous, falſe,
And ſelfiſh eye.

Syph. Avenging Juno, hear ?
And canſt thou think to juſtify thyſelf ?
I bluſh to hear thee, traitreſs !

Soph. Oh, my ſoul !
Canſt thou hear this, this baſe opprobrious language,
And yet be tamely calm ?---Well, well, for once
It ſhall be ſo---in pity to thy madneſs---
Impatient ſpirit, down !---Yes, Syphax, yes,
Yes, I will greatly juſtify myſelf ;
Even by the conſort of the thundering Jove,

Who

Who binds the holy marriage-vow, be judg'd.
And every public heart, not meanly loft
In little low purfuits, to wretched felf
Not all devoted, will abfolve me too.
But in the tempeft of the foul, when rage,
Loud indignation, unattending pride,
And jealoufy confound it, how can then
The nobler paffions, how can they be heard?
Yet let me tell thee——
    Syph. Thou canft tell me nought.
Away! away! nought but illufion, falfhood——
    Soph. My heart will burft, in honour to myfelf,
If here I fpeak not; though thy rage, I know,
Can never be convinc'd, yet fhall it be
Confounded.----And muft I renounce my freedom?
Forgo the power of doing general good?
Muft yield myfelf the flave, the barbarous triumph
Of infolent, enrag'd, inveterate Rome?
And all for nothing but to grace thy fall?
Nay by myfelf to perifh for thy pleafure?
For thee, the Romans may be mild to thee;
But I, a Carthaginian, I, whofe blood
Holds unrelenting enmity to theirs;
Who have myfelf much hurt them, and who live
Alone to work them woe; what, what can I
Hope from their vengeance, but the very dregs
Of the worft fate, the bitternefs of bondage?
Yet thou, kind man, wouldft in thy generous love,
Wouldft have me fuffer that; be bound to thee,
For that dire end alone, beyond the ftretch
Of nature and of law.
    Syph. Confufion! Law!
I know the laws permit thee, the grofs laws
That rule the vulgar. I'm a captive, true;
And therefore mayft thou plead a fhameful right
To leave me to my chains—But fay, thou bafe one!
Ungrateful! fay, for whom am I a captive?
For whom thefe many years with war, and death,
Defeats, and defolation have I liv'd?
For whom has battle after battle bled?
For whom my crown, my kingdom, and my all,
Been vilely caft away? For whom this day,

This

'This very day, have I been stain'd with slaughter,
With yon last reeking field?---For one, ye gods,
Who leaves me for the victor, for the wretch
I hold in utter endless detestation.
Fire! fury! hell!---Oh, I am richly paid!——
But thus it is to love a woman---Woman!
The source of all disaster, all perdition!
Man in himself is social, would be happy,
Too happy; but the gods, to keep him down,
Curs'd him with woman! fond, enchanting, smooth,
And harmless-seeming woman; while at heart
All poisons, serpents, tigers, furies, all
That is destructive, in one form combin'd,
And gilded o'er with beauty!

   Soph. Hapless man!
I pity thee; this madness only stirs
My bosom to compassion, not to rage.
Think as you list of our unhappy sex,
Too much subjected to your tyrant force;
Yet know that all, we were not all, at least,
Form'd for your trifles, for your wanton hours.
Our passions too can sometimes soar above
The houshold task assign'd us, can expand
Beyond the narrow sphere of families,
And take in states into the panting heart,
As well as yours, ye partial to yourselves!
And this is my support, my joy, my glory,
The conscience that my heart abhors all baseness,
And of all baseness most ingratitude.
This sure affronted honour may declare,
With an unblushing cheek.

   Syph. False, false as hell!
False as your sex!' when it pretends to virtue.
You talk of honour, conscience, patriotism.
A female patriot!---Vanity!---Absurd!
Even doating dull credulity would laugh
To scorn your talk.   Was ever woman yet
Had any better purpose in her eye,
Than how to please her pride or wanton will?
In various shapes, and various manners, all,
All the same plagues, or open, or conceal'd,

Soph. Muſt I then, muſt I, Syphax,
Give thee a bitter proof of what I ſay ?
I would not ſeem to heighten thy diſtreſs,
Not in the leaſt inſult thee ; thou art fallen,
So fate ſevere has will'd it, fallen by me.
I therefore have been patient ; from another,
Such language, ſuch indignity, had fir'd
My ſoul to madneſs.   But ſince driven ſo far,
I muſt remind thy blind injurious rage
Of our unhappy marriage.
    Syph. Horror !—Oh !
Blot it, eternal night !
    Soph. Allow me, Syphax !
Hear me but once ! If what I here declare
Shines not with reaſon and the cleareſt truth,
May I be baſe, deſpis'd, and dumb for ever !
I pray thee think, when unpropitious Hymen
Our hands united, how I ſtood engag'd.
I need not mention what full well thou know'ſt.
But pray recall, was I not flatter'd ? young ?
With blooming life elate, with the warm years
Of vanity ? ſunk in a paſſion too,
Which few reſign ? Yet then I married thee,
Becauſe to Carthage deem'd a ſtronger friend ;
For that alone.   On theſe conditions, ſay,
Didſt thou not take me, court me to thy throne ?
Have I deceiv'd thee ſince ? Have I diſſembled ?
To gain one purpoſe, e'er pretended what
I never felt ? Thou canſt not ſay I have.
And if that principle, which then inſpir'd
My marrying thee, was right, it cannot now
Be wrong.   Nay, ſince my native city wants
Aſſiſtance more, and ſinking calls for aid,
Muſt be more right——
    Syph. This reaſoning is inſult !
    Soph. I'm ſorry that thou doſt oblige me to it.
Then in a word take my full-open'd ſoul.
All love, but that of Carthage, I deſpiſe.
I formerly to Maſiniſſa thee
Preferr'd not, nor to thee now Maſiniſſa,
But Carthage to you both.   And if preferring
Thouſands to one, a whole collected people,

                                        All

All nature's tendernefs, whate'er is facred,
The liberty, the welfare of a ftate,
To one man's frantic happinefs, be fhame:
Here, Syphax, I invoke it on my head!
This fet afide; I, carelefs of myfelf,
And, fcorning profperous ftate, had ftill been thine,
In all the depth of mifery proudly thine!
But fince the public good, the law fupreme,
Forbids it; I will leave thee with a kingdom,
The fame I found thee, or not reign myfelf.
Alas! I fee thee hurt—Why cam'ft thou here,
Thus to inflame thee more?

   Syph. Why, forcerefs? Why?
Thou complication of all deadly mifchief!
Thou lying, foothing, fpecious, charming fury!
I'll tell thee why—To breathe my great revenge;
To throw this load of burning madnefs from me;
To ftab thee!——

   Soph. Ha!——

   Syph. And, fpringing from thy heart,
To quench me with thy blood!   [*Phœnifla interpofes.*

   Soph. Oh, give me way!
Phœnifla, tempt not thou his brutal rage.
Me, me, he dares not murder; if he dares,
Here let his fury ftrike; for I dare die.
What holds thy trembling point?

   Phœn. Guards!

   Soph. Seize the king.
But look you treat him well, with all the ftate
His dignity demands.

   Syph. Goodnefs from thee
Is the worft death—The Roman trumpets!—Ha!
Now I bethink me, Rome will do me juftice.
Yes, I fhall fee thee walk the flave of Rome;
Forget my wrongs, and glut me with the fight.
Be that my beft revenge.

   Soph. Inhuman! that,
If there is death in Afric, fhall not be.

       Enter Lælius.

   Læl. Syphax! alas, how fallen! how chang'd! from
I here beheld thee once in pomp and fplendor;   [what
At that illuftrious interview, when Rome

                And

And Carthage met beneath this very roof,
Their two great generals, Afdrubal and Scipio,
To court thy friendſhip.   Of the ſame repaſt
Both gracefully partook, and both reclin'd
On the ſame couch ; for perſonal diſtaſte
And hatred ſeldom burn between the brave.
Then the ſuperior virtues of the Roman
Gain'd all thy heart.   Even Afdrubal himſelf,
With admiration ſtruck and juſt deſpair,
Own'd him as dreadful at the ſocial feaſt
As·in the battle.   This thou may'ſt remember ;
And how thy faith was given before the gods,
And ſworn and ſeal'd to Scipio ; yet how falſe
Thou ſince haſt prov'd, I need not now recount.
But let thy ſufferings for thy guilt atone,
The captive for the king.   A Roman tongue
Scorns to purſue the triumphs of the ſword
With mean upbraidings.

   Syph. Lælius, 'tis too true.
Curſe on the cauſe !

   Læl. But where is Maſiniſſa ?
The brave young victor, the Numidian Roman !
Where is he, that my joy, my glad applauſe,
From envy pure, may hail his happy ſtate ?
Why that contemptuous ſmile ?

   Syph. Too credulous Roman !
I ſmile to think how that this Maſiniſſa,
This Rome-devoted hero, muſt ſtill more
Attract thy praiſes by a late exploit.
In every thing ſuccefsful.

   Læl. What is this ?
Theſe public ſhouts ? A ſtrange unuſual joy
O'er all the captive city blazes wide.
What wanton riot reigns to-night in Cirtha,
Within theſe conquer'd walls ?

   Syph. This, Lælius, is
A night of triumph o'er my conqueror,
O'er Maſiniſſa.

   Læl. Maſiniſſa ! How ?

   Syph. Why he to-night is married to my Queen.

   Læl. Impoſſible !

Syph. Yes, she, the fury! she,
Who put the nuptial torch into my hand,
That set my throne, my palace, and my kingdom,
All in a blaze.   She now has seiz'd on him;
Will turn him soon from Rome.   I know her power;
Her lips distil unconquerable poison.
Oh, glorious thought!—Will sink this hated youth,
Will crush him deep, beneath the mighty ruin
Of falling Carthage.
    Læl. Can it be? Amazement!
    Syph. Nay, learn it from himself.   He comes—Away!
Ye furies, snatch me from his sight! for hell,
Its tortures all are gentle to the presence
Of a triumphant rival.   [*Exit.*
    Læl. What is man?

Enter Masinissa.

    Maf, Thou more than partner of this glorious day!
Which has from Carthage torn her chief support,
And tottering left her, I rejoice to see thee.
To Cirtha welcome, Lælius.   Thy brave legions
Now taste the sweet repose by valour purchas'd;
This city pours refreshment on their toils.
I order'd Narva——
    Læl. Thanks to Masinissa.
All that is well.   I here observ'd the King,
But loosely guarded.   True, indeed, from him
There is not much to fear.   The dangerous spirit,
Still not unworthy fear, our matchless prize,
Is his imperious Queen, is Sophonisba.
The pride, the rage of Carthage live in her.
How, where is she?
    Maf. She, Lælius? In my care.
Think not of her; I'll answer for her conduct.
    Læl. Yes, if in chains.   Till then, believe me, Prince,
It were as hopeful answering for the winds,
That their broad pinions would not rouze the desart,
Or that their darted lightning will be harmless,
As promise peace from her.   But why so dark?
You shift your place; your countenance grows warm.
It is not usual this in Masinissa.
Pray, what offence can asking for the Queen,
The Roman captive, give?

Maf.

Maf. Lælius, no more.
You know my marriage—Syphax has been bufy.
It is unkind to dally with my paffion.

Læl. Ah, Mafiniffa! was it then for this,
Thy hurry hither from the recent battle?
Is the firft inftance of the Roman bounty
Thus, thus abus'd? They give thee back thy kingdom,
And in return are of their captive robb'd;
Of all they valued, Sophonifba.

Maf. Robb'd!
How, Lælius? Robb'd!

Læl. Yes, Mafiniffa, robb'd.
What is it elfe? But I, this very night,
Will here affert the majefty of Rome,
And, mark me, tear her from the nuptial bed.

Maf. Oh, gods! Oh, patience! As foon, fiery Roman,
As foon thy rage might from her azure fphere
Tear yonder moon. The man that feizes her,
Shall fet his foot firft on my bleeding heart:
Of that be fure. And is it thus ye treat
Your firm allies? Thus kings in friendfhip with you?
Of human paffions ftrip them? Slaves indeed,
If thus deny'd the common privileges
Of nature, what the weakeft creatures claim,
A right to what they love.

Læl. Out, out! For fhame!
This paffion makes thee blind. Here is a war,
Which defolates the nations, has almoft
Laid wafte the world. How many widows, orphans,
And love-lorn virgins pine for it in Rome!
Even her great fenate droops, her nobles fail,
Her Circus fhrinks, her every luftre thins;
Nature herfelf, by frequent prodigies,
Seems at this havock of her works to fichen;
And our Aufonian plains are now become
A horror to the fight. At each fad ftep,
Remembrance weeps. Yet her, the greateft prize
It hitherto has yielded; her, whofe charms
Are only turn'd to whet its cruel point,
Thou to thy wedded breaft haft taken her,
Haft purchas'd thee her beauties by a fea
Of thy protector's blood, and on a throne

Set her, this day recover'd by their arms.
Canft thou thyfelf, thou, think of it with patience?
Nor to a Roman mention king.   A Roman
Would fcorn to be a king.   The Roman people
Took liberty from out the very duft,
And for great ages urg'd it to the fkies,
The dread of kings!
  Maf. Be not fo haughty, Lælius.
It fcarce becomes the gentle Scipio's friend;
Suits not thy wonted eafe, the tender manners
I ftill have mark'd in thee.   I honour Rome;
But honour too myfelf, my vows, my Queen;
Nor will, nor can I tamely hear thee threaten
To feize her like a flave.
  Læl. I will be calm
This thy rafh deed, this unexpected fhock,
Such a peculiar injury to me,
Thy friend and fellow-foldier, has perhaps
Snatch'd me too far: for haft thou not difhonour'd,
By this laft action, a fuccefsful war,
Our common charge, entrufted us by Scipio?
  Maf. Ay, there it is.   Has not thy vain ambition
(Oh, where is friendfhip!) plann'd her for thy triumph?
To think on't, death! to think it is difhonour.
At fuch a fight, the warrior's eye might wet
His burning cheek; and all the Roman matrons,
Who line the laurel'd way, afham'd, and fad,
Turn from a captive brighter than themfelves.
But Scipio will be milder.
  Læl. I difdain
This thy furmife, and give it up to Scipio.
Thofe paffions are not comely.   Here to-morrow
Comes the Proconful.   Mean time, Mafiniffa,
Ah, harden not thyfelf in flattering hope!
Scipio is mild, but fteady—Ha! the Queen.
I think fhe hates a Roman—and will leave thee.   [*Exit.*
                Enter Sophonifba.
  Soph. Was not that Roman Lælius, as I enter'd,
Who parted gloomy hence?
  Maf. Madam, the fame.
  Soph. Unhappy Afric! fince thefe haughty Romans
Have in this lordly manner trod thy courts.

                        E   I read

I read his fresh reproaches in thy face;
The lesson'd pupil in thy fallen look,
In that forc'd smile which sickens on thy cheek.

Maf. Oh, say not so, thou rapture of my soul !
For while I see thee, meditate thy charms,
I smile as cordial as the sun in May ;
Deep from the heart, in every sense of joy,
I fondly smile.

Soph. Nay, tell me, Masinissa,
How feels their tyranny, when 'tis brought home ?
When, lawless grown, it touches what is dear ?
Pomp for a while may dazzle thoughtless man,
False glory blind him ; but there is a time,
When ev'n the slave in heart will spurn his chains,
Nor know submission more.   What said his pride ?

Maf. His disappointment for a moment only
Burst in vain passion, and————

Soph. You stood abash'd ;
You bore his threats, and tamely silent heard him,
Heard the fierce Roman mark me for his triumph.
Oh, bitter !

Maf. Banish that unkind suspicion.
The thought enflam'd my soul.   I vow'd my life,
My last Massylian, to the sword, ere he
Should touch thy freedom with the least dishonour.
But that from Scipio————

Soph. Scipio !

Maf. That from him————

Soph. I tell thee, Masinissa, if from him
I gain my freedom, from myself conceal it.
I shall disdain such freedom.

Maf. Sophonisba !
Thou all my heart holds precious ! doubt no more.
Nor Rome, nor Scipio, nor a world combin'd
Shall tear thee from me, till out-stretch'd I lie,
A nameless wretch.

Soph. If thy protection fails,
Of this at least be sure, be very sure,
To give me timely death.

Maf. Cease thus to talk
Of death, of Romans, of unkind ambition.
My softer thoughts those rugged themes refuse,

Can

Can turn alone to love.   All, all but thee,
All nature is a paffing dream to me :
Fix'd in my view, thou doft for ever fhine,
Thy form forth-beaming from the foul divine.
A fpirit thine which mortals might adore ;
Defpifing love, and thence creating more.
Thou the high paffions, I the tender prove ;
Thy heart was form'd for glory, mine for love.

[Exeunt.

END of the FOURTH ACT.

A C T   V.

Enter Mafiniffa and Narva.

MASINISSA.

HAIL to the joyous day ! With purple clouds
The whole horizon glows.   The breezy Spring
Stands loofely floating on the mountain-top,
And deals her fweets around.   The fun too feems,
As confcious of my joy, with brighter eye
To look abroad the world ; and all things fmile
Like Sophonifba.   Love and friendfhip fure
Have mark'd this day from out their choiceft ftores,
For beauty rais'd by dignity and virtue,
With all the graces, all the loves embellifh'd.
Oh, Sophonifba's mine ! and Scipio comes !
  Nar. My Lord, the trumpets fpeak his near approach.
  Maf. I want his fecret audience.   Leave us, Narva.

[Exit Narva.

Enter Scipio.

Scipio ! more welcome than my tongue can fpeak !
Oh, greatly, dearly welcome !
  Scipio. Mafiniffa,
My heart beats back thy joy.   A happy friend,
With laurel green, with conqueft crown'd, and glory ;
Rais'd by his prudence, fortitude and valour,
O'er all his foes ; and on his native throne,
Amidft his refcu'd fhouting fubjects fet.
Say, can the gods, in lavifh bounty, give
A fight more pleafing ?

E 2

Maf.

Maf. My great friend and patron;
It was thy timely, thy reftoring arm,
That brought me from the fearful defart-life,
To live again in ftate, and purple fplendor.
And now I wield the fceptre of my fathers,
See my dear people from the tyrant's fcourge,
From Syphax freed ; I hear their glad applaufes ;
And, to compleat my happinefs, have gain'd
A friend worth all.   Oh, gratitude, efteem,
And love like mine, with what divine delight
Ye fill the heart !

    Scipio. Heroic youth ! thy virtue
Has earn'd whate'er thy fortune can beftow.
It was thy patience, Mafiniffa ; patience,
A champion clad in fteel, that in the wafte
Attended ftill thy ftep, and fav'd my friend
For better days.   What cannot patience do ?
A great defign is feldom fnatch'd at once ;
'Tis patience heaves it on.   From favage nature
'Tis patience that has built up human life,
The nurfe of arts ; and Rome exalts her head,
An everlafting monument of patience.

    Maf. If I have that, or any virtue, Scipio,
'Tis copy'd all from thee.

    Scipio. No, Mafiniffa,
'Tis all unborrow'd ; the fpontaneous growth
Of nature in thy breaft.   Friendfhip, for once,
Muft, tho' thou blufheft, wear a liberal tongue ;
Muft tell thee, noble youth, that long experience
In councils, battles, many a hard event,
Has found thee ftill fo conftant, fo fincere,
So wife, fo brave, fo generous, fo humane,
So well attemper'd, and fo fitly turn'd
For what is either great or good in life,
As cafts diftinguifh'd honour on thy country,
And cannot but endear thee to the Romans.
For me, I think my labours all repaid,
My wars in Afric.   Mafiniffa's friendfhip
Smiles at my foul.   Be that my deareft triumph,
To have affifted thy forlorn eftate,
And lent a happy hand in raifing thee
To thy paternal throne, ufurp'd by Syphax.

The

The greateſt ſervice could be done my country,
Diſtracted Afric, and mankind in general,
Was aiding ſure thy cauſe.   To put the power
The public power, into the good man's hand,
Is giving plenty, life, and joy to millions.
But has my friend, ſince late we parted armies,
Since he with Lælius acted ſuch a brave,
Auſpicious part againſt the common foe,
Has he been blameleſs quite ? Has he conſider'd,
How pleaſure often on the youthful heart,
Beneath the roſy, ſoft diſguiſe of love,
(All ſweetneſs, ſmiles, and ſeeming innocence)
Steals unperceiv'd, and lays the victor low ?
I would not, cannot put thee to the pain——
It pains me deeper—of the leaſt reproach.
Let thy too faithful memory ſupply
The reſt. [*Pauſing.*] Thy ſilence, that dejected look,
That honeſt colour fluſhing o'er thy cheek,
Impart thy better ſoul.
  Maſ. Oh, my good Lord !
Oh, Scipio ! love has ſeiz'd me, tyrant love
Inthralls my ſoul.   I am undone by love.
  Scipio. And art thou then to ruin reconcil'd ?
Tam'd to deſtruction ? Wilt thou be undone ?
Reſign the towering thought, the vaſt deſign,
With future glories big ; the warrior's wreath,
The glittering files, the trumpet's ſprightly clang,
The praiſe of ſenates, an applauding world,
The patriot's ſtatue, and the hero's triumph,
All for a ſigh, all for a ſoft embrace,
For a gay tranſient fancy, Maſiniſſa ?
For ſhame, my friend ! for honour's ſake, for glory,
Sit not with folded arms, deſpairing, weak,
And careleſs all, till certain ruin comes ;
Like a ſick virgin ſighing to the gale,
Unconquerable love !
  Maſ. How chang'd indeed !
The time has been, when, fir'd from Scipio's tongue,
My ſoul had mounted in a flame with his.
Where is ambition flown ? Hopeleſs attempt !
Can love like mine be quell'd ? Can I forget

E 3

What

What still poſſeſſes, charms my thoughts for ever?
Throw ſcornful from me what I hold moſt dear?
Not feel the force of excellence? To joy
Be dead, and undelighted with delight?
Soft; let me think a moment——No, no, no!
I am unqeual to thy virtue, Scipio.
  Scipio. Fie, Maſiniſſa, fie! By heavens, I bluſh
At thy dejeſtion, this degenerate language!
What, periſh for a woman! ruin all,
All the fair deeds which an admiring world
Hopes from thy riſing day, only to ſooth
A ſtubborn fancy, a luxurious will!
How muſt it, think you, found in future ſtory,
Young Maſiniſſa was a virtuous prince,
And Afric ſmil'd beneath his early ray;
But that a Carthaginian captive came,
By whom untimely in the common fate
Of love he fell? The wife will ſcorn the page;
And all thy praiſe be ſome fond maid exclaiming,
Where are thoſe lovers now?—Oh, rather, rather,
Had I ne'er ſeen the vital light of heaven,
Than like the vulgar live, and like them die!
Ambition ſickens at the very thought.
To puff and buſtle here from day to day,
Loſt in the paſſions of inglorious life,
Joys which the careleſs brutes poſſeſs above us;
And when ſome years, each duller than another,
Are thus elaps'd, in nauſeous pangs to die,
And paſs away, like thoſe forgotten things,
That ſoon become as they had never been.
  Maſ. And am I dead to this?
  Scipio. The gods, young man,
Who train up heroes in misfortune's ſchool,
Have ſhook thee with adverſity, with each
Illuſtrious evil, that can raiſe, expand,
And fortify the mind. Thy rooted worth
Has ſtood theſe wint'ry blaſts, grown ſtronger by them.
Shall then, in proſperous times, while all is mild,
All vernal, fair, and glory blows around thee,
Shall then the dead ſerene of pleaſure come,
And lay thy faded honours in the duſt?
  Maſ. O gentle Scipio! ſpare me, ſpare my weakneſs.

Scipio. Remember Hannibal—A signal proof,
A fresh example of destructive pleasure.
He was the dread of nations, once of Rome,
When from Bellona's bosom, nurs'd in camps,
And hard with toil, he down the rugged Alps
Rush'd in a torrent over Italy;
Unconquer'd, till the loose delights of Capua
Sunk his victorious arm, his genius broke,
Perfum'd, and made a lover of the hero.
And now he droops in Bruttium, fear'd no more,
Sinks on our borders, like a scatter'd storm.
Remember him, and yet resume thy spirit,
Ere it is quite dissolv'd.

   Maf. Shall Scipio stoop
Thus to regard, to teach me wisdom thus,
And yet a stupid anguish at my heart
Repel whate'er he says?—But why, my Lord,
Why should we kill the best of passions, love?
It aids the hero, bids ambition rise,
Turns us to please, inspires immortal deeds,
Even softens brutes, and makes the good more good.

   Scipio. There is a holy tenderness indeed,
A nameless sympathy, a fountain-love,
Branch'd infinite from parents to their children,
From child to child, from kindred on to kindred,
In various streams, from citizen to citizen,
From friend to friend, from man to man in general,
That binds, supports, and sweetens human life.
But is thy passion such?———Lift, Masinissa,
While I the hardest office of a friend
Discharge, and, with a necessary hand,
A hand, tho' harsh at present, really tender,
I paint this passion. And if then thou still
Art bent to sooth it, I must sighing leave thee
To what the gods think fit.

   Maf. Oh, never, Scipio!
Oh, never leave me to myself! Speak on;
I dread, and yet desire thy friendly hand.

   Scipio. I hope that Masinissa need not now
Be told, how much his happiness is mine;
With what a warm benevolence I'd spring
To raise, confirm it, to prevent his wishes.

Oh,

Oh, luxury to think!—But while he rages,
Burns in a fever, fhall I let him quaff
Delicious poifon for a cooling draught,
In foolifh pity to his thirft? Shall I
Let a fwift flame confume him as he fleeps,
Becaufe his dreams are gay? Shall I indulge
A frenzy flafh'd from an infectious eye?
A fudden impulfe, unapprov'd by reafon;
Nay, by thy cool deliberate thought condemn'd,
Refolv'd againft? A paffion for a woman,
Who has abus'd thee bafely, left thy youth,
Thy love, as fweet, as tender as the fpring,
The blooming hero for the haughty tyrant;
And now who makes thy fheltering arms alone
Her laft retreat, to fave her from the vengeance,
Which even her very perfidy to thee
Has brought upon her head?—Nor is this all;
A woman, who will ply her deepeft arts,
(Ah, too prevailing! as appears already)
Will never reft, till Syphax' fate is thine;
'Till friendfhip weeping flies; we join no more
In glorious deeds, and thou fall off from Rome?
I too could add, that there is fomething mean,
Inhuman in thy paffion.   Does not Syphax,
While thou rejoiceft, die? The generous heart
Should fcorn a pleafure which gives others pain.
If this, my friend, all this confider'd deep,
Alarm thee not, not rouze thy refolution,
And call the hero from his wanton flumber,
Then Mafiniffa's loft.

　　Maf. Oh, I am pierc'd!
In every thought am pierc'd! 'Tis all too true—
I wifh I could refufe it.   Whither, whither,
Thro' what enchanted wilds have I been wandering?
They feem'd Elyfium, the delightful plains,
The happy groves of heroes and of lovers.
But the divinity that breathes in thee
Has broke the charm, and I am in a defart,
Far from the land of peace.   It was but lately,
That a pure joyous calm o'erfpread my foul,
And reafon tun'd my paffions into blifs;
When love came hurrying in, and with rafh hand,

Mix'd

Mix'd them delirious, till they now ferment
To mifery.   There is no reafoning down
This deep, deep anguifh, this continual pang:
A thoufand things, whene'er my raptur'd thought
Runs back a little.   But I will not think—
And yet I muft.   Oh, gods! that I could lofe
What a fond few hours' memory has grav'd
On adamant!

   Scipio. But one ftrong effort more,
And the fair field is thine—A conqueft far
Excelling that o'er Syphax.   What remains,
Since now thy madnefs to thyfelf appears,
But an immediate, manly refoution
To fhake off this effeminate difeafe,
Thefe foft ideas, which feduce thy foul,
Make it all idle, unafpiring, weak,
A fcene of dreams, to puff them to the winds,
And be my former friend, thyfelf, again.
I joy to find thee touch'd by generous motives,
And that I need not bid thee recollect
Whofe awful property thou haft ufurp'd;
Need not affure thee, that the Roman people,
The fenators of Rome, will never fuffer
A dangerous woman, their devoted foe,
A woman, whofe irrefragable fpirit
Has in great part fuftain'd this bloody war,
Whofe charms corrupted Syphax from their fide,
And fir'd embattled nations into rage;
Will never fuffer her, when gain'd fo dear,
To ruin thee too, taint thy faithful breaft,
And kindle future war.   No, fate itfelf
Is not more fteady to the right than they.
And where the public good but feems concern'd,
No motive their impenetrable hearts,
Nor fear nor tendernefs can touch—Such is
The fpirit that has rais'd imperial Rome.

   Maf. Ah, killing truth! But, I have promis'd, Scipio,
Have fworn to fave her from the Roman power.
My plighted faith is pafs'd, my hand is given;
And, by the confcious gods, who mark'd my vows,
The whole united world fhall never have her;
For I will die a thoufand, thoufand deaths,

With

With all Maſſylia in one field expire,
Ere to the loweſt wretch, much more to her
I love, to Sophoniſba, to my Queen,
I violate my word.

   Scipio. My heart approves
Thy reſolution, thy determin'd honour.
For ever ſacred be thy word, and oath.
Virtue by virtue will alone be clear'd,
And ſcorns the crooked methods of diſhonour.
But, thus divided, how to keep thy faith
At once to Rome and Sophoniſba; how
To ſave her from our chains, and yet thyſelf
From greater bondage: this thy ſecret thought
Can beſt inform thee.

   Maſ. Agony! Diſtraction!
Theſe wilful tears——Oh, look not on me, Scipio!
For I'm a child again.

   Scipio. Thy tears are no reproach.
Tears oft look graceful on the manly cheek.
The cruel cannot weep.　Even friendſhip's eye
Gives thee the drop it would refuſe itſelf.
I know 'tis hard, wounds every bleeding nerve
About thy heart, thus to tear off thy paſſion.
But for that very reaſon, Maſiniſſa,
'Tis hop'd from thee.　The harder, thence reſults
The greater glory.　Why ſhould we pretend
To conquer, rule mankind, be firſt in power,
In great aſſemblies, honour, place, and pleaſure,
While ſlaves at heart, while by fantaſtic turns
Our frantic paſſions rage? The very thought
Should turn our pomp to ſhame, our ſweet to bitter,
And, when the ſhouts of millions meet our ears,
Whiſper reproach.　Oh, ye celeſtial powers!
What is it, in a torrent of ſucceſs,
To bear down nations, and o'erflow the world?
All your peculiar favour.　Real glory
Springs from the ſilent conqueſt of ourſelves;
And without that, the conqueror is nought,
Save the firſt ſlave.　Then rouze thee, Maſiniſſa;
Nor in one weakneſs all thy virtues loſe.
And, Oh, beware of long, of vain repentance!

   Maſ. Well, well, no more—It is but dying too. [*Exit.*
                                 Scipio.

Scipio. I wish I have not urg'd the truth to rigour.
'here is a time when virtue grows severe,
'oo much for nature, and even almost cruel.

Enter Lælius.

'oor Masinissa, Lælius, is undone;
etwixt his passion and his reason tost
n miserable conflict.

  Læl. Entering, Scipio,
e shot athwart me, nor vouchsaf'd one look.
Iung on his clouded brow I mark'd despair,
nd his eye glaring with some dire resolve.
ast o'er his cheek too ran the hasty tear.
t were great pity that he should be lost!

  Scipio. By heavens, to lose him were a shock, as if
loft thee, Lælius, lost my dearest brother,
ound up in friendship from our infant years.
thousand lovely qualities endear him,
)nly too warm of heart.

  Læl. What shall be done?

  Scipio. Here let it rest, till time abates his passion.
Jature is nature, Lælius, let the wise
ay what they please. But, now, perhaps he dies——
Iaste, haste, and give him hope. I have not time
'o tell thee what—Thy prudence will direct.
Vhatever is consistent with my honour,
Iy duty to the public, and my friendship
'o him himself, say, promise, shall be done.
hope returning reason will prevent
)ur farther care.

  Læl. I fly with joy.

  Scipio. His life
Jot only save, but Sophonisba's too;
'or both, I fear, are in this passion mix'd:

  Læl. It shall be done.   [*Exit.*

  Scipio. If friendship pierces thus,
Vhen Love pours in his added violence,
Vhat are the pangs which Masinissa feels!   [*Exit.*

Enter Sophonisba *and* Phœnissa.

  Soph. Yes, Masinissa loves me—Heavens, how fond!
Jut yet I know not what hangs on my spirit,
dismal boding; for this fatal Scipio,
dread his virtues, this prevailing Roman,

Even

Even now, perhaps, deludes the generous King,
Fires his ambition with miftaken glory,
Demands me from him; for full well he knows,
That, while I live, I muft intend their ruin.
    Phœn. Madam, thefe fears————
    Soph. And yet it cannot be.
Can Scipio, whom ev'n hoftile fame proclaims
Of perfect honour, and of polifh'd manners,
Smooth, artful, winning, moderate, and wife,
Make fuch a wild demand? Or, if he could,
Can Mafiniffa grant it? Give his Queen,
Whom love and honour bind him to protect,
Yield her a captive to triumphant Rome?
'Tis bafenefs to fufpect it; 'tis inhuman.
What then remains?——Suppofe they fhould refolve,
By right of war, to feize me for their prize.
Ay, there it kills! What can his fingle arm,
Againft the Roman power; that very power
By which he ftands reftor'd? Diftracting thought!
Still o'er my head the rod of bondage hangs.
Shame on my weaknefs! This poor catching hope,
This tranfient tafte of joy, will only more
Imbitter death.
    Phœn. A moment will decide.
Madam, till then————
    Soph. Would I had dy'd before!
And am I dreaming here? Here, from the Romans,
Befeeching I may live to fwell their triumph?
When my free fpirit fhould ere now have join'd
That great affembly, thofe devoted fhades,
Who fcorn'd to live till liberty was loft,
But ere their country fell, abhorr'd the light.
Whence this pale flave? He trembles with his meffage.

    Enter a Slave with a letter and poifon from Mafiniffa.

    Slave. [*Kneeling.*] This, Madam, from the King, and
      this.
    Soph. Ha! Stay———   [*Reads the letter.*
Rejoice, Phœniffa! give me joy, my friend!
For here is liberty. My fears are air.
The hand of Rome can never touch me more.
Hail, perfect freedom, hail!
                                   Phœn.

Phœn. How, what, my Queen!
Ah! what is this?   [*Pointing to the poifon.*
  Soph. The firft of bleffings, death.
  Phœn. Alas, alas! can I rejoice in that?
  Soph. Shift not thy colour at the found of death;
For death appears not in a dreary light,
Seem not a blank to me; a lofing all
Thofe fond fenfations, thofe enchanting dreams,
Which cheat a toiling world from day to day,
And form the whole of happinefs they know.
It is to me perfection, glory, triumph.
Nay, fondly would I chufe it, tho' perfuaded
It were a long dark night without a morning,
To bondage far prefer it; fince it is
Deliverance from a world where Romans rule,
Where violence prevails—And timely too—
Before my country falls; before I feel
As many ftripes, as many chains, and deaths,
As there are lives in Carthage.   Glorious charter!
By which I hold immortal life and freedom;
Come, let me read thee once again—and then,
To thy great purpofe.   [*Reads the letter aloud.*

    " Mafiniffa to his Queen.
    " 'The gods know with what pleafure I would have
kept my faith to Sophonifba in another manner. But
fince this fatal bowl can alone deliver thee from the Romans, call to mind thy father, thy country, that thou haft
been the wife of two kings; and act up to the dictates of
thy own heart. I will not long furvive thee."

Oh, 'tis wond'rous well!
Ye gods of death, who rule the Stygian gloom!
Ye who have greatly dy'd! I come, I come!
I die contented, fince I die a queen;
By Rome untouch'd, unfullied by their power;
So much their terror, that I muft not live.
And thou, go tell the King, if this is all
The nuptial prefent he can fend his bride,
I thank him for it. But that death had worn
An eafier face before I trufted him.
His poifon, tell him too, he might have fpar'd;
Thefe times may want it for himfelf, and I

Live not of such a cordial unprovided.
Add, hither had he come, I could have taught
Him how to die.   I linger not, remember,
I stand not shivering on the brink of life ;
And, but these votive drops, which, grateful, thus,

                                      [*Taking the poison.*

To Jove the high deliverer I shed,
Assure him that I drank it, drank it all,
With an unalter'd smile——Away.   [*Drinks.*
                                       [*Exit Slave.*
My friend,   [*To* Phœp.
In tears, my friend ! Dishonour not my death
With womanish complaints.   Weep not for me,
Weep for thyself Phœnissa, for thy country,
But not for me.   There is a certain hour,
Which one would wish all undisturb'd and bright,
No care, no sorrow, no dejected passions,
And that is when we die, when hence we go,
Ne'er to be seen again.   Then let us spread
A bold exalted wing, and the last voice
We hear, be that of wonder and applause.
    Phœn. Who with the patriot wishes not to die !
    Soph. And is the sacred moment then so near ?
The moment, when yon sun, those heavens, this earth,
Hateful to me, polluted by the Romans,
And all the busy, slavish race of men,
Shall sink at once, and straight another state,
New scenes, new joys, new faculties, new wonders,
Rise on a sudden round ; but this the gods
In clouds and horror wrap, or none would live.
How liberal is death ! Methinks, I seem
To touch the happy shore.   Behind me frowns
A stormy sea, with tossing mortals thick ;
While, unconfin'd and green, before me lies
The land of bliss, and everlasting freedom ;
Where walk the mighty dead, all of one mind,
One blooming smile, one language, and one country.
Oh, to be there ! My breast begins to burn ;
My tainted heart grows sick.   Ah, me, Phœnissa !
How many virgins, infants, tender wretches,
Must feel these pangs, ere Carthage is no more !
Soft—lead me to my couch—My shivering limbs

Do this laſt office, and then reſt for ever.
I pray thee, weep not; pierce me not with groans.
The King too here! Nay, then my death is full.
    Enter Maſiniſſa, Lælius, *and* Narva.
 Maſ. Has Sophoniſba drank this curſed bowl?
Oh, horror, horror! what a ſight is here?
 Soph. Had I not drank it, Maſiniſſa, then
I had deſerv'd it.
 Maſ. Exquiſite diſtreſs!
Oh, bitter, bitter fate! and this laſt hope
Compleats my woe.
 Soph. When will theſe ears be deaf
To miſery's complaint? Theſe eyes be blind
To miſchief wrought by Rome?
 Maſ. Too ſoon, too ſoon!
Ah, why ſo haſty? But a little while,
Hadſt thou delay'd this horrid draught, I then
Had been as happy as I now am wretched.   [ing?
 Soph. What means this talk of hope, of coward wait-
 Maſ. What have I done? Oh, heavens! I cannot think
Without diſtraction, hell, and burning anguiſh,
On my raſh deed! But, while I talk, ſhe dies.
And how, what, where am I, then? Say, canſt thou
Forgive me, Sophoniſba?
 Soph. Yes, and more,
More than forgive thee, thank thee, Maſiniſſa.
Hadſt thou been weak, and dally'd with my freedom,
'Till by proud Rome enſlav'd, that injury
I never had forgiven.
 Maſ. I came with life.
Lælius and I from Scipio haſted hither;
But death was here before us. This vile poiſon!
 Soph. With life! There was ſome merit in the poiſon;
But this deſtroys it all. And couldſt thou think
Me mean enough to take it? Oh, Phœniſſa!
This mortal toil is almoſt at an end——
Receive my parting ſoul.
 Phœn. Alas, my Queen!
 Maſ. Dies, dies, and ſcorns me! Mercy, Sophoniſba!
Grant one forgiving look, while yet thou canſt;
Or death itſelf, the grave cannot relieve me:
But, with the Furies join'd, my frantic ghoſt

F 2

Will

Will howl for ever.   Quivering and pale!
Have I done this?
  Soph. Come nearer, Mafiniffa.
Out, ftubborn nature!
  Maf. Mifery! Thefe pangs
To me transferr'd were eafe.   A moment only,
An agonizing moment, while I have
An age of things to fay!
  Soph. We, but for Rome,
Might have been happy.   Rouze thee now, my foul!
The cold deliverer comes.   Be mild to Syphax.
In my furviving friend behold me ftill.
Farewel—'Tis done—Oh, never, never, Carthage,
Shall I behold thee more!   [*Dies.*
  Maf. Dead, dead, Oh, dead!
Is there no death for me?
                    [*Snatches Lælius's fword to ftab himfelf.*
  Læl. Hold, Mafiniffa!
  Maf. And wouldft thou make a coward of me, Lælius?
Have me furvive that murder'd excellence?
Did fhe not ftir? Ha! Who has fhock'd my brain?
It whirls, it blazes!—Was it thou, old man?
  Narva. Alas, alas!—good Mafiniffa, foftly.
Let me conduct thee to thy couch.
  Maf. The grave
Were welcome.   But ye cannot make me live:
Opprefs'd with life!—Off!—crowd not thus around me;
For I will hear, fee, think no more.   Thou fun,
Keep up thy hated beams; and all I want
Of thee, kind earth, is an immediate grave.
Ay, there fhe lies—Why to that pallid fweetnefs
Can not I, nature, lay my lips, and die?
                              [*Throws himfelf befide her.*
  Læl. See there the ruins of the noble mind,
When from calm reafon paffion tears the fway.
What pity fhe fhould perifh!——Cruel war!
'Tis not the leaft misfortune in thy train,
That oft by thee the brave deftroy the brave.
She had a Roman foul; for every one
Who loves, like her, his country, is a Roman.
Whether on Afric's fandy plains he glows,
Or lives untam'd among Riphæan fnows.

If parent liberty the breaſt inflame,
The gloomy Lybian then deſerves that name;
And, warm with freedom, under frozen ſkies,
In fartheſt Britain Romans yet may riſe.

End of the Fifth Act.

EPI.

EPILOGUE.

By a FRIEND.

NOW, I'm afraid the modest taste in vogue
Demands a strong, high-season'd epilogue;
Else might some silly soul take pity's part,
And odious virtue sink into the heart.

   Our squeamish author scruples this proceeding;
He says it hurts sound morals and good breeding:
Nor Sophonisba would he here produce,
A glaring model of no private use.
Ladies, he bid me say, behold your Cato:
What tho' no stoic she, nor read in Plato?
Yet sure she offer'd, for her country's sake,
A sacrifice, which Cato could not make——
Already, now, these wicked men are sneering,
Some wresting what one says, and others leering.
I vow, they have not strength for—public spirit:
'That, ladies, must be your superior merit.

   Mercy forbid! we should lay down our lives,
Like these old, Punic, barbarous, heathen wives.
Spare christian blood——But sure the devil's in her,
Who for her country would not lose a pinner.
Lard! how could such a creature shew her face?
How?—Just as you do there—thro' Brussels lace.
The Roman fair, the public in distress,
Gave up the dearest ornaments of dress.
How much more cheaply might you gain applause!
One yard of ribbon, and two ells of gauze.
And gauze each deep-read critic must adore;
Your Roman ladies dress'd in gauze all o'er.
Should you, fair patriots, come to dress so thin,
How clear might all your—sentiments be seen!
To foreign looms no longer owe your charms;
Nor make their trade more fatal than their arms.

Each

Each Britifh dame, who courts her country's praife,
By quitting thefe outlandifh modes, might raife
(Not from yon powder'd band, fo thin and fpruce)
Ten able-bodied men, for—public ufe.

   But now a ferious word about the play.
Aufpicious fmile on this his firft effay :
Ye generous Britons ! your own fons infpire ;
Let your applaufes fan their native fire :
Then other Shakefpeares yet may rouze the ftage,
And other Otways melt another age.

A
NUPTIAL SONG,

Intended to have been inferted in the FOURTH ACT.

COME, gentle Venus, and affuage
  A warring world, a bleeding age :
For nature lives beneath thy ray,
The wint'ry tempefts hafte away,
A lucid calm invefts the fea,
Thy native deep is full of thee ;
And flowering earth, where'er you fly,
Is all o'er fpring, all fun the fky.
A genial fpirit warms the breeze ;
Unfeen, among the blooming trees,
The feather'd lovers tune their throat,
The defart growls a foften'd note,
Glad o'er the meads the cattle bound,
And love and harmony go round.
  But chief, into the human heart
You ftrike the dear, delicious dart ;
You teach us pleafing pangs to know,
To languifh in luxurious woe,

To

To feel the generous paſſions riſe,
Grow good by gazing, mild by ſighs ;
Each happy moment to improve,
And fill the perfect year with love.
   Come, thou delight of heav'n and earth,
To whom all creatures owe their birth ;
Oh, come, red-ſmiling ! tender, come ;
And yet prevent our final doom :
For long the furious God of War
Has cruſh'd us with his iron car,
Has rag'd along our ruin'd plains,
Has curs'd them with his cruel ſtains,
Has clos'd our youth in endleſs ſleep
And made the widow'd virgin weep.
Now let him feel thy wonted charms ;
Oh, take him to thy twining arms !
And while thy boſom heaves on his,
While deep he prints the humid kiſs,
Ah, then, his ſtormy heart controul,
And ſigh thyſelf into his ſoul !
   Thy ſon too, Cupid, we implore,
To leave the green Idalian ſhore ;
But he, ſweet god, our only foe,
Long let him draw the twanging bow,
Transfix us with his golden darts,
Pour all his quiver on our hearts,
With gentler anguiſh make us ſigh,
And teach us ſweeter deaths to die.

M.ʳˢ **HOPKINS** in the Character of **ARETHUSA**

Yes—I must have thy Kingdoms—must have thee.

PHILASTER.

A TRAGEDY.

As altered from BEAUMONT and FLETCHER,

AND PERFORMED AT THE

Theatre-Royal in Covent-Garden.

DISTINGUISHING ALSO THE

VARIATIONS OF THE THEATRE,

Regulated from the Prompt-Book,

By PERMISSION of the MANAGERS,

By Mr. WILD, Prompter.

LONDON:
Printed for JOHN BELL, near *Exeter-Exchange*, in the *Strand.*
MDCCLXXVIII.

On comparing this play with the original, the reasons
assigned by the editor in his advertisement, for the alterations he had presumed to make, were so obvious, it was
judged to be more acceptable to the reader in its present
form, than as originally written.

ADVERTISEMENT.

THE prefent age, though it has done honour to its own difcernment by the applaufes paid to Shake-fpeare, has, at the fame time, too grofsly neglected the other great mafters in the fame fchool of writing. The pieces of Beaumont and Fletcher in particular, (to fay nothing of Jonfon, Maffinger, Shirley, &c.) abound with beauties, fo much of the fame colour with thofe of Shakefpeare, that it is almoft unaccountable, that the very age which admires one, even to idolatry, fhould pay fo little attention to the others; and, while almoft every poet or critic, at all eminent in the literary world, have been ambitious of diftinguifhing themfelves, as editors of Shakefpeare, no more than two folitary editions of Beaumont and Fletcher, and one of thofe of a very late date, have been publifhed in the prefent century.

The truth is, that nature indeed is in all ages the fame; but modes and cuftoms, manners and languages, are fubject to perpetual variation. Time infenfibly renders writings obfolete and uncouth, and the gradual intro-duction of new words and idioms brings the older forms into difrepute and difufe. But the intrinfic merit of any work, though it may be obfcured, muft for ever remain; as antique coins, or old plate, though not current or fafhionable, ftill have their value, according to their weight.

The injuries of modern innovation in the ftate of letters may be in a great meafure repaired, by rendering the writings of our old authors familiar to the public, and bringing them often before them. How many plays are there of Shakefpeare, now in conftant acting, of which the directors of the theatres would fcarce hazard the reprefentation, if the long-continued, and, as it were, traditional approbation of the public had not given a fanction to their irregularities, and familiarized the

diction;

diction! The language even of our Liturgy and Bible, if we may venture to mention them on this occasion, would perhaps soon become obsolete and unintelligible to the generality, if they were not constantly read in our churches. The stile of our authors, especially in this play, is often remarkably plain and simple, and only raised or enriched by the sentiments. It is the opinion of Dryden, that even " Shakespeare's language is a little " obsolete in comparison of theirs ; and that the English " language in them arrived to its highest perfection ; " what words have since been taken in, being rather " superfluous, than necessary."

Philaster has always been esteemed one of the best productions of Beaumont and Fletcher; and, we are told by Dryden, was the first play that brought them into great reputation. The beauties of it are indeed so striking and so various, that our authors might in this play almost be said to rival Shakespeare, were it not for the many evident marks of imitation of his manner. The late editors of Beaumont and Fletcher conceive, that the poets meant to delineate, in the character of Philaster, a Hamlet racked with the jealousy of Othello; and there are several passages, in this play, where the authors have manifestly taken fire from similar circumstances and expressions in Shakespeare, particularly some, that will readily occur to the reader, as he goes along, from Othello, Hamlet, Cymbeline, and Lear.

To remove the objections to the performance of this excellent play on the modern stage, has been the chief labour, and sole ambition, of the present editor. It may be remembered, that The Spanish Curate, The Little French Lawyer, and Scornful Lady, of our authors, as well as The Silent Woman of Jonson, all favourite entertainments of our predecessors, have, within these few years, encountered the severity of the pit, and received sentence of condemnation. That the uncommon merit of such a play as Philaster might be universally acknowledged and received, it appeared necessary to clear it of ribaldry and obscenity, and to amend a gross indecency in the original constitution of the fable, which must have checked the success due to the rest of the
piece,

piece, nay, indeed, was an infuperable obftacle to its reprefentation.

But though the inaccuracies and licentioufnefs of the piece were inducements (according to the *incudi reddere* of Horace) to put it on the anvil again, yet nothing has been added more than was abfolutely neceffary, to make it move eafily on the new hinge, whereon it now turns : nor has any thing been omitted, except what was fuppofed to have been likely to obfcure its merit, or injure its fuccefs. The pen was drawn, without the leaft hefitation, over every fcene now expunged, except the firft fcene of the third act, as it ftands in the original ; in regard to which, the part that Philafter fuftains in it occafioned fome paufe : but, on examination, it feemed that Dion's falfification of facts in that fcene was inconfiftent with the reft of his character, though very natural in fuch a perfon as Megra : and though we have in our times feen the fudden and inftantaneous tranfitions from one paffion to another remarkably well reprefented on the ftage, yet Philafter's emotions appeared impoffible to be exhibited with any conformity to truth or nature. It was therefore thought advifable to omit the whole fcene ; and it is hoped, that this omiffion will not be difapproved, and that it will not appear to have left any void or chafm in the action ; fince the imputed falfehood of Arethufa, after being fo induftrioufly made public to the whole court, might very naturally be imagined to come to the knowledge of Philafter in a much-fhorter interval, than is often fuppofed to elapfe between the acts ; or even between the fcenes of fome of our old plays.

The fcenes in the fourth act, wherein Philafter, according to the original play, wounds Arethufa and Bellario, and from which the piece took its fecond title of Love lies a bleeding, have always been cenfured by the critics. They breathe too much of that fpirit of blood, and cruelty, and horror, of which the Englifh tragedy hath often been accufed. The hero's wounding his miftrefs hurt the delicacy of moft; and his maiming Bellario fleeping, in order to fave himfelf from his purfuers, offended the generofity of all. This part of the fable, therefore, fo injurious to the character of Philafter, it

was judged abfolutely requifite to alter; and a new turn
has been given to all thofe circumftances : but the change
has been effected by fuch fimple means, and with fo much
reverence to the original, that there are hardly ten lines
added on account of the alteration.

The reft of the additions or alterations may be feen at
once, by comparing the prefent play with the original ;
if the reader does not, on fuch occafions, of himfelf too
eafily difcover the patch-work of a modern hand.

There is extant in the works of the Duke of Buckingham, who wrote The Rehearfal, and altered The Chances,
an alteration of this play, under the title of The Refto-
ration, or Right will take Place. The duke feems to
have been very ftudious to difguife the piece, the names
of the Dramatis Perfonæ, as well as the title, being entirely changed ; and the whole piece, together with the
prologue and epilogue, feeming intended to carry the air
of an oblique political fatire on his own times. However that may be, the Duke's play is as little (if not
lefs) calculated for the prefent ftage, as the original of
our authors. The character of Thrafomond (for fo the
Duke calls the Spanifh prince) is much more ludicrous
than the Pharamond of Beaumont and Fletcher. Few of
the indecencies or obfcenities in the original are removed ;
and with what delicacy the adventure of Megra is ma-
naged, may be determined from the following fpecimen
of his Grace's alteration of that circumftance, not a
word of the following extract being to be found in Beaumont and Fletcher.

Enter the Guard, bringing in Thrafomond, *in Drawers,
muffled up in a Cloak.*

Guard. Sir, in obedience to your commands,
We ftopt this fellow ftealing out of doors.
                              [*They pull off his cloak.*
Agremont. Who's this, the prince ?
Cleon. Yes ; he is incognito.
King. Sir, I muft chide you for this loofenefs !
You've wrong'd a worthy lady ; but no more.
                                        Thra-

7

Thrasomond. Sir, I came hither but to take the air.
Cleon. A witty rogue, I warrant him.
Agremont. Ay, he's a devil at his answers.
King. Conduct him to his lodgings.

If to move the passions of pity and terror are the two chief ends of tragedy, there needs no apology for giving that title to the play of Philaster. If Lear, Hamlet, Othello, &c. &c. notwithstanding the casual introduction of comic circumstances in the natural course of the action, are tragedies; Philaster is so too. The Duke of Buckingham entitles his alteration a tragi-comedy; but that word, according to its present acceptation, conveys the idea of a very different species of composition; a play, like The Spanish Friar, or Oroonoko, in which two distinct actions, one serious and the other comic, are unnaturally woven together; as absurd a medley (in the opinion of Addison) as if an epic writer was to undertake to throw into one poem the adventures of Æneas and Hudibras.

As to the form in which the piece is now submitted to the public, some, perhaps, will think that the editor has taken too many liberties with the original, and many may censure him for not having made a more thorough alteration. There are, it must be confessed, many things still left in the play, which may be thought to lower the dignity of tragedy, and which would not be admitted in a fable of modern construction: but where such things were in nature, and inoffensive, and served at the same time as so many links in the chain of circumstances that compose the action, it was thought better to subdue in some measure the intemperance of the scenes of low humour, than wholly to reject or omit them. It would not have been in the power, nor indeed was it ever in the intention or desire, of the editor, to give Philaster the air of a modern performance; no more than an architect of this age would endeavour to embellish the magnificence of a Gothick building with the ornaments of the Greek or Roman orders. It is impossible for the severest reader to have a meaner opinion of the editor's share in the work than he entertains of it himself. Something, however,

was

2

was neceſſary to be done; and the reaſons for what he has done have already been aſſigned; nor can he repent of the trouble he has taken, at the inſtance of a friend, whom he is happy to oblige, when he ſees himſelf the inſtrument of reſtoring Philaſter to the theatre, of diſplaying new graces in Mrs. Yates, and of calling forth the extraordinary powers of ſo promiſing a genius for the ſtage as Mr. Powell.

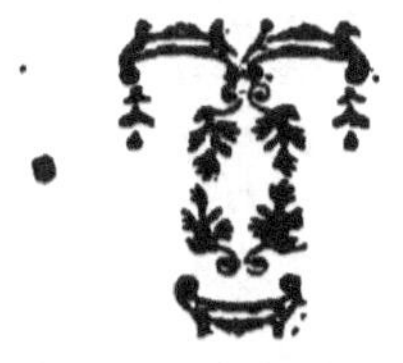

P R O L O G U E.

Written by George Colman, Esq. on Mr. Powell's
first Appearance at Drury-Lane.

WHILE modern tragedy, by rule exact,
    Spins out a thin-wrought fable, act by act,
We dare to bring you one of those bold plays,
Wrote by rough English wits in former days;
Beaumont and Fletcher! those twin stars, that run
Their glorious course round Shakespeare's golden sun;
Or when Philaster Hamlet's place supplied,
Or Bessus walk'd the stage by Falstaff's side.
Their souls, well pair'd, shot fire in mingled rays,
Their hands together twin'd the social bays,
Till fashion drove, in a refining age,
Virtue from court, and nature from the stage.
Then nonsense, in heroics, seem'd sublime;
Kings rav'd in couplets, and maids sigh'd in rhime.
Next, prim, and trim, and delicate, and chaste,
A hash from Greece and France, came modern taste.
Cold are her sons, and so afraid of dealing
In rant and fustian, they ne'er rise to feeling.
O say, ye bards of phlegm, say, where's the name
That can with Fletcher urge a rival claim?
Say, where's the poet, train'd in pedant schools,
Equal to Shakespeare, who o'erleapt all rules?
Thus of our bards we boldly speak our mind;
A harder task, alas, remains behind:
To-night, as yet by public eyes unseen,
A raw, unpractis'd novice fills the scene.
Bred in the city, his theatric star
Brings him at length on this side Temple-Bar;
Smit with the muse, the ledger he forgot,
And when he wrote his name, he made a blot.
Him while perplexing hopes and fears embarrass,
Skulking (like Hamlet's rat) behind the arras,
Me a dramatic fellow-feeling draws,
Without a fee, to plead a brother's cause.
Genius is rare; and while our great comptroller,
No more a manager, turnt arrant stroller,
Let new adventurers your care engage,
And nurse the infant suplings of the stage!

DRAMATIS PERSONÆ.

MEN.

	Drury-Lane	*Covent-Garden.*
King,	Mr. Branfby.	Mr. L'Eftrange.
Philafter,	Mr. Powell.	Mr. Melmoth.
Pharamond,	Mr. Lee.	Mr. Clinch.
Dion,	Mr. Burton.	Mr. Hull.
Cleremont,	Mr. Caftle.	Mr. Davis.
Thrafiline,	Mr. Ackman.	Mr. Thompfon.
Captain,	Mr. Baddely.	Mr. Dunftall.
Countryman,	Mr. Parfons.	Mr. Cufhing.
Meffengers,	{ Mr. Fox. { Mr. Marr.	
Woodmen,	{ Mr. Watkins. { Mr. Strange.	Mr. Fox.

WOMEN.

		Drury-Lane	*Covent-Garden.*
Arethufa,		Mifs Bride.	Mrs. Mattocks.
Euphrafia, difguifed under the name of			
Bellario,		Mrs. Yates.	Mrs. Melmoth.
Megra, a *Spanifh* Lady,		Mrs. Lee.	Mifs Sherman.
Galatea,		Mifs Mills.	Mrs. Whitfield.
Lady,		Mrs. Hippifley.	Mifs Pearce.

SCENE, *SICILY.*

PHILASTER.

₊ *The lines marked with inverted commas, 'thus,' are omitted in the representation.*

ACT I.

SCENE, *an Antichamber in the Palace.*

Enter Dion, Cleremont, *and* Thrafiline.

CLEREMONT.

HERE's nor lords, nor ladies.

Dion. Credit me, gentlemen, I wonder at it. They received ſtrict charge from the King to attend here. Beſides, it was loudly publiſhed, that no officer ſhould forbid any gentleman that deſired to attend and hear.

Cler. Can you gueſs the cauſe ?

Dion. Sir, it is plain, about the Spaniſh Prince, that's come to marry our kingdom's heir, and be our ſovereign.

Cler. Many, that will ſeem to know much, ſay, ſhe looks not on him like a maid in love.

'*Thra.* They ſay too, moreover, that the Lady Megra (ſent hither by the Queen of Spain, Pharamond's mother, to grace the train of Arethuſa, and attend her to her new home, when eſpouſed to the Prince) carries herſelf ſomewhat too familiarly towards Pharamond ; and it is whiſpered, that there is too cloſe an intercourſe between him and that lady.

Dion. Troth, perhaps there may ; tho' the multitude (that ſeldom know any thing but their own opinions) ſpeak what they would have. But the Prince, before his own approach, received ſo many confident meſſages from the ſtate, and bound himſelf by ſuch indiſſoluble engagements, that I think their nuptials muſt go forwards, and that the Princeſs is reſolved to be ruled.

Cler.

Cler. Sir, it is thought, with her he shall enjoy both these kingdoms of Sicily and Calabria.

Dion. Sir, it is, without controversy, so meant. But 'twill be a troublesome labour for him to enjoy both these kingdoms with safety, the right heir to one of them living, and living so virtuously; especially, the people admiring the bravery of his mind, and lamenting his in-juries.

Cler. Who, Philaster?

Dion. Yes, whose father, we all know, was by our late King of Calabria unrighteously deposed from his fruitful Sicily. Myself drew some blood in those wars, which I would give my hand to be washed from.

Cler. Sir, my ignorance in state-policy will not let me know why, Philaster being heir to one of these kingdoms, the King should suffer him to walk abroad with such free liberty.

Dion. Sir, it seems your nature is more constant than to enquire after state-news. But the King, of late, made a hazard of both the kingdoms of Sicily and his own, with offering but to imprison Philaster; at which the city was in arms, not to be charmed down by any state-order or proclamation, till they saw Philaster ride through the streets, pleased, and without a guard; at which they threw their hats and their arms from them, some to make bonfires, some to drink, all for his deliverance. Which, wise men say, is the cause the King labours to bring in the power of a foreign nation to awe his own with. [*Flourish.*

Thra. Peace; the King.

SCENE *draws, and discovers the* King, Pharamond, Arethusa, *and Train.*

King. To give a stronger testimony of love
Than 'sickly' promises, ' (which commonly
' In princes find both birth and burial
' In one breath)' we have drawn you, worthy Sir,
To make your fair indearments to our daughter,
And worthy services known to our subjects,
' Now lov'd and wonder'd at.' Next, our intent
To plant you deeply, our immediate heir
Both to our blood and kingdoms. ' For this lady,
' (The

' (The beſt part of your life, as you confirm me,
' And I believe) though her few years and ſex
' ,Yet teach her nothing but her fears and bluſhes;
' Think not, dear Sir, theſe undivided parts,
' That muſt mould up a virgin, are put on
' To ſhew her ſo, as borrow'd ornaments,
' To ſpeak her perfect love to you, or add
' An artificial ſhadow to her nature.'
Laſt, noble ſon, (for ſo I now muſt call you)
What I have done thus public, is ' not only
' To add a comfort in particular
' To you or me, but all; and' to confirm
The nobles, and the gentry of theſe kingdoms,
By oath to your ſucceſſion, which ſhall be
Within this month at moſt.

   Pha. Kiſſing your white hand, miſtreſs, I take leave,
To thank your royal father; and thus far
To be my own free trumpet.   Underſtand,
Great King, and theſe your ſubjects, gentlemen,
Believe me, in a word, a prince's word,
There ſhall be nothing to make up a kingdom
Mighty and flouriſhing, defenced, fear'd,
Equal to be commanded and obey'd,
But through the travels of my life I'll find it,
And tie it to this country.   And I vow,
My reign ſhall be ſo eaſy to the ſubject,
That ev'ry man ſhall be his prince himſelf,
And his own law: (yet I his prince and law)
And, deareſt lady, let me ſay, you are
The bleſſed'ſt living; for, ſweet Princeſs, you
Shall make him yours for whom great queens muſt die.

   Thra. Miraculous!

   Cler. This ſpeech calls him Spaniard, being nothing but
A large inventory of his own commendations.
But here comes one more worthy thoſe large ſpeeches,
Than the large ſpeaker of them.

      Enter Philaſter.

   Phi. Right noble Sir, as low as my obedience,
And with a heart as loyal as my knee,
I beg your favour.

   King. Riſe; you have it, Sir.
Speak your intents, Sir.

               Phi.

Phi. Shall I speak them freely?
Be still my royal Sovereign———
  King. As a subject,
We give you freedom.
  Dion. Now it heats.
  Phi. Then thus I turn
My language to you, Prince, you, foreign man.
Ne'er state, nor put on wonder; for you must
Indure me, and you shall.   This earth you tread on,
(A dowry, as you hope, with this fair Princess)
By my dead father (Oh, I had a father,
Whose memory I bow to!) was not left
To your inheritance, and I up and living,
Having myself about me, and my sword,
The souls of all my name, and memories,
These arms and some few friends, besides the gods,
To part so calmly with it, and sit still,
And say, I might have been.   I tell thee, Pharamond,
When thou art king, look I be dead and rotten,
And my name ashes.   For, hear me, Pharamond,
This very ground thou goest on, this fat earth,
My father's friends made fertile with their faiths,
Before that day of shame, shall gape, and swallow
Thee and thy nation, like a hungry grave,
Into her hidden bowels.   Prince, it shall;
By Nemesis, it shall.
  King. You do displease us.
You are too bold.
  Phi. No, Sir, I am too tame,
Too much a turtle, a thing born without passion,
A faint shadow, that every drunken cloud sails over,
And maketh nothing.
  Pha. What you have seen in me to stir offence
I cannot find, unless it be this lady,
Offer'd into mine arms, with the succession,
Which I must keep, though it hath pleas'd your fury
To mutiny within you.   The King grants it,
And I dare make it mine.   You have your answer.
  Phi. If thou wert sole inheritor to him
That made the world his, and were Pharamond
As truly valiant as I feel him cold,
And ring'd among the choicest of his friends,

And

And from this presence, spite of all these stops,
You should hear further from me.
 King. Sir, you wrong the Prince.
I gave you not this freedom to brave our best friends;
You do deserve our frown. Go to; be better temper'd.
 Phi. It must be, Sir, when I am nobler us'd.
 King. Philaster, tell me
The injuries you aim at in your riddles.
 Phi. If you had my eyes, Sir, and sufferance,
My griefs upon you, and my broken fortunes,
My wants great, and now nought but hopes and fears,
My wrongs would make ill riddles to be laughed at.
Dare you be still my King, and right me not?
 King. Go to;
Be more yourself, as you respect our favour;
You'll stir us else. Sir, I must have you know,   [we
That you're, and shall be, at our pleasure, ' what fashion
'- Will put upon you.' Smooth your brow, or, by the
   gods——
 Phi. I am dead, Sir; you're my fate. It was not I
Said I was wrong'd.' I carry all about me
My weak stars led me to, all my weak fortunes.
Who dares in all this presence speak, (that is
But man of flesh, and may be mortal) tell me,
I do not most entirely love this Prince,
And honour his full virtues?
 King. Sure he's possess'd!
 Phi. Yes, with my father's spirit. It's here, O King!
A dangerous spirit; now he tells me, King,
I was a king's heir, bids me be a king,
And whispers to me, these be all my subjects.
'Tis strange, he will not let me sleep, but dives
Into my fancy, and there gives me shapes
That kneel, and do me service, cry me king.
But I'll suppress him; he's a factious spirit,
And will undo me. Noble Sir, your hand;
I am your servant.
 King. Away; I do not like this.
For this time I pardon your wild speech.
       [*Exeunt* King, Pha. Are. *and train.*
 Dion. See how his fancy labours. Has he not
Spoke home, and bravely? What a dangerous train

Did he give fire to! How he shook the King!
Made his soul melt within him, and his blood
Run into whey! It stood upon his brow,
Like a cold winter dew.

   Phi. Gentlemen,
You have no suit to me; I am no minion.
You stand, methinks, like men that would be courtiers,
If you could well be flatter'd at that price,
Not to undo your children. You're all honest.
Go, get you home again, and make your country
A virtuous court, to which your great ones may,
In their diseased age, retire, and live recluse.

   Cle. How do you, worthy Sir?

   Phi. Well, very well,
And so well, that, if the King please, I find
I may live many years.

   Dion. The King must please,
Whilst we know what you are, and who you are,
Your wrongs and injuries. Shrink not, worthy Sir,
But add your father to you; in whose name
We'll waken all the gods, and conjure up
The rods of vengeance, the abused people,
Who, like to raging torrents, shall swell high,
And so begirt the dens of these male-dragons,
That, through the strongest safety, they shall beg
For mercy at your sword's point.

   Phi. Friends, no more;
Our ears may be corrupted. 'Tis an age
We dare not trust our wills to. Do you love me?

   Thra. Do we love heav'n and honour?

   Phi. My Lord Dion,
You had a virtuous gentlewoman call'd you father:
Is she yet alive?

   Dion. Most honour'd Sir, she is;
And for the penance but of an idle dream,
Has undertook a tedious pilgrimage.

Enter a Lady.

   Phi. Is it to me, or any of these gentlemen you come?

   Lady. To you, brave Lord; the Princess would intreat
your present company.

   Phi. Kiss her fair hand, and say, I will attend her.

   Dion. Do you know what you do?

Phi.

Phi. Yes ; go to see a woman.

Cler. But do you weigh the danger you are in ?

Phi. Danger in a sweet face !

Her eye may shoot me dead, or those true red
And white friends in her face may steal my soul out ;
There's all the danger in't.   But be what may,
Her single name hath armed me.   [*Exit.*

Dion. Go on ;
And be as truly happy as thou art fearless.
Come, gentlemen, let's make our friends acquainted,
Left the King prove false.   -   -   [*Exeunt.*

SCENE *changes to another apartment.*

Enter Arethusa *and a Lady.*

Are. Comes he not ?

Lady. Madam ?

Are. Will Philaster come ?

Lady. Dear Madam, you were wont
To credit me at first.

Are. But didst thou tell me so ?
I am forgetful, and my woman's strength
Is so o'ercharg'd with danger like to grow
About my marriage, that these under things
Dare not abide in such a troubled sea.
How look'd he, when he told thee he would come ?

Lady. Why, well.

Are. And not a little fearful?

Lady. Fear, Madam ! sure he knows not what it is.

Are. You are all of his faction ; the whole court
Is bold in praise of him ; whilst I
May live neglected, and do noble things,
As fools in strife throw gold into the sea,
Drown'd in the doing.   But I know he fears.

Lady. Fear, Madam ! Methought his looks hid more
Of love than fear.

Are. Of love ! to whom ? To you ?
Did you deliver those plain words I sent
With such a winning gesture, and quick look,
That you have caught him ?

Lady. Madam, I mean to you.

Are. Of love to me ! Alas ! thy ignorance
Lets thee not see the crosses of our births.

Nature, that loves not to be question'd why
She did or this, or that, but has her ends,
And knows she does well, never gave the world
Two things so opposite, so contrary,
As he and I am.

   Lady. Madam, I think I hear him.

   Are. Bring him in.   *[Exit Lady.*
You gods, that would not have your dooms withstood,
Whose holy wisdoms at this time it is
To make the passion of a feeble maid
The way unto your justice, I obey.

        Re-enter Lady and Philaster.

   Lady. Here is my Lord Philaster.

   Are. Oh! 'tis well.
Withdraw yourself.   *[Exit Lady.*

   Phi. Madam, your messenger
Made me believe you wish'd to speak with me.

   Are. 'Tis true, Philaster.
Have you known,
That I have ought detracted from your worth ?
Have I in person wrong'd you ? Or have set
My baser instruments to throw disgrace
Upon your virtues ?

   Phi. Never, Madam, you.

   Are. Why then should you, in such a public place,
Injure a princess, and a scandal lay
Upon my fortunes, ' fam'd to be so great,'
Calling a great part of my dowry in question ?

   Phi. Madam, ' this truth, which I shall speak, will
‘ Foolish. But’ for your fair and virtuous self,   *[seem.*
I could afford myself to have no right
To any thing you wish'd.

   Are. Philaster, know,
I must enjoy these kingdoms of Calabria
And Sicily. By fate, I die, Philaster,
If I not calmly may enjoy them both.

   Phi. I would do much to save that noble life;
Yet would be loth to have posterity
Find in our stories, that Philaster gave
His right unto a sceptre and a crown,
To save a lady's longing.

                       Are.

Are. Nay, then, hear;
I muſt, and will have them, and more.
Phi. What more ? Say, you would have my life;
Why, I will give it you; for it is of me
A thing ſo loath'd and unto you that aſk
Of ſo poor uſe, I will unmov'dly hear.
Are. Fain would I ſpeak; and yet the words are ſuch
I have to ſay, and do ſo ill beſeem
The mouth of woman, that I wiſh them ſaid,
And yet am loth to utter them. Oh, turn
Away thy face! a little bend thy looks!
Spare, ſpare me, Oh, Philaſter!
Phi. What means this?
Are. But that my fortunes hang upon this hour,
But that occaſion urges me to ſpeak,
And that perverſely to keep ſilence now
Would doom me to a life of wretchedneſs,
I could not thus have ſummon'd thee, to tell thee,
The thoughts of Pharamond are ſcorpions to me,
More horrible than danger, pain, or death!
Yes—I muſt have thy kingdoms—muſt have thee.
Phi. How, me!
Are. Thy love! without which, all the land
Diſcovered yet, will ſerve me for no uſe,
But to be buried in.
Phi. Is't poſſible?
Are. With it, it were too little to beſtow
On thee. Now, though thy breath may ſtrike me dead,
(Which, know, it may) I have unripp'd my breaſt.
Phi. Madam, you are too full of noble thoughts,
To lay a train for this contemned life,
Which you may have for aſking. To ſuſpect
Were baſe, where I deſerve no ill. Love you!
By all my hopes, I do, above my life.
But how this paſſion ſhould proceed from you.
So violently———
Are. Another ſoul into my body ſhot,
Could not have fill'd me with more ſtrength and ſpirit,
Than this thy breath. But ſpend not haſty time
In ſeeking how I came thus. 'Tis the gods,
The gods, that make me ſo; and ſure our love
Will be the nobler, and the better bleſs'd,

In that the secret justice of the gods
Is mingled with it. Let us leave and part,
Left some unwelcome guest should fall betwixt.
　　Phi. 'Twill be ill,
I should abide here long.
　　Are. 'Tis true, and worse
You should come often. How shall we devise
To hold intelligence, that our true loves,
On any new occasion, may agree,
What path is best to tread.
　　Phi. I have a boy,
Sent by the gods, I hope, to this intent,
Not yet seen in the court. Hunting the buck,
I found him sitting by a fountain-side,
Of which he borrow'd some to quench his thirst,
And paid the nymph again as much in tears.
A garland lay by him, made by himself,
Of many several flowers, bred in the bay,
Stuck in that mystic order, that the rareness
Delighted me; but ever when he turned
His tender eyes upon them, he would weep,
As if he meant to make them grow again.
Seeing such pretty helpless innocence
Dwell in his face, I ask'd him all his story;
He told me, that his parents gentle dy'd,
Leaving him to the mercy of the fields,
Which gave him roots; and of the crystal springs,
Which did not stop their courses; and the sun,
Which still, he thank'd him, yielded him his light;
Then took he up his garland, and did shew
What every flower, as country people hold,
Did signify; and how all, ordered thus,
Express'd his grief; and to my thoughts did read
The prettiest lecture of his country art
That could be wish'd; so that, methought, I could
Have studied it. I gladly entertain'd him,
Who was as glad to follow; and have got
The trustiest, loving'st, and the gentlest boy,
That ever master kept. Him will I send
To wait on you; and bear our hidden love.
　　　　　　　Enter Lady.
　　Are. 'Tis well; no more.
　　　　　3

Lady.

Lady. Madam, the Prince is come to do you fervice.

Are. What will you do, Philafter, with yourfelf?
Dear, hide thyfelf. Bring in the Prince.

Phi. Hide me from Pharamond!
When thunder fpeaks, which is the voice of Jove,
Though I do reverence, yet I hide me not.

Are. Then, good Philafter, give him fcope and way
In what he fays; for he is apt to fpeak
What you are loth to hear. For my fake do.

Phi. I will.

Enter Pharamond.

Pha. My princely miftrefs, as true lovers ought,
I come to kifs thefe fair hands; and to fhew,
In outward ceremonies, the dear love
Writ in my heart.

Phi. If I fhall have an anfwer no direftlier,
I am gone.

Pha. To what would he have an anfwer?

Are. To his claim unto the kingdom.

Pha. I did forbear you, Sir, before the King.

Phi. Good Sir, do fo ftill; I would not talk with you;

Pha. But now the time is fitter.

Phi. Pharamond,
I loath to brawl with fuch a blaft as thou,
Who art nought but a valiant voice. But if
Thou fhalt provoke me further, men will fay,
Thou wert, and not lament it.

Pha. Do you flight
My greatnefs fo, and in the chamber of the Princefs?

Phi. It is a place, to which, I muft confefs,
I owe a reverence; but wer't the church,
Ay, at the altar, there's no place fo fafe,
Where thou dar'ft injure me, but I dare punifh thee.
' Farewel.' [*Exit.*

Pha. Infolent boafter! offer but to mention
Thy right to any kingdom——

Are. Let him go;
He is not worth your care.

Pha. My Arethufa!
I hope our hearts are knit; and yet fo flow
State ceremonies are, it may be long
Before our hands be fo. If then you pleafe,

Being

Being agreed in heart, let us not wait
For pomp and circumstance, but solemnize
A private nuptial, and anticipate
Delights, and so foretaste our joys to come.
    Are. My father, Sir, is all in all to me;
Nor can I give my fancy or my will
More scope than he shall warrant.   When he bids
My eye look up to Pharamond for lord,
I know my duty; but, till then, farewel.   [*Exit.*
    Pha. Nay, but there's more in this—some happier man;
Perhaps Philaster——'Sdeath! let me not think on't—
She must be watch'd—He too must be ta'en care of,
Or all my hopes of her and empire rest
Upon a sandy bottom——If she means
To wed me, well; if not, I swear revenge.
                                                 [*Exit.*

ND of the FIRST ACT.

A C T   II.

SCENE, *an Apartment in the Palace.*

Enter Philaster *and* Bellario.

PHILASTER.

AND thou shalt find her honourable, boy;
    Full of regard unto thy tender youth.
For thine own modesty, and for my sake,
Apter to give, than thou wilt be to ask,
Ay, or deserve.
    Bel. Sir, you did take me up
When I was nothing; and only yet am something,
By being yours.   You trusted me, unknown;
And that which you are apt to construe now
A simple innocence in me, perhaps
Might have been craft, the cunning of a boy
Harden'd in lies and theft; yet ventur'd you
To part my miseries and me; for which
I never can expect to serve a lady,
That bears more honour in her breast than you.
    Phi. But, boy, it will prefer thee; thou art young,
And bear'st a childish, overflowing love
                                                 To.

To them that clap thy cheeks, and speak thee fair.
But when thy judgment comes to rule those passions,
Thou wilt remember best those careful friends,
That plac'd thee in the noblest way of life.
She is a princess I prefer thee to.

Bel. In that small time that I have seen the world,
I never knew a man hasty to part with
A servant he thought trusty. I remember,
My father would prefer the boys he kept
To greater men than he; but did it not,
Till they were grown too saucy for himself.

Phi. Why, gentle boy, I find no fault at all
In thy behaviour.

Bel. Sir, if I have made
A fault of ignorance, instruct my youth;
I shall be willing, if not apt, to learn.
Age and experience will adorn my mind
With larger knowledge; and if I have done
A wilful fault, think me not past all hope
For once. What master holds so strict a hand
Over his boy, that he will part with him
Without one warning? Let me be corrected,
To break my stubbornness, if it be so,
Rather than turn me off, and I shall mend.

Phi. Thy love doth plead so prettily to stay,
That, trust me, I could weep to part with thee.
Alas, I do not turn thee off! thou know'st,
It is my business that doth call thee hence;
And when thou art with her, thou dwell'st with me.
Think so, and 'tis so; and when time is full,
That thou hast well discharg'd this heavy trust,
Laid on so weak a one, I will again
With joy receive thee; as I live, I will.
Nay, weep not, gentle boy; 'tis more than time
Thou didst attend the Princess.

Bel. I am gone.
But since I am to part with you, my Lord,
And none knows whether I shall live to do
More service for you, take this little prayer:
Heav'n bless your loves, your fights, all your designs;
May sick men, if they have your wish, be well;
And Heav'n hate those you curse, tho' I be one. [*Exit.*
                                                          Phi.

Phi. The love of boys unto their lords is ſtrange !
I have read wonders of it : yet this boy,
For my ſake, if a man may judge by looks
And ſpeech, would out-do ſtory.   I may ſee
A day to pay him for his loyalty.　　　　　　*[Exit.*

SCENE changes to Arethuſa's Apartment.

Enter Arethuſa and a Lady.

Are. Where's the boy ? Where's Bellario ?
Lady. Within, Madam.
Are. Gave you him gold to buy him cloaths ?
Lady. I did.
Are. And has he done't ?
Lady. Madam, not yet.
Are. 'Tis a pretty, ſad talking boy, is it not ?
Enter Galatea.
Oh, you are welcome ! What good news ?
　Gal. As good as any one can tell your Grace,
That ſays ſhe has done that you would have wiſh'd.
　Are. Haſt thou diſcovered then ?
　Gal. I have.   Your Prince,
Brave Pharamond,'s diſloyal.
　Are. And with whom ?
　Gal. Ev'n with the lady we ſuſpect ; with Megra.
　' *Are.* Oh, where ! and when ?
　' *Gal.* I can diſcover all.'
　Are. The King ſhall know this ; and if deſtiny,
To whom we dare not ſay, It ſhall not be,
Have not decreed it ſo in laſting leaves,
Whoſe ſmalleſt characters were never chang'd,
This hated match with Pharamond ſhall break.
Run back into the preſence, mingle there
Again with other ladies ; leave the reſt
To me.　　　　　　　　　　　　　*[Exit* Gal.
Where's the boy ?
　Lady. Within, Madam.
　Are. Go, call him hither.　　　　　*[Exit Lady.*
Enter Bellario.
Why art thou ever melancholy, Sir ?
You are ſad to change your ſervice.   Is't not ſo ?
　Bel. Madam, I have not chang'd ; I wait on you,
To do him ſervice.

Are.

Are. Thou difclaim'ft in me.
Tell me, Bellario ; thou canft fing and play ?
  Bel. If grief will give me leave, Madam, I can.
  Are. Alas ! what kind of grief can thy years know?
Had'ft a crofs mafter when thou went'ft to fchool ?
Thou art not capable of other grief.
Thy brows and cheeks are fmooth as waters be,
When no breath troubles them.　Believe me, boy,
Care feeks out wrinkled brows, and hollow eyes,
And builds himfelf caves to abide in them.
Come, Sir, tell me truly, does your lord love me ?
  Bel. Love, Madam ! I know not what it is.
  Are. Canft thou know grief, and never yet knew'ft love ?
Thou art deceiv'd, boy.　Does he fpeak of me,
As if he wifh'd me well ?
  Bel. If it be love,
To forget all refpect of his own friends,
In thinking on your face ; if it be love,
To fit crofs-arm'd, and figh away the day,
Mingled with ftarts, crying your name as loud,
And haftily, as men i' the ftreets do fire ;
If it be love, to weep himfelf away,
When he but hears of any lady dead,
Or kill'd, becaufe it might have been your chance ;
If, when he goes to reft, (which will not be)
'Twixt ev'ry prayer he fays, he names you once,
As others drop a bead, be to be in love,
Then, Madam, I dare fwear he loves you.
  Are. Oh !
You are a cunning boy, taught to deceive,
For your lord's credit.　But thou know'ft, a falfehood
That bears this found, is welcomer to me,
Than any truth, that fays, he loves me not.
Lead the way, boy.　Do you attend me too ;
'Tis thy lord's bufinefs haftes me thus. Away. [*Exeunt.*

   SCENE *changes to another Apartment in the Palace.*

    Enter Megra *and* Pharamond.
  Meg. What then am I ? A poor neglected ftale !
Have I then been an idle toying fhe,
To fool away an hour or two withal,
And then thrown by for ever ?
C

Pha.

Ha. Nay, have patience.

Meg. Patience! I shall go mad! Why, I shall be
A mark for all the pages of the court
To bend their wit upon.

Pha. It shall not be.
She whose dishonour is not known abroad,
Is not at all dishonour'd.

Meg. Not dishonour'd!
Have we then been so chary of our fame,
So cautious, think you, in our course of love,
No blot of calumny has fall'n upon it? Say,
What charm has veil'd Suspicion's hundred eyes,
And who shall stop the cruel hand of Scorn?

Pha. Cease your complaints, reproachful and unkind!
What could I do? Obedience to my father,
My country's good, my plighted faith, my fame,
Each circumstance of state and duty, ask'd
The tender of my hand to Arethusa.

Meg. Talk not of Arethusa! She, I know,
Would fain get rid of her most precious bargain.
She is for softer dalliance; she has got
A cherub, a young Hylas, an Adonis!

Pha. What mean you?

Meg. She, good faith, has her Bellario!
A boy—about eighteen—a pretty boy!
Why, this is he that must, when you are wed,
Sit by your pillow, like a young Apollo,
Sing, play upon the lute, with hand and voice
Binding your thoughts in sleep. She does provide him
For you, and for herself.

Pha. Injurious Megra!
Oh, add not shame to shame! To rob a lady
Of her good name thus, is an heinous sin,
Not to be pardon'd: yet, though false as hell,
'Twill never be redeem'd, if it be sown
Amongst the people, fruitful to increase
All evil they shall hear.

Meg. It shall be known:
Nay, more, by Heav'n, 'tis true! a thousand things
Speak it beyond all contradiction true.
Observe how brave she keeps him: how he stands
For ever at her beck. There's not an hour,

Sacred

Sacred howe'er to female privacy,
But he's admitted ;- and in open court,
Their tell-tale eyes hold soft discourse together.
Why, why is all this ? Think you she's content
To look upon him ?
      Pha. Make it but appear,
That she has play'd the wanton with this stripling,
All Spain, as well as Sicily, shall know
Her foul dishonour.   I'll disgrace her first,
Then leave her to her shame.
      Meg. You are resolv'd ?
      Pha. Most constantly.
      Meg. The rest remains with me.
I will produce such proofs, that she shall know
I did not leave our country, and degrade
Our Spanish honour and nobility,
To stand a mean attendant in her chamber,
With hoodwink'd eyes, and finger on my lips.
What I have seen, I'll speak ; what known, proclaim ;
Her story shall be general as the wind,
And fly as far.   I will about it straight.
Expect news from me, Pharamond.   Farewel.   [*Exit.*
      Pha. True or not true, one way I like this well ;
For I suspect the Princess loves me not.
If Megra's charge prove malice, her own ruin
Must follow, and I'm quit of her for ever.
But if she makes suspicions truths ; or if,
Which were as deep confusion, Arethusa
Disdain'd our proffer'd union, and Philaster
Stand foremost in her heart, let Megra's charge
Wear but the semblance and the garb of truth,
They shall afford me measure of revenge.
I will look on with an indifferent eye,
Prepar'd for either fortune ; or to wed,
If she prove faithful, or repulse her sham'd.   [*Exit.*

SCENE, the Presence Chamber.

Enter Dion, Cleremont, Thrasiline, Megra, *and* Galatea.

      Dion. Come, ladies, shall we talk a round ?
      Gal. 'Tis late.
      Meg. 'Tis all
My eyes will do, to lead me to my bed.

C 2

Enter

Enter Pharamond.

Thra. The Prince!

Pha. Not a-bed, ladies! You're good sitters up.
What think you of a pleasant dream, to last
'Till morning?

Enter Arethusa *and* Bellario.

Are. 'Tis well, my Lord; you're courting of ladies.
Is't not late, gentlemen?

Cle. Yes, Madam.

Are. Wait you there.   [*Exit* Arethusa.

Meg. She's jealous, as I live! Look you, my Lord,
The Princess has a boy.

Pha. His form is angel-like.

Dion. Serves he the Princess?

Thra. Yes:

Dion. 'Tis a sweet boy.

Pha. Ladies all, good rest. I mean to kill a buck
To-morrow morning, ere you've done your dreams.
                                        [*Exit* Phar.

Meg. All happiness attend your Grace.   Gentlemen,
Gal. All good night.   [good rest.
                            [*Exeunt* Gal. *and* Meg.

Dion. May your dreams be true to you.
What shall we do, gallants? 'Tis late.   The King
Is up still.   See, he comes, and Arethusa
With him.

Enter King, Arethusa, *and* Guard.

King. Look your intelligence be true.

Are. Upon my life, it is.   And I do hope
Your Highness will not tie me to a man,
That in the heat of wooing throws me off,
And takes another.

Dion. What should this mean?

King. If it be true,
That lady had much better have embrac'd
Cureless diseases.   Get you to your rest.
                            [*Exeunt* Are. *and* Bel.

You shall be righted.   Gentlemen, draw near.
Haste, some of you, and cunningly discover
If Megra be in her lodging.

Cle. Sir,
She parted hence but now, with other ladies.
                                              King.

King. I would speak with her,
Dion. She's here, my Lord.

Enter Megra.

King. Now, lady of honour, where's your honour
No man can fit your palate, but the Prince. [now?
Thou troubled sea of sin; thou wilderness,
Inhabited by wild affections, tell me,
Had you none to pull on with your courtesies
But he that must be mine, and wrong my daughter?
By all the gods! all these, and all the court
Shall hoot thee, and break scurvy jests upon thee,
Make ribald rhimes, and fear thy name on walls.

Meg. I dare, my Lord, your hootings and your clamours.
Your private whispers, and your broader sleerings,
Can no more vex my soul, than this base carriage,
The poor destruction of a lady's honour,
The publishing the weakness of a woman.
But I have vengeance yet in store for some,
Shall, in the utmost scorn you can have of me,
Be joy and nourishment.

King. What means the wanton?
D'ye glory in your shame?

Meg. I will have fellows,
Such fellows in't, as shall make noble mirth.
The princess, your dear daughter, shall stand by me,
On walls, and sung in ballads, any thing.—

King. My daughter!

Meg. Yes, your daughter, Arethusa,
The glory of your Sicily, which I,
A stranger to your kingdom, laugh to scorn.
I know her shame, and will discover all;
Nay, will dishonour her. I know the boy
She keeps, a handsome boy, about eighteen;
Know what she does with him, and where, and when.
Come, Sir, you put me to a woman's madness,
The glory of a fury.

King. What boy's this

Meg. Alas, good minded Prince!
You know not these things: I will make them plain.
I will not fall alone: what I have known
Shall be as public as a print: all tongues
Shall speak it, as they do the language they

C 3

Are

Are born in, as free and commonly : I'll set it
Like a prodigious star, for all to gaze at ;
And that so high and glowing, other realms,
Foreign and far, shall read it there ; and then
Behold the fall of your fair princess too.   [*Exit.*

   King. Has she a boy ?
   Cle. So, please your grace, I've seen
A boy wait on her, a fair boy.
   King. Away ; I'd be alone. Go, get you to your
      quarters.   [*Exeunt.*
            Manet King.
You gods, I see, that who unrighteously
Holds wealth or state from others, shall be curst
In that which meaner men are blest withal :
Ages to come shall know no male of him
Left to inherit, and his name shall be
Blotted from earth. If he have any child,
It shall be crosly match'd. The gods themselves
Shall sow wild strife between her lord and her ;
Or she shall prove his curse who gave her being.
Gods ! if it be your wills—But how can I
Look to be heard of gods, who must be just,
Praying upon the ground I hold by wrong ?   [*Exit.*

       END of the SECOND ACT.

A C T III.

SCENE, *The Court.*

Enter Philaster.

PHILASTER.

OH, that I had a sea
  Within my breast, to quench the fire I feel !
More circumstances will but fan this fire.
It more afflicts me now, to know by whom
This deed is done, than simply that 'tis done.
Woman, frail sex ! the winds that are let loose
From the four several corners of the earth,
And spread themselves all over sea and land,
Kiss not a chaste one ! Taken with her boy !

                         Oh,

Oh, that, like beasts, we could not grieve ourselves,
With what we see not ! Bulls and rams will fight
To keep their females standing in their sight;
But take 'em from them, and you take at once
Their spleens away ; and they will fall again,
Unto their pastures, growing fresh and fat ;
And taste the water of the springs as sweet
As 'twas before, finding no start in sleep.
But miserable man—See, see, you gods,
                              [*Seeing* Bellario *at a distance.*

He walks still ! and the face you let him wear
When he was innocent, is still the same,
Not blasted.   Is this justice? Do you mean
To intrap mortality, that you allow
Treason so smooth a brow ?
                    Enter Bellario.

I cannot now
Think he is guilty.
    Bel. Health to you, my Lord!
The princess doth commend her love, her life,
And this unto you.   ·   [*Gives a letter.*
    Phi. Oh, Bellario !
Now I perceive she loves me; she does shew it
In loving thee, my boy ; sh'as made thee brave.
    Bel. My Lord, she has attired me past my wish,
Past my desert ; more fit for her attendant,
Though far unfit for me, who do attend.
    Phi. Thou art grown courtly, boy.   O, let all women,
                                     [*Reads.*

That love black deeds, learn to dissemble here !
Here, by this paper she does write to me,
As if her heart were mines of adamant
To all the world besides ; but, unto me
A maiden snow that melted with my looks.
Tell me, my boy, how doth the princess use thee?
For I shall guess her love to me by that.
    Bel. Scarce like her servant, but as if I were
Something allied to her, or had preserv'd
Her life three times by my fidelity :
As mothers fond do use their only sons ;
As I'd use one that's left unto my trust,

                                            For

For whom my life should pay, if he met harm;
So she does use me.

  Phi. Why, this is wondrous well:
But what kind language does she feed thee with?

  Bel. Why, she does tell me, she will trust my youth
With all her loving secrets; and does call me
Her pretty servant; bids me weep no more
For leaving you; she'll see my services
Rewarded; and such words of that soft strain,
That I am nearer weeping when she ends
Than 'ere she spake.

  Phi. This is much better still.

  Bel. Are you not ill, my Lord?

  Phi. Ill! No, Bellario.

  Bel. Methinks your words
Fall not from off your tongue so evenly,
Nor is there in your looks that quietness,
That I was wont to see.

  Phi. Thou art deceiv'd, boy:
And she stroaks thy head?

  Bel. Yes.

  Phi. And does clap thy cheeks?

  Bel. She does, my Lord.

  Phi. And she does kiss thee, boy? ha!

  Bel. How, my Lord!

  Phi. She kisses thee?

  Bel. Not so, my Lord.

  Phi. Come, come, I know she does.

  Bel. No, by my life.

  Phi. Why, then, she does not love me. Come, she does,
I bade her do it; I charg'd her by all charms
Of love between us, by the hope of peace
We should enjoy, to yield thee all delights.
Tell me, gentle boy,
Is she not past compare? Is not her breath
Sweet as Arabian winds, when fruits are ripe?
Is she not all a lasting mine of joy?

  Bel. Ay, now I see why my disturbed thoughts
Were so perplex'd. When first I went to her,
My heart held augury; you are abus'd;
Some villain has abus'd you: I do see
Whereto you tend. Fall rocks upon his head,

That put this to you ! 'tis some subtle train,
To bring that noble frame of yours to nought.

Phi. Thou think'st I will be angry with thee ; come,
Thou shalt know all my drift : I hate her more
Than I love happiness ; and plac'd thee there,
To pry with narrow eyes into her deeds.
Hast thou discover'd ? Is she fall'n to lust,
As I would wish her ? Speak some comfort to me.

Bel. My Lord, you did mistake the boy you sent :
Had she a sin that way, hid from the world,
Beyond the name of sin, I would not aid
Her base desires ; but what I came to know
As servant to her, I would not reveal,
To make my life last ages.

Phi. Oh, my heart !
This is a salve worse than the main disease.
Tell me thy thoughts ; for I will know the least
That dwells within thee, or will rip thy heart
To know it ; I will see thy thoughts as plain
As I do now thy face.

Bel. Why, so you do.
She is (for ought I know) by all the gods,
As chaste as ice ; but were she foul as hell,
And I did know it thus, the breath of kings,
The points of swords, tortures, nor bulls of brass,
Should draw it from me.

Phi. Then it is no time
To dally with thee ; I will take thy life,
For I do hate thee ; I cou'd curse thee now.

Bel. If you do hate, you could not curse me worse ;
The gods have not a punishment in store
Greater for me, than is your hate.

Phi. Fie, fie !
So young and so dissembling ! Tell me when
And where thou didst possess her, or let plagues
Fall on me strait, if I destroy thee not !

Bel. Heav'n knows, I never did : and when I lie
To save my life, may I live long and loath'd !
Hew me asunder, and, whilst I can think,
I'll love those pieces you have cut away
Better than those that grow ; and kiss those limbs,
Because you made them so.

Phi.

Phi. Fear'ſt thou not death ?
Can boys contemn that ?
  Bel. Oh, what boy is he
Can be content to live to be a man,
That ſees the beſt of men thus paſſionate,
Thus without reaſon ?
  Phi. Oh, but thou doſt not know
What 'tis to die.
  Bel. Yeſ, I do know, my Lord ;
'Tis leſs than to be born ; a laſting ſleep,
A quiet reſting from all jealouſy ;
A thing we all purſue : I know, beſides,
It is but giving over of a game
That muſt be loſt.
  Phi. But there are pains, falſe boy,
For perjur'd ſouls ; think but on theſe, and then
Thy heart will melt, and thou wilt utter all.
  Bel. May they fall all upon me whilſt I live,
If I be perjur'd, or have ever thought
Of that you charge me with ! If I be falſe,
Send me to ſuffer in thoſe puniſhments
You ſpeak of ; kill me.
  Phi. Oh, what ſhou'd I do ?
Why, who can but believe him ? He does ſwear
So earneſtly, that if it were not true,
The gods would not endure him.   Riſe, Bellario :
Thy proteſtations are ſo deep, and thou
Doſt look ſo truly, when thou uttereſt them,
That though I know 'em falſe, as were my hopes,
I cannot urge thee further : but thou wert
To blame to injure me, for I muſt love
Thy honeſt looks, and take no vengeance on
Thy tender youth. A love from me to thee
Is firm whate'er thou doſt. It troubles me,
That I have call'd the blood out of thy cheeks,
That did ſo well become them.   But, good boy,
Let me not ſee thee more : ſomething is done,
That will diſtract me, that will make me mad,
If I behold thee ; if thou tender'ſt me,
Let me not ſee thee.
  Bel. I will fly as far
As there is morning, 'ere I give diſtaſte

To

To that moſt honour'd mind. But through theſe tears,
Shed at my hopeleſs parting, I can ſee
A world of treaſon practis'd upon you,
And her, and me. Farewel, for evermore!
If you ſhall hear, that ſorrow ſtruck me dead,
And after find me loyal, let there be
A tear ſhed from you in my memory,
And I ſhall reſt at peace.   [*Exit* Bel.

  Phi. Bleſſing be with thee,
Whatever thou deſerv'ſt! Oh, where ſhall I
Eaſe my breaking heart? Nature, too unkind,
That gave no medicine for a troubled mind! [*Exit* Phil.

SCENE, Arethuſa's Apartment.

Enter Arethuſa.

  Are. I marvel, my boy comes not back again.
But that I know my love will queſtion him
Over and over; how I ſlept, wak'd, talk'd!
How I remembered him, when his dear name
Was laſt ſpoke! ' and how, when I ſigh'd, wept, ſung,'
And ten thouſand ſuch! I ſhould be angry at his ſtay.

Enter King.

  King. What, at your meditations! Who attends you?
  Are. None but my ſingle ſelf; I need no guard;
I do no wrong, nor fear none.
  King. Tell me, have you not a boy?
  Are. Yes, Sir.
  King. What kind of boy?
  Are. A page, a waiting-boy.
  King. A handſome boy?
  Are. I think he be not ugly;
Well qualified, and dutiful, I know him;
I took him not for beauty.
  King. He ſpeaks, and ſings, and plays?
  Are. Yes, Sir.
  King. About eighteen?
  Are. I never aſk'd his age.
  King. Is he full of ſervice?
  Are. By your pardon, why do you aſk?
  King. Put him away.
  Are. Sir!

King.

King. Put him away; 'has done you that good service
Shames me to speak of.

Are. Good Sir, let me understand you.

King. If you fear me,
Shew it in duty; put away that boy.

Are. Let me have reason for it, Sir, and then
Your will is my command.

King. Do you not blush to ask it? Cast him off,
Or I shall do the same to you. ' You're one
' Shame with me, and so near unto myself,
' That,' by my life, I dare not tell myself
What you have done.

Are. What have I done, my Lord?

King. Understand me well;
There be foul whispers stirring—Cast him off,
And suddenly do it.   Farewel.   [*Exit* King.

Are. Where may a maiden live securely free,
Keeping her honour safe? Not with the living:
They feed upon opinions, errors, dreams,
And make 'em truths.   They draw a nourishment
Out of defamings, grow upon disgraces,
And when they see a virtue fortified
Strongly above the battery of their tongues,
Oh, how they cast to sink it: and defeated
(Soul-sick with poison) strike the monuments
Where noble names lie sleeping!

Enter Philaster.

Phi. Peace to your fairest thoughts, my dearest mistress!

Are. Oh, my dear servant, I have a war within me.

Phi. He must be more than man, that makes these
Run into rivers. Sweetest fair, the cause?   [crystals,
And as I am your slave, ' tied to your goodness,
' Your creature made again from what I was,
' And newly spirited,' I'll right your honours.

Are. Oh, my best love; that boy!

Phi. What boy?

Are. The pretty boy you gave me———

Phi. What of him?

Are. Must be no more mine.

Phi. Why?

Are. They are jealous of him.

Phi. Jealous! who?

Are. The King.

Phi. Oh, my fortune!
Then 'tis no idle jealoufy.   Let him go.

Are. Oh, cruel,
Are you hard-hearted too? Who fhall now tell you,
How much I lov'd you? Who fhall fwear it to you,
And weep the tears I fend? Who fhall now bring you
Letters, rings, bracelets, lofe his health in fervice?
Wake tedious nights in ftories of your praife?
' Who now fhall fing your crying elegies,
' 'And ftrike a fad foul into fenfelefs pictures,
' And make them mourn?' Who fhall take up his lute,
And touch it, till he crown a filent fleep
Upon my eye-lid, making me dream and cry,
Oh, my dear, dear Philafter.

Phi. Oh, my heart!
Would he had broken thee, that made thee know
This lady was not loyal! Miftrefs, forget
The boy, I'll find thee a far better one.

Are. Oh, never, never, fuch a boy again,
As my Bellario.

Phi. 'Tis but your fond affection.

Are. With thee, my boy, farewel for ever
All fecrecy in fervants : farewel faith,
And all defire to do well for itfelf :
Let all that fhall fucceed thee, for thy wrongs,
Sell and betray chafte love!

Phi. And all this paffion for a boy?

Are. He was your boy; you gave him to me, and
The lofs of fuch muft have a mourning for.

Phi. Oh, thou forgetful woman!

Are. How, my Lord?

Phi. Falfe Arethufa!
Haft thou a medicine to reftore my wits,
When I have loft 'em? If not, leave to talk,
And to do thus.

Are. Do what, Sir? ' Would you fleep?'

Phi. ' For ever, Arethufa.' Oh, you gods!
Give me a worthy patience : have I ftood
Naked, alone, the fhock of many fortunes?
Have I feen mifchiefs numberlefs and mighty
Grow like a fea upon me? Have I taken

Danger as stern as death into my bosom,
And laugh'd upon it, made it but a mirth,
And flung it by ? Do I live now like him,
Under this tyrant king, that languishing
Hears his sad bell, and sees his mourners ? Do I
Bear all this bravely, and must sink at length
Under a woman's falsehood ? Oh, that boy,
That cursed boy ! None but a villain boy,
To wrong me with !

 Are. Nay, then I am betray'd;
I feel the plot cast for my overthrow ;
Oh, I am wretched !

 Phi. Now you may take that little right I have
To this poor kingdom : give it to your boy !
For I have no joy in it. Some far place
Where never womankind durst set her foot,
For bursting with her poisons, must I seek,
And live to curse you :
There dig a cave, and preach to birds and beasts
What woman is, and help to save them from you.
How heav'n is in your eyes, but in your hearts
More hell than hell has; how your tongues, like scorpions,
Both heal and poison : how your thoughts are woven
With thousand changes in one subtle web,
And worn so by you. How that foolish man,
That reads the story of a woman's face,
And dies believing it, is lost for ever.
How all the good you have is but a shadow,
I'th' morning with you, and at night behind you,
Past and forgotten. How your vows are frost,
Fast for a night, and with the next sun gone.
How you are, being taken all together,
A mere confusion, and so dead a chaos,
That love cannot distinguish. These sad texts,
Till my last hour, I am bound to utter of you.
So farewel all my woe, all my delight !   [*Exit.*

 Are. Be merciful, ye gods, and strike me dead.
What way have I deserv'd this ? Make my breast
Transparent as pure crystal, that the world,
Jealous of me, may see the foulest thought
My heart holds. Where shall a woman turn her eyes,
To find out constancy ? ' Save me,' how ' black,'

         Enter

Enter Bellario.

'And' guiltily, methinks, that boy looks now!
Oh, thou diſſembler, that, before thou ſpak'ſt,
Wert in thy cradle falſe! Sent to make lies,
And betray innocents; thy Lord and thou
May glory in the aſhes of a maid
Fool'd by her paſſion; but the conqueſt is
Nothing ſo great as wicked. Fly away,
Let my command force thee to that, which ſhame
Should do without it. If thou underſtoodſt
The loathed office thou haſt undergone,
Why, thou wouldſt hide thee under heaps of hills,
Leſt men ſhould dig and find thee.

   Bel. Oh, what god.
Angry with men, hath ſent this ſtrange diſeaſe
Into the nobleſt minds? Madam, this grief
You add unto me is no more than drops
To ſeas, for which they are not ſeen to ſwell;
My lord hath ſtruck his anger through my heart,
And let out all the hope of future joys;
You need not bid me fly; I come to part,
To take my lateſt leave.
I durſt not run away in honeſty,
From ſuch a lady, like a boy that ſtole,
Or made ſome grievous fault. Farewel! The gods
Aſſiſt you in your ſuff'rings! Haſty time
Reveal the truth to your abuſed lord,
And mine; that he may know your worth! Whilſt I
Go ſeek out ſome forgotten place to die.   [*Exit.*

   Are. Peace guide thee! thou haſt overthrown me once,
Yet, if I had another heaven to loſe,
Thou, or another villain, with thy looks,
Might talk me out of it.

Enter a Lady.

   Lady. Madam, the King would hunt, and calls for you
With earneſtneſs.

   Are. I attend him.
Diana, if thou canſt rage with a maid,
As with a man, let me diſcover thee
Bathing, and turn me to a fearful hind,
That I may die purſu'd by cruel hounds,
And have my ſtory written in my wounds.   [*Exeunt.*

END of the THIRD ACT.

D 2

A C T

ACT IV.

SCENE, *a Wood.*

Enter Philaster.

PHILASTER.

OH, that I had been nourish'd in these woods
  With milk of goats, and acorns, and not known
The right of crowns, nor the dissembling trains
Of women's looks; but digg'd myself a cave,
' Where I, my fire, my cattle, and my bed,
' Might have been shut together in one shed ;'
And then had taken me some mountain girl,
Beaten with winds, chaste as the harden'd rocks
Whereon she dwells; that might have strew'd my bed
With leaves, and reeds, and with the skins of beasts
Our neighbours; ' and have borne at her big breasts
' My large coarse issue !' This had been a life
Free from vexation !

Enter Bellario.

Bel. Oh, wicked men !
An innocent may walk safe among beasts :
Nothing assaults me here.   See, my griev'd lord
Looks as his foul were searching out the way
To leave his body.   Pardon me, that must
Break thro' thy last command ; for. I must speak :
You, that are griev'd, can pity ; hear, my Lord.

Phi. Is there a creature yet so miserable,
That I can pity ?

Bel. Oh, my noble Lord,
View my strange fortune, and bestow on me,
According to your bounty (if my service
Can merit nothing) so much as may serve
To keep that little piece I hold of life
From cold and hunger.

Phi. Is it thou ? ' Begone !'
Go, sell those misbeseeming cloaths thou wear'st,
And feed thyself with them.

Bel. Alas ! my Lord, I can get nothing for them :
The silly country people think 'tis treason
To touch such gay things.

Phi.

Phi. Now, by my life, this is
Unkindly done, to vex me with thy fight;
Thou'rt fall'n again to thy diffembling trade:
How fhouldft thou think to cozen me again?
Remains there yet a plague untry'd for me?
Ev'n fo thou wept'ft, and look'd'ft, and fpok'ft, when firft
I took thee up: curfe on the time! If thy
Commanding tears can work on any other,
Ufe thy old art, I'll not betray it. Which
Way wilt thou take, that I may fhun thee? for
Thine eyes are poifon unto mine; and I
Am loth to grow in rage. This way, or that way?

Bel. Any will ferve. But I will chufe to have
That path in chace that leads unto my grave.

[Exeunt feverally.

Enter Dion *and the* Woodmen.

Dion. This is the ftrangeft fudden chance! You,
woodman!——

1 *Wood.* My Lord ' Dion.'

Dion. Saw you a lady come this way on a fable horfe
ftudded with ftars of white?

2 *Wood.* Was fhe not young ' and tall?'

Dion. Yes. Rode fhe to the wood, or to the plain?

2 *Wood.* Faith, my Lord, we faw none. [*Exeunt* Wood.

Dion. Pox of your queftions then!

Enter Cleremont.

What, is fhe found?

Cle. Nor will be, I think. There's already a thoufand fatherlefs tales amongft us; fome fay, her horfe run
away with her; fome, a wolf purfued her; others, it
was a plot to kill her; and that armed men were feen in
the wood: but, queftionlefs, fhe rode away willingly.

Enter King *and* Thrafiline.

King. Where is fhe?

Cle. Sir, I cannot tell.

King. How is that?
Sir, fpeak you where fhe is.

Dion. Sir, I do not know.

King. You have betray'd me, you have let me lofe
The jewel of my life. Go, bring her me,
And fet her here before me; 'tis the King
Will have it fo. Alas! what are we kings?

D 3

Why

Why do you, gods, place us above the rest;
To be ferv'd, fear'd, and ador'd, till we
Believe we hold within our hands your thunder:
And when we come to try the pow'r we have,.
There's not a leaf ftirres at our threatenings.
I have finn'd, 'tis true, and here found to be punifh'd;
Yet would not then be punifh'd.

Enter Pharamond and Galatea.

King. What, is fhe found?
Pha. No, we have ta'en her horfe.
He gallop'd empty by; there is fome treafon:
You, Galatea, rode with her into the wood; why left you
  Gal. She did command me.   [her?
  King. You're all cunning to obey us for our hurt;
But I will have her.
Run all, difperfe yourfelves; the man that finds her,
Or (if fhe be kill'd) the traitor; I'll make him great.
  Pha. Come, let us feek.
  King. Each man a feveral way; here I myfelf.
[Exeunt.

SCENE, Another Part of the Wood.

Enter Arethufa.

Ar. Where am I now? Feet, find me out a way,
Without the counfel of my troubled head;
I'll follow you boldly about thefe woods,
O'er mountains, thorough brambles, pits, and floods:
Heaven, I hope, will eafe me.   I am fick.

Enter Bellario.

Bel. Yonder's my lady; heav'n knows, I want nothing,
Becaufe I do not wifh to live; yet I
Will try her charity.   O hear, you that have plenty,
And from that flowing ftore, drop fome on dry ground: fee,
The lively red is gone to guard her heart;   [*She faints.*
I fear, fhe faints. Madam, look up; fhe breathes not;
Open once more thofe rofy twins, and fend
Unto my Lord, your lateft farewel; Oh, fhe ftirs:
How is it, Madam? Speak fome comfort.
  Ar. 'Tis not gently done,
To put me in a miferable life,
And hold me there; I pray thee, let me go,
I fhall do beft without thee; I am well.

Enter Philaster.

Phi. I am to blame to be so much in rage:
I'll tell her coolly, when and where I heard
This killing truth.   I will be temperate
In speaking, and as just in hearing it.   [good gods,
Oh, monstrous! [*Seeing them,*] Tempt me not, ye gods!
Tempt not a frail man! what's he, that has a heart,
But he must ease it here?

Bel. My Lord, help the Princess.

Are. I am well, forbear.

Phi. Let me love lightning, let me be embrac'd
And kiss'd by scorpions, or adore the eyes
Of basilisks, rather than trust the tongues
Of hell-bred women! Some good gods look down,
And shrink these veins up; stick me here a stone,
Lasting to ages in the memory
Of this damn'd act! Hear me, you wicked ones!
You have put hills of fire into this breast,
Not to be quench'd with tears; for which may guilt
Sit on your bosoms! at your meals, and beds,
Despair await you! What, before my face?
Poison of asps between your lips! Diseases
Be your best issues! Nature make a curse,
And throw it on you!

Are. Dear Philaster, leave
To be enrag'd, and hear me.

Phi. I have done:
Forgive my passion.   Not the calmed sea,
When Æolus locks up his windy brood,
Is less disturb'd than I.   I'll make you know it.
Dear Arethusa, do but take this sword,
And search how temperate a heart I have;
Then you, and this your boy, may live and reign
In sin, without controul.   Wilt thou, Bellario?
I pr'ythee, kill me; ' thou art poor, and may'st
' Nourish ambitious thoughts, when I am dead:
' This way were freer.'

Are. Kill you!

Bel. Not for a world.

Phi. I blame not thee,
Bellario; thou hast done but that which gods
Would have transform'd themselves to do! ' Begone,
                                        ' Leave

' Leave me without reply; this is the laft
' Of all our meeting. Kill me with this fword!
' Be wife, or worfe will follow; we are two
' Earth cannot bear at once.' Refolve to do, or fuffer.

Are. If my fortunes be fo good to let me fall
Upon thy hand, I fhall have peace in death.
Yet tell me this, will there be no flanders,
No jealoufies in the other world, no ill there?

Phi. None.

Are. Shew me then the way.

Phi. Then guide
My feeble hand, you that have pow'r to do it!
For I muft perform a piece of juftice. If your youth
Have any way offended heav'n, let pray'rs
Short and effectual reconcile you to it.

Enter a Country Fellow.

Coun. I'll fee the King if he be in the foreft; I have
hunted him thefe two hours; if I fhould come home
and not fee him, my fifters would laugh at me.
There's a courtier with his fword drawn, by this hand,
upon a woman, I think.

Are. I am prepar'd.

Phi. Are you at peace?

Are. With heav'n and earth.

Phi. May they divide thy foul and body!

Coun. Hold, daftard! offer to ftrike a woman!

                                          [*Preventing him.*

Phi. Leave us, good friend.

Are. What ill-bred man art thou, thus to intrude thy-
' Upon our private fports, our recreations?' [felf

Coun. I underftand you not; but I know the knave
wou'd have hurt you.

Phi. Purfue thy own affairs; it will be ill   [me to.
To multiply blood upon my head, which thou wilt force

Coun. I know not your rhetorick; but I can lay it on,
if you offer to touch the woman.

Phi. Slave, take what thou deferv'ft.   [*They fight.*

Are. Heav'ns guard my Lord!

Bel. Unmanner'd boor!—my Lord!——
                                     [*Interpofing, is wounded.*

Phi. I hear the tread of people: I am hurt.
The gods take part againft me, cou'd this boor

                                       Have

Have held me thus elfe ? I muſt ſhift for life,
Though I do loath it.   [*Ex.* Phil. *and* Bel.
    Coun. I cannot follow the rogue.

Enter Pharamond, Dion, Cleremont, Thraſiline, *and*
                    Woodmen.

    Pha. What art thou ?
    Coun. Almoſt kill'd I am for a fooliſh woman ; a knave
would have hurt her.
    Pha. The princeſs, gentlemen !
    Dion. 'Tis above wonder ! Who ſhould dare do this ?
    Pha. Speak, villain, who would have hurt the Prin-
    Coun. Is it the Princeſs ?   [ceſs ?
    Dion. Ay.
    Coun. Then I have ſeen ſomething yet.
    Pha. But who would have hurt her ?
    Coun. I told you, a rogue ; I ne'er ſaw him before, I.
    Pha. Madam, who was it ?
    Are. Some diſhoneſt wretch ;
Alas ! I know him not, and do forgive him.
    Coun. He's hurt himſelf, and ſoundly too, he can-
not go far ; I made my father's old fox fly about his ears.
    Pha. How will you have me kill him ?
    Are. Not at all,
'Tis ſome diſtracted fellow.
If you do take him, bring him quick to me,
And I will ſtudy for a puniſhment,
Great as his fault.
    Pha. I will.
    Are. But ſwear.
    Pha. By all my love, I will :
Woodmen, conduct the Princeſs to the King,
And bear that wounded fellow unto dreſſing :
Come, gentlemen, we'll follow the chace cloſe.
            [*Ex.* Are. Pha. Dion. Cle. Thra. *and* 1 Woodman.
    Coun. I pray you, friend, let me ſee the King.
    2 Wood. That you ſhall, and receive thanks.
    Coun. If I get clear of this, I'll go ſee no more gay
fights.   [*Exeunt.*
            SCENE, *another Part of the Wood.*
            Enter Bellario, *with a ſcarf.*
    Bel. Yes, I am hurt ; and would to heav'n it were
A death's wound to me ! I am faint and weak

                    With—

With loſs of blood : my ſpirits ebb a-pace :
A heavineſs near death ſits on my brow,
And I muſt ſleep : bear me, thou gentle bank,
For ever, if thou wilt; you ſweet ones all,
Let me unworthy preſs you : I cou'd wiſh,
I rather were a corſe ſtrew'd over with you,
Than quick above you. ' Dulneſs ſhuts mine eyes,
' And I am giddy.' Oh ! that I could take
So found a ſleep, that I might never wake.

Enter Philaſter.

Phi. I have done ill ; my conſcience calls me falſe.
What ſtrike at her, that would not ſtrike at me !
When I did fight, methought, I heard her pray
The gods to guard me. She may be abus'd,
And I a loathed villain. If ſhe be,
She'll not diſcover me ; the ſlave has wounds,
And cannot follow, neither knows he me.
Who's this ? Bellario ſleeping ! If thou beeſt
Guilty, there is no juſtice that thy ſleep
Should be ſo found ; and mine, whom thou haſt wrong'd,
So broken.

Bel. Who is there ? My Lord Philaſter !
[*A cry within.*
Hark ! You are purſu'd; fly, fly my Lord ! and ſave
Yourſelf.

Phi. How's this ! would'ſt thou I ſhould be ſafe ?

Bel. Elſe were it vain for me to live. Oh, ſeize,
My Lord, this offer'd means of your eſcape !
The Princeſs, I am ſure, will ne'er reveal you ;
They have no mark to know you, but your wounds ;
I, coming in betwixt the boor and you,
Was wounded too.   To ſtay the loſs of blood
I did bind on this ſcarf, which thus
I tear away. Fly ! and 'twill be believed
'Twas I aſſail'd the Princeſs.

Phi. O heavens !
What haſt thou done ? Art thou then true to me ?

Bel. Or let me periſh loath'd ! Come, my good Lord,
Creep in amongſt thoſe buſhes. Who does know,
But that the gods may ſave your much-lov'd breath ?

Phi. Oh, I ſhall die for grief ! What wilt thou do ?

Bel. Shift for myſelf well : peace, I hear 'em come !
Within.

Within. Follow, follow, follow; that way they went.

Bel. With my own wounds I'll bloody my own fword!
I need not counterfeit to fall; heav'n knows
That I can ftand no longer.

Enter Pharamond, Dion, Cleremont, Thrafiline, &c.

Pha. To this place we have track'd him by his blood.

Cle. Yonder, my Lord, creeps one away.

Dion. Stay, Sir, what are you?

Bel. A wretched creature wounded in thefe woods
By beafts! relieve me, if your names be men,
Or I fhall perifh!

Dion. This is he, my Lord,
Upon my foul, affail'd her; 'tis the boy,
That wicked boy, that ferv'd her.

Pha. Oh, thou wretch!
What caufe could'ft thou fhape
To hurt the Princefs?

Bel. Then I am betray'd.

Dion. Betray'd! no, apprehended.

Bel. I confefs,
Urge it no more, that, big with evil thoughts,
I fet upon her, and did make my aim
Her death. For charity, let fall at once
The punifhment you mean, and do not load
This weary flefh with tortures!

Pha. I will know
Who hir'd thee to this deed.

Bel. My own revenge,

Pha. Revenge, for what?

Bel. It pleas'd her to receive
Me as her page, and, when my fortunes ebb'd,
That men ftrid o'er them carelefs, fhe did fhower
Her welcome graces on me, and did fwell
My fortunes, till they overflow'd their banks,
Threat'ning the men that croft 'em; when, as fwift
As ftorms arife at fea, fhe turn'd her eyes
To burning funs upon me, and did dry
The ftreams fhe had beftow'd, leaving me worfe,
And more contemn'd than other little brooks,
Becaufe I had been great. In fhort, I knew

I

I could

I could not live, and therefore did defire
To die reveng'd.

Pha. If tortures can be found,
Long as thy natural life, prepare to feel
The utmoft rigour.

Cle. Help to lead him hence.

Philafter *comes forth.*

Phi. Turn back, you ravifhers of innocence!
Know ye the price of that you bear away
So rudely?

Pha. Who's that?

Dion. 'Tis the Lord Philafter.

Phi. 'Tis not the treafure of all kings in one,
The wealth of Tagus, nor the rocks of pearl
That pave the court of Neptune, can weigh down
That virtue.　It was I affail'd the Princefs.
Place me, fome god, upon a pyramid,
Higher than hills of earth, and lend a voice
Loud as your thunder to me, that from thence
I may difcourfe to all the under-world
The worth that dwells in him!

Pha. How's this?

Bel. My Lord, fome man
Weary of life, that would be glad to die.

Phi. Leave thefe untimely courtefies, Bellario.

Bel. Alas! he's mad; come, will you lead me on?

Phi. By all the oaths that men ought moft to keep,
And gods do punifh moft, when men do break,
He touch'd her not.　Take heed, Bellario,
How thou doft drown the virtues thou haft fhown,
With perjury.　By all that's good, 'twas I;
You know, fhe ftood betwixt me and my right.

Pha. Thy own tongue be thy judge.

Cle. It was Philafter.

Dion. Is't not a brave boy?
Well, Sirs, I fear me, we are all deceiv'd.

Phi. Have I no friend here?

Dion. Yes.

Phi. Then fhew it; fome
Good body lend a hand to draw us nearer.
Would you have tears fhed for you when you die?
Then lay me gently on his neck, that there

I may weep floods, [*They lead him to* Bellario] and breathe
          out my fpirit ;
'Tis not the wealth of Plutus, nor the gold
Lock'd in the heart of earth, can buy away
This arm-full from me.   You hard-hearted men,
More ftony than thefe mountains, can you fee
Such clear pure blood drop, and not cut your flefh
To ftop his life ? To bind whofe bitter wounds,
Queens ought to tear their hair, and with their tears
Bathe them.   Forgive me, thou that art the wealth
Of poor Philafter !

    Enter King, Arethufa, *and a Guard.*

 King. Is the villain ta'en ?
 Pha. Sir, here be two confefs the deed ; but fay it was
Philafter.
 Phi. Queftion it no more, it was.
 King. The fellow that did fight with him, will tell us.
 Are. Ah, me ! I know he will.
 King. Did not you know him ?
 Are. No, Sir ; if it was he, he was difguifed.
 Phi. I was fo.   Oh, my ftars ! that I fhould live ftill.
 King. Thou ambitious fool !
Thou, that haft laid a train for thy own life ;
' Now I do mean to do, I'll leave to talk.'
Bear him to prifon.
 Are. Sir, they did plot together to take hence
This harmlefs life ; fhould it pafs unreveng'd,
I fhould to earth go weeping : grant me then
(By all the love a father bears his child)
The cuftody of both, and to appoint
Their tortures and their death.
 King. 'Tis granted : take them to you, with a guard,
Come, princely Pharamond, this bufinefs paft,
We may with more fecurity go on
To your intended match.   [*Exeunt.*

END of the FOURTH ACT.

E

ACT

A C T V.

SCENE, *the Palace*.

Enter Philaster, Arethusa, *and* Bellario.

' ARETHUSA.

' NAY, dear Philaster, grieve not! we are well!
' *Bel.* Nay, good my Lord, forbear; we are won-
d'rous well.
' *Phi.* Oh, Arethusa! Oh, Bellario! leave to be kind:
' I shall be shot from heav'n, as now from earth,
' If you continue so. I am a man,
' False to a pair of the most trusty ones
' That ever earth bore. Can it bear us all?
' Forgive, and leave me! but the King hath sent
' To call me to my death: Oh, shew it me,
' And then forget me. And for thee, my boy,
' I shall deliver words will mollify
' The hearts of beasts, to spare thy innocence.
' *Bel.* Alas, my Lord, my life is not a thing
' Worthy your noble thoughts; 'tis not a life,
' 'Tis but a piece of childhood thrown away:
' Should I outlive you, I should then outlive
' Virtue and honour; and, when that day comes,
' If ever I shall close these eyes but once,
' May I live spotted for my perjury,
' And waste my limbs to nothing!
' *Are.* And I (the woful'st mind that ever was,
' Forc'd with my hands to bring my Lord to death)
' Do by the honour of a virgin swear,
' To tell no hours beyond it.
' *Phi.* Make me not hated so.
' People will tear me, when they find you true
' To such a wretch as I; I shall die loath'd.
' Enjoy your kingdoms peaceably, whilst I
' For ever sleep forgotten with my faults,
' Ev'ry just servant, ev'ry maid in love,
' Will have a piece of me, if you be true.
' *Are.* My dear Lord, say not so.
' *Bel.* A piece of you!
' He was not born of woman, that can cut
' It and look on.

' *Phi.* Take me in tears betwixt you ;
' For elſe my heart will break with ſhame and ſorrow.
' *Are.* Why, 'tis well.
' *Bel.* Lament no more.
' *Phi.* What would you have done
' If you had wrong'd me baſely, and had found
' My life no price, compar'd to yours ? For love, Sirs,
' Deal with me plainly.
' *Bel.* 'Twas miſtaken, Sir.
' *Phi.* Why, if it were ?
' *Bel.* Then, Sir, we would have aſk'd your pardon,
' *Phi.* And have hope to enjoy it ?
' *Are.* Enjoy it ! ay.
' *Phi.* Would you, indeed ? be plain.
' *Bel.* We would, my Lord.
' *Phi.* Forgive me then.
' *Are.* So, ſo.
' *Bel.* 'Tis as it ſhould be now.
' *Phi.* Lead to my death.   [*Exeunt.*'

SCENE, the Preſence Chamber.

Enter King, Dion, Cleremont, *and* Thraſiline.
King. Gentlemen, who ſaw the Prince ?
Cle. So pleaſe you, Sir, he's gone to ſee the city,
And the new platform, with ſome gentlemen
Attending on him.
King. Is the Princeſs ready
To bring her priſoner out ?
Thra. She waits your grace.
King. Tell her we ſtay.

Enter a Meſſenger.

Meſ. Where's the King ?
King. Here.
Meſ. To your ſtrength, O King,
And reſcue the prince Pharamond from danger ;
He's taken priſoner by the citizens,
Fearing the Lord Philaſter.

' *Enter another Meſſenger.*

' *Meſ.* Arm, arm, O King, the city is in mutiny,
' Led by an old grey ruffian, who comes on
' In reſcue of the lord Philaſter.   [*Exit.*'
King. Away to th' citadel ; I'll ſee them ſafe,

E 2   And

And then cope with thefe burghers : let the guard
And all the gentlemen give ftrong attendance.   [*Exit.*

Cle. The city up! This was above our wifhes.

Dion. Well, my dear countrymen, if you continue,
and fall not back upon the firft broken fhin, I'll have you
chronicled, and chronicled, and cut and chronicled, and
fung in all-to-be-praifed fonnets, and graved in new brave
ballads, that all tongues fhall troule you *in fæcula fæculo-
rum*, my kind can-carriers.

Thra. What if a toy take them i'th' heels now, and
they all run away, and cry, the devil take the hind-
moft ?

Dion. Then the fame devil take the foremoft too, and
fouce him for his breakfaft! ' If they all prove cowards,
' my curfes fly among them and be fpeeding ! May they
' have murrains reign to keep the gentlemen at home,
' unbound in eafy freeze ! May the moths branch their
' velvets ! May their falfe lights undo them, and difcover
' preffes, holes, ftains, and oldnefs in their ftuffs, and
' make them fhop-rid !' May they keep whores and
horfes, and break ; and live mewed up with necks of
beef and turnips ! May they have many children, and
none like the father ! May they know no language but
that gibberifh they prattle to their parcels, unlefs it be
the Gothic Latin they write in their bonds, and may
they write that falfe, and lofe their debts !

Enter the King.

King. 'Tis Philafter,
None but Philafter, muft allay this heat ;
They will not hear me fpeak ; but call me tyrant.
My daughter and Bellario too declare,
Were he to die, that they would both die with him.
Oh, run, dear friend, and bring the lord Philafter ;
Speak him fair ; call him prince ; do him all
The courtefy you can ; commend me to him.
I have already given orders for his liberty.

Cle. My Lord, he's here.

Enter Philafter.

King. Oh, worthy Sir, forgive me ; ' do not make
' Your miferies and my faults meet together,
' To bring a greater danger. Be yourfelf,
' Still found amongft difeafes.' I have wrong'd you,

' And

' And though I find it laſt, and beaten to it,
' Let firſt your goodneſs know it.'   Calm the people,
And be what you were born to: take your love,
And with her my repentance, ' and my wiſhes,
' And all my pray'rs :' by th' gods, my heart ſpeaks this :
And if the leaſt fall from me not perform'd,
May I be ſtruck with thunder.
     Phi. Mighty Sir,
I will not do your greatneſs ſo much wrong,
As not to make your word truth ; free the Princeſs
And the poor boy, and let me ſtand the ſhock
Of this mad ſea-breach, which I'll either turn
Or periſh with it.
     King. Let your own word free them.
     Phi. Then thus I take my leave, kiſſing your hand,
And hanging on your royal word : be kingly,
And be not mov'd, Sir ; I ſhall bring you peace,
Or never bring myſelf back.
     King. All the gods go with thee.   [*Exeunt.*

SCENE, a Street in the City.

Enter an old Captain and Citizens with Pharamond.

     Cap. Come, my brave myrmidons, let us fall on,
Let our caps ſwarm, my boys,   -
And your nimble tongues forget your mothers'
Gibberiſh, of what do you lack, and ſet your mouths
Up, children, till your pallats fall frighted half a
Fathom, paſt the cure of bay-ſalt and groſs pepper,
And then cry Philaſter, brave Philaſter.
     All. Philaſter! Philaſter!
     Cap. How do you like this, my Lord Prince ?
     Pha. I hear it with diſdain, unterrified ;
Yet ſure humanity has not forſook you ;
You will not ſee me maſſacred, thus coolly butcher'd by
          numbers ?
Enter Philaſter.
     All. Long live Philaſter, the brave prince Philaſter
     Phi. I thank you, gentlemen ; but why are theſe
Rude weapons brought abroad, to teach your hands
Uncivil trades ?
     Cap. My royal Roſiclear,
We are thy myrmidons, thy guard, thy roarers ;

E 3

An

And when thy noble body is in durance,
Thus we do clap our mufty murrions on,
And trace the ftreets in terror. Is it peace,
Thou Mars of men? Is the king fociable,
And bids thee live? Art thou above thy foemen,
And free as Phœbus? Speak; if not, this ftand
Of royal blood fhall be abroach, a-tilt, and run
Even to the lees of honour.

   Phi. Hold and be fatisfied; I am myfelf,
Free as my thoughts are; by the gods, I am.

   Cap. Art thou the dainty darling of the king?
Art thou the Hylas to our Hercules?
Is the court navigable, and the prefence ftuck
With flags of friendfhip? If not, we are thy caftle,
And this man fleeps.

   Phi.. I am what I defire to be, your friend;
I am what I was born to be, your prince.

   Pha. Sir, there is fome humanity in you;
You have a noble foul; forget my name,
And know my mifery; fet me fafe aboard
From thefe wild Canibals, and, as I live,
I'll quit this land for ever.

   Phi. I do pity you: friends, difcharge your fears;
Deliver me the Prince.
Good, my friends, go to your houfes, and by me have
Your pardons, and my love;
And know, there fhall be nothing in my pow'r
You may deferve, but you fhall have your wifhes.

   All. Long mayft thou live, brave Prince!
Brave Prince! brave Prince!   [*Exeunt* Phi. *and* Pha.

   Cap. Go thy ways; thou art the king of courtefy:
fall off again, my fweet youths; come, and every man
trace to his houfe again, and hang his pewter up; then
to the tavern, and bring your wives in muffs: we will
have mufic, and the red grape fhall make us dance, and
rife, boys.   [*Exeunt.*

SCENE,

SCENE *changes to the Court.*

Enter King, Arethusa, Galatea, Megra, Cleremont,
Dion, Thrasiline, Bellario, *and Attendants.*

King. Is it appeas'd?
Dion. Sir, all is quiet as the dead of night,
As peaceable as sleep.   My lord Philaster
Brings on the Prince himself.
King. Kind gentleman!
I will not break the least word I have giv'n
In promise to him.   I have heap'd a world
Of grief upon his head, which yet I hope
To wash away.

Enter Philaster *and* Pharamond.

Cle. My Lord is come.
King. My son!
Blest be the time, that I have leave to call
Such virtue mine! ' Now thou art in mine arms,
' Methinks I have a salve unto my breast
' For all the stings that dwell there :' streams of grief
That I have wrong'd thee, and as much of joy
That I repent it, issue from mine eyes :
Let them appease thee ; take thy right ; take her,
She is thy right too, and forget to urge
My vexed soul with that I did before.
Phi. Sir, it is blotted from my memory,
Past and forgotten : for you, prince of Spain,
Whom I have thus redeem'd, you have full leave
To make an honourable voyage home.
And if you would go furnish'd to your realm
With fair provision, I do see a lady,
Methinks, would gladly bear you company.
Meg. Shall I then alone
Be made the mark of obloquy and scorn?
Can shame remain perpetually in me,
And not in others? Or have princes salves -
To cure ill names, that meaner people want?
Phi. What mean you?
Meg. You must get another ship
To bear the Princess and the boy together.
Dion. How now!
Meg. I have already publish'd both their shames.

' Ship

' Ship us all four, my Lord; we can endure
' Weather and wind alike.'
    King. Clear thou thyself, or know not me for father.
    Are. This earth, how false it is! What means is left
For me to clear myself? It lies in your belief.
My Lord; believe me, and let all things else
Struggle together to dishonour me.
    Bel. Oh, stop your ears, great King, that I may speak
As freedom would: then I will call this lady
As base as be her actions. Hear me, Sir;
Believe your heated blood when it rebels
Against your reason, sooner than this lady.
    Phi. This lady! I will sooner trust the wind
With feathers, or the troubled sea with pearl,
Than her with any thing: believe her not!
Why, think you, if I did believe her words,
I would outlive them? Honour cannot take
Revenge on you; then what were to be known
But death?
    King. Forget her, Sir, since all is knit
Between us: but I must request of you
One favour, and will sadly not be denied.
    Phi. Command, whate'er it be.
    King. Swear to be true
To what you promise.
    Phi. By the l'ow'rs above,
Let it not be the death of her or him,
And it is granted.
    King. Bear away the boy
To torture. I will have her clear'd or buried.
    Phi. Oh, let me call my words back, worthy Sir;
Ask something else: bury my life and right
In one poor grave; but do not take away
My life and fame at once.
    King. Away with him, it stands irrevocable.
    Bel. Oh, kill me, gentlemen!
    ' *Dion.* No, help, Sirs.'
    Bel. Will you torture me?
    King. Haste there; why stay you?
    Bel. Then I shall not break my vow,
You know, just gods, though I discover all.
    King. How's that? Will he confess?

Dion.

Dion. Sir, fo he fays.

King. Speak then.

Bel. Great king, if you command
This lord to talk with me alone, my tongue,
Urg'd by my heart, fhall utter all the thoughts
My youth hath known, and ftranger things than thefe
You hear not often.

King. Walk afide with him.

                [Dion *and* Bel. *walk afide together.*

Dion. Why fpeak'ft thou not ?

Bel. Know you this face, my Lord ?

Dion. No.

Bel. Have you not feen it, nor the like ?

Dion. Yes, I have feen the like, but readily
I know not where.

Bel. I have been often told
In court, of one Euphrafia, a lady,
And daughter to you ; betwixt whom and me,
They, that would flatter my bad face, would fwear
There was fuch ftrange refemblance, that we two
Could not be known afunder, dreft alike.

Dion. By Heav'n, and fo there is.

Bel. For her fair fake,
Who now doth fpend the fpring-time of her life
In holy pilgrimage, move to the King,
That I may 'fcape this torture.

Dion. But thou fpeak'ft
As like Euphrafia, as thou doft look.
How came it to thy knowledge that fhe lives
In pilgrimage ?

Bel. I know it not, my Lord.
But I have heard it, yet do fcarce believe it.

Dion. Oh, my fhame, is it poffible ? Draw near,
That I may gaze upon thee : art thou fhe ?
' Or elfe her murderer ?' Where wert thou born ?

Bel. In Siracufa.

Dion. What's thy name ?

Bel. Euphrafia.

Dion. 'Tis juft ; 'tis fhe ; now I do know thee ; Oh,
That thou hadft died, and I had never feen
Thee nor my fhame.

Bel. Would I had died, indeed ! I wifh it too ;

And

And fo I muſt have done by vow, ere publiſhed
What I have told ; but that there was no means
To hide it longer ; yet I joy in this,
The Princefs is all clear.
   King. What have you done?
   Dion. All is difcover'd.
   Are. What is difcover'd ?
   Dion. Why, my ſhame ;
It is a woman ; let her fpeak the reſt.
   Phi. How ! that again.
   Dion. It is a woman.
   Phi. Bleſt be you pow'rs that favour innocence !
It is a woman, Sir ! hark, gentlemen !
It is a woman. Arethufa, take
My foul into thy breaſt, that would be gone
With joy ; it is a woman—thou art fair,
And virtuous ſtill to ages, 'fpight of malice.
   King. Speak you ; where lies his ſhame ?
   Bel. I am his daughter.
   Phi. The gods are juſt.
But, Bellario,
(For I muſt call thee ſtill fo) tell me, why
Thou didſt conceal thy fex ; it was a fault ;
A fault, Bellario, though thy other deeds
Of truth outweigh'd it : all thefe jealoufies
Had flown to nothing, if thou hadſt difcover'd,
What now we know.
   Bel. My father oft would fpeak
Your worth and virtue, and as I did grow
More and more apprehenfive, I did thirſt
To fee the man fo prais'd ; but yet all this
Was but a maiden-longing, to be loſt
As foon as found ; till fitting in my window,
Printing my thoughts in lawn, I faw a god
I thought (but it was you) enter our gates ;
My blood flew out, and back again as faſt,
As I had puff'd it forth and fuck'd it in
Like breath ; then was I call'd away in haſte
To entertain you. Never was a man,
Heav'd from a ſheep-cote to a fcepter, rais'd
So high in thoughts as I ; you left a kifs
Upon thefe lips then, which I mean to keep

From

From you for ever; I did hear you talk,
Far above finging; after you were gone,
I grew acquainted with my heart, and fearch'd
What ftirr'd it fo: alas! I found it love;
Yet far from ill, for could I have but liv'd
In prefence of you, I had had my end;
For this I did delude my noble father
With a feign'd pilgrimage, and drefs'd myfelf
In habit of a boy; and, for I knew
My birth no match for you, I was paft hope
Of having you: and underftanding well
That when I made difcovery of my fex,
I could not ftay with you; I made a vow,
By all the moft religious things a maid
Could call together, never to be known,
Whilft there was hope to hide me from mens' eyes,
For other than I feem'd, that I might ever
Abide with you; then fat I by the fount,
Where firft you took me up.
 King. Search out a match
Within our kingdom, where and when thou wilt,
And I will pay thy dowry; and thyfelf
Wilt well deferve him.
 Bel. Never, Sir, will I
Marry; it is a thing within my vow.
 Phi. I grieve, fuch virtues fhould be laid in earth
Without an heir. Hear me, my royal father,
Wrong not the freedom of our fouls fo much,
To think to take revenge of that bafe woman;
Her malice cannot hurt us; fet her free
As fhe was born, faving from fhame and fin.
 King. Well! Be it fo. You, Pharamond,
Shall have free paffage, and a conduct home
Worthy fo great a prince; when you come there,
Remember, 'twas your faults that loft you her,
And not my purpos'd will.
 Pha. I do confefs it;
And let this confeffion
Spread an oblivion o'er my follies paft.
 King. It fhall—All is forgot;
Now join your hands in one. Enjoy, Philafter,
This kingdom, which is yours, and after me

Whatever I call mine ; my bleffing on you !
All happy hours be at your marriage-joys,
That you may grow yourfelves over all lands,
And live to fee your plenteous branches fpring
Where-ever there is fun !——Let princes learn
By this to rule the paffions of their blood ;
For, what Heav'n wills, can never be withftood.

END of the FIFTH ACT.

M.rs YATES in the Character of *VIRGINIA*.

For tho' I love, yet still I am a Roman.

BELL'S EDITION.

VIRGINIA.

A TRAGEDY.

LONDON:

Printed for JOHN BELL, near *Exeter-Exchange*, in the *Strand*.

MDCCLXXVIII.

T O

THE RIGHT HONOURABLE

T H E

EARL AND COUNTESS OF COVENTRY,

THIS TRAGEDY,

IN GRATEFUL ACKNOWLEDGMENT

OF THEIR

POWERFUL PROTECTION AND FAVOUR,

IS INSCRIBED,

BY THEIR MOST OBLIGED,

A N D

MOST OBEDIENT HUMBLE SERVANT,

THE AUTHOR.

[illegible]

[illegible]

[illegible]

[illegible]

[illegible]

[illegible]

[illegible]

[illegible]

[illegible]

PROLOGUE.

Written and spoken by Mr. GARRICK.

PROLOGUES, like compliments, are loss of time;
 'Tis penning bows, and making legs in rhyme;
'Tis cringing at the door with simp'ring grin,
When we should shew the company within——
So thinks our bard, who, stiff in classic knowledge,
Preserves too much the buckram of the college.
Lord, Sir! said I, an audience must be woo'd,
And, lady-like, with flattery pursu'd;
They nauseate fellows that are blunt and rude.
Authors should learn to dance, as well as write——
Dance at my time of life! Zounds, what a fight!
Grown gentlemen ('tis advertis'd) do learn by night.
Your modern prologues, and such whims as these,
The Greeks ne'er knew—turn, turn to Sophocles——
I read no Greek, Sir—when I was at school,
Terence had prologues; Terence was no fool——
He had; but why? (reply'd the bard in rage)
Exotics, monsters, had possess'd the stage,
But we have none, in this enlighten'd age!
Your Britons now, from gallery to pit,
Can relish nought, but sterling, Attic wit.
Here, take my play, I meant it for instruction;
If rhymes are wanting for its introduction,
E'en let that nonsense be your own production.
Off went the poet—It is now expedient,
I speak as manager, and your obedient.
I, as your cat'rer, would provide you dishes,
Dress'd to your palates, season'd to your wishes——

Say

Say but you're tir'd with boil'd and roaſt at home,
We too can ſend for niceties from Rome ;
To pleaſe your taſtes will ſpare nor pains nor money,
Diſcard ſirloins, and get you maccaroni.
Whate'er new guſto for a time may reign,
Shakeſpeare and beef muſt have their turn again.
    If novelties can pleaſe, to-night we've two ;
Tho' Engliſh both, yet ſpare them, as they're new——
To one at leaſt your uſual favour ſhew ;
A female aſks it, can a man ſay no ?
Should you indulge our * novice, yet unſeen,
And crown her with your hands a tragic queen ;
Should you with ſmiles a confidence impart,
To calm thoſe fears which ſpeak a feeling heart ;
Aſſiſt each ſtruggle of ingenuous ſhame,
Which curbs a genius in its road to fame :
With one wiſh more her whole ambition ends——
She hopes ſome merit, to deſerve ſuch friends.

---

* A new actreſs.

ADVER.

ADVERTISEMENT.

THE Author cannot suffer this tragedy to be published, without acknowledging the obligations he is under to Mr. Garrick, not only for his masterly performance in the representation—(that is, nothing new) and for his prologue and epilogue, which have met with universal applause, but likewise for his friendly advice, by which the play is certainly rendered much more dramatic than it was at first. By the same advice, some passages are restored in the printing, which were omitted in the representation. The reader, perhaps, may excuse this small addition to the length of the scenes; but with the spectator, brevity will atone for a number of deficiencies.

Mrs. Cibber, in particular, and the other performers, in general, should have the author's thanks, for the great justice they have done him, did not the applause of the town make any thing that he could say unnecessary.

DRA-

DRAMATIS PERSONÆ.

MEN.

	Drury-Lane.
Appius,, chief of the Decemvirs,	Mr. Moffop.
L. *Virginius*, a plebeian centurion,	Mr. Garrick.
Lucius Icilius, a young plebeian, late tribune of the people,	Mr. Rofs.
Claudius, a patrician, a dependant on *Appius*,	Mr. Davies.
Rufus, a plebeian, a creature of *Claudius*,	Mr. Mozeen.
Caius, freedman to L. *Virginius*,	Mr. Clough.

WOMEN.

Virginia, daughter to L. *Virginius*,	Mrs. Cibber.
Marcia, fifter to *Claudius*,	Mrs. Graham.
Plautia, *Virginia*'s nurfe and governefs,	Mrs. Bennet.

Guards, lictors, attendants, &c.

SCENE, *ROME*.

VIR.

VIRGINIA.

ACT I.

SCENE, *an Apartment in* Claudius's *House in Rome.*

Enter Claudius *and* Rufus.

CLAUDIUS.

RUFUS, didſt mark Virginius, with what ſcorn
    He ey'd us, as we paſs'd his gates but now ?
    Ruf. Old age, and frantic dreams of Rome and glory,
Have turn'd his viſionary brain.
    Claud. Saw'ſt thou
With what impetuous haſte and eager looks
He iſſued forth ?
    Ruf. What is the cauſe ?
    Claud. A ſummons
Is juſt arriv'd, that calls him to the camp ;
A battle is expeſted ev'ry hour.
'Tis lucky, and will favour the deſign
Of our Decemvir on his beauteous daughter.
    Ruf. This raſh purſuit of a contraſted maid,
I fear, will have ſome fatal end.   Should Appius
Employ his pow'r——I tremble at the thought!
Virginius is ador'd throughout the tribes ;
His ſilver hairs, his honour, his rough eloquence,
Would fire all Rome.   We muſt find out ſome way
To turn him from ſo deſperate a courſe.
    Claud. Impoſſible and vain !—His headlong paſſions
Mock all controul.   Of that no more.   I tell thee,
No choice is left, but to contrive the means
To ſooth her to his arms.
    Ruf. To ſooth her, Claudius !
Thou know'ſt ſhe is contraſted ; nay, with fondneſs

She

Claud. [illegible] Pondering'd;
[illegible] of Appius' message with Virginia,
And [illegible] the [illegible]
[illegible] blood [illegible].
[illegible]; [illegible]
[illegible]; but [illegible]
Is of plebeian [illegible].

   Ref. How [illegible] this?

   Claud. With [illegible], deep [illegible]; [illegible],
And her [illegible], who are all [illegible]——
[illegible] I hear her [illegible].   Go, Refus; [illegible]
To Appius; tell him, that [illegible],
Obedience to his will; and [illegible] her son
Will let him know th' [illegible], and seize his [illegible].

                                         [*Exit* [illegible]

             Enter Marcus.

   Mar. I come [illegible]
Your own [illegible].

   Claud. Marcus, [illegible]
My soul [illegible]; but [illegible]
Her [illegible], hopes, and [illegible]; [illegible]
Each [illegible], and each [illegible] with [illegible] Marcus.

   Mar. Then [illegible].   Thus [illegible]
Becomes a [illegible].   [*illegible*]

   Claud. Too [illegible].
Thy [illegible] I own, thy [illegible].   Let me call thee
The [illegible] my soul [illegible] with.

   Mar. My [illegible],
Thy [illegible] are all my own; and if the world
[illegible], to [illegible],
I'll give my [illegible], my life, my all, as freely
As I give [illegible] this or I deserve.

   Claud. Oh, Marcus!
Virginia——she, she is the cause!
   Mar. Virginia!
My dear and [illegible] friend!——When [illegible]?
This [illegible] I [illegible]——

   Claud. [*illegible*] Where, Virginia!
Expect her here——Oh, [illegible]——
   Mar. Shall I [illegible]
From [illegible], I were to [illegible] his [illegible]——

                                              [*Exit*

Know then, this day Icilius secretly
Intends to enter Rome.
   Claud. Heav'ns! on what cause?
Ha!—sure he has not heard—It cannot be——   [*Aside.*
   Mar. Th'impatience of a lover.   Thro' my means,
He begs to meet the object of his wishes ;
To steal a look, to breathe a sigh, no more.
   Claud. But knows Virginia his intent ?
   Mar. She does not ;
I only sent t' intreat her to pass hither.
   Claud. Marcia, I do conjure thee, by the gods,
By all thou hold'st most dear, attend and hear me!
Prevent their meeting, break this fatal match,
Or Appius, stung to frenzy, will commit
Some act of desperation——Oh, 'twill save
Thy friends, thy brother, Appius, nay Virginia
And Rome itself, perhaps, from instant ruin !   [*Think,*
   Mar. Ah, Claudius ! whither wouldst thou lead me ?—
Think, what I owe to friendship and to honour.
   Claud. Honour commands all private ties should yield
To public good. Wouldst thou behold our streets
Strewn with the carcases of slaughter'd citizens,
And Tyber's wave run purple with their blood ?
Ha, civil discord, Marcia !
   Mar. Gods, cut short
My thread of life, ere that dread hour arrives !
   Claud. 'Tis ev'n at hand, and, like a horrid comet,
Hangs o'er our fated heads, portending plagues,
And gen'ral desolation to mankind !
   Mar. Why dost thou tempt me with these shapes of
To my perdition ? I dare be unhappy,   [*terror,*
Unhappy, but not base. Oh, my Virginia !
Companion of my youth ! the tender band
Of amity, that link'd our infancy,
Grew with our growth, and ripen'd with our years,
Shall I now break the sacred knot with treason ?
Icilius too—a friend !—What have I said ?
A friend !—Ah, Marcia ! would he were no more !
But, hush, my sighs ! [*Aside.*] How shall I look on him,
When he shall know, that Marcia was the serpent
That stung his heart ?

Claud. Icilius?——hear me, Marcia——
If thou would ft fave Icilius from deftruction,
Burft all the ties that bind him to Virginia;
By heav'ns, his very life, his being, all,
Depend on thy compliance,
    Mar. Ha!—his life!—
Saidft thou his life!—be ftill, my trembling heart. [*Afide.*
    Claud. Diforder'd!   [*Afide.*
    Mar. Muft Icilius' life then pay
The purchafe of his love?
    Claud. 'Tis as I wifh'd——   [*Afide.*
Can Marcia afk?—fhould Appius' hopes be blafted,
Think'ft thou he'd e'er endure a hated rival
Should live to triumph o'er him, and poffefs
The prize he loft?—To pierce Icilius' heart,
And glut his fierce revenge, Appius would wade
Thro' feas of blood!
    Mar. Look down, ye pitying gods,
Or I am loft!   [*Afide.*
    Claud. Diflodge this fatal image,
That fills Virginia's breaft; make room for Appius;
Truft me the time will come, when ev'n Icilius
Shall thank thy care, and blefs the hand that fav'd him.
A more aufpicious love fhall crown his wifhes,
And kinder ftars fhall reign!
    Mar. I dare not, cannot——
    Claud. Enough——thou haft decreed Icilius' fall,
And all muft go to wreck.   [*Going.*
    Mar. Diftract me not!——
Oh, ftay!——tho' I fhould try to plead for Appius,
What could I hope?—Repulfe, reproach, and fhame
At once would dafh th' attempt——
    Claud. To plead for Appius!——
Feeble and vain!—Thou muft fow difcord, Marcia,
Between the lovers; Appius then may profper.
    Mar. Moft foul, and horrid!
    Claud. 'Tis a righteous fraud
To cheat 'em into fafety——but no more——
Heav'n points the only way to peace and blifs;
If thou wilt not purfue it, take th' event.
    Mar. Oh, love! Oh, virtue! how ye tear this heart! [*Afide.*
Means Appius nobly? Does he purpofe marriage,
And holy rites?

B

Claud.

Claud. 'Tis his foul's utmoſt wiſh
To call Virginia his, and by a claim,
The proudeſt blood of Rome might glory in.
                    Enter a Slave.
    Slave. The daughter of Virginius is arriv'd,
And entering now the gates.   [*Exit* Slave.
    Claud. Now, Marcia, hear me.
Let me go forth to meet her, let me ſeize
The bleſt occaſion, and in ſofteſt terms
Sooth her young boſom with th' illuſtrious conqueſt
Her charms have made—I'll tell her thou art abſent—
Soon to return——— She muſt not ſee Icilius———
Beware of that———leave me to plead for Appius———
I'll blazon out the purity and ardor
Of his bright flame, his dignity, and merit;
I'll warm with love, or dazzle with ambition,
Her heart, if it be caſt in woman's mould:
Marcia, farewel! Be conſtant, and remember,
Thy friends, thy country, all, demand this ſervice!
                                    [*Exit* Claudius.

    Mar. Thy country and thy friends demand this ſer-
Ah, me!—he little thinks what paſſes here!   [vice—
                            [*Striking her breaſt.*

What conflicts!——what deſpair!——He little knows
The buſy, ſecret ſpring, that heaves unſeen
Within this beating breaſt, and drives me on
To do a deed!——Relentleſs, cruel love!
What ravage haſt thou made within this boſom!
Which nature faſhion'd in her ſofteſt mould,
And fitted it for truth and gentle pity!
But thou haſt ruin'd all!——Thou haſt let in
The furies, and their horrid train upon me!
Thou haſt undone poor Marcia!——Oh, Icilius!
Why did I ever ſee thy fatal form!
Why didſt thou chuſe me out to be thy friend,
And tell to me the ſtory of thy love,
Warm from the heart!—the flame infected me!
And can I ſee thee bleed?—Oh, love and fortune,
Guard the dear youth!——Reſerve your ſharpeſt bolts
For me!—Witneſs, ye gods, I am content
To be a wretch———But bleſs, Oh, bleſs Icilius!
                                    [*Exit* Mar.
                            SCENE,

SCENE, *The Forum.*

Enter **L.** Virginius *and* Caius.

L. Vir. Say'ſt thou Horatius is ſet free ?

Caius. This morn,
By an expreſs command from the Decemvirs,
The Lictors have releas'd him.

L. Vir. Then 'tis well——
I but delay'd my march till he was ſafe——
But by the gods, this outrage touches nearly,
And calls for quick redreſs ——Our ſenators
Thus wrong'd for riſing in the cauſe of liberty !——
Valerius ſilenc'd, and the brave Horatius
Condemn'd to bonds and death !

Caius. 'Tis now pretended,
The earneſt interceſſion of the ſenate
Hardly obtain'd this boon.

L. Vir. Mean, ſhallow art !
If he is freed, their fears, and not their mercy,
Have loos'd his chains !   Their dreaded pow'r now ſhakes !
They feel it too—Laſt night th'incens'd plebeians,
Gathering in deſperate throngs around the ſenate,
With their repeated clamours ſcar'd the colour
From their pale cheeks, till on their ſeat of judgment
They trembled, Caius ! Nay their hundred lictors—
But ſee, where Appius comes, their chief——

Caius. Virginius,
Retire—tempt not his rage—Your noble friend
Is ſafe—The camp demands your ſervice now——
Avoid his ſight : nor with your preſence rouze
The ſmother'd flames of diſcord.

L. Vir. Shall I fly
From Appius ?—Here I'll ſtay and dare his worſt !
And if his brutal pride provoke my anger,
I ſwear, ev'n from the fulneſs of my heart
I'll pour it on him !

Caius. Yet be calm ——

L. Vir. No more——
When bold oppreſſion ſtalks, let come what may,
Honour and age ſhall hold their courſe——

[Exit Caius.

B 2

Enter

Enter Appius.

Ap. Virginius,
Your friend yet lives; the senate have prevail'd;
And their united pray'rs at length have sav'd him
From the Tarpeian rock——Advise him well
To curb his insolence—Let him beware
How he again affronts the sovereign pow'r
With that seditious tongue, unless he means
To pay the forfeit with his life.

L. Vir. 'Tis well——
Th' imperial stile of kings and Tarquin's reign
Seem now return'd; and we must learn to tremble,
When Appius thunders!

Ap. Think'st thou the Decemvirate,
In whom the majesty of Rome resides,
So weak in strength or counsel, that each citizen
Commission'd by his pride, shall dare unquestion'd
T' arraign their power and office, give a loose
To his invective rage, and brave his masters?
But say, Virginius, why art thou a foe?
Thou hast not felt the weight of sov'reign power,
Thy family, tho' of plebeian rank,
Rever'd, and honour'd; favour and distinction,
Have still pursu'd thy steps, and grac'd thy virtues;
Why then such spleen to the Decemvirate?
Why so much care to foster and support
Th' unruly tribes?

L. Vir. Because I love mankind;
And therefore am an enemy to tyrants.

Ap. Call'st thou these clods mankind? things made for
To be impell'd or check'd, goaded or curb'd,   [use,
As higher spirits direct?

L. Vir. It seems then, Appius,
The Roman people are mere flocks and herds,
Permitted for a while to graze and fatten,
Then to be fleec'd, or slaughter'd at thy will.

Ap. Not all, Virginius—some must draw the yoke,
And carry burdens.

L. Vir. Insolent usurper!
Dar'st thou to triumph in a nation's sorrows?
Nay revel o'er her ruins? Righteous gods!

                                        Brought

Brought ye your boafted laws from Greece, to trample .
On thofe of nature and your groaning country ?

Ap. By heav'ns, thou mov'ft my laughter more than
Want ye your Confuls, your feditious Tribunes, [wrath!
To drive th' ungovern'd herd at your own lift ?
For this, ye feek the rabble, make harangues,.
Complain of wrongs, and fpeech it in the Forum.

L. Vir. Foe to thy country! What's that impious power,
Which the Decemvirate abufe fo grofly,
Firft gain'd by fraud, now held by violence ?
Is't not mere facrilege, and ufurpation ?
With all the fatal arts of dark ambition,
Did ye not practife on the tribes, to pave
Your way to empire ? Nay, thou haughty tyrant,.
Their chief, whofe fierce and barb'rous pride was wont •
To fpurn the commons, quickly learn'dft to fmooth
That rugged brow, and court the dregs of Rome !
The populace thus moulded to your purpofe,
Ye threw afide the mafk, and with bold robbery,
Seiz'd fovereign power !

  Ap. Ay, and will hold it too,.
In fpite of thee, Valerius and Horatius !

  L. Vir: Valerius and Horatius once were names
Fatal to tyrants ! Their great anceftors.
Once join'd their virtues 'gainft the haughty Tarquins,.
Together fluic'd their veins in honour's caufe,
And purchas'd immortality !——Will thefe,.
Who wear their father's names, forget their glories ?
No, proud Decemvir; thou fhalt find their fpirits
Live in their fons ! Some fparks of liberty,
In Roman breafts, tho' faint, yet ftill alive,
Blown by their breaths, may kindle to a flame :.
The gen'rous fire fhall catch from foul to foul,.
O'erbear all oppofition, blaft our foes,.
Purge off the foul infection we've contracted,.
And melt this droffy age, to pureft gold !

  Ap. Why then, the fate of the Decemvirate
Is fixt, it feems, and here their pow'r muft end;.
For fo the great Virginius has decreed !

  L. Vir. Thou triumph'ft, tyrant!—but the time will
(Perhaps is not far off) when thy mifdeeds,   [come,.
Accumulated, ripe for punifhment,

B. 3.   Shall

Shall burſt upon thy head, wake ſlumb'ring vengeance,
And juſtify the gods!—Rome feels at length
Thy galling chain, and pants to ſhake it off;
The miſt, that popular favour threw around thee,
Is vaniſh'd, and ſhe ſees thee as thou art!
Cover'd with crimes!—Fraud, rapine, perjury!
Now ſtarts to light the murder of brave Siccius,
And thy baſe hand red with his patriot blood!
    Ap. Confuſion!——
    L. Vir. Ha, Decemvir!—does it ſting thee?
With murder luſt is coupled! thy fell boſom
No pity knows!—The cries of innocence,
The lover's groans, the pangs of huſbands, parents,
Are but as goads to ſpur thy brutal appetite!
But think not yet our ſpirits are ſo tam'd,
So broke by conſtant wrongs—With inſtant march,
I'll join the camp—the gallant bands ſhall know,
While they drop blood for Rome, what chains are forging
To fetter thoſe victorious hands that ſav'd
Their country!—yes, Decemvir!—and 'ere long
Expect their thanks!——   [*Exit L. Virginius.*
    Ap. By heav'ns, thou haſt awak'd,
A fire that ſhall conſume thee!—Have I tam'd
The fierceſt ſpirits in Rome, quell'd the proud ſenate,
And bent their necks beneath my yoke, to ſhrink,
When a grey-headed ruffian ſtorms—Shalt thou
Controul my will?—Thy daughter, proud plebeian,
Shall quit thy inſolence! Appius from her
Shall ſeek redreſs, and on her panting boſom,
Receive the dear amends!
                    Enter Claudius.
    Ap. Now, Claudius, now——
What bring'ſt thou from the lovely fair?
    Claud. Repulſe——
Reproach, deſpair———nay ſcarce her fears ſuppreſs'd
Her riſing ſcorn——Icilius reigns unrivall'd
Within her breaſt, nor is there room for Appius.
    Ap. Shall Appius then at laſt become the ſcoff
Of a plebeian girl?—That haughty Appius,
Who with a nod has taught the ſtate to tremble?
No——by the gods ſhe's mine!——
    Claud. Conſider, Appius———

Ap. Away——she shall be mine—her fate's decreed——
I check'd my impetuous wishes, 'till her father
Had turn'd his back on Rome, nay, bore his insolence
Till I e'en burst with rage——————Then, but I mark'd
His daughter for my prey, I'd like a tyger
Leap'd at his throat !——But now, my boiling blood
No more can brook restraint——I am repuls'd,
And vengeance shall have way !——————I will possess her,
Tho' all Rome sink to lowest Tartarus,
And drag me headlong with her cumb'rous ruins !
   Claud. Is this the hero, whose superior greatness
Has won an empire?
   Ap. Claudius, I am mad !——
I'm on the rack !—My soul, with all her functions,
Chain'd down and prison'd, that she cannot stir
To shake her heavy load off, and escape
From this devouring fire !
   Claud. Now, gods above
Whom we adore, what spell has chang'd thee thus ?
And backward turn'd the course of thy strong nature,
Inflexible till now ?—— Severe, unmov'd,
Defying love's sweet pow'rs, and all his train
Of gentle sighs and wishes !
   Ap. Wouldst thou have me
Tell o'er the tale of my dishonour ?——Dwell on
Each point and circumstance of my defeat,
And parcel out my shame ?——Thou shalt be satisfy'd,
If the hot blood, that rises to my cheeks,
Choak not all utterance.——One fatal morn,
As I was seated on my throne of judgment,
In th' open Forum, the attendant crowd
Awaiting my decrees, my eyes were struck
With a young damsel that past slowly by me,
Attended only by one female slave.
Oh, Venus, what a grace !—What heavenly sweetness !
What looks!—On th' instant, troubled and disorder'd,
Trembling all o'er, I felt a pain unusual,
Yet mix'd with strange delight, shoot nimbly thro' me,
And thrill in ev'ry vein !— Quite fixt and motionless
Some time I sat, nor heard the noisy orator
Haranguing long and loud !——————My senses all
Seal'd up, except these eyes, which still pursu'd her:
                                        When

When fuddenly I rofe from my tribunal,
Difmifs'd the crowd, and gath'ring up my robe
In hafte, I followed her.
     Claud. Great Hercules !
Couldft thou fee this ?———
     Ap. Before I quite had reach'd her,
She enter'd, with her flave, the public fchools,
By cuftom deftin'd to our Roman maids ;
Here fuddenly I ftopp'd———here I ftood rooted———
My eyes devouring her !——
     Claud. Ye powers of love,
Who fhall henceforth oppofe your boundlefs fway ?
     Ap. Thus I remain'd entranc'd ;. and at my eyes.
Drank in her beauties, and with them deep draughts.
Of poifon, how delicious !—If fhe mov'd,
What grace !—Or if fhe mingled in the dance
Among the blooming virgins, Dian's felf,
Amidft her woodland nymphs fhe feem'd !———At length,
The exercifes o'er, a lyre fhe took,
A deep-ftrung lyre, and to harmonious chords
Pour'd out fuch melting ftrains, as would have ftaid
Th' uplifted arm of angry Jove, in act
To deal his thunder on a guilty world !
     Claud. In what bright forms a raptur'd lover's fancy.
Paints the all-perfect fair one ?———But proceed !
What follow'd this ?
     Ap At laft, the fports being ended,
She iffued forth ——— When ftrait the eyes of all
Were turn'd on her alone——— Surpris'd, abafh'd.
Her lovely face o'erfpread with rofy blufhes,
That witnefs'd fweet confufion, fhe let drop
Her veil, and homeward mov'd with decent pace,.
Timid and filent !——Ever fince that day,
That fatal day, my foul has known no reft.!
The venom'd fhaft ftill rankles in my bofom :
Still, as I pafs that way, I ftop and gaze !———
A monftrous fight !———Rome's awful magiftrate.
A laughter to the people !
     Claud. This fond paffion.
I fee has taken root.---But fay, great Appius,
Couldft thou, infpir'd with love fo delicate,
For fuch a charming maid, fo foft, fo perfect,

Couldft

Couldſt thou uſe force?—What!—lock thy furious hand
In her torn hair, and drag her, ſhrieking loud,
Invoking heav'n and earth, and curſing thee!
Injure, perhaps, and wound with thy abuſes
Her poliſh'd limbs!—By violence tear from her
Joys of a moment, inſincere, unripe,
Not half poſſeſs'd!

   Ap. Oh! Claudius, I will own to thee, with bluſhes,
This untam'd heart is melted to the ſoftneſs
Of a fond, loveſick maid!—Fain would I win
Her gentle ſoul, poſſeſs her pure affections!
But, Oh, in vain!—Force then muſt be employ'd;
The deſperate, only remedy——

   Claud. Hold, Appius!——
What if ſome luckier chance might yet prevail,
And give her to your wiſhes, charm'd and willing?
Were not that well?——

   Ap. Thou mean'ſt to trifle with me!——
But have a care!

   Claud. Know then my anxious zeal,
Still lab'ring in your ſervice, prompted me
To crave my ſiſter's aid; who won at length,
By my unwearied pray'r, at length conſents
To undertake our cauſe.

   Ap. That may be ſomething——
She is Virginia's friend——

   Claud. 'Tis an event
I ſcarce could hope—And what has mov'd her to't,
Unleſs a ſecret paſſion for Icilius,
Unwarily have ſtol'n upon her peace—

   Ap. Oh, gods, that were ſuch fortune!

   Claud. Diſcord, Appius,
Muſt firſt deſtroy their peace—let jealouſy
Diſtil her bane to taint their growing loves!
Light up reſentment! Fan the dang'rous fire
With dark ſurmiſes, hints, invented tales,
'Till it burſt all the tender bands in ſunder,
That knit their ſouls! Then ſeize the bleſt occaſion,
Then preſs her home; and ere the ſudden breach
Their jars have made, is cloſ'd, ſtep in between,
And ſever them for ever!

                                 Ap.

Ap. Now, by heav'ns,
Some whifp'ring deity infpir'd the thought!
It may fucceed---and then!---I'll fly this moment,
And throw me at her feet!---With fighs, and tears,
And all the moving eloquence of love,
I'll try to melt her heart! For who can paint
The energy, the tranfports of a lover?
Methinks I'm fick of pow'r without Virginia!
I feel a void! There's fomething wanting here!
                              [*Striking his breaft.*

Come then, fweet God of love, and crown my wifhes,
And touch the lovely maid with equal fire!
I'm wild with tranfport!---Oh, ye tedious hours,
Add feathers to your wings! that I may prove
The united joys of empire and of love!   [*Exeunt.*

END of the FIRST ACT.

A C T   II.

SCENE, Marcia's *Apartment.*

Marcia *and* Icilius, *meeting.*

MARCIA.

LUCIUS Icilius, welcome!
    Icil. Gen'rous Marcia,
Compos'd of faith and honour, conftant ever!
Accept fuch thanks, as one beyond all bounds
Oblig'd, can pay!---May the bleft gods above
Reward thy truth, and, at thy greateft need,
Grant me a friend as noble as thyfelf!
Oh, Marcia!---I have feen——
    Mar. What means, Icilius,
This ftrange diforder?
    Icil. But this morn I left
Our camp---In one fhort hour, the fpace I meafur'd
'Twixt Algidum and Rome, and fondly hop'd
In Marcia's friendfhip and Virginia's love
To banifh all my cares.——But, as I pafs'd

Virginius'

Virginius' gates, thefe eyes beheld a fight
That curdled up my blood!——The tyrant Appius
Was coming forth.——What may this mean?
   Mar. Icilius,
How fhall I anfwer thee?——In vain, alas!
Would I conceal what thou too foon muft know!
   Icil. My heart mifgives me! Does the high-thron'd
        villain
Attempt my love?—Oh, vengeance, vengeance, Marcia!
Or is't a lover's vain furmife?——
   Mar. Oh, no!——
   Icil. I fhall grow mad!—diftracting, horrid thoughts
Crowd faft upon me!—Marcia, if thy foul
Be not infenfible to ev'ry touch
Of friendfhip, or of pity; if the pangs
Of bleeding love, and tort'ring jealoufy
Can move thee, fpeak!—Reveal my mifery!
Sufpence is death!
   Mar. Icilius, that I pity thee,
The heav'ns bear witnefs for me!
   Icil. Ah, Virginia!
Thou fhalt have juftice; nor fhall the curft Appius
Invade thy helplefs innocence unpunifh'd!
   Mar. Icilius, think of that no more—His pow'r
Mocks all refiftance! His impetuous will,
Alone the meafure of all right and wrong!
Inflexible his foul; nor would he change
His deftin'd purpofe, though the fuppliant earth
Were humbled to his feet.
   Icil. Away——his pow'r
I reck not.—But be fure if he attempt
Againft Virginia aught, this hand fhall reach him
Through his arm'd lictors, though each deadly axe
Were levell'd at this head.
   Mar. Some dread event,
I fear, will be the iffue of this ftrife,
Unlefs fome pitying god look down on Rome,
And either melt the ftubborn foul of Appius,
Or move Icilius for his country's fake,
(His country threaten'd to be drench'd in blood!)]
Greatly to quit his claim, and fhew the force
Of Roman virtue.

Icil.

Icil. Do I hear aright?——
Amazement!—This from thee —Marcia!—the friend
Of my Virginia!---Marcia, whose soft pity.
Was wont to be the balm of all my woes?

   Mar. Ah, Lucius! Couldst thou read within my breast
In what deep characters thy woes are grav'd;
Knew'st thou, thy hapless fate alone extorts
The bitter, but yet neceffary counfel;
Then wouldst thou know too, Marcia is not wanting
In pity to Icilius, nor in faith.
To his Virginia

   Icil. Still obfcure and ftrange——
Some myft'ry yet behind---But, Marcia, fay,
If I could part from all my foul holds dear,
Tear from my panting breaft this rooted paffion,
And quite forget that e'er I lov'd Virginia!
What would become of her?—That dear, kind maid!
What would be her defpair, her loft condition,
Should I, on whofe firm truft her gentle foul
Relies, forfake her?

   Mar. Is all this diftrefs
For her alone?---Left fhe fhould over-grieve
For fuch a lofs?

   Icil. What dark and dreadful meaning
Lurks underneath thefe words?

   Mar. The mighty gods
Direct thee for the beft!

   Icil. Thou mak'ft me tremble!
And yet I know not why---Thou canft not mean——
Ah, no!---Let me fhun that!---My very foul
Shudd'ring ftarts back, as from a precip'ce,
To look that way!---I dare not think fuch ruin!—
For were fhe falfe!——

   Mar. Icilius, calm thy fpirit——
And ftand prepar'd for all---Think it not ftrange,
E'en though Virginia fhould——

   Icil. Stop, Marcia, ftop!
Think whither thou art going!---Oh, my heart!
What feel I here!---The damps of death are on me!---
What was't?---Thou faid'ft ev'n tho' Virginia fhould---
Should what?—— Speak!——

Mar.

Mar. Lucius, my heart bleeds for thee!
Compose this agony—Alas! I meant
To say, ev'n though she should consent, alarm'd
By danger, and perhaps too, her young bosom
Warm'd with ambition, and the flatt'ring hopes——

   Icil. Ruin'd!—Betray'd!—Undone!---She's false!--
     'Tis so!——
Virginia's false!—Oh, may the righteous gods
Avenge me!---But yet hold---Can it then be?——
Say, art thou not deceiv'd?---I know thou art---
Can I forget, in our first hours of love,
How her young heart, unpractis'd in deceit,
Spoke through her eyes, and fondly told the secret
Her tongue conceal'd?---But then, at length, when
By my soft flame, and melted into tenderness, [warm'd
In broken words, unutterably sweet,
Hiding her crimson blushes in my bosom,
And sighing soft, she own'd she lov'd Icilius!
That my soul sicken'd with excess of bliss?

   Mar. Why, what a wretch am I!—Can I bear this?
                         [*Aside.*

   Icil. Could she be thus, yet afterwards betray me
For Appius?---High and proud, rugged, severe,
Ill-pair'd with her in temper, as in years?
It cannot be——

   Mar. It seems thou know'st not, Lucius,
The force of vanity in female hearts.
Well may it shake Virginia's constancy,
To see a lover kneeling at her feet,
Who, with a nod, commands imperial Rome;
To see, where'er she turns her wand'ring eyes,
The capitol, the forum, the comitia,
Fill'd with the glories of his ancestors!
Statues and trophies! monuments! inscriptions!
Then fancy pictures the arm'd lictors standing
In order rank'd before her palace gate,
To wait her coming forth; while she assumes
Distinguish'd place amidst the noble matrons.
Alas! Icilius, these are charms too mighty
For our weak spirits!

Let me begone!---The light grows odious to me!
Away—to th' camp—there 'midst the throng of arms,
Seek from the savage Æqui that relief
My woes demand!---Secure, at least, to find
A faith more firm, and a less cruel foe!
Yet ere I quit these hated walls for ever,
Once more I will behold the perjur'd maid;
I will! and in the bitterness of soul
Upbraid her with my wrongs!   [*Going.*

    Mar. Yet stay, Icilius!
For mercy, but a moment stay, and hear me!
                       [*Exit* Icilius.

He's gone!---What have I done?---A horrid deed!
Methinks I dread to look within myself,
I am so black, so guilty!---Let me hide me
From thought---I dare not think---Ah, poor Virginia!
Abus'd Icilius!---Wretched, wretched Marcia!   [*Exit.*

SCENE, Virginia's *Apartment.*

Plautia *and* Virginia.

    Plaut. My dearest child, take comfort ——
    Vir. Oh, my Plautia!
My more than mother!---Thou, whose tender care
Nurs'd up my infant weakness, now my friend!
What comfort can I know, when all I love
Is far away, expos'd to ev'ry chance
Of cruel war!---That dear, that faithful breast,
Where my soul lives, where ev'ry wish and hope,
As to their center tend, perhaps this moment
Bleeds by some hostile spear!---while fatal Appius
Most basely in his absence, dares invade
The peace and honour of the maid he loves!
    Plaut. The gods, my child, shall shield thee from his
           violence!
    Vir. I do submit me to their gracious will.
Perhaps my death—I know not---Methinks, Plautia,
But for Icilius, I could wish to die!
And something whispers to my boding soul,
(A still and secret voice that speaks within)
Ere long I shall!
    Plaut. Banish these idle terrors—
The fears of fancy——

                                 Vir.

Vir. Plautia, but laft night
The vifion of Lucretia ftood before me!
    Plaut. Alas, my child! it was a dream---no more——
    Vir. A dream!——this mid-day fun not now beholds me
With fenfes more awake!---methinks I fee
And hear her ftill!---that more than human form!
That voice! that action! grave, majeftic, fad!
Daughter, fhe faid (pointing to a large wound
On her fair bofom, that yet dropp'd with blood)
Behold Lucretia, who for glóry died!
Remember, that this path is always open
To virtue, and to fame!---Then fighing, thus!
She parted from my fight!——
    Plaut. 'Twas terrible!
    Vir. Oh, 'twas a hint from fate---my father abfent---
Icilius too---myfelf, a helplefs maid,
Expos'd to all the infolence of power——
Plautia, this mighty fhade in pity came
T'affift my virtue, by her great example,
And teach me how to die!
    Plaut. Virginia, hear me——
Truft to my cautious age and ripe experience;
Ere long thy father will return---with him
Icilius comes---till then be mild with Appius:
Sooth his wild rage; deprive him not of hope;
Left arm'd with pow'r, and ftung by thy rafh fcorn,
Like a fell wolf, the fhepherd far away,
He wrong thy helplefs innocence.
    Vir. Oh, Plautia!
Muft I diffemble? flatter? muft I act
A part my foul abhors?---unfkill'd in arts,
That falfe ones ufe!——
    Plaut. Compell'd by ftrong neceffity,
Such fraud is virtue.
    Vir. What will fate do with me!
Oh, heav'ns! fupport me, Plautia, or I fink——
Look where the tyrant comes!---I cannot bear
The terror of his prefence!
    Plaut. Now beware,
How you provoke his rage;---be conftant, firm,
And meet him with a fettled brow.   [*Exit* Plautia.

        Enter

Enter Appius.

Vir. Lord Appius !

Ap. Forgive this rashness, fair Virginia,
That I presume t'appear before you, thus
Unwelcome to your eyes, and half forbid !
But, Oh, the torments not to be endur'd,
The agonies I feel ! They drive me on
Against all hope !---I would obey, but cannot !
My trembling limbs unbidden bear me to thee,
And my fond soul wants power to check their course ;
Ah, then ! if thou haft pity in thy nature,
If e'er that tender bosom heav'd with sighs,
At some sad tale of wretched, hopeless love,
Bleeding, distracted, torn with wild despair,
Look, look on me ! for all that woe is mine !

Vir. It ill befits the glory of great Appius
To mock an humble maid——

Ap. Alas, Virginia !
Mock thee ?—but well I know thou canst not mean it !
Mock thee ?—By heav'ns, all greatness, power, and pride,
Empire, and rule, degraded fall before thee,
And vanish into nothing !—Turn not from me !

Vir. My Lord, my Lord !—without reproach and
How may a Roman virgin dare to listen　　　　[shame
To words like these ?---and in a father's absence ?
And what can the great high-born Appius mean,
But scorn, and ruin to Virginia ?

Ap. Cruel !
Thou know'st——

Vir. My Lord, I know my humble lot
Has plac'd me far beneath you ; yet this heart
Is not less sensible of shame and baseness,
Than if it beat with high patrician blood.

Ap. By heav'ns, thou wrong'st my meaning and my
My love is pure as thy own rosy blushes !　　　[honour ;

Vir. My Lord, you wrong yourself, you wrong your
And that of your immortal ancestors,　　　　[glory,
By such a mean pursuit——some noble dame——

Ap. Talk not of others !---Thou alone hast empire,
Within this breast !-- Others there are, 'tis true,
And noble too---but, ah, how unlike thee !
My soul grows dull, and sickens at their sight——

Oh,

Oh, charming maid! Thou'rt of a different mould!
Thy fweetnefs, innocence, and artlefs truth,
Thy namelefs graces, and thy virtues join'd,
Ennoble thee above all high defcent,
And dignify my choice! and here, I fwear
I mean thee for my bride!
 Vir. Away, my Lord···
Have you forgot th' inviolable law
Yourfelf ordain'd, that interdicts fuch union?
 Ap. Have I deferv'd fo little of my country,
As not to claim an inftant revocation
Of any law that dooms me to be wretched?
Before to-morrow's fun awake the world,
It fhall be done——
 Vir. I muft not, dare not hear
Language like this---My Lord, let me intreat you
To leave me till my father be return'd;
The daughter of a Roman citizen
Cannot without a ftain admit fuch vifits.
 Ap. Cruel!---What banifh me from thy lov'd fight
For days!---whole days and nights!---it muft not be!
Here let me fall, and breathe my faithful vows!
Here, on the fpotlefs altar of thy hand,
Swear endlefs truth and love!   [*Kneeling.*
 Vir. Rife, rife my Lord!   [*Alarmed.*
     Enter Icilius.
 Icil. Ha!—do I fee aright!
 Vir. Icilius here!
 Ap. He here!---curft chance!——
 Icil. By all the pow'rs above,
'Tis fo! ev'n as fhe faid! fure my kind genius
Guided me here, that this fond, credulous heart
Might doubt no more, nor longer be abus'd
By one fo falfe! fo fatal!
 Vir. Ah, Icilius!
What mean thefe words?---Think'ft thou——
 Icil. Madam, 'tis well——
You have done nobly, while this wretch, this drudge,
Was abfent, lab'ring in the fields of death!
You've made a choice moft worthy of you. Appius,
Alone could merit fuch a heart as yours?
'Tis true, your vows are mine; but what are vows?
     C 3   Your

Your mounting spirit scorns to fly at less
Than empire!——Diadems perhaps, and sceptres!
Fit recompence for Appius! mighty Appius!
The righteous lawgiver! the glorious patron
Of liberty, and father of his country!

Ap. Insolent Tribune, hence! Dost thou presume
With scurril taunts?——

Icil. What, thou art champion for her!---
She well deserves it——

Vir. Is this well, Icilius?---
From thee this usage?

Ap. By the gods, sweet maid,
I will revenge thy wrongs; they're mine!---Plebeian!
Thy speech, as base as thy ignoble birth,
Shall cost thee dear!---Respect restrains my rage,
Or with this arm I would chastise thee hence!
                    [*Laying his hand on his sword.*

Icil. By heav'ns, Decemvir, but unsheath thy sword,
And thou o'erpay'st my wrongs---I'll call thee noble!---
But I forgot---thy outrage is entrusted
To safer hands---to lictors, guards, and armies.
        [Appius *coming up fiercely with his sword drawn,*
            Virginia *rushes between.*

Vir. For mercy hold!---Oh, spare my soul these ter-
Nor drive me to despair!——   [rors,

Ap. Thou lovely fair
Compose thy breast!---here at thy feet I lay
My sword and my resentment, and disclaim
Anger, ambition, pride, and ev'ry passion,
But love!——

Icil. Is't come to this?---Gods, she avows
Her perfidy, nor thinks me worth the pains
Ev'n of a little poor dissimulation!

Vir. His anguish touches me; but conscious pride,
And injur'd honour, after such an outrage,
Forbid that he should know it---[*Aside.*] Yes---perhaps
'Tis true; and thou dost well to think me false;
Thou seest I labour not t'evade the charge,
Nor do I deign an answer!

Ap. This goes well——
I'll interpose no longer——

Icil. Yes, I fee,
That heart, which once I thought the gift of heav'n
To blefs my days, is fold to bafe ambition;
That venal heart!---not giv'n, but fold!---Go then,
Thou perjur'd maid! enjoy thy guilty greatnefs!
Go! a new Tullia! help they impious Tarquin
To trample on thy country's bleeding bofom!
Like her, triumphant on thy haughty car,
Drive o'er thy rev'rend father's mangled corfe,
And think no road too fhort, that leads to empire!
    Vir. Go thou! nor longer dare to violate
My ears with thy licentious, brutal fpeech!
Go, where I never may behold thee more!
    Ap. Why this exceeds my hopes!---I thank thee,
        Marcia!   [*Afide.*
    Icil. Yes, falfe one, I will go!---I fee my prefence
Is irkfome grown to thee; yes, I will go,
And where thou never fhalt behold me more!
Come, ye fierce Æqui, pierce this breaft! Here make
A paffage for my ftreaming blood!---The torrent
Shall wafh away Virginia's fatal image!
I too, as well as fhe, will thank the hand
That gives the blow!
    Vir. Refentment, grief, and pity,
Tear up my foul!---Alas, thefe ftarting tears
Will tell what paffes here!   [*Afide, ftriking her breaft.*
    Icil. Now, cruel maid,
Farewel!---a long, and laft farewel for ever!
I will not call upon the mighty gods
To punifh thee, or to avenge my wrongs——
No—while this breath of life remains, I cannot,
I cannot curfe Virginia!---that lov'd name,
That once lov'd name, is dear to me ev'n ftill!
This only---'midft the glories of thy triumph,
Mayft thou remember, not without a pang,
Him whom thou haft undone!, the wretch Icilius!
Who lov'd thee with fuch---but no more---Farewel.
                                              [*Going.*

    Vir. Oh, ftay, yet ftay, Icilius!
    Ap. No, let him go.   [*Exit* Icilius.
And elfewhere vent his bafe plebeian infolence,
While Appius at thy feet—
                                              Vir.

Vir. Off!---hold me not!—
What, is he gone ?—Diftraction ! madnefs ! death !—
Return, return, Icilius——
         [*Attempting to follow, but held by* Appius.
   Ap. Fair Virginia,
He merits not thy love; defpife, forget him ;
And, Oh, let faithful Appius bending thus,
Embracing thus thy knees !
   Vir. [*Still ftruggling to follow* Icilius, *but held by* Ap-
         pius.] My life ! my Lucius !
He's gone ! for ever gone !—hence, barb'rous tyrant !
Pollute me not with thy infected touch,.
Nor longer blaft my fight with fuch a monfter !
Is't not enough thou haft undone my peace,
Blotted my fame, drove from my longing eyes
My only love, defpairing, bent on death,
Stabb'd to the heart with the empoifon'd thought
That his Virginia's falfe ?—And would thy cruelty
Yet farther torture me ?
   Ap. Ha, is it thus ?——
Doft thou then own thy love for him, thy hate
For me ?—'tis well—by Heav'ns, I thank thy rage!
It has forc'd out, before thou wert aware,
The fecret of thy foul, conceal'd till now,
And all thy arts unveil'd !—but for this chance
I had been fool'd !—thy looks of feeming mildnefs,
Thy gentle foothing fpeech, and foft demeanor
(Hollow and falfe !) had almoft vanquifh'd me,
And chang'd my fix'd refolves,—but fince 'tis thus
I'm fpurn'd, and my fond, generous, ardent paffion
Thus treated——
   Vir. Hence, with thy detefted paffion,
To fiends and furies, black as thy own foul,
If fuch there be ! and leave me to the forrows
Which thou haft heap'd upon me !
   Ap. Now, by Hercules,
Appius again fhall be himfelf---proud fair,
Thou haft thy wifh---hence, trifling love, begone !
I give thee to the winds ! my paffion's o'er,
And nought but lufty appetite remains,
Which, fpite of all thy peevifh fcorn and rage,
I will indulge to fuch luxurious height,

                                        That

That gorg'd at length, and glutted, it shall sicken,
And turn away from thy pall'd charms with loathing!
Nor shall my vengeance rest unsatisfied——
Icilius---He, thy minion! soon shall find
What 'tis to have pull'd down on his crush'd head
The wrath of Appius!---Now, go storm and rage!
Thou shalt have cause!——For ere to-morrow's sun
Be sunk to rest, I'll meet thee, haughty maid,
As mighty Jove met Semele!—in thunder!

            [*Exit* Appius.

Vir. [*After some pause, and looking wildly about her.*]
  Where shall I fly!---Terror, remorse, despair,
Surround me!---Heav'n and earth abandon me!——
Icilius gone---perhaps to death---Thou wretch!
Whose fatal pride has plung'd thee in this gulph
Of horror, view thyself, and then grow mad!
Distraction!---is there no relief for woe
Like mine?—No hope in store?—Quick, let me fly!—
Oh, bear me, winds, to my Icilius' bosom,
Ere stung with grief and rage, he quit for ever
These hated walls!—Retard his flight, ye pow'rs!
And let these streaming eyes and breaking heart
To gentle pity melt the gen'rous youth,
And clear my love, my honour, and my truth. [*Exit.*

END of the SECOND ACT.

A C T III.

SCENE, Marcia's *Apartment.*

Appius, Claudius, *and* Marcia.

CLAUDIUS.

HAST thou well weigh'd th'event? Consider, Appius,
 When once the attempt is made, there's no retreat;
To fail were ruin.
 Ap. Cease thy groundless fears;
Th' event is sure; thy claim is plausible;
Thy proofs most clear; my hardy veterans,
That crowd in throngs, all ready to avouch
Whate'er I dictate; and myself thy judge.

              Thou

Thou art ungrateful, Claudius—Ha !—methinks
Thou art much bound to me, who strive to gain thee
So fair a slave !---What say'st thou, gentle Marcia ?

Mar. This black contrivance startles me---this shews me
My own offence---what, seize her as a slave !
A free-born maid ! and with hir'd perjury,
Miscreants suborn'd, and bought for gold, despoil her
Of liberty, of innocence, of peace,
Of spotless fame !——Thou canst not be so base !

Ap. It seems that Marcia then, of all her sex,
Is turn'd an advocate for faith, and honour !

Mar. Upbraid me well thou may'st—my own sad heart,
Conscious of guilt, upbraids me yet more bitterly,
And tells me, the severe reproach is just ;
Yet, thanks to the blest gods, at length these eyes
Are open'd, and my slumb'ring virtue wakes !

Ap. Hence, all ye idle sects of vain philosophers !
Sages, and moralists, and prating sophists !
Hence, with your pedant wisdom !—I'll no more on't---
Let me learn truth and virtue from a woman !
Now, Marcia, hear (to shew the deep effects
Of thy reproof) that yet before the star
Of night arise, thou shalt behold Virginia,
Thy friend Virginia, claim'd, prov'd, and adjudg'd
A slave in th' open Forum ; a born slave——
Mark me, and by my sentence too; fair Marcia.

    Mar. Thou sprung from gods ! and dost thou claim
        descent
From Hercules, who purg'd the earth of monsters !

  Claud. Marcia, no more——

    Mar. Away, vile sycophant !
I will not call thee brother !——This base counsel
Was thine : 'tis such pernicious flatterers,
Such busy, ready, fawning slaves, as thou art,
That choak, and stifle truth, poison all virtue,
And curse mankind with tyrants and oppressors !

  Claud. 'Tis deeply spoke---but whence this sudden
For if I err not, who of late, but Marcia,   [change ?
To forward Appius' wish !---Whose arts contriv'd
To make a breach between two faithful lovers,
And to effect it, broke through all the ties
Of holy friendship ?

Ap.

Ap. Claudius, peace——perhaps
The all-perfect Marcia thinks our groffer fenfe
Could ne'er difcover lurking at her heart
The little wanton god, who fometimes loves
To fport with fuch high virtue !——
　　Claud. Doft thou blufh,
Degenerate maid ?---Was this the fecret fpring
Of all thy zeal for Appius, all thy cares
For poor Virginia, and her threaten'd honour ?
And now thy hopes are loft, would'ft thou affume
A virtue which thou know'ft not ?
　　Ap. Worthy Marcia,
(To quit the licence of thy fpeech) learn this——
'Tis vice defeated, baffled, difappointed,
That makes fuch virtuous profelytes as thou art,
And fills the world with prating hypocrites !
　　Mar. What fhall I fay ! Alas, what anfwer make
To this deep charge !---forgive me, pitying Heav'n !
And, Oh, ye haplefs pair, whom I have injur'd,
Forgive me too ! while thus with confcious blufhes
I own my fault——I own, 'twas treach'rous love,
That firft feduc'd my wand'ring fteps from virtue ;
Yet guilty, and unhappy as I am,
My foul ftarts back with horror from a crime
Like this---'tis true, while Appius meant with honour
To wooe Virginia for his virtuous bride,
I aided, though by means not wholly juft ;
But this is fuch perdition ! words are wanting
To give a name to it !---Oh, Appius !---Claudius !
Quit, quit betimes this fatal enterprize,
Nor call down thunder on your impious heads !
　　Ap. Away, fhe dreams——let's leave her——this way
　　　　Claudius.　　　　[*Exeunt* Appius *and* Claudius.
　　Mar. All's loft---there is no hope---nothing can fhake
The dreadful refolution he has taken——
What fcenes of blood and rage do I forefee !
Mifguided, wretched Marcia ! with what mifcreants
Haft thou combin'd !---Now learn how dangerous
It is to venture near the verge of bafenefs :
A gen'rous mind fhould never dare to quit
Virtue's firm hold ; that gone, that facred anchor
Once parted from, there is no ftop——down drives

The

The defp'rate bark before the foaming torrent,
Breaks on a rock, and finks to rife no more!
But, Oh, that injur'd maid! that dear Virginia!
She little thinks what frightful mifchiefs wait her!
Much lefs what treach'rous hand has lent its aid,
To her undoing!---Quick, let me fly---Ay, yet
Prevent, if poffible, th'uplifted blow!
'Tis worfe than death!--Yes, thou fhalt know my guilt,
In fpite of fhame thou fhalt; and if there be
A way for thee to 'fcape, although the paffage
Lie through this heart, I'll pierce it for Virginia!

                              [*Exit* Marcia.

SCENE, Icilius's *Tent in the* Roman *Camp at* Algidum;
     Firft an alarm, then a retreat is founded.

         Icilius enters difordered, as from fight.
  Icil. Will nothing rid me of my mifery!
Do I in vain provoke the forward foe
To end me!--Oh, Virginia!--falfe Virginia!----
Great gods, behold me here, a wretch complete,
The work of your own hands, in all your wrath!
'Tis death muft give me eafe--in the ftill urn
Virginia's perfidy and all my woes
Shall fleep: reft then, my heart, nor let a groan
Efcape to tell Virginius, his falfe daughter
Has ruin'd all thy peace! She has bafely fold
Her love---for wealth and pride!
                        [*Walking about difodered.*
Virginius here!   [*Surprized.*
        Enter L. Virginius.
  L. Vir. Ay, here Icilius ----
Now, in the name of all the gods, what means
This wild defpair, that fhuns the light? I mark'd thee,
When to the camp thou cam'ft---there on thy vifage
O'erfpread with ghaftly pale, I faw a grief
That ftruck my heart---Art thou refolv'd on death?
Why elfe rufh defp'rate on a thoufand fwords,
As ev'n but now thou didft, as if to court it?
Alas, Icilius! little doft thou fhow
Regard for me, and lefs for poor Virginia,
Whofe life, whofe being, hangs on thine!

                                     Icil.

Icil. Oh, torture!
But yet I muſt diſſemble. [*Aſide.*] Say, Virginius,
Much honour'd, and much lov'd! ſay, is it ſtrange,
A Roman ſhould forget the thoughts of danger,
When glory, and his country's wrongs, inſpire him?

L. Vir. This falſe reſerve, Icilius, is unworthy
Both of thyſelf and me. Is our alliance
So hateful, that for refuge thou wouldſt fly
Into the arms of death? Perhaps Virginia,
Too fond, has ſurfeited thy ſickly flame,
And now is cheap in thy eſteem. If ſo,
I will abſolve thee from this odious contract;
And duty, and ſubmiſſion to a father,
Shall teach her, howſoe'er it wring her heart,
Without complaint, or aught but ſilent tears,
Unmurm'ring to reſign thee.

Icil. Down, my heart!
Down, ſwelling grief! [*Aſide.*] Virginius, hear me ſpeak;
If e'er my ſoul, ſince firſt ſhe could diſtinguiſh
Among mankind, wiſh'd other than to be
Join'd in indiſſoluble bonds to thee,
Thy blood, and all thy virtues, may the gods
Abandon me this.hour! Then wound me not
So deep, to think that ought in thy alliance
Is irkſome to me; much leſs, that Virginia
Has ſurfeited my love with too much kindneſs.
Ah, no!—Perhaps I may—I know not why——
But to myſelf, methinks, my ſoul ſeems heavier
Than ſhe was wont to be; and I would rouze me
By action. This diſtemp'rature of mind,
This wayward ſicklineſs, that has no name,
Is one of thoſe conditions human nature
Holds her frail tenement by——But it will paſs——

L. Vir. Words, words, mere words!—I ſee, thro' all
A black corroding grief, that gnaws thy heart; [this veil,
Which ſince thou'rt obſtinate to hide—No more——
I've done—This only, then farewel—Whene'er
Thy need requires, I tell thee, old Virginius
Has yet a heart that's firm, a hand to aid thee
Againſt the world combin'd. But have a care,
Take heed, young man—My friendſhip and my honour
Muſt not be trifled with—This touches both——

D

This

This mean referve !—By heav'ns, I know no art ;
For I have nought to hide.   But in thy breaft
I find that other maxims rule.   There's myftery,
And deep difguife, which noble minds difdain.
There's fomething dark—and where 'tis dark—'tis foul.
                                        [*Exit angrily.*

  Icil. At length he's gone.   This was a trying conflict.
With rage and grief fupprefs'd, my heart was burfting,
Yet fcorn'd complaint.   No, fhould I ftoop to ufe
A father's pow'r, to gain a forc'd confent,
And hug a wretched carcafe in my arms,
The nobler part, the mind, all over ftain'd,
Blotted and fcrawl'd with Appius' hated image ?
Could I bear this ? No.   Could the angry gods
Add aught to the full load of woe I bear,
It would be thus, thus to poffefs Virginia !
                  Enter a Guard with Caius.
  Guard. A meffenger
To Lucius Icilius from Rome.
  Caius. This, from Valerius, to his friend Icilius
I am commiffion'd to deliver.   [*Prefenting a letter.*
  Icil. Valerius ! Ha ! what may this meffage mean ?
      [*Reads.*]   .   [*Afide.*

  " Valerius to Icilius fends health.
  " Thefe fhall inform you, that your prefence and aid
are here moft neceffary, in defence of the unhappy Virginia, againft the attempts of the enraged Appius, who,
finding all his arts to feduce her vain, now threatens open
violence.   The diftreffed maid, whofe truth and conftancy
your unjuft fufpicions have much wronged, is prepared to
give moft fignal, tho' fatal, proofs of both, unlefs you interpofe your timely fuccour.   Farewel."

Heavens ! can it be ?—I fee Valerius' hand
A witnefs to its truth.   Can I have been
So fatally deceiv'd ?—My heart mifgives me !
  Caius. Icilius, pardon me—th' extremity
In which I left Valerius and his friends,
Demands my utmoft hafte.   I hav't, befides,
In charge, to let Virginius know what ruin
Awaits his moft unhappy child.
  Icil. Oh, Caius !
                                              I know

I know thee now ; Virginius' faithful freedman.
Alas ! for pity, tell me, if thou know'ft
Aught of Virginia——What has driv'n the tyrant
To this precipitate courfe ?
    Caius. A frefh repulfe,
Which, urg'd with too much bitternefs and fcorn,
Has fir'd him ev'n to madnefs, and he breathes
Nought but revenge and violence.   I faw,
Ere I departed, at her father's houfe,
The haplefs maid, all fainting, drown'd in tears ;
With her Valerius, and her uncle Numitor,
Horatius, Plautia, Marcia, Claudius' fifter,
Who, weeping, afks forgivenefs, owns fome treach'ry
She has been guilty of ; and 'tis from her
Appius' defigns are known.
    Icil. Why, then, there lives not
A wretch fo curs'd as I ! [*Afide.*] Oh, Caius ! hafte,
Lofe not a moment—Hence ! [*Exit* Caius.] Virginia !—
Torn with remorfe and fhame, defpair and love,
I fly, thou dear, thou gen'rous, faithful maid,
To thy relief.   Grant me, all-gracious Heav'n,
But one blefs'd hour, to wipe my guilt away,
To pierce the tyrant's heart, and to protect
My injur'd love ; the next, decree my fall.   [*Exit.*

    ·S C E N E, Virginia's *Apartment.*

        Enter Virginia *and* Marcia.
    Mar. Yet let me call myfelf thy friend, Virginia !
And fhall I faithful add,
Tho' for a while mifled by fatal love,
That wand'ring and deceitful fire, I ftray'd,
Wide erring from the paths of truth and honour ?
Yes, let this fhame, thefe tears, wafh out the ftain.
Oh, might I live to fee thee fafe from treafon,
And blefs'd with love, my foul could afk no more !
But if the fates, averfe, have doom'd, fweet maid,
That thou muft fall, for glory fall, thy Marcia,
Once the companion of thy youth and truft,
Tho' now a wretch, fhall nobly perifh with thee.
    Vir. Marcia, once more belov'd, and faithful too !
I fee thee now, I know thee by that virtue
I once fo lov'd, and brighter now than ever !
                D 2   The

The intervening mift, that paffion rais'd,
Is clear'd away, and all is fair again.

Mar. This goodnefs weighs me down. My heart's too
To fpeak—then let me thus pour out my thanks,   [full
My grateful tears, in thy forgiving bofom.

Vir. Ah, my lov'd Marcia! 'tis enough—too much.
I'm fatisfy'd. Urge then no more a fault
Thy haplefs paffion caus'd. 1 know too well
The tyrant pow'r of love; Icilius' charms,
How irrefiftible.

Mar. Thou haft reftor'd me
To life and happinefs!

Vir. From this fweet union
My breaft derives new hopes; and may the pow'rs
That watch o'er innocence look down propitious!
But chiefly thou, bright goddefs, Chaftity!
Thou, to whofe honour ancient Rome decreed
Temples and altars, when thy own Lucretia
For glory bled! do thou protect thy votary
From violence and fhame!

Enter Plautia.

Plaut. Thy uncle, Numitor,
Without expects thee. News of great import
Are from the camp but now arriv'd. All Rome
Is in confufion; what the circumftance,
He can deliver. We muft now attend him.   [*Exeunt*:

S C E N E, *a Garden.*

Enter Appius:

Ap. Wherefore did trifling love's ignoble fire
Melt this firm breaft? My foul was form'd for empire,
For war; to guide the car, to wield the fword,
Or in the fenate teach the ftubborn fathers
My will was law, and my decrees were fate.
But now the war, the tumult is within: [Marcia!
It rages here. [*Pointing to his breaft.*] Deferted too by
Curfe on her ill-tim'd fears, and coward virtue!

Enter Rufus *to him haftily.*

Ruf. Appius, I come with news to fhake all fpirits
But thine. From different quarters meffengers,
Breathlefs with heat and fpeed, are juft arriv'd,
Who tell of the defeat of both our armies;

On

On the firſt onſet, the perfidious cohorts
Turn'd back, and fled ; not broken by the enemy,
But reſolute beforehand not to conquer,
'Thro' hate and ſpleen to the decemvirate,
Leſt aught of happy ſhould befal the ſtate
Beneath their government.
   Ap. Malicious gods !
From this time I renounce your temples, altars,
Your falſe, precarious aid ; and on this arm
And this firm ſpirit alone will build my fortune.
What, is the fatal news divulg'd ?
   Ruf. 'Tis ſpread
Thro' univerſal Rome ; the madding populace
Tumultuous riſe ; confuſion, havock, ſpoil,
Are all on foot.
   Ap. Oh, for the bolts of Jove,
To wield amongſt them !—Yet this very night,
Whate'er befal, I ſwear to ſacrifice
That peeviſh, ſcornful maid, that racks me thus,
To love and to revenge !
   Ruf. Surely, my Lord,
'Twere ſafer to defer the execution
'Of your deſign, till this moſt dang'rous ſtorm
Be overblown———
   Ap. No, by my great progenitor,
Alcides, I will on ! Like him, I'll combat
This many-headed monſter, this baſe hydra,
The raſcal people, to the utmoſt verge
Of life and death !
   Ruf. Howe'er, theſe dire commotions
Should inſtantly be quell'd ; we muſt aſſuage
The preſent heat.
   Ap. Go thou, and find out Claudius ;
Bid him inform my colleagues of this news :
Let them aſſemble ſtraight, in Mars's temple,
The ſenate—We muſt uſe them now—We want
Their popular name, and their authority,
To quell the rabble rout. This done, let Claudius
Repair to me before I meet the ſenate :
For I'll not quit, or ſlack, for this impediment,
The courſe I have reſolv'd. The proud Virginia,
Before another ſun gilds theſe ſeven hills,

D 3

Shall

Shall yet be mine; nor shall the curs'd Icilius
Escape this arm. Then let to-morrow come;
And if I fall, I fall with glorious ruin!
Secure of blifs, whate'er my fortune prove,
I'll triumph, glutted with revenge and love!

                                             [*Exeunt.*

END of the THIRD ACT.

A C T   IV.

SCENE, *an Apartment in* Virginius's *House.*

Enter Virginia, Plautia, *and* Marcia.

VIRGINIA.

WHAT doft thou tell me? My Icilius come?
    Plaut. The flaves without have feen him hur-
With eager looks and pace.   [rying hither,
   Mar. Let me retire;
I dare not look on him. The wretched Marcia
Muft needs be horror to his eyes.
   Vir. No, Marcia,
Thou fhalt remain, and he fhall know thy fervices,
And all thy generous friendfhip.
                       Enter Icilius.
   Icil. My Virginia!
                [*After fome paufe, as recollecting himfelf.*
Alas! forgive me, that I call thee fo.
I had forgot I was a wretch, a criminal,
And muft not call thee mine. The fight of thee
Had banifh'd for a moment from my memory
My deep dy'd guilt, and call'd back former times,
And happier fcenes, when all was peace and love.
Yet hear me; for I afk thee not for pardon;
I afk thee not to give me back that love,
Which once was all the treafure of this heart;
I've fquander'd it away, and muft not murmur
That nothing now is left me but mere mifery,
To fill the aching void.
   Vir. My vows are heard!
He is return'd, and full of truth and love!   [*Afide.*
                                                 Icil.

Icil. Turn not away, but hear me; for, I fwear,
The dang'rous cloud that's burfting o'er thy head,
Once paft, with patient grief I will endure
Whate'er thy utmoft rigour fhall impofe.

Vir. No more; I cannot bear it. Yes, my Lucius,
I'm thine, for ever thine ! My kindling heart,
At thy approach, with fympathetic love,
To meet thee fprings, and with thy gen'rous flame
Tranfported, longs to mix its faithful fires.

Icil. Gods, gods ! this is too much ! fuch fudden blifs
Pouring upon me !—Sure I'm in a dream !
Some fweet illufion, that thus mocks my fancy
With fhadowy fcenes of joy !—Here let me fall,
And breathe my fighs——   [*Kneeling.*

Vir. [*Raifing him.*] How fweet it is to love !
Methinks my bofom feels as if fome treafure,
Long loft, were now, by an immediate act
Of Heav'n's own bounty, to my hopes reftor'd.

Icil. Is't poffible ? Ah, let me prefs thee thus
Againft my trembling breaft, and hold thee faft !
                                           [*Embracing.*
Thus folding thee, thus, let thy pitying heart
Tell mine, in nimble beatings, thou forgiv'ft me,
That I am blefs'd, and thou art ever mine !
Ha ! do my eyes deceive me ? Marcia here !

Vir. If thy Virginia's love indeed be precious
In Lucius' eyes, next to the gracious gods,   [perhaps,
Behold the gen'rous friend, [*Pointing to* Mar.] to whom,
Thou ow'ft that yet fhe lives ; that without fhame
She dares look up, and fondly gaze upon thee !
Thou dear, kind maid ! [*Embracing* Mar.] without whofe
      timely fuccour
The loft Virginia had perhaps this moment
Been a defpis'd, difhonour'd, wretched flave.
Oh, Lucius !——

Mar. Ceafe, Virginia, to opprefs
His gen'rous mind. Thou know'ft, th' unhappy Marcia
Has lefs deferv'd his pardon than his fcorn.

Icil. No more, fair Marcia ; let nought inaufpicious,
Let no unkind remembrance now pollute
This perfect blifs. Haft thou not fav'd Virginia ?
And can I e'er repay the mighty debt ?

                                                 I do

I do believe thy foul is virtuous, noble,
Tho' for a while thy guardian genius flumber'd,
Neglectful of his charge —— But yet, my heart,
Thou muft not know repofe.   [*Afide.*
   Vir. What means my Lucius?
There's fomething lab'ring in thy breaft.
   Icil. Thou dear,
Lov'd maid! my foul, long tofs'd in troubles,
Amidft thefe tranfports, for a while fufpended
Her racking cares, and catch'd at hope too foon.
   Vir. Oh, eafe my throbbing bofom!
   Icil. My Virginia!
The jewel I had loft, I have recover'd!
But, Oh, not yet fecur'd! For, know, to render
All oppofition to his defp'rate purpofe
Hopelefs and vain, the tyrant has affembled
His crew of ruffians from all parts. The levies
New rais'd; are juft arriv'd in dreadful throngs,
And awe the trembling city. No affiftance,
No human aid can now defend thy innocence;
Nothing but flight.
   Vir. Ye guardian pow'rs, protect me!
Where fhall I fly?——
   Icil. Compofe thy troubled breaft:
All may be well. With a fond lover's care
I would attend thy fteps, and guard my treafure
From ev'ry ill; but, Oh! imperious honour
Forbids me now to leave my wretched country
A prey to faction, tyranny, and rapine,
That reign within thefe walls; while the proud foe,
With fire and fword, advancing to our gates,
Threatens to lay imperial Rome in duft.
Thy uncle Numitor will be the guide
And partner of thy flight; he will conduct thee
To Ardea, where the good Herminius, bound
By ties of blood, and ancient friendfhip, dwells;
His facred hearth, and hofpitable gods
Are ready to receive thee.
   Vir. Ah, my Lucius!
How tranfient was the momentary joy
That fwell'd my eager hopes!—Methinks I feel
                  A fhivering,

A fhivering, like the approach of death!
Sure fome prefage!——
   Icil. Thou deareft maid! have comfort.
Are there not gods above? When virtue fuffers,
'Tis their own caufe. But let us hafte; the fenate
Is now affembling. Let us feize the occafion .
(While Claudius and the fierce Decemvir meet them)
To lead thee hence. When once th' impending ftorm,
That's gathering o'er our heads, be overblown,
Thou quickly fhalt return to blefs thefe eyes:
Then fettled calms, and gentle peace, fhall footh
Each anxious care; aufpicious Love fhall prune
His ruffled wings, and point each fhaft with gold;
And facred Hymen light his nuptial torch;
To guide us on our way to endlefs blifs.   *[Exeunt.*

SCENE, *a Street in Rome.*

   Enter Appius, Rufus, *and* Claudius.
  Ap. Icilius now in Rome!
  Ruf. By your command,
Watching in yon retreat, I faw him enter
Virginius' gates.
  Ap. Confufion! we're difcover'd!
There's fome defign on foot. Is thy band ready?
                         [To Claudius.
  Claud. They're all prepar'd.
  Ap. Ha, Claudius! look, look yonder!
They're coming forth this inftant. Marcia too!
'Tis fhe who has betray'd us——There they go——
See, Numitor conducts my lovely prize!
By Heav'ns, Icilius quits her, and returns!——
Fortune, I thank thee!—Claudius, now advance
With all thy force, and meet them in the front
That way——On my tribunal thou fhalt find me.
              [Exeunt Claud. *and* Ruf.
Now, my propitious ftars, fhine out! Now fpeed
My glorious hopes, that I may tafte the fweets
That wait on empire! Let the vulgar herd,
By flow purfuits of art, and patient labour,
Attain their ends; but let me, like a god,
At once ftretch out my arm, and feize my joy! *[Exit.*

SCENE,

SCENE, *the Gate Collina in Rome.*

While a march is playing, L. Virginius *enters with a band
of soldiers.*

L. Vir. At length, my valiant friends, and fellow-fol-
We tread the parent foil, where firft we drew   [diers,
Our breath.   This is no time for ftudied forms
Of fpeech.   With hurry'd march, and wounds unheal'd,
We've left our camp, and here are come, to conquer
Or die.   There is no mean ; our hard oppreffor,
Already victor o'er our laws, our liberties,
Our fortunes and our lives, is not content,
Unlefs he may extend his wide dominion,
Over our honours too : our maids, our matrons,
Muft glut his impious luft ; force muft compel,
Where treafon can't feduce — My child, Virginia,
My age's darling, whom my choice and word
Had long fince deftin'd to the brave Icilius,
Your tribune, muft be forc'd from my embrace,
To a loath'd purpofe.   Will ye bear it, Romans ?
Say, fhall your old centurion, bent with years,
And cumb'rous arms, who on his breaft yet bears
The mark of many a wound, in battle fhar'd
With you, my brave companions, now at laft
Be ftabb'd with fuch a fight ? A helplefs daughter,
In vain imploring aid, dragg'd to pollution ?
No, in each eye I read your noble purpofe,
To die, or free your finking, bleeding country,
From this pernicious tyrant————
          Enter Marcia *to* L. Virginius *haftily.*
Mar. Ah, Virginius !
L. Vir. Marcia, what mean thefe wild and frighted
This breathlefs hafte ?   [looks,
Mar. Virginia, Oh, Virginia !———
My treach'rous brother———
L. Vir. Ha ! Virginia, faidft thou ?
Claudius !—Virginia !—Ye avenging gods !———
Why join'ft thou thus their names ?—Speak, thou dear
Tho' thy perfidious brother be a traitor,   [maid !
Thy faithful, gen'rous breaft holds no alliance
With his black crimes.

Mar.

Mar. Yes, thou brave son of Rome!
I am a wretch! I've wrong'd thee, basely wrong'd thee!
The tale's too long to tell; but I've betray'd
My friend, my trust, nor dare I to prophane
The sacred name of faithful.   But I'll die,
Or purge my guilt away.

    L. Vir. [*Hastily.*] Where is my daughter?   [A slave!
    Mar. Torn from my arms! She's lost! she's gone!—
    L. Vir. A slave! What mean'st thou ?—Death and
Where is she?   [madness!—Speak—
    Mar. Ah! where now she is I know not.
But, some few minutes since, my impious brother,
Attended by a band of ruffians, seiz'd her,
As we were coming forth, and dragging her,
Spite of the gath'ring crowd, to the tribunal
Of the Decemvir, claim'd her for his slave.

    L. Vir. My friends, my fellow citizens, my country-
Say, shall a Roman suffer wrongs like these ?   [men!
    Mar. Then started forth a train of perjur'd miscreants,
With ready witness to support th' imposture;
And the fierce judge, without remorse or shame,
At once pronounc'd her doom.   Icilius then
Rush'd in between; a desp'rate tumult rose;
Daggers were drawn; a mingled cry was heard;
Blood stream'd on ev'ry side; the women fled,
Loud shrieking.   Soon the torrent bore away
Virginia from my side.   'Midst the confusion,
Your name and your arrival were proclaim'd.
That instant, spurr'd by friendship, grief, and duty,
I flew to find you out, and to relate
The horrid tale.   Farewel! These swelling eyes
Shall ne'er be clos'd in sleep, till I have found
Where my perfidious brother has conceal'd
The injur'd maid.   [*Exit.*

    L. Vir. Oh, miserable Rome!
To sure destruction doom'd ? Oh, Mars, Quirinus!
Our tutelar gods! where slept your watchful care,
When, in an evil hour, your blinded sons,
Misjudging, trusted to the grasp of tyranny
Their precious birthright, freedom; nay, held out
Their hands for bonds ?——Away, my friends, away!

                        Arm'd

Arm'd as we are, let's ruſh into the Forum,
And inſtantly aſſault our curs'd oppreſſor.
Let us not drag our chains a moment longer;
Let us not think we live, till we are free.
Away, to conquer, or to die !   [*Going.*

Enter Icilius.

Icil. Virginius,
A moment hold.   Where doſt thou run ?
    L. Vir. Icilius,
My ſon ! where is Virginia ?—Ha, ſpeak ! where,
Where haſt thou left my child ?—Diſtraction ! death !—
Without her ?——Could not love and glory teach thee
To've ſeen her piecemeal torn before thine eyes,
And afterwards to've dragg'd her quiv'ring limbs
To greet her father, rather than have left her
A prey to tyranny and luſt ?
    Icil. Virginius,
But ſtay and hear me——
    L. Vir. Too, too long I've ſtaid !
My lov'd Virginia ! had thy wretched father
Been near thee, never hadſt thou known this ſhame !
    Icil. Thou couldſt have done no more——
    L. Vir. Away, away !
    Icil. Why this is madneſs, rage—   [*Impatiently.*
    L. Vir. [*Surveying him.*] I ſee thee living—
Yet ſee not her—   [*Raiſing his voice.*
    Icil. Virginius, if th' impatience
Of thy juſt grief, had left me pauſe for ſpeech,
Ere this I had inform'd thee, that thy daughter
Lives yet unhurt, her freedom, and her honour
Safe and inviolate——
    L. Vir. Thank the bleſs'd gods !
Still may ſhe be their care !—But yet, Icilius—
Safe, and inviolate !—Why then not with thee ?
    Icil. Know then, this is the cauſe : When I oppos'd
Appius' unrighteous judgment, which decreed
Virginia to the cuſtody of Claudius
'Till thy return—
    L. Vir. What, has not the Decemvir
Adjudg'd her Claudius' ſlave ?

2

Icil.

Icil. With patience hear me——
He would, by abfolute and final fentence,
Without repeal, have doom'd her Claudius' flave,
Had not the venerable Numitor
Stood forth, and with an eloquence, which grief,
Such grief alone could minifter, expos'd
The cruelty and the iniquity
Of fuch a fhamelefs fentence, to deprive
A father and a Roman of his child,
Unheard——The murm'ring throng was fir'd, and Ap-
Compell'd to refpite his unjuft decree   [pius
'Till thy return——But mark the bafe condition!
E'en that the lovely maid fhould be confign'd
To the falfe charge of the pernicious Claudius,
Till her reputed father fhould appear
T' affert his right:
    L. Virg. Perfidious, treach'rous villain!
So fhould my innocent child in that dark interval
Have fuffer'd wrongs beyond all cure!
    Icil. My blood
No more could brook reftraint—I rufh'd on Claudius,
And tore her from his hold; the pitying crowd
Took part in my diftrefs, and foon beat off
The lictors: ftrait the ribald crew of Appius
Fell on; a bloody fray enfu'd, and all
Was going to wreck; when 'midft the throng appear'd
Horatius and Valerius; both belov'd,
Both favour'd of the people—They at length
So far prevail'd, that the Decemvir granted,
Pretending care for peace and public weal,
(Tho' inly ftung to madnefs) that Virginia
Should reft with Numitor till thy return,
And final iffue of the caufe: to him
I then refign'd my precious charge; thro' crowds
Of fhouting Romans, he conducted her
In fafety home.   It now remains with thee,
To think in this diftrefsful exigence
What courfe is beft.
    L. Virg. What beft?—Oh, righteous gods!
Was it for this ye gave me this dear child?
Was it for this my early care nurs'd up
Her blooming youth, and in that gracious form

                         E   Infus'd

Infus'd a noble and ingenuous spirit,
To have it now disputed, after all,
If she be mine or not?—If she shall live,
As she was bred, in freedom and in honor,
The virtuous daughter of a Roman citizen,
Or sunk in everlasting infamy,
The slave and harlot of a villain?——Ah!——
That thought is death! I'll not endure it longer!
I'll know the worst.—This torturing suspense
Is insupportable!—
   Icil. What wouldst thou do?
By force redress thy wrongs, and hazard all
Upon one desp'rate cast?—Be more advis'd,
And wait till—
   L. Virg. Wait! When ev'ry hour's delay
Cries out dishonour on me!---No, by Heav'ns,
The shameful cause shall be this day decided!
Another sun shall never more behold
Virginius crouching, and deprefs'd with fear
Of being father to a strumpet!
   Icil. Gods!
Wilt thou rush headlong to destruction? Aid
The tyrant's foul design, and wait thy doom
From his corrupt tribunal?---This base claim
Of Claudius, and his prosecuted right,
Thou know'st is mere delusion, a vile mockery
Of justice and wilt thou---
   L. Virg. No more, Icilius---
But be persuaded that Virginius knows
The duty of a father and a Roman.
   Icil. Think on the tyrant's strength---
What counterpoise
Canst thou oppose to such unequal weight?
What valour 'gainst such odds?---'Tis sure perdition
And must I see, with patient eyes, my love,
My hopes all sacrific'd?---
   L. Virg. I pray thee leave me---
My breast is all confusion. If my grief,
Our ancient friendship, or my pray'r can touch thee,
Be this the proof—A while avoid Virginia;
Forget the ties of love, and all th' engagements
Of plighted faith—Till this base cause is ended,

I dare

I dare not call her mine, nor can I give,
Or thou receive the doubtful gift with honour.
Now, my try'd warriors, if your old Centurion,
Whene'er he led you forth to arms and glory,
Sustain'd the shock of battle with the foremost,
And, drop for drop, pour'd out his blood with yours,
Now comes the time to claim your love, your aid ;
To you, and to the gods, I trust my doom,
And stand or fall with liberty and Rome.

END of the FOURTH ACT.

ACT V.

SCENE, *An Apartment in* L. Virginius's *House.*

L. VIRGINIUS.

THE time draws near : and fate comes hast'ning on
    Virginia's fate and mine—I must compose
This tempest here, and settle all within
To meet whate'er may fall—Distracting doubts,
Be still !---Ye horrid shapes of fear, avaunt !---
Alas, in vain ! My lab'ring soul can find
No rest—Where'er she turns, terror starts up
To thwart her way—Oh, my belov'd Virginia !
Should'st thou be torn from me !—Let me not think on't !
Alas, she comes this way !—I must not see her—
She melts me so !---I cannot---   [*Turning away.*

Enter Virginia.

Virg. Sir, my father !
Turn not away,——what have I done ?——
    L. *Virg.* Virginia,
Why dost thou come to waken with thy presence
Those tender thoughts, those soft remembrances,
That war upon my firmness ?---Fly, my child,
Fly from a wretched parent, whom the wrath
Of fate pursues---perhaps I must forget
I ever was a father !

E 2   *Virg.*

Virg. Oh, my heart!
Do you forſake me too! Ah, whither, whither,
Wilt thou betake thee now, undone Virginia,
When ev'n a father's arms are ſhut againſt thee!
Oh, Sir! (ſince now the tender name, my infancy
Firſt learn'd to liſp, muſt ever be forgot)
What ſhould I think ?—Am I indeed not yours?
Or do you ſcorn to acknowledge me your daughter,
Stain'd as I am, and branded for a ſlave!
    L. Virg. My tears will choak me! [*Aſide.*] Go, re-
          tire, my daughter————
Thou art my own! my deareſt, tendereſt child!
I glory that thou art!---Go in a while---
Let me collect myſelf---The ſight of thee
Diſarms me of all ſtrength, all pow'r, and ſhakes
My firmeſt reſolutions!
    Virg. Muſt I go,
Thus doubtful of my fate, thus driven from you?
Behold the poor Virginia at your feet!   [*Kneeling.*
Behold theſe falling tears!——whatever be
The purpoſe of your ſoul (it muſt be noble,
Since 'tis my father's.) Oh, unfold it all!
I will not ſhrink, but meet it as becomes
A Roman maid, and daughter to Virginius!   [while;
    L. Virg. She cleaves my heart! [*aſide.*] Repoſe thyſelf a
Within few moments I return—Mean time
Avoid Icilius—let not heedleſs paſſion
Thwart my command, but, as thou lov'ſt, obey. [*Exit.*
    Virg. What can this mean ?——My father's ſtrict com-
T' avoid Icilius—The ſtrange war of paſſions   [mand
Conflicting in his breaſt, his broken voice,
His ſtarts, his eager looks, all, all declare,
Some dread event is near!
            Enter Icilius.
    Icil. Alas, Virginia !—
We're loſt—thy cruel father's ſavage honour
Is hurrying to deſtroy us! but ev'n now
I met him going forth, and would have ſpoke—
When frowning ſtern—Forbear, he cry'd, Içilius,
To thwart me thus, and fiercely paſt along.
I know his fatal purpoſe—Oh, Virginia!
Urg'd by the Furies, he is gone to claim
                                        Imme-

Immediate judgment, and provoke a sentence
That will undo us all————

   Virg. Farewel, farewell!   *[Weeping.*

   Icil. And wilt thou leave me thus to my despair?
Can thy own heart consent t' abandon me?
Or is Icilius such a stranger there,
That thou canst banish his remembrance from thee
Without a pang; nay, ev'n with cold indifference?

   Virg. Alas! 'too well thou know'st this heart, Icilius,
To think that ever cold indifference
Can harbour there—my duty, not my wishes,
Commands me hence; his will, which ever was
And ever must be sacred to Virginia.

   Icil. 'Tis well—thy duty bids thee tear this heart,
And thou obey'st—how pow'rful is thy duty!
But Oh, Virginia, Oh, how weak thy love.

   Virg. Cruel Icilius!

   Icil. Yet I swear to heav'n,
I will not leave thee till this day be past,
Tho' men and gods oppose—Thou art my own——
I will defend thee, and my rights in thee,
While I have life, nor trust to other aid;
Where'er thou goest, I will pursue thy steps,
And join my fate with thine.

   Virg. Away, Icilius!—
It seems, thou know'st me not---Hast thou forgot,
I am Virginius' daughter?---Wouldst thou cancel
The bond of my obedience?---Learn to render
Thy passion worthier of thyself and me!
Learn to respect my duty, and my glory;
For tho' I love, yet still I am a Roman!

   Icil. Farewel to all my hopes!—Virginia's heart,
Which once I fondly thought my own, it seems,
Is Roman all!. and in the blaze of glory,
Love's weaker flame is lost!

            Enter Plautia *and* Marcia.

   Plau. My child! thy father
Impatient of his wrongs, this moment waits
To lead thee to the judgment-seat of Appius!
Our streets are throng'd—Rome pours her numbers forth,
All anxious for thy fate—My heart is broke
With tenderness, and sorrow!

Mar. Thou dear maid,
Whom I have injur'd! fee, the wretched Marcia,
Sinking with guilt and grief and fhame, is come
To follow thy fad fteps, and loud proclaim
To heav'n and earth, ev'n in the face of Appius,
And her falfe brother, the detefted perfidy
They have contriv'd againft thee!
    Vir. My kind Marcia,
All will be well — Methinks my foul feems arm'd
With heav'n-imparted ftrength; and lighter grown
Than ufual, is beginning to fhake off
Thefe earthy bands that hold her—Now, my Lucius,
Once more farewel—forgive the few harfh words,
Which while my tongue pronounc'd, my heart difclaim-
       ed;
For Oh, that I have ever fondly lov'd thee,
And ever will, till the laft pulfe of life
Shall ceafe to beat within this conftant heart,
Let this embrace, and this, perhaps the laft [*Embracing.*
That e'er fhall bind thee to Virginia's breaft,
Bear witnefs!
    Icil. Oh, my foul!—here let me grow! [*Embracing.*
And twift my vital thread with thine fo faft,
The envious Fates fhall be oblig'd to clofe
Th' inexorable fhears on both at once!
    Vir. Icilius, I muft leave thee!
    Icil. May the gods
Abandon me, if aught fhall now divide us!
No, fince t'is defp'rate courfe is fix'd, Virginia,
Myfelf will guide thee to this bafe tribunal,
Where rob'd iniquity fits high enthron'd,
To tread on innocence!—Now, ye juft pow'rs,
Whom we adore, exert your dreaded influence!
Now ftrike on virtue's fide; confound the guilty,
Succour th' oppreft, and fhow that ye are gods!
                        [*Exeunt.*

S C E N E Appius's *Tribunal in the Forum, A nume-*
       rous train of Lictors, Guards, &c.
Enter Appius *and* Claudius. *They come forward to the*
       front of the ftage.

    Ap. Is all prepar'd?

                           Clau.

Clau. Nothing is wanting—Guards
Are plac'd in ev'ry quarter——Three ſtrong cohorts
Poſſeſs the Forum, and forbid acceſs
To all but friends——Virginius' followers,
A deſp'rate, raging band, juſt hot from war,
We unawares ſurpris'd, ſecur'd, diſarm'd them ;
Not without blood——

 Ap. That's well, my truſty Claudius,
By Heav'n that's well !—but how haſt thou diſpos'd
Thy ſiſter Marcia ?—Ha !—ſhe may be dangerous !
She knows too much, and is too keen a foe.

Clau. Rufus has my command, if ſhe approach,
To ſeize and inſtantly convey her home ;
He likewiſe has't in charge to apprehend
Icilius, as a rebel, and to bear him
Without delay to priſon.

 Ap. 'Tis enough——
I'm ſatisfied—and yet methinks---Ah, Claudius !
There's ſomething heavy here, that weighs me down——
I know not what——

Clau. There's no retreating now---
The die is thrown——

 Ap. I hear 'em coming---Now,
My genius ! Now, be mighty, and ſupport me !

[Appius aſcends the Tribunal.

Appius, *ſeated on his Tribunal.* Claudius *below.* L. Virginius *enters, leading by the hand his daughter* Virginia.
 Plautia, *with a train of weeping matrons following.*
 Lictors, Guards, *&c. cloſe up each ſide of the ſtage, leaving only the front open.*

 Ap. Romans, you ſee me from this awful ſeat
A ſecond time conſtrain'd to render judgment,
In a determin'd cauſe ; our laws, 'tis true,
Our rights, our cuſtoms, all cry out aloud
Againſt ſuch violation ; but, alas !
So the neceſſity of theſe bad times
Demands ; for bold ſedition ſtalks abroad
With ſuch gigantic ſtrides, that Juſtice ſelf
Is forc'd to quit her path !---I'll not repeat
The high indignities, the outrages,
The inſults offer'd to the ſov'reign magiſtrate ;

No,

No, Romans, let my wrongs forgotten die---
It is not for revenge, but law, I stand;
The sacred tables, and the even course
Of steady justice---This is Appius' aim---
Romans, I've done---Let either side stand forth---
I rest in equal poise to weigh the right.
   Clau. Then let my right prevail---My proofs thou
        know'st---
This ancient slave---a witness to the birth
Of that young maid, in my own house---my freedman
Davus---who, with the mother's privity
Sold her to childless Numitoria,
Virginius' wife---
   Ap. These proofs, so long conceal'd.
Why now produc'd?
   Clau. Does Appius ask the cause?
Does he?---'Tis well---thou shalt be satisfied;
But then complain not after, when thou hear'st
Ungrateful truths---
   Ap. What mean these obscure hints,
These dark surmises?---Speak---I dare thy worst.
   Clau. Know then, it is for thee I prosecute
This odious, this unpopular claim---For thee
Am loaded with the bitter hate, and rage
Of all the Commons.
   Ap. Traitor!---How?---for me?---
   Clau. For thee---Thy desp'rate, inauspicious love
For this young maid, known to all Rome---(Nay, frown
      not---)
Threaten'd a union, which the sacred tables
Have doom'd accurs'd---My freedman, struck with horror,
To think a slave should stain the Appian race,
Disclos'd his guilt, till then conceal'd from me;
I urge my right, to snatch thee from destruction.
   Ap. I'm not to learn, that boldest censure lives
In basest mouths---The herd will still affect
To know and reason deep!---But couldst thou think
I meant to blot my name with such perdition?
   Clau. Forgive my fears, if they have done thee wrong;
Thy glory was the cause; therefore unmov'd
I wait thy final sentence; if Virginius
Have aught t' object, now let him urge it home.
L. Vir.

L. Vir. Thou traitor !---I have hitherto been silent,
And patiently have heard that impious tongue
Wrong Heav'n and earth !---only that I might learn
The full extent of this abhorr'd contrivance ;
Glaring, as is the day, to ev'ry eye !
But, Oh, thou pander slave !---think'ft thou, Virginius
Will deign an anfwer to the perjur'd tale ?
Difprove thofe caitiffs, whom thou haft produc'd,
And wait a fentence from that faithlefs judge,
Who leagu'd with thee---

Ap. Virginius, fuch intemp'rance
Befpeaks a doubtful caufe---Were I indeed
The tyrant thou pretend'ft, what hinders me,
But that this moment, feizing the advantage
Thy infolence and outrage gives, I might
Proceed to inftant judgment, and ftand juftify'd,
To envy's felf ?---Think then, and be advis'd,
While yet 'tis time---If thou haft aught to offer
That can avail thee, or invalidate
Th' accufer's claim, fpeak free, thou fhalt be heard
With favour ; nay, by Heav'ns, myfelf will joy
To fee this innocent, haplefs, virtuous maid,
Whom I admire and pity, fav'd from ruin.

L. Vir. Oh, Jove, the thunderer !---This temperate
How calm, how cool he meditates oppreffion !   [villain !
With what ferenity he gives the ftab !
Thou tyrant, who, if Juftice had her courfe,
Trembling and pale, ought'ft now to ftand before
The terrible tribunal of the people,
To give account of all thy crimes !---Think'ft thou
There is that peafant flave, who could be gull'd
By fuch apparent fraud !---Behold the Forum
Block'd up with troops !---My friends, by bafe furprize
O'erpower'd, in chains !---Ev'n now, a band of ruffians
Burft forth, and feiz'd Icilius---Nay, with violence,
The gen'rous Marcia (Ah, too nobly good,
To be allied to a perfidious brother !)
They feiz'd, they dragg'd along the ftreets of Rome !
Becaufe fhe could unfold thee, lay thee open,
With all the foul corruption of thy heart,
To public view !---Thou feeft I know thee, Appius ;
Spare then all farther feigning---Thou'ft play'd o'er

Thy

Thy part affign'd ; now be thyfelf again,
Th' oppreffive, bloody, bold, rapacious tyrant !
And fnatch'd by open force !

   Ap. Thou infolent,
Audacious rebel ! Think'ft thou to patch up
Thy rotten plea, by ribaldry and railing ?
Or with thy clam'rous cries, extort thro' fear,
What right denies thee ?---No, thy venom'd rage
Shall burft thee, ere I fhrink ?---Claudius, thou haft,
By fair and open proof, by living witnefs,
Supported well thy claim ; which this foul railer
Refufes to reply to, but by flander :
Take then thy own ; for this is my award ;
Which, by the Gods, and the offended majefty
Of Juftice, unrevoked fhall ftand---So, hence,
And take her with thee.

   Clau. I thank thee, Apiups---Come——we muft re-
       tire---   [*Laying hold of* Virginia.

   Vir. Off !——Touch me not !——infidious, treach'-
     rous monfter !

   [*She ftruggling*, Claudius *endeavours to force her away.*
Oh, gods !---help, help !---my father ! Romans ! help !
Save me !

   Clau. In vain thou ftruggleft---Thou muft hence
With me—and fhalt—Thou art my flave, young maid ;
Know thy condition ; and henceforward learn
Obedience to my pleafure——

   Vir. Triumph o'er
A lifelefs corfe thou may'ft, and thefe torn limbs,
Stiff'ning in death, trail after thee——but never,
No, never think, while fenfe and vital heat
Inform this earthly mafs, to part me from
The ftock where firft I grew !   [*Clinging to her father.*

   L. Vir. No more, my daughter---
Thou feeft refiftance is in vain——We muft
Fulfil our deftiny : there is no help :
Submit thee then, and, arm'd with patience, fuit
Thy mind to thy hard fortune.

   Vir. Righteous Heaven !
What, does my father give me up ?——Does he
Confirm the cruel fentence pafs'd upon me ?——
Behold me then a flave !——Here, thou remorfelefs,

Thou

Thou perjur'd minifter!---Here---bind thefe limbs!
In fervile fetters, manacle thefe hands!
This wretched frame fhall not be fubject long
To thy inhuman power!---Come then---drag me
To dungeons, death and darkpefs——

   L. Vir. Hold, Virginia—
Appius, thou feeft I yield, nor dare I longer.
Contend againft the fov'reign pow'r; the law,
That robs me of my daughter, tho' fevere,
I do fubmit to; and I pray forgive
A wretched father, if my unweigh'd fpeech
Have been, too bitter : now, before I go
For ever to lofe fight of this poor maid,
Whom certainly I always thought my own,
And as my own have lov'd, and bred, and cherifh'd ;
If thou haft pity, grant this one requeft ;
The privilege but of a few fad moments,
To breathe out all the anguifh of my foul,
And glut myfelf with grief—'Twill be fome eafe,
Before we part, to take a laft farewel,
To fold her in my trembling arms once more,
And rain my bitter tears into her bofom,
Ere I refign her !

   Ap. Be it fo---but let
A guard, for more fecurity, attend.

   L. Vir. 'Tis well——I thank ye——This way, Vir-
     ginia——

   Vir. My beating heart !   [*Following.*
   L. Vir. Support me, gods !   [*Afide.*
   [L. Virginius *and his daughter come forward on the ftage.*
   L. Vir. My child !
Ah, my belov'd Virginia !
   Vir. My dear father !
   L. Vir. I cannot utter it !—When I would fpeak,
My heart-ftrings tremble, and affrighted nature
Backward recoils !—My child !---muft it then be ?
Muft I forget all feelings of a father,
And of a man ?---Muft I blot out all traces
From this diftracted brain, of what I have been ?
How I have lov'd, how train'd up thee, fweet maid,
Now for pollution mark'd ?---Oh, bloody Appius !---
Gods, gods !---if ye are juft !---Draw nearer to me---
                        [*To* Virginia.

Let me weep over thee a while---and then——
Canſt thou not gueſs!---Oh, ſay, and ſpare my tongue
The dreadful word!---Canſt thou read the purpoſe
That ſhakes me thus!
   Vir. What may this mean?
   L. Vir. Seeſt thou
This mortal point?——   *[Pulling out the dagger.*
   Vir. 'Tis as my boding heart
Preſag'd---here then my cares and danger end. . *[Aſide.*
My father, tho' my ſex and years, till now
Unvers'd in ſorrow, ſtart to look on death;
Tho' nature ſtruggles hard, and fain would ward
The fatal blow, that cuts off all my hopes;
Yet my ſoul feels, and owns the deed is noble,
And worthy of my father!
   L. Vir. 'Tis cruel, but yet glorious!---Thou muſt die,
To ſave thee from perdition!---Think, Oh, think
What 'tis to live a ſlave! the butt and mark
Of hourly ſhame and inſult!---think upon
Thy youth, thy innocence and maiden bloom,
Stain'd and defac'd by barb'rous luſt and outrage:
Think when the brutal tyrant ſhall be cloy'd,
To have thy rifled beauties then conſign'd
To th' next groſs ruffian and the next---Diſtraction!
   Vir. Quick, quick, diſpatch——
Tear up my boſom with thy ſteel, but ſpare
To rend my ſoul with ſounds like theſe---Oh, ſtrike!---
   L. Vir. Thus then---[*Lifting the dagger.*] my hand
        ſhrinks back, and ev'ry nerve
Stiffens with horror!---turn aſide, my eyes,
Nor view the bloody deed!---
   Vir. No more, my father——
Oh, gods!---We are obſerv'd!---They'll tear me from
      thee!
Here ſtrike!---Oh, let me aid thy trembling hand!
A moment loſt conſigns me o'er to ſhame!
   L. Vir. Juſt gods!---[*Looking up to Heaven.*] thus
       then---and thus——   *[Stabbing her.*
The only way I can, I ſet thee free!
   Ap. What has he done! [*Starting up on his Tribunal.*
   Plaut. Oh, horrid, cruel, father!
She ſinks!---She dies!---Help!--- [*Runs to ſupport her.*
                              L. Vir.
I

L. Virg. [*Holding up the dagger to* Appius.] Appius,
    with this blood
Thee, and thy impious head, I thus devote
To the infernal gods !   [*Exit, holding up the dagger.*
  Ap. Perdition seize me,
But he has murder'd her !—Attach him, Lictors,
And bear him instant—What noise is that ?
           [*A tumultuous noise is heard without.*

    Enter Rufus *to* Appius, *haftily.*

  Ruf. My Lord, Icilius, refcu'd by the populace,
Is coming at their head ; the guards on poft
They have broke through, and bear down all before 'em.
  Ap. Confusion !—I'm betray'd !—The flaves have fold
  Claud. Let us efcape, before it be too late—   [me !
We muft give way to th' torrent—
  Ap. No, this arm
Shall ftem it—and the troops that fled, fhall conquer,
When Appius leads them on—Away ! [*To* Claudius. Ap-
    pius *defcends in hafte from his tribunal, and goes out*
    with Claudius.

    Enter Marcia, *with a train of weeping matrons.*

  Mar. [*Seeing* Virginia's *body.*] Oh !
Support me !—here !—here is a fight !—turn here,
And ftiffen into ftone !—See that fweet bofom,
All gor'd and bloody, heaving yet in death !
Look on her quiv'ring lips, and that dead pale
That creeps o'er all her bloom !   [*A loud fhout is heard.*

    Then enters Icilius *at the head of the people.*

  Icilius. [*Seeing the body, he is ftruck with horror, and ftands*
    fixed in aftonifhment for fome time—at laft he kneels
    down by her.] My Virginia !
[Virginia *at the found of his voice, endeavours to raife*
    herfelf—She looks at him for fome time, unable to fpeak ;
    then finks down, and with a groan expires.
  Icilius. [*Starting up from the ground.*] Oh, blaft thefe
    eyes,
Some fpeedy fire from heav'n !—dry up all fight !
Left looking here, I ftrike againft the gods,
That doom'd me fuch a wretch !   Gone, gone for ever !
             F   It

It is not to be borne !——the only way
Is thus !——   [*Going to stab himself,*

          Enter L. Virginius, *who catches his arm.*

    L. Vir. What means thy rage ?---Look here !——his
          impious blood
Smokes on my dagger's point !
                         [*Holding up the bloody dagger.*
    Icil. [*Struggling.*] Unhand me, murd'rer !——
Thou butcher of thy child !—there, parricide !
Behold thy triumph there !——
                         [*Pointing to* Virginia's *body.*
    L. Vir. [*Weeping.*] My old heart splits with sorrow !
Sweet hapless flow'r !
Untimely cropt by the fell planter's hand !
My eyes weep blood to look on what I've done——
And yet 'twas pity nerv'd my arm to strike
The blow !
    Icil. Distraction seize thee !—then strike here !
Give me thy pity too !
    L. Vir. Icilius, hear me——
Look on the cold remains of that dear maid—
She sleeps in peace and honour !—Wouldst thou rather
Behold her thus, or stain'd with foul pollution ?
——Now, as thou art a Roman,
Declare——
    Icil. Away !---I wish to die, Virginius——
    L. Vir. To die ?—Are Rome and glory then forgot ?
At sight of this hot knife, smoking with blood,
All Rome was fir'd, and aided my old arm
To reach the tyrant's heart !—And shall we now
Give up these glorious hopes ?---The Roman name
Again shall rise ? Again fair liberty
Smile o'er th' afflicted land !---For such a jewel,
A patriot breast must know no price too dear ;
Not ev'n a daughter's blood !---Remember Tarquin,
His exil'd race, and Brutus' guilty sons,
Great Curtius, Cocles, and th' Horatian brothers !
Heroes of old, who for their country bled,
And all th' illustrious list of mighty dead !
Warm'd with their distant rays, let us aspire
To trace their steps, and emulate their fire ;
          4   T'extend

T' extend our fame beyond this narrow ſpan,
And in the Roman to forget the man!

END of the FIFTH ACT.

E P I L O G U E.

Written by Mr. GARRICK.

THE poet's pen, can like a conjurer's wand,
    Or kill, or raiſe his heroine at command;
And I ſhall, ſpirit-like, before I ſink,
Not courteouſly enquire, but tell you what you think.
From top to bottom, I ſhall make you ſtare,
By hitting all your judgments to a hair.
*And firſt, with you above, I ſhall begin---**
Good-natur'd ſouls, they're ready all to grin.
Though twelve-pence ſeat you there, ſo near the cieling,
The folks below can't boaſt a better feeling.
No high bred prud'ry in your region lurks,
You boldly laugh and cry, as Nature works.
Says John to Tom, (ay---there they ſit together,
As honeſt Britons as e'er trod on leather:)
" 'Tween you and I, my friend, 'tis very vild,
That old Vergeenus ſhould have ſtuck his child:
I would have bang'd him for't, had I been ruler,
And duck'd that Apus too, by way of cooler."
Some maiden-dames, who hold the middle-floor,
And fly from naughty man at forty four; †
With turn'd-up eyes, applaud Virginia's 'ſcape,
And vow they'd do the ſame to ſhun a rape;
So very chaſte, they live in conſtant fears,
And apprehenſion ſtrengthens with their years.
Ye bucks, who from the pit your terrors ſend,
Yet love diſtreſſed damſels to befriend;

*** Upper Gallery.**   **† Middle Gallery.**

You

EPILOGUE.

You think this tragic joke too far was carried;
And wish, to set all right, the maid had married:
You'd rather see (if so the fates had will'd)
Ten wives. be kind, than one poor virgin kill'd.
May I approach unto the boxes, pray---
And there search out a judgment on the play?
In vain, alas! I should attempt to find it---
Fine ladies see a play, but never mind it———
'Tis vulgar to be mov'd by acted passion,
Or form opinions, till they're fix'd by fashion.
Our author hopes, this fickle goddess Mode,
With us will make, at least, nine days abode;
To present pleasure he contracts his view,
And leaves his future fame, to time and you.

M. MASSEY in the Character of CHRISTINA
—— don't you know me Sir?

BELL'S EDITION.

GUSTAVUS VASA,

THE

DELIVERER OF HIS COUNTRY.

A TRAGEDY.

Written by HENRY BROOKE, *Esq.*

AS INTENDED TO HAVE BEEN PERFORMED AT THE

Theatre-Royal in Drury-Lane.

LONDON:

Printed for JOHN BELL, near *Exeter-Exchange*, in the *Strand*.

MDCCLXXVIII.

A PREFATORY

DEDICATION

TO THE

SUBSCRIBERS.

AS I esteemed it my happiness to live under a government where national liberty was established by law, and the rights of subjects interwoven with their allegiance, so I ever thought it my safety to act with such allowable freedom, as did not contradict any of our written and known regulations.

Tho' inconsiderable in myself, I am yet a subject of Great-Britain; and the privileges of her meanest member are dear to the whole constitution.

Among those privileges, I claim that of justifying my conduct, I claim that of defending my property, and wish I could do both, without giving disgust, even to those by whose censures I am a sufferer.

When I wrote the following sheets, I had studied the ancient laws of my country, but was not conversant with her present political state. I did not consider things minutely; in the general view, I liked our constitution, and zealously wished that the religion, the laws, and liberties of England might ever be sacred and safe. I had nothing to fear or hope from party or preferment. My attachments were only to truth; I was conscious of no other principles, and was far from apprehending that such could be offensive.

A 2

I took

I took my fubject from the Hiftory of Sweden, one of thofe Gothic and glorious nations, from whom our form of government is derived, from whom Britain has inherited thofe unextinguifhable fparks of liberty and patriotifm, that were her light through the ages of ignorance and fuperftition, her flaming fword turned every way againft invafion, and that vital heat which has fo often preferved her, fo often reftored her, from inteftine malignities. Thofe are the fparks, the gems, that alone give true ornament and brightnefs to the crown of a Britifh monarch; that give him freely to reign over the free, and fhall ever fet him above the princes of the earth, till corruption grows univerfal, till fubjects wifh to be flaves, and Kings know not how to be happy.

I was pleafed with the fimilitude between the principles, and, as I may fay, between the natural conftitutions of Sweden and Britain. I looked no further for fentiments, than as they arofe from facts; and for the facts I am indebted to hiftory: nay, I ingenuoufly confefs, I was fo far from a view of merit with the difaffected, that I looked upon this performance as the higheft compliment I could pay the prefent eftablifhment—Such was my ignorace, or fuch is my misfortune.

Many are the difficulties a new author has to encounter in introducing his play on the ftage. I had the good fortune to furmount them. This piece was about five weeks in rehearfal; the day was appointed for acting; I had difpofed of many hundred tickets; and imagined I had nothing to fear, but from the weaknefs of the performance.

But, then it was, that where I looked for approbation, I met with repulfe. I was condemned and punifhed in my works, without being accufed of any crime; and made obnoxious to the government under which I live, without having it in my power to alter my conduct, or knowing in what inftance I had given offence.

However fingular and unprecedented this treatment may appear, had I conceived it to be the intention of the legiflature, I fhould have fubmitted without complaining; or had any, among hundreds who have perufed the manufcript, obferved but a fingle line that might inadvertently
tend

tend to fedition or immorality, I would then have been the firft to ftrike it out; I would now be the laft to publifh it.

Had the dignity of the Lord Chamberlain's office condefcended, as fome would infinuate, to a theatrical examination of the drama, to a critical inquifition of the conduct, the unities, and tricks of fcenery, even fo I might have hoped for equal indulgence with farces, pantomimes, and other performances of like tafte and genius.

But this is not the cafe ; the Lord Chamberlain's office is alone concerned in thofe reafons which gave birth to the ftatute ; it is to guard againft fuch reprefentations as he may conceive to be of pernicious influence in the commonwealth ; this is the only point to which his prohibitions are underftood to extend, and his prohibition lays me under the neceffity of publifhing this piece, to convince the public, that (though of no valuable confequence) I am at leaft inoffenfive.

Patriotifm, or the love of country, is the great and fingle moral which I had in view through this play. This love (fo fuperior in its nature to all other interefts and affections) is perfonated in the character of Guftavus. It is the love of national welfare ; national welfare is national liberty ; and he alone that can be confcious of it, he alone can contribute to the fupport of it, who is perfonally free.

By perfonal freedom I mean that ftate refulting from virtue, or reafon ruling in the breaft, fuperior to appetite and paffion ; and by national freedom, I mean a fecurity (arifing from the nature of a well-ordered conftitution) for thofe advantages and privileges that each man has a right to, by contributing as a member to the weal of that community.

The monarch, or head of fuch a conftitution, is as the father of a large and well-regulated family ; his fubjects are not fervants, but fons ; their care, their affections, their attachments are reciprocal, and their intereft is one, is not to be divided.

This is truly to reign ; this only is to reign. How glorious, how extenfive, is the prerogative of fuch a monarch ! He is fuperior to fubjects, each of whom is equal to any monarch, who is only fuperior to flaves. He is fceptered in the hearts of his people, from whence he di-

rects

rects their hands with double force and energy. His office partakes of the divine inclination, by being exerted to no other end but the happiness of a people.

Oh, never may any subtleties, any insinuations, raise groundless jealousies in a people so governed! never may they be influenced to imagine that such a prince is invading their rights, while he is only solicitous to confirm and preserve them!

And never may any ministry, any adulation, seduce such a prince from that his true interest and honour!

I should not have had the assurance to solicit a subscription in favour of sentiments that any circumstance could ever make me retract. These, and these only, are the principles of which you are patrons; and the honourable names prefixed * to this performance, lay me under such a future obligation of conduct, as shall ever make me cautious of forfeiting the advantages I receive from them. They are also to me a lasting memorial of that gratitude with which I am,

Your most obliged, most faithful,

And most humble servant,

HENRY BROOKE.

---

* The author was favoured with a very numerous and respectable subscription.

PRO-

PROLOGUE.

*B*RITONS! *this night presents a state distress'd,*
   Tho' brave, yet vanquish'd; and tho' great, oppress'd;
Vice, rav'ning vulture, on her vitals prey'd,
Her peers, her prelates, fell corruption sway'd;
Their rights, for pow'r, th' ambitious weakly sold,
The wealthy, poorly, for superfluous gold.
Hence wasting ills, hence sev'ring factions rose,
And gave large entrance to invading foes;
Truth, justice, honour fled th' infected shore,
For freedom, sacred freedom, was no more.
   Then, greatly rising in his country's right,
Her hero, her deliverer, sprung to light;
A race of hardy, northern sons he led,
Guiltless of courts, untainted, and unread,
Whose inborn spirit spurn'd th' ignoble fee,
Whose hands scorn'd bondage, for their hearts were free.
   Ask ye what law their conqu'ring cause confess'd?
Great nature's law, the law within the breast;
Form'd by no art, and to no sect confin'd,
But stamp'd by Heav'n upon th' unletter'd mind.
   Such, such, of old, the first-born natives were,
Who breath'd the virtues of Britannia's air;
Their realm, when mighty Cæsar vainly sought,
For mightier freedom against Cæsar fought,
And rudely drove the fam'd invader home,
To tyrannize o'er polish'd—venal Rome.
   Our bard, exalted in a free-born flame,
To ev'ry nation would transfer this claim:
He to no state, no climate bounds his page,
He bids the moral beam thro' ev'ry age;
Then be your judgment gen'rous as his plan,
Ye sons of freedom!—save the friend of man.

DRA-

[8]

DRAMATIS PERSONÆ.

MEN.

Criftiern, King of Denmark and Nor-
way, and Ufurper of Sweden, Mr. Wright.
Trollio, a Swede, Archbifhop of Upfal,
and Vicegerent to *Criftiern*, Mr. Cibber.
Peterfon, a Swedifh nobleman, fecretly
of the Danifh party, and friend to
Trollio, - - Mr. Turbutt.
Laertes, a young Danifh Nobleman, at-
tendant to *Criftina*,   - Mr. Woodward.
Guftavus, formerly General of the
Swedes, and firft coufin to the de-
ceafed King,   - Mr. Quin.
Arvida, of the royal blood of Sweden,
friend and coufin to *Guftavus*, Mr. Milward.
Anderfon, Chief Lord of Dalecarlia, Mr. Mills.
Arnoldus, a Swedifh Prieft, and chaplain
in the copper mines of Dalecarlia, Mr. Havard.
Sivard, Captain of the Dalecarlians, Mr. Ridout.

WOMEN.

Criftina, daughter to *Criftiern*, Mrs. Giffard.
Augufta, Mother to   Mrs. Butler.
 Guftavus,   } Prifoners in
Guftava, Sifter to } *Criftiern's*
 Guftavus, a child, } camp,   Mifs Cole.
Mariana, attendant and confident to
Criftina,   - - Mrs. Chetwood.

Soldiers, Peafants, Meffengers, and Attendants.

Scene, Dalecarlia, a northern province in Sweden.

GUSTA-

GUSTAVUS VASA.

ACT I.

SCENE, *the infide of the Copper-Mines in Dalecarlia.*

Enter Anderfon, Arnoldus, *and Servants, with torches.*

ANDERSON.

YOU tell me wonders.
 Arn. Soft, behold, my Lord,
       [*Points behind the fcenes.*
Behold him ftretch'd, where reigns eternal night,
The flint his pillow, and cold damps his fov'ring;
Yet, bold of fpirit, and robuft of limb,
He throws inclemency afide, nor feels
The lot of human frailty.
 And. What horrors hang around! the favage race
Ne'er hold their den but where fome glimm'ring ray
May bring the cheer of morn——What then is he?
His dwelling marks a fecret in his foul,
And whifpers fomewhat more than man about-him.
 Arn. Draw but the veil of his apparent wretchednefs,
And you fhall find his form is but affum'd,
To hoard fome wond'rous treafure lodg'd within.
 And. Let him bear up to what thy praifes fpeak him,
And I will win him, fpite of his referve,
Bind him with facred friendfhip to my foul,
And make him half myfelf.
 Arn. 'Tis nobly promis'd;
For worth is rare, and wants a friend in Sweden:
And yet I tell thee, in her age of heroes,
When nurs'd by freedom, all her fons grew great,
And ev'ry peafant was a prince in virtue.
I greatly err, or this abandon'd ftranger
Had fteppd the firft for fame, tho' now he feeks
To veil his name, and cloud his fhine of virtues;
For there is danger in them.

                And.

And. True, Arnoldus.
Were there a prince throughout the fcepter'd globe,
Who fearch'd out merit for its due preferment,
With half that care our tyrant feeks it out
For ruin, happy, happy were that ftate,
Beyond the golden fable of thofe pure
And earlieft ages——Wherefore this, good Heav'n?
Is it of fate, that who affumes a crown
Throws off humanity?

Arn. So Criftiern holds.
He claims our country as by right of conqueft,
A right to ev'ry wrong.　Ev'n now 'tis faid,
The tyrant envies what our mountains yield
Of health or aliment; he comes upon us,
Attended by a num'rous hoft, to feize
Thefe laft retreats of our expiring liberty.

And. Say'ft thou?

Arn. This rifing day, this inftant hour,
Thus chafed, we ftand upon the utmoft brink
Of fteep perdition, and muft leap the precipice,
Or turn upon our hunters.

And. Now, Guftavus!
Thou prop and glory of inglorious Sweden,
Where art thou, mightieft man?—Were he but here——
I'll tell thee, my Arnoldus, I beheld him,
Then when he firft drew fword, ferene and dreadful,
As the brow'd evening ere the thunder break;
Fór foon he made it toilfome to our eyes
To mark his fpeed, and trace the paths of conqueft?
In vain we follow'd where he fwept the field;
'Twas death alone could wait upon Guftavus.

Arn. He was indeed whate'er our wifh could form him.

And. Array'd and beauteous in the blood of Danes,
Th' invaders of his country, thrice he chafed
This Criftiern, this fell conqu'ror, this ufurper,
With rout and foul difhonour at his heels,
To plunge his head in Denmark.

Arn. Nor ever had the tyrant known return,
To tread our necks, and blend us with the duft,
Had he not dar'd to break thro' ev'ry law
That fanctifies the nations; feiz'd our hero,

The

The pledge of fpecious treaty, tore him from us,
And led him chain'd to Denmark.

And. Then we fell.
If ftill he lives, we yet may learn to rife;
But never can I dare to reft a hope
On any arm but his.

Arn. And yet, I truft,
This ftranger, that delights to dwell with darknefs,
Unknown, unfriended, compafs'd round with wretched-
Conceals fome mighty purpofe in his breaft,   [nefs,
Now lab'ring into birth.

And. When came he hither?

Arn. Six moons have chang'd upon the face of night,
Since here he firft arriv'd, in fervile weeds,
But yet of mien majeftic.   I obferv'd him,
And ever as I gaz'd, fome namelefs charm,
A wond'rous greatnefs, not to be conceal'd,
Broke thro' his form, and aw'd my foul before him,
Amid thefe mines he earns the hireling's portion,
His hands out-toil the hind, while on his brow
Sits patience, bathed in the laborious drop
Of painful induftry——I oft have fought,
With friendly tender of fome worthier fervice,
To win him from his temper; but he fhuns
All offers, yet declin'd with graceful act,
Engaging beyond utt'rance.   And at eve,
When all retire to fome domeftic folace,
He only ftays, and, as you fee, the earth
Receives him to her dark and cheerlefs bofom,

And. Has no unwary moment e'er betray'd
The labours of his foul, fome fav'rite grief,
Whereon to raife conjecture?

Arn. I faw, as fome bold peafants late deplor'd
Their country's bondage, fudden paffion feiz'd
And bore him from his feeming; ftraight his form
Was turn'd to terror, ruin fill'd his eye,
And his proud ftep appear'd to awe the world;
When check'd, as thro' an impotence of rage,
Damp fadnefs foon ufurp'd upon his brow,
And the big tear roll'd graceful down his vifage.

And. Your words imply a man of much importance.

Arn. So I fufpected, and at dead of night

Stole

Stole on his flumbers; his full heart was bufy,
And oft his tongue pronounc'd the hated name
Of—bloody Criftiern——There he feem'd to paufe,
And, recollected to one voice, he cry'd,
Oh, Sweden! Oh, my country! Yet I'll fave thee.
 And. Forbear; he rifes——Heav'ns, what majefty!
     Enter Guftavus.
Your pardon, ftranger, if the voice of virtue,
If cordial amity from man to man,
And fomewhat that fhould whifper to the foul,
To feek and cheer the fuff'rer, led me hither,
Impatient to falute thee.   Be it thine
Alone to point the path of friendfhip out,
And my beft pow'r fhall wait upon thy fortunes.
 Guf. Yes, gen'rous man! there is a wond'rous teft,
The trueft, worthieft, nobleft caufe for friendfhip;
Dearer than life, than int'reft, or alliance.
And equal to your virtues.
 And. Say, unfold.
 Guf. Art thou a foldier, a chief lord in Sweden,
And yet a ftranger to thy country's voice,
That loudly calls the hidden patriot forth?
But what's a foldier? What's a lord in Sweden?
All worth is fled or fall'n; nor has a life
Been fpar'd, but for difhonour; fpar'd to breed
More flaves for Denmark, to beget a race
Of new-born virgins for th' unfated luft
Of our new mafters.   Sweden, thou art no more!
Queen of the north! thy land of liberty,
Thy houfe of heroes, and thy feat of virtues,
Is now the tomb where thy brave fons lie fpeechlefs,
And foreign fnakes engender.
 And. Oh, 'tis true!
But wherefore? To what purpofe?
 Guf. Think of Stockholm.
When Criftiern feiz'd upon the hour of peace,
And drench'd the hofpitable floor with blood,
Then fell the flow'r of Sweden, mighty names!
Her hoary fenators, and gafping patriots.
The tyrant fpoke, and his licentious band
Of blood-train'd miniftry were loos'd to ruin.
Invention wanton'd in the toil of infants

   I   Stabb'd

Stabb'd on the breaft, or reeking on the points
Of fportive javelins. Hufbands, fons, and fires,
With dying ears drank in the loud defpair
Of fhrieking chaftity. The wafte of war
Was peace and friendfhip to this civil maffacre.
Oh, heav'n and earth! Is there a caufe for this?
For fin without temptation, calm, cool villainy,
Delib'rate mifchief, unimpaffion'd luft,
And fmiling murder? Lie thou there, my foul:
Sleep, fleep upon it, image not the form
Of any dream but this, till time grows pregnant,
And thou canft wake to vengeance.   [forth.
    And. Thou'ft greatly mov'd me. Ha! thy tears ftart
Yes, let them flow, our country's fate demands them;
I too will mingle mine, while yet 'tis left us
To weep in fecret, and to figh with fafety.
But wherefore talk of vengeance? 'Tis a word
Should be engraven on the new-fall'n fnow,
Where the firft beam may melt it from obfervance.
Vengeance on Criftiern! Norway and the Dane,
The fons of Sweden, all the peopled north,
Bends at his nod——My humbler boaft of pow'r
Meant not to cope with crowns.
    Guf. Then what remains
Is briefly, this; your friendfhip has my thanks,
But muft not my acceptance. Never—no——
Firft fink, thou baleful manfion, to the centre,
And be thy darknefs doubled round my head,
Ere I forfake thee for the blifs of Paradife,
To be enjoy'd beneath a tyrant's fceptre:
No, that were wilful flavery——Freedom is
The brilliant gift of Heav'n, 'tis reafon's felf,
The kin of Deity——I will not part it.
    And. Nor I, while I can hold it; but, alas!
That is not in our choice.
    Guf. Why? Where's that pow'r whofe engines are of
To bend the brave and virtuous man to flavery?   [force
Bafe fear, the lazinefs of luft, grofs appetites,
Thefe are the ladders, and the groveling foot-ftool,
From whence the tyrant rifes on our wrongs,
Secure and fcepter'd in the foul's fervility.
He has debauch'd the genius of our country,

B

And

And rides triumphant, while her captive fons
Await his nod, the filken flaves of pleafure,
Or fetter'd in their fears.

And. I apprehend you.
No doubt, a bafe fubmiffion to our wrongs
May well be term'd a voluntary bondage:
But think the heavy hand of pow'r is on us;
Of pow'r, from whofe imprifonment and chains
Not all our free-born virtue can protect us.

Guf. 'Tis there you err; for I have felt their force;
And had I yielded to enlarge thefe limbs,
Or fhare the tyrant's empire, on the terms
Which he propos'd, I were a flave indeed.
No, in the deep and deadly damp of dungeons,
The foul can rear her fceptre, fmile in anguifh,
And triumph o'er oppreffion.

And. Oh, glorious fpirit! Think not I am flack
To relifh what thy noble fcope intends;
But then the means, the peril, and the confequence!
Great are the odds, and who fhall dare the trial?

Guf. I dare.
Oh, wert thou ftill that gallant chief
Whom once I knew! I could unfold a purpofe,
Would make the greatnefs of thy heart to fwell,
And burft in the conception.

And. Give it utt'rance.
Perhaps there lie fome embers yet in Sweden,
Which, waken'd by thy breath, might rife in flames,
And fpread vindictive round. You fay you know me;
But give a tongue to fuch a caufe as this,
And if you hold me tardy in the call,
You know me not. But thee I've furely known;
For there is fomewhat in that voice and form,
Which has alarm'd my foul to recollection:
But 'tis as in a dream, and mocks my reach.

Guf. Then name the man whom it is death to know,
Or, knowing, to conceal——and I am he.

And. Guftavus! Heav'ns! 'Tis he! 'tis he himfelf!

Enter Arvida, fpeaking to a Servant.

Arv. I thank you, friend; he's here; you may retire.

[Exit Servant.
And.

And. Good morning to my noble gueſt ; you're early.
                   [Guſtavus *walks apart.*
  Arv. I come to take a ſhort and haſty leave.
'Tis ſaid, that from the mountain's neighb'ring brow
The canvas of a thouſand tents appears,
Whitening the vale——Suppoſe the tyrant there ;
You know my ſafety lies not in the interview——
Ha ! what is he, who, in the ſhreds of ſlavery
Supports a ſtep ſuperior to the ſtate
And inſolence of ermine ?
  Guſ. Sure that voice
Was once the voice of friendſhip and Arvida !
  Arv. Ha ! Yes, 'tis he !—ye pow'rs, it is Guſtavus !
  Guſ. Thou brother of adoption ! In the bond
Of ev'ry virtue wedded to my ſonl,
Enter my heart ; it is thy property.
  Arv. I'm loſt in joy, and wond'rous circumſtance.
  Guſ. Yet, wherefore, my Arvida, wherefore is it,
That in a place, and at a time like this,
We ſhould thus meet ? Can Criſtiern ceaſe from cruelty ?
Say, whence is this, my brother ? How eſcap'd you ?
Did I not leave thee in the Daniſh dungeon ?
  Arv. Of that hereafter.   Let me view thee firſt.
How graceful is the garb of wretchedneſs,
When worn by virtue ! Faſhions turn to folly ;
Their colours tarniſh, and their pomps grow poor
To her magnificence.
  Guſ. Yes, my Arvida ;
Beyond the ſweeping of the proudeſt train
That ſhades a monarch's heel, I prize theſe weeds ;
For they are ſacred to my country's freedom.
A mighty enterprize has been conceiv'd,
And thou art come auſpicious to the birth,
As ſent to fix the ſeal of heav'n upon it.
  Arv. Point but thy purpoſe—let it be to bleed——
  Guſ. Your hands, my friends.
  All. Our hearts.
  Guſ. I know they're brave.
Of ſuch the time has need, of hearts like yours,
Faithful and firm, of hands inur'd and ſtrong ;
For we muſt ride upon the neck of danger,
And plunge into a purpoſe big with death.
B 2

And.

And. Here let us kneel, and bind us to thy side.
By all——

Guſ. No, hold—if we want oaths to join us,
Swift let us part, from pole to pole aſunder.
A cauſe like ours is its own ſacrament;
Truth, juſtice, reaſon, love, and liberty,
Th' eternal links that claſp the world, are in it;
And he who breaks their ſanction, breaks all law,
And infinite connection.

Arn. True, my Lord.

And. And ſuch the force I feel.

Arv. And I.

Arn. And all.

Guſ. Know then, that ere our royal Stenon fell,
While this my valiant couſin and myſelf,
By chains and treach'ry lay detain'd in Denmark,
Upon a dark and unſuſpected hour,
The bloody Criſtiern ſought to take my head.
Thanks to the ruling Pow'r, within whoſe eye
Imboſom'd ills, and mighty treaſons roll,
Prevented of their blackneſs——I eſcap'd,
Led by a gen'rous arm, and ſome time lay
Conceal'd in Denmark; for my forfeit head
Became the price of crowns.   Each port and path
Was ſhut againſt my paſſage; till I heard
That Stenon, valiant Stenon fell in battle,
And freedom was no more.   Oh, then what bounds
Had pow'r to hem the deſp'rate? I o'erpaſs'd them,
Travers'd all Sweden, thro' ten thouſand foes,
Impending perils, and ſurrounding tongues,
That from himſelf enquir'd Guſtavus out.
Witneſs, my country, how I toil'd to wake
Thy ſons to liberty—In vain; for fear,
Cold fear, had ſeiz'd on all——Here laſt I came,
And ſhut me from the ſun, whoſe hateful beams
Serv'd but to ſhew the ruins of my country.
When here, my friends, 'twas here, at length, I found,
What I had left to look for, gallant ſpirits,
In the rough form of untaught peaſantry.

And. Indeed they once were brave; our Dalecarlians
Have oft been known to give a law to kings;
And as their only wealth has been their liberty,

From

From all th' unmeasur'd graspings of ambition
Have held that gem untouch'd—tho' now 'tis fear'd——
   Guf. It is not fear'd—I say, they still shall hold it.
I've search'd these men, and find them like the soil,
Barren without, and to the eye unlovely,
But they've their mines within ; and this the day
In which I mean to prove them.
   Arn. Oh, Gustavus !
Most aptly haft thou caught the paffing hour
Upon whose critical and fated hinge
The ftate of Sweden turns.
   Guf. And to this hour
I've therefore held me in this darkfome womb,
That fends me forth as to a fecond birth
Of freedom, or thro' death to reach eternity.
This day, return'd with ev'ry circling year,
In thoufands pours the mountain peafants forth,
Each with his batter'd arms and rufty helm,
In fportive difcipline well train'd, and prompt
Againft the day of peril.   Thus difguis'd,
Already have I ftirr'd their latent fparks
Of flumb'ring virtue, apt as I could wifh,
To warm before the lighteft breath of liberty.
   Arn. How will they kindle, when, confefs'd to view,
Once more their lov'd Guftavus ftands before them,
And pours his blaze of virtues on their fouls !
   Arv. It cannot fail.
   And. It has a glorious afpect.
   Arv. Now, Sweden, rife and re-affert thy rights,
Or be for ever fall'n.
   And. Then be it fo.
   Arn. Lead on, thou arm of war,
To death or victory.
   Guf. Let us embrace.
Why, thus, my friends, thus join'd in fuch a caufe
Are we not equal to a hoft of flaves ?
You fay the foe's at hand—Why, let them come;
Steep are our hills, nor eafy of accefs,
And few the hours we afk for their reception ;
For I will take thefe ruftic fons of liberty
In the firft warmth and hurry of their fouls ;
And fhould the tyrant then attempt our heights,
B 3

He

He comes upon his fate——Arise, thou sun !
Haste, haste to rouze thee to the call of liberty,
That shall once more salute thy morning beam,
And hail thee to thy setting.
   Arn. O bless'd voice !
Prolong that note but one short day thro' Sweden,
And tho' the sun and life should set together,
It matters not——we shall have liv'd that day.
   Arv. Were it not worth the hazard of a life
To know if Cristiern leads his pow'rs in person,
And what his scope intends ? Be mine that task,
Ev'n to the tyrant's tent I'll win my way,
And mingle with his councils.
   Gust. Go, my friend.
Dear as thou art, whene'er our country calls,
Friends, sons, and sires should yield their treasure up,
Nor own a sense beyond the publick safety.
But tell me, my Arvida, 'ere thou goest,
Tell me what hand has made thy friend its debtor,
And giv'n thee up to freedom and Gustavus ?
   Arv. Ha ! let me think of that, 'tis sure she loves him.
                                 [*Aside.*

Away thou skance and jaundice eye of jealousy,
That tempts my soul to sicken at perfection ;
Away ! I will unfold it————To thyself
Arvida owes his freedom.
   Gust. How, my friend ?   [dungeon
   Arv. Some months are pass'd since in the Danish
With care emaciate, and unwholesome damps
Sick'ning I lay, chain'd to my flinty bed,
And call'd on death to ease me——strait a light
Shone round, as when the ministry of heav'n
Descends to kneeling saints. But Oh ! the form
That pour'd upon my sight———Ye angels speak !
For ye alone are like her ; or present
Such visions pictur'd to the nightly eye
Of fancy trans'd in bliss. She then approach'd,
The softest pattern of embodied meekness,
For pity had divinely touch'd her eye,
And harmoniz'd her motions———Ah, she cry'd,
Unhappy stranger, art not thou the man
Whose virtues have endear'd thee to Gustavus ?
                                         Gust.

Guſt. Guſtavus did ſhe ſay?
Arv. Yes, yes, her lips
Breath'd forth that name with a peculiar ſweetneſs.
Loos'd from my bonds, I roſe, at her command,
When, ſcarce recov'ring ſpeech, I would have kneel'd,
But haſte thee, haſte thee for thy life, ſhe cry'd;
And O, if e'er thy envied eyes behold
Thy lov'd Guſtavus; ſay, a gentle foe
Has giv'n thee to his friendſhip.
   Guſt. You've much amaz'd me! Is her name a ſecret?
   Arv. To me it is———but you perhaps may gueſs.
   Guſt. No, on my word.
   Arv. You too had your deliv'rer.
   Guſt. A kind, but not a fair one—Well, my friends!
Our cauſe is ripe, and calls us forth to action.
Tread ye not lighter? Swells not ev'ry breaſt
With ampler ſcope to take your country in,
And breath the cauſe of virtue? Riſe, ye Swedes!
Riſe greatly equal to this hour's importance.
On us the eyes of future ages wait,
And this day's arm ſtrikes forth deciſive fate;
This day, that ſhall for ever ſink———or ſave;
And make each Swede a monarch———or a ſlave.

END of the FIRST ACT.

ACT II.

SCENE *The Camp.*

Enter Criſtiern, *Attendants,* &c. Trollio *meets him.*

TROLLIO.

ALL hail, moſt mighty of the thrones of Europe!
  The morn ſalutes thee with auſpicious brightneſs,
No vapour frowns prophetic on her brow,
But the clear ſun, who travels with thy arms,
Still ſmiles, attendant on thy growing greatneſs;
His evening eye ſhall ſee thee peaceful lord
Of all the north, of utmoſt Scandinavia;

Whence

Whence thou may'ſt pour thy conqueſts o'er the earth,
'Till fartheſt India glows beneath thy empire,
And Lybia knows no regal name but yours.

    Criſt. Yes, Trollio, I confeſs the godlike thirſt,
Ambition, that wou'd drink a ſea of glory.
But what from Dalecarlia ?

    Troll. Late laſt night,
I ſent a truſty ſlave to Peterſon,
And hourly wait ſome tidings.

    Criſt. Think you ?—Sure
The wretches will not dare ſuch quick perdition.

    Troll. I think they will not—Tho' of old I know them
All born to broils, the very ſons of tumult ;
Waſte is their wealth, and mutiny their birthright,
And this the yearly fever of their blood,
Their holiday of war ; a day apart,
Torn out from peace, and ſacred to rebellion.
Oft has their battle hung upon the brow
Of yon wild ſteep, a living cloud of miſchiefs,
Pregnant with plagues, and empty'd on the heads
Of many a monarch.

    Criſt. Monarchs they were not,
Pageants of wax, the mouldings of the populace,
Tame, paultry idols, ſcepter'd up for ſhew,
And garniſh'd into royalty—No, Trollio,
Kings ſhould be felt if they wou'd find obedience ;
The beaſt has ſenſe enough to know his rider :
When the knee trembles, and the hand grows ſlack,
He caſts for liberty ; but bends and turns
For him that leaps with boldneſs on his back,
And ſpurs him to the bit.

*Enter a Gentleman Uſher, and ſeveral Peaſants, who kneel
and bow at a diſtaace.*

    Criſt. What ſlaves are thoſe ?
    Gent. My gracious liege, your ſubjects.
    Criſt. Whence ?
    Gent. Of Sweden,
From Angermannia, from Helſingia ſome,
Some from Gemtian and Nerician provinces.
    Criſt. Their buſineſs.

Gent.

Gent. They come to speak their griefs.

Crist. Their griefs! their insolence!
Is not the camel mute beneath his burden?
Were they not born to bear? Away!——Hold! come,
What wou'd these murmurers?

Gent. Most royal Cristiern,
They say they have but one—one gracious King,
And yet are bow'd beneath a host of tyrants,
Talk-masters, soldiers, gatherers of subsidies,
All officers of rapine, rape, and murder;
Will-doing potentates, the lords of licence,
Who weigh their sweat and blood, and heavier shame,
Ev'n as a feather puff'd away in sport,
The pastime of a gale.

Crist. I'll hear no more,
I know ye, well I know ye, ye base supplicants;
Fear is the only worship of your souls,
And ever where ye hate, ye yield obeysance.
Wretches! Shall I go poring on the earth,
Lest my imperial foot should tread on emmets?
Is it for you I must controul my soldier,
And coop my eagles from their carrion? No—
Are ye not commoners, vile things in nature,
Poor pricelefs peasants? slaves can know no property!
Out of my sight!   [*Exeunt Peasants.*
    Enter Arvida *guarded, and a Gentleman.*

Arv. Now, fate, I'm caught, and what remains is ob-
Gent. A prisoner, good my lord.   [vious.
Crist. When taken?
Gent. Now, ev'n here, before your tent;
I mark'd his careless action, but his eye
Of studied observation—then his port
And base attire ill suiting——I enquir'd,
But found he was a stranger.

Crist. Ha! observe.
(Damn'd affectation) what a sullen scorn
Knits up his brow, and frowns upon our presence.
What——ay——thou wou'dst be thought a mystery,
Some greatness in eclipse——Whence art thou, slave?
Silent! Nay, then—Bring forth the torture there——
A smile! Damnation!——How the wretch assumes
The wreck of state, the suff'ring soul of majesty.
                    What

What have we no pre-eminence, no claim?
Doſt thou not know thy life is in our pow'r?
　Arv. 'Tis therefore I deſpiſe it.
　Criſt. Matchleſs inſolence!
What art thou? Speak!
　Arv. Be ſure no friend to thee;
For I'm a foe to tyrants.
　Criſt. Fiends and fire!——
A whirlwind tear thee, moſt audacious traitor. [*Criſtiern.*
　Arv. Do, rage and chafe, thy wrath's beneath me,
How poor thy pow'r, how empty is thy happineſs,
When ſuch a wretch, as I appear to be,
Can ride thy temper, harrow up thy form,
And ſtretch thy ſoul upon the rack of paſſion.　　[hence!
　Criſt. I'll know thee—I will know thee! Bear him
Why, what are Kings, if ſlaves can brave us thus?
Go, Trollio, hold him to the rack—Tear, ſearch him,
Prove him thro' ev'ry poignance, ſting him deep.
　　　　　　　　　[*Exit* Trollio *with* Arvida *guarded.*
　　　　　Enter a Meſſenger as in haſte.
　Criſt. What wou'd'ſt thou, fellow?
　Meſſ. O my ſovereign lord,
I am come faſt and far, from ev'n 'till morn,
Five times I've croſs'd the ſhade of ſleepleſs night
Impatient of thy preſence.
　Criſt. Whence?
　Meſſ. From Denmark;
Commended from the conſort of thy throne
To ſpeed and privacy.　　　　　　　　　[ſpeak out,
　Criiſt. Your words wou'd taſte of terror,—Wretch,
Nor dare to tremble here——for didſt thou bear
Thy tidings from a thouſand leagues around,
Unmov'd, I move the whole, the cent'ring nave,
Where turns that mighty circle——Speak thy meſſage.
　Meſſ. A ſecret malady, my gracious liege,
Some factious vapour, riſen from off the ſkirts
Of ſouthmoſt Norway, has diffus'd its bane,
And rages now within the heart of Denmark.
　Criſt. It muſt not, cannot, 'tis impoſſible!
What, my own Danes? Nay, then the world wants weed-
I will not bear it——Hell! I'd rather ſee,　　[ing.
This earth a deſart, deſolate and wild,

　　　　　　　　　　　　　　　　　And

Ard like the lion ftalk my lonely round,
Famifh'd and roaring for my prey.———Call Trollio,
I'll have men ftudied, deeply read in mifchiefs.

Enter a Servant, who kneels and delivers a letter.

Crift. From whom?
Serv. From Peterfon.
Crift. To Trollio ——— Right.   [*Reads.*
How's this?——Be gone————
Go all——without there——wait my pleafure.
O curfe! How hell has tim'd its plagues!
            Enter Trollio.
Crift. Come near, my Trollio.
We've heard ill news from Denmark—that's a trifle———
But here's to blaft thy eyes——Read———
    Troll. Ha! Guftavus!
So near us, and in arms!   [time
    Crift. What's to be done? Now, Trollio, now's the
To fubtilize thy foul, found every depth,
And waken all the wond'rous ftatefman in thee.
For I muft tell thee (fpite of pride and royalty,
Of guarding armies, and of circling nations
That bend beneath my nod) this curs'd Guftavus
Invades my fhrinking fpirits, awes my heart,
And fits upon my flumbers ——————All in vain
Has he been daring, and have I been vigilant;
Spite of himfelf he ftill evades the hunter,
And if there's pow'r in heav'n or hell it guards him.
When was I vanquifh'd, but when he oppos'd me?
When have I conquer'd, but when he was abfent?
His name's a hoft, a terror to my legions.
And by my tripled crown, I fwear, Guftavus,
I'd rather meet all Europe for my foe,
Than fee thy face in arms!
    Troll. Be calm, my liege;
And liften to a fecret big with confequence,
That gives thee back the fecond man on earth
Whofe valour cou'd plant fears around thy throne;
Thy pris'ner———
    Crift. What of him?
    Trol. The prince Afvida.
    Crift. How!

                                              Troll.

Troll. The fame.

Crift. My royal fugitive?

Troll. Moft certain.

Crift. Now then 'tis plain who fent him hither.

Troll. Yes.   [me——

Pray give me leave, my Lord——a thought comes crofs

If fo he muft be ours——   [*Paufes.*

Your pardon for a queftion——Has Arvida

E'er feen your beauteous daughter, your Criftina?

  Crift. Never—yes—poffibly he might, that day

When the proud pair, Guftavus and Arvida,

Thro' Copenhagen drew a length of chain,

And grac'd my chariot wheels—but why the queftion?

  Troll. I'll tell you—while e'en now he ftood before us

I mark'd his high demeanour, and my eye

Claim'd fome remembrance of him, tho' in clouds

Doubtful and diftant, but a nearer view

Renew'd the characters effac'd by abfence,

Yet, left he might prefume upon a friendfhip

Of ancient league between us, I diffembled,

Nor feem'd to know him———— On he proudly ftrode,

As who fhould fay, Back, fortune, know thy diftance!

'Thus fteadily he pafs'd, and mock'd his fate.

When, lo! the Princefs to her morning walk

Came forth attended————quick amazement feiz'd

Arvida at the fight; his fteps took root,

A tremor fhook him; and his alt'ring cheek

Now fudden flufh'd, then fled its wonted colour;

While with an eager and intemp'rate look

He bent his form, and hung upon her beauties.

  Crift. Ha! Did our daughter note him?

  Troll. No, my Lord;

She pafs'd regardlefs——Strait his pride fell from him,

And at her name he ftarted.

'Then heav'd a figh, and caft a look to heav'n,

Of fuch a mute, yet eloquent emotion,

As feem'd to fay, Now, fate, thou haft prevail'd,

And found one way to triumph o'er Arvida!

  Crift. But whither wou'd this lead?

  Troll. Lift, lift, my Lord!

While thus his foul's unfeated, fhook by paffion,

Cou'd we engage him to betray Guftavus————

                                        Crift.

Crist. O empty hope! Impossible, my Trollio,
Do I not know him, and the curs'd Gustavus?
Both fix'd in resolution deep as hell,
And proud as high Olympus!
  Troll. Ah, my liege,
No mortal footing treads so firm in virtue,
As always to abide the slipp'ry path,
Nor deviate with the bias ——— Some have few,
But each man has his failing, some defect
Wherein to slide temptation——Leave him to me.
  Crist. I know thou hast a serpentizing genius,
Canst wind the subtlest mazes of the soul,
And trace her wand'rings to the source of action.
If thou canst bend this proud one to our purpose,
And make the lion crouch, 'tis well———if not,
Away at once, and sweep him from remembrance.
  Troll. Then I must promise deep.
  Crist. Ay, any thing; out-bid ambition.
  Troll. Love?   [him:
  Crist. Ha! Yes—our daughter too—if she can bribe
But then to win him to betray his friend?
  Troll. O doubt it not, my Lord—for if he loves,
As sure he greatly does, I have a stratagem
That holds the certainty of fate within it.
Love is a passion whose effects are various,
It ever brings some change upon the soul,
Some virtue, or some vice, 'till then unknown,
Degrades the hero, and makes cowards valiant.
  Crist. True, when it pours upon a youthful temper,
Open and apt to take the torrent in;
It owns no limits, no restraint it knows,
But sweeps all down tho' heav'n and hell oppose;
Ev'n virtue rears in vain her sacred mound,
Raz'd in its rage, or in its swellings drown'd. [*Exeunt:*

SCENE *opens and discovers* Arvida *in chains, guards pre-*
  paring instruments of death and torture. He advances in
  confusion.

  Arv. Off, off, vain cumbrance, ye conflicting thoughts!
Leave me to heav'n. O peace!——It will not be———
Just when I rose above mortality,
To pour her wond'rous weight of charms upon me!

C

                                                      At

At fuch a time, it was, it was too much !
To pluck the foaring pinion of my foul,
While eagle-ey'd fhe held her flight to heav'n,
O'er pain and death triumphant ! Help, ye faints,
Angelic minifters, defcend, defcend !
And lift me to myfelf; hold, bind my heart
Firm and unfhaken in th' approaching ruin,
The wreck of earth-born frailty ! and, O heav'n !
For ev'ry pang thefe tortur'd limbs fhall feel,
Defcend in ten-fold bleffings on Guftavus !
Yes, blefs him, blefs him ! Crown his hours with joy,
His head with glory, and his arms with conqueft ;
Set his firm foot upon the neck of tyrants,
And be his name the balm of every lip
That breathes thro' Sweden ! Worthieft to be ftil'd
Their friend, their chief, their father, and their king !

Enter Trollio.

   Troll. Unbind your prifoner.
   Arv. How ?
   Troll. You have your liberty,
And may depart unqueftion'd.
   Arv. Do not mock me.
It is not to be thought, while pow'r remains,
That Criftiern wants a reafon to be cruel.
But let him know I wou'd not be oblig'd.
He who accepts the favours of a tyrant
Shares in his guilt ; they leave a ftain behind them.
   Troll. You wrong the native temper of his foul ;
Cruel of force, but never of election :
Prudence compell'd him to a fhew of tyranny ;
Howe'er thofe politicks are now no more,
And mercy in her turn fhall fhine on Sweden.
   Arv. Indeed ! It were a ftrange, a blefs'd reverfe,
Devoutly to be wifh'd, but then the caufe,
The caufe, my Lord, muft furely be uncommon.
May I prefume ?
Perhaps a fecret.
   Troll. No——or if it were,
The boldnefs of thy fpirit claims refpect,
And fhould be anfwer'd. Know, the only man,
In whom our monarch ever knew repulfe,

Is

Is now our friend ; that terror of the field,
Th' invincible Guftavus.
  Arv. Ha ! friend to Criftiern ? Guard thyfelf, my heart !
                                         [Afide.
Nor feem to take alarm——Why, good my Lord,
What terror is there in a wretch profcrib'd,
Naked of means, and diftant as Guftavus ?
  Troll. There you miftake—Nor knew we till this hour
The danger was fo near——From yonder hill
He fends propofals, back'd with all the pow'rs
Of Dalecarlia, thofe licentious refolutes,
Who, having nought to hazard in the wreck,
Are ever foremoft to foment a ftorm.
  Arv. I were too bold to queftion on the terms.
  Troll. No—truft me, valiant man, whoe'er thou art,
I wou'd do much to win a worth like thine,
By any act of fervice, or of confidence.
The terms Guftavus claims, indeed, are haughty ;
The freedom of his mother and his fifter,
His forfeit province, Gothland, and the ifles
Submitted to his fceptre——But the league,
The bond of amity, and lafting friendfhip,
Is, that he claims Criftina for his bride.
You ftart, and feem furpriz'd.
  Arv. A fudden pain
Juft ftruck athwart my breaft——But fay, my Lord,
I thought you nam'd Criftina.
  Troll. Yes.
  Arv. O torture ?   *[Afide.*
What of her, my good Lord ;
  Troll. I faid, Guftavus claim'd her for his bride.
  Arv. His bride ! his wife !
You did not mean his wife ! Do fiends feel this ? *[Afide.*
Down, heart, nor tell thy anguifh ? I'ray excufe me,
Did you not fay, the Princefs was his wife ?
Whofe wife, my Lord ?
  Troll. I did not fav what was, but what muft be.
  Arv. Touching Guftavus, was it not ?
  Troll. The fame.
  Arv. His bride !
  Troll. I fay his bride, his wife ; his lov'd Criftina !
Criftina, fancied in the very prime

C 2

And

And youthful smile of nature; form'd for joys
Unknown to mortals.   You seem indispos'd.
   Arv. The crime of constitution—Oh, Gustavus! [*Aside.*
This is too much!—And think you then, my Lord—
What, will the royal Cristiern e'er consent
To match his daughter with his deadliest foe?
   Troll. What should he do? War else must be eternal.
Besides, some rumours from his Danish realms
Make peace essential here.
   Arv. Yes, peace has sweets,
That Hybla never knew; it sleeps on down,
Cull'd gently from beneath the Cherub's wings;
No bed for mortals——Man is warfare——All
A hurricane within: yet friendship stoops,
And gilds the gloom with falsehood—smiles and varnish!
For still the storm grows high, and then no shore
No rock to split on! 'Twere a kind perdition
To sink ten thousand fathoms at a plunge,
And fasten on oblivion————there we hold
And all is——   [*Faints.*
   Troll. Help, bear him up.   O potency of love!
That plucks this noble fabrick from his base.
Bend, bend him forward—He revives—How fare you?
   Arv. I know not—yet a dagger were most friendly.
Return me, Trollio, O return me back
To death, to racks! Undone, undone Arvida!
   Troll. Is't possible, my Lord! the Prince Arvida!
My friend!   [*Embraces him.*
   Arv. Confusion to the name!   [*Turns.*
   Troll. Why this, good heav'n? And wherefore thus
     disguis'd?
   Arv. Yes, that accomplish'd traitor, that Gustavus;
While he sat planning private scenes of happiness,
O well dissembled! He, be sent me hither;
My friendly, unsuspecting heart a sacrifice,
To make death sure, and rid him of a rival.
   Troll. A rival! Do you then love Cristiern's daughter?
   Arv. Name her not, Trollio; since she can't be mine:
Gustavus! how, ah! how hast thou deceiv'd me!
Who could have look'd for falshood from thy brow?
Whose heav'nly arch was as the throne of virtue,
Thy eye appear'd a sun to chear the world,
                        Thy

Thy bosom truth's fair palace, and thy arms,
Benevolent, the harbour for mankind.
   Troll. What's to be done ? Believe me, valiant Prince,
I know not which most sways me to thy int'rests,
My love to thee, or hatred to Gustavus.   [quickly !
   Arv. Wou'd you then save me ? Think, contrive it
Lend me your troops—by all the pow'rs of vengeance,
Myself will face this terror of the north,
This son of fame—this—O Gustavus—What ?
Where had I wander'd ?—Stab my bleeding country !
Save, shield me from that thought.
   Troll. Retire, my Lord ;.
For see, the Princess comes.
   Arv. Where, Trollio, where ?
Ha! Yes, she comes indeed! her beauties drive
Time, place, and truth, and circumstance before them !
Perdition pleases there—pull—tear me from her !
Yet must I gaze—but one—but one look more,
And I were lost for ever..   [*Exeunt.*
    Enter Cristina, Mariana, *and Attendants.*
   Cristina. Forbid it, shame! forbid it, virgin modesty.
No, no, my friend, Gustavus ne'er shall know it.
O I am over-paid with conscious pleasure ;.
The sense but to have sav'd that wond'rous man,
Is still a smiling cherub in my breast,
And whispers peace within.   [quence,.
   Mar. 'Tis strange a man, of his high note and conse--
Shou'd so evade the busy search of thousands ;
That six long months have shut him from enquiry,
And not an eye can trace him to his covert.
   Cristina. Once 'twas not so, each infant lisp'd, Gustavus !
It was the fav'rite name of ev'ry language,
His slightest motions fill'd the world with tidings ;
Wak'd he, or slept, fame watch'd th'important hour,
And nations told it round.
   Mar. I've heard, my Princess,
What time Gustavus lay detain'd in Denmark,
Your royal father sought the hero's friendship,
And offer'd ample terms of peace and amity.
   Cristina. He did ; he offer'd that, my Mariana,
For which contending monarchs su'd in vain,
He offer'd me, his darling, his Cristina ;
       C 3   But

But I was flighted, flighted by a captive,
Tho' kingdoms fwell'd my dower.
   Mar. Amazement fix me,
Rejected by Guftavus!
   Criftina. Yes, Mariana;——but rejected nobly.
Not worlds cou'd win him to betray his country!
Had he confented, I had then defpis'd him.
What's all the gaudy glitter of a crown?
What, but the glaring meteor of ambition,
That leads a wretch benighted in his errors.
Points to the gulph, and fhines upon deftruction.
   Mar. You wrong your charms, whofe pow'r might re-
Things oppofite in nature—Had he feen you!— [concile
   Criftina. He has, my Mariana, he has feen me.
I'll tell thee——yet while inexpert of years,
I heard of bloody fpoils, the wafte of war,
And dire conflicting man; Guftavus' name
Superior rofe, ftill dreadful in the tale:
Then firft he feiz'd my infancy of foul,
As fomewhat fabled of gigantic fiercenefs,
Too huge for any form; he fcar'd my fleep,
And fill'd my young idea.   Not the boaft
Of all his virtues, graces only known
To him, and heav'nly natures! cou'd erafe
The ftrong impreffion; 'till that wond'rous day
In which he met my eyes.   But O, O heav'n!
O love, and all ye cordial pow'rs of paffion!
What then was my amazement! he was chain'd,
Was chain'd, my Mariana! Like the robes
Of coronation, worn by youthful kings,
He drew his fhackles.   The Herculean nerve
Braced his young arm; and foften'd in his cheek
Liv'd more than woman's fweetnefs! Then his eye!
His mein! his native dignity! He look'd,
As tho' he led captivity in chains,
And all were flaves around.
   Mar. Did he obferve you?
   Criftina. He did: for as I trembled, look'd and figh'd,
His eyes met mine; he fix'd their glories on me.
Confufion thrill'd me then, and fecret joy,
Faft throbbing, ftole its treafures from my heart,
And mantling upward, turn'd my face to crimfon.
I wifh'd

I wifh'd——but did not dare to look——he gaz'd;
When fudden, as by force, he turn'd away,
And would no more behold me.
    ·*Enter* Laertes.
 Laer. Ah, bright imperial maid! my royal miftrefs!
 Criftina. What wou'dft thou fay? Thy looks fpeak
   terror to me.
 Laer. O you are ruin'd facrific'd, undone!
I heard it all; your cruel, cruel father
Has fold you,·giv'n you up a fpoil to treafon,
The purchafe of the nobleft blood on earth——
Guftavus!————
 Criftina. Ah! What of him? Where, where is he?
 Laer. In Dalecarlia, on fome great defign,
Doom'd in an hour to fall by faithlefs hands:
His friend, the brave, the falfe, deceiv'd Arvida,
Ev'n now prepares to lead a band of ruffians
Beneath the winding covert of the hill,
And feize Guftavus, obvious to the fnares
Of friendfhip's fair diffemblance. And your father
Has vow'd your beauties to Arvida's arms,
The purchafe of his falfehood.
 Criftina. Shield me, heav'n!
Firft, duty, break thy filial bands in funder,
And blot the name of parent from the world!
Is there no lett, no means of quick prevention?
 Laer. Behold my life ftill chain'd to thy direction,
My will fhall have a wing for ev'ry word,
That breathes thy mandate.
 Criftina. Will you, good Laertes?
Alas, I fear to overtafk thy friendfhip,
Say, will you fave me then——O go, hafte, fly!
Acquaint Guftavus———— if, if he muft fall,
Let hofts that hem this fingle lion in,
Let nations hunt him down——let him fall nobly.
 Laer. I go, my Princefs——Heav'n direct me to him!
          [*Exit.*
 Criftina. I wou'd pray too, to fave me from pollution;
Detefted ftain, the touch of the betrayer!
But mighty love the partial pray'r arrefts,
And leaves me only anxious for Guftavus.
For him cold fears my fainting bofom chill,
His cares diftract me, and his dangers kill;

Ye pow'rs ! if deaf to all the vows I make,
Yet shield Gustavus, for Gustavus' sake ;
Protect his virtues from a faithless foe,
And save your only image, left below.

[Exeunt.

End of the Second Act.

A C T   III.

SCENE, Mountains of Dalecarlia.

Enter Gustavus, as a Peasant—Dalecarlians following.

GUSTAVUS.

YE men of Sweden, wherefore are ye come ?
   See ye not yonder, how the locusts swarm,
To drink the fountains of your honour up,
And leave your hills a desart——Wretched men !
Why came ye forth ? Is this a time for sport ?
Or are ye met with song and jovial feast,
To welcome your new guests, your Danish visitants ?
To stretch your supple necks beneath their feet,
And fawning lick the dust ?—Go, go, my countrymen,
Each to your several mansions, trim them out,
Cull all the tedious earnings of your toil
To purchase bondage——Bid your blooming daughters,
And your chaste wives to spread their beds with softness ;
Then go ye forth, and with your proper hands
Conduct your masters in : conduct the sons
Of lust and violation——O Swedes, Swedes !
Heav'ns ! are ye men, and will ye suffer this ?

Enter Arnoldus, who talks apart with Gustavus.

1st Dale. How my blood boils !
2d Dale. Who is this honest spokesman ;
3d Dale. What, know ye not Rodolphus of the mines ?
A better lab'rer ne'er struck steel to stone.
Gus. There was a time, my friends ! a glorious time ;
When, had a single man of your forefathers
Upon the frontier met a host in arms,
His courage scarce had turn'd ; himself had stood,

Alone

Alone had ſtood the bulwark of his country.
Your ſires were known but by their manly fronts,
On their black brows, enthron'd, ſat liberty,
The awe of honour, and contempt of death.
   1ſt Dale. We are not baſtards.
   2d Dale. No.
   3d Dale. We're Dalecarlians.
   Guſ. Come, come ye on then. Here I take my ſtand!
Here, on the brink, the very verge of liberty;
Altho' contention riſe upon the clouds,
Mix heav'n with earth, and roll the ruin onward;
Here will I fix, and breaſt me to the ſhock,
'Till I, or Denmark fall.
   Siv. And who art thou?
That thus wou'dſt ſwallow all the glory up
That ſhou'd redeem the times? Behold this breaſt,
The ſword has till'd it; and the ſtripes of ſlaves
Shall ne'er trace honour here: ſhall never blot
The fair inſcription——Never ſhall the cords
Of Daniſh inſolence bind down theſe arms
That bore my royal maſter from the field.
   Guſ. Ha! Say you, brother? Were you there—O grief!
Where liberty and Stenon fell together?
   Siv. Yes, I was there—A bloody field it was,
Where conqueſt gaſp'd, and wanted breath to tell,
Its o'er-toil'd triumph. There, our bleeding King,
There Stenon on this boſom made his bed,
And rolling back his dying eyes upon me:
Soldier, he cried, if e'er it be thy lot
To ſee my valiant couſin, great Guſtavus,
Tell him——for once, that I have fought like him,
And wou'd like him have——
Conquer'd—he ſhou'd have ſaid—but there, O there
Death ſtopt him ſhort.
   Guſ. Come to my arms, and let me hide thy tears,
For I have caught their ſoftneſs—O Danes, Danes!
You ſhall weep blood for this. Shall they not, brother?
Yes, we will deal our might with thrifty vengeance,
A life for ev'ry blow, and when we fall,
There ſhall be weight in't; like the tort'ring tow'rs
That draw contiguous ruin.

Siv.

Siv. Brave, brave man!
My foul admires thee—By my father's fpirit,
I wou'd not barter fuch a death as this
For immortality! Nor we alone—
Here be the trufty gleanings of that field
Where laft we fought for freedom : here's rich poverty,
'Tho' wrapp'd in rags, my fifty brave companions,
Who thro' the force of fifteen thoufand foes
Bore off their King, and fav'd his great remains. [Captain,
　Guf. Give me your hands, thofe valiant hands.—Why,
We could but die alone, with thefe we'll conquer.
My fellow lab'rers too————What fay ye, friends?
Shall we not ftrike for't?
　All. Death ; victory or death !
No bonds, no bonds !
　Arn. Spoke like yourfelves—Ye men of Dalecarlia,
Brave men and bold ! Whom ev'ry future age,
Tongues, nations, languages, and rolls of fame
Shall mark for wond'rous deeds, achievements won
From honour's dang'rous fummit, warriors all !
Say, might ye chufe a chief, for high exploits,
From the firft annal, to the lateft praife
That breathes a hero's name—Speak, name the man
Who then fhould meet your wifh ?
　Siv. Forbear the theme.
Why wou'dft thou feek to fink us with the weight
Of grievous recollection ? O Guftavus !
Cou'd the dead wake, thou wert that man of men,
Firft of the foremoft.
　Guf. Didft thou know Guftavus ?　　　　　　[worth
　Siv. Know him ! O heav'n ! what elfe, who elfe was
The knowledge of a foldier ? That great day,
When Criftiern, in his third attempt on Sweden,
Had fum'd his pow'rs and weigh'd the fcale of fight :
On the bold brink, the very pufh of conqueft,
Guftavus rufh'd, and bore the battle down ;
In his full fway of prowefs, like leviathan
That fcoops his foaming progrefs on the main,
And drives the fhoals along—forward I fprung,
All emulous, and lab'ring to attend him ;
Fear fled before, behind him rout grew loud,
And diftant wonder gaz'd—At length he turn'd,
And having ey'd me with a wond'rous look

　　　　　　　　　　　　　　　　　　Of

Of fweetnefs mix'd with glory—Grace ineftimable!
He pluck'd this bracelet from his conqu'ring arm
And bound it here—My wrift feem'd treble nerv'd;
My heart fpoke to him, and I did fuch deeds
As beft might thank him—But from that blefs'd day
I never faw him more—yet ftill to this,
I bow, as to the relicks of my faint:
Each morn I drop a tear on ev'ry bead,
Count all the glories of Guftavus o'er,
And think I ftill behold him.

   Guf. Rightly thought;
For fo thou doft, my foldier.
Give me my arms—Off, off, ye dark difguifes!
For I will be myfelf. Behold your general,
Guftavus! Come once more to lead ye on
To laurel'd victory, to fame, to freedom!

   1ſt Dale. Is it?
   2d Dale. Yes.
   3d Dale. No.
   4th Dale. 'Tis he!
   5th Dale. 'Tis he!
   6th Dale. 'Tis he!   *[A ſhout.*
   Siv. Strike me, ye pow'rs!——It is illufion all!
It cannot.
   Guf. What, no nearer?
   Siv. 'Tis, it is!——   *[Falls and embraces his knees.*
   Guf. O fpeechlefs eloquence!
Rife to my arms, my friend.
   Siv. Friend! faid you, friend?
O my heart's Lord! My conqu'rer! my!——
   Guf. Approach, my fellow foldiers, your Guftavus
Claims no precedence here: friendfhip like mine
Throws all refpects behind it——'tis enough——
I read your joys, your tranfports in your eyes;
And wou'd, O, wou'd I had a life to fpend,
For ev'ry foldier here! whofe ev'ry life's
Far dearer than my own; dearer than aught,
Except your liberty, except your honour.
Perifh Guftavus, 'ere this facred fun,
That lights the reft of Sweden to their fhame,
Should blufh upon your chains! Why faid I chains!

   I   To

To fouls like yours, I fhould have talk'd of triumphs,
Empire, and fame, and hazards imminent,
Occafions wifh'd, for glory——hafte, brave men !
Collect your friends to join us on the inftant ;
Summon our brethren to their fhare of conqueft,
And let loud echo, from her circling hills,
Sound freedom, 'till the undulation fhake
The bounds of utmoft Sweden.
   [*Exeunt* Dalecarlians, *crying* Guftavus, Guftavus, liberty !
               Enter Anderfon.
   And. There was a glorious found !
   Guf. Yes, Anderfon,
The long-wifh'd hour is come——the ftorm is up,
And wrecks will follow.   Where they are to light
Let Heav'n determine.   Well, my noble friend,
Has Peterfon fet out ?
   And. He has, this inftant ;
And bears your pacquet to the tyrant's camp.
   Guf. What think you of his zeal ?
   And. In truth, my Lord,
It wears a gallant fhow.
   Guf. 'Tis fpecious all,
Flafh without fire, the lightning of a cloud
That carries darknefs in the rear—— For Peterfon,
To fpread my letters through the camp of Criftiern,
And feek for fuccours in the jaws of death,
It fhew'd too bold, too much the flaming patriot.
Befide, I know him for the friend of Trollio.
   And. Why would you then employ him ?
   Guf. There's the myftery.
'Tis not his faith, but treachery I truft to.
My letters are directed to the chiefs
Of thofe inglorious mercenary Swedes,
Whom Criftiern has feduced to join his hoft,
And turn the fword of conqueft on their country ;
To each of thofe I have addrefs'd in terms
Of fpecial correfpondence, meant to rouze
The jealoufy of Criftiern ; as I think
My pacquet can't efcape him——What enfues ?
The tyrant hence concludes himfelf betray'd,
Sifts all his legions, thins the ranks of fight,
And leaves them open to our bold invafion.
                                 But

But grant that Peterſon deceive my aim,
And hold the rank of viitue ; then the Swedes
May waken to the glorious call of honour.
So——ev'ry way it ſaves us from the guilt
Of Swedes encount'ring Swedes, and ſpares the blood
Of brethren, though revolted.
    And. On my ſoul,
This is a ſtratagem that ſaps the miner,
Makes treaſon turn a traitor to itſelf;
And mock its own deſigns.
    Guſ. Oh, noble friend, faſt winds the great machine
That ſtrikes the fate of Sweden---Go, my Anderſon,
Aſſemble all thy brave adherents round thee,
With warlike inſpiration warm their ſouls,
And haſte to join me here.
    And. I will, my Lord.   [*Exit.*
                Enter Laertes.
    Laer. Thy preſence nobly ſpeaks the man I wiſh, Guſ-
    Guſ. Yes. Thou haſt a hoſtile garb,   [tavus.
Ha! ſay---Art thou Laertes? If I err not,
There is a friendly ſemblance in that face,
Which anſwers to a fond impreſſion here,
And tells me I'm thy debtor——my deliv'rer!
    Laer. No, valiant prince, you over-rate my ſervice,
There is a worthier object of your gratitude
Whom yet you know not---Oh, I have to tell——
But then to gain your credit, muſt unfold
What haply ſhould be ſecret——Be it ſo;
You are all honour.
    Guſ. Let me to thy mind,
For thou haſt wak'd my ſoul into a thought
That holds me all attention.
    Laer. Mightieſt man!
To me alone you held yourſelf oblig'd
For life and liberty—Had it been ſo,
I were more bleſs'd, with retribution juſt
To pay thee for my own : for on the day
When by your arm the mighty Thraces fell,
Fate threw me to your ſword—You ſpar'd my youth,
And in the very whirl and rage of fight
Your eye was taught compaſſion—from that hour
                    D   I vow'd

I vow'd my life the flave of your rememb'rance;
And often, as Criftina, heav'nly maid!
The miftrefs of my fervice, queftion'd me
Of wars and vent'rous deeds, my tidings came
Still freighted with thy name, until the day
In which yourfelf appear'd, to make praife fpeechlefs.
Criftina faw you then, and on your fate
Dropp'd a kind tear; and when your noble fcorn
Of proffer'd terms provok'd her father's rage
To take the deadly forfeit; fhe, fhe only,
Whofe virtues watch'd the precious hour of mercy,
All trembling, fent my fecret hand to fave you;
Where, through a pafs unknown to all your keepers,
I led you forth, and gave you to your liberty.

   Guf. Oh, I am funk, o'erwhelm'd with wond'rous good-
But were I rich, and free as opening mines   [nefs!
That teem their golden wealth upon the world,
Still I were poor, unequal to her bounty.
Nor can I longer doubt whofe gen'rous arm
In my Arvida, in my friend's deliverance,
Gave double life, and freedom to Guftavus.

   Laer. A fatal prefent! Ah, you know him not;
Arvida is mifled, undone by paffion;
Falfe to your friendfhip, to your truft unfaithful.

   Guf. Ha! hold!

   Laer. I muft unfold it.

   Guf. Yet forbear:
This way—I hear fome footing—pray you, foft——
If thou haft aught to urge againft Arvida,
The man of virtue, tell it not the wind;
Left flander catch the found, and guilt fhould triumph.
                            [*Exeunt.*

       Arvida *entering, fpeaks to a Soldier.*
   Arv. He's here——bear back my orders to your fel-
That not a man, on peril of his life,   [lows
Advance in fight till call'd.

   Sold. My Lord, I will——

   Arv. Have I not vow'd it, faithlefs as he is,
Have I not vow'd his fall? Yet, good Heav'n!
Why ftart thefe fudden tears? On, on I muft,
For I am half way down the dizzy fteep,
Where my brain turns---A draught of Lethe now---
Oh, that the world would fleep---to wake no more!
                               Or

Or that the name of friendſhip bore no charm
To make my nerve unſteady, and this ſteel
Flee backward from its taſk ! It ſhall be done.
Empire ! Criſtina ! though th' affrighted ſun
Start back with horror of the direful ſtroke,
It ſhall be done.   Calm, calm the hell within,
Thy looks may elſe turn traitors---Ha, he comes !
How ſteadily he looks, as Heav'n's own book,
The leaf of truth, were open'd on his aſpect.
Up, up, dark miniſter——his fate call out
[*Puts up the dagger.*

To nobler execution ; for he comes
In oppoſition, ſingly, man to man,
As though he brav'd my wiſh.
Enter Guſtavus.
　[*They look for ſome time on each other ;* Arvida *lays
　　his hand on his ſword, and withdraws it by turns ;
　　then advances irreſolutely.*
Guſ. Is it then ſo ?
Arv. Defend thyſelf.
Guſ. No——ſtrike——
I would unfold my boſom to thy ſword,
But that I know the wound you give this breaſt
Would doubly pierce thy own.
Arv. I know thee not——
It is the time's eclipſe, and what ſhould be
In nature, now is namelefs.
Guſ. Ah, my brother !
Arv. What wouldſt thou ?
Guſ. Is it thus we two ſhould meet ?
Arv. Art thou not falſe ? Deep elſe, Oh, deep indeed
Were my damnation.
Guſ. Dear, unhappy man !
My heart bleeds for thee.   Falſe I'd ſurely been,
Had I like thee been tempted.
Arv. Ha ! Speak, fpeak,
Did thou not ſend to treat with Criſtiern ?
Guſt. Never.
I know thy error, but I know the arts,
The frauds, the wiles, that practis'd on thy virtue ;
Firm how you ſtood, and tow'r'd above mortality ;
'Till in the fond unguarded hour of love,

D 2

The

The wily undermining 'Trollio came,
And won thee from thyfelf—a moment won thee:
For ftill thou art Arvida, ftill the man
On whom thy country calls for her deliv'rance.
Already are her braveft fons in arms,
Mark, how they fhout, impatient of our prefence,
To lead them on to a new life of liberty,
To fame, to conqueft---Ha, Heav'n guard my brother,
Thy cheek turns pale, thy eye is wild upon me,
Wilt thou not anfwer me?
 Arv. Guftavus!
 Guf. Speak.
 Arv. Have I not dream'd?
 Guf. No other I efteem it.
Where lives the man whofe reafon flumbers not?
Still pure, ftill blamelefs, if at wonted dawn
Again he wakes to virtue.
 Arv. Oh, my dawn
Muft foon be dark.   Confufion diffipates,
To leave me worfe confounded.
 Guf. Think no more on't.
Come to my arms, thou deareft of mankind!
 Arv. Stand off! Pollution dwells within my touch,
And horror hangs around me---Cruel man!
Oh, thou haft doubly damn'd me with this goodnefs;
For refolution held the deed as done,
That now muft fink me---Hark! I'm fummon'd hence,
My audit opens! Poife me! for I ftand
Upon a fpire, againft whofe fightlefs bafe
Hell breaks his wave beneath.   Down, down I dare not,
And up I cannot look, for juftice fronts me.
Thou fhalt have vengeance, though my purpling blood
Were nectar for heav'n's bowl, as warm and rich,
As now 'tis bafe, it thus fhould pour for pardon.
  [Guftavus *catches his arm, and in the ftruggle the dag-*
   ger falls.
 Guf. Ha! Hold, Arvida---No, I will not lofe thee---
Forbid it, Heav'n! thou fhalt not rob me fo;
No, I will ftruggle with thee to the laft,
And fave thee from thyfelf.   Oh, anfwer me!
Wilt thou forfake me? Anfwer me, my brother,
My beft Arvida.
           Arv.

Arv. I would fpeak to thee——
But let it be by filence——Oh, Guftavus!
   Guf. Say but you'll live.
   Arv. Oh!
   Guf. For my fake.
   Arv. Yes, take me;
Expofe me, cage me, brand me for the tool
Of crafted villains, for the verieft flave,
On whom the bend of each contemptuous brow
Shall look with loathing. Ah, my turpitude
Shall be the vile comparative for knaves
To boaft and whiten by!
   Guf. Not fo, not fo.
Who knows no fault, my friend, knows no perfection.
The rectitude that Heav'n appoints to man
Leads on through error; and the kindly fenfe
Of having ftray'd, endears the road to blifs;
It makes Heav'n's way more pleafing! Oh, my brother,
'Tis hence a thoufand cordial charities
Derive their growth, their vigour, and their fweetnefs.
This fhort lapfe
Shall to thy future foot give cautious treading,
Erect and firm in virtue.
   Arv. Give me leave.   [*Offers to pafs.*
   Guf. You fhall not pafs.
   Arv. I muft.
   Guf. Whither?
   Arv. I know not——Oh, Guftavus!
   Guf. Speak.
   Arv. You can't forgive me.
   Guft. Not forgive thee!
   Arv. No.
Look there.   [*Points to the dagger.*
And yet when I refolv'd to kill thee,
I could have died---indeed I could---for thee
I could have died, Guftavus!
   Guf. Oh, I know it.
A gen'rous mind, though fway'd a-while by paffion,
Is like the fteely vigour of the bow,
Still hold its native rectitude, and bends
But to recoil more forceful. Come, forget it.

D 3   *Enter*

Enter a Dalecarlian.

Dale. My Lord, as I now pass'd the mountain's brow,
I spy'd some men, whose arms, and strange attire,
Give cause for circumspection.

Guf. Danes, perhaps;
Haste, intercept their passage to the camp.　　[*Exit Dal.*

Arv. Those are the Danes that witness to my shame.

Guf. Perish th' opprobrious term ! not so, Arvida ;
Myself will be the guardian of thy fame ;
Trust me, I will---Our friends approach---Oh, clear,
While I attend them, clear that cloud, my brother,
That sits upon the morning of thy youth ;
It hangs too near the heart of thy Gustavus.　　[*Exit.*

Arv. Of thy Gustavus ! Oh, wretch, wretch, cursed
　　. wretch !
What is this time and place, and toys of circumstance ;
That wind our actions, so, as Heav'n's own hand
What's done may not unravel ?---Pardon may !——
There's the Lethean sweet, the snow of heav'n,
New blanching-o'er the Negro front of guilt,
That to the eye of mercy all appears
Fair as th' unwritten page---yet self-convict,
Tho' Heav'n's free pow'r should pardon, where's my peace ?
Thus, thus to be driven out from my own breast !
To 'have no shed, no shelt'ring nook at home
To take reflection in ! How looks the wretch
Whose heart cries villain to itself ? I'll not
Endure its battery---Somewhat must be done
Of high import ere night, that I may sleep,
Or wake for ever.

Enter Gustavus, *followed by the* Dalecarlians, Anderson,
　　Arnoldus, Sivard, *Officers, &c.*

　　1*st Dale.* Let us all see him !
　　2*d Dale.* Yes, and hear him too.
　　3*d Dale.* Let us be sure 'tis he himself.
　　4*th Dale.* Our general.
　　5*th Dale.* And we will fight while weapons can be found.
　　6*th Dale.* Or hands to wield them.
　　7*th Dale.* Get on the bank, Gustavus.
　　And. Do, my Lord.
　　Guf. My countrymen !——

1*st*

1ſt Dale. Ho! hear him.
2d Dale. Peace!
3d Dale. Peace!
4th Dale. Peace!
Guſ. Amazement I perceive hath fill'd your hearts,
And joy for that your loſt Guſtavus, 'ſcap'd
Thro' wounds, impriſonments, and chains, and deaths,
Thus ſudden, thus unlook'd for ſtands before ye.
As one eſcap'd from cruel hands I come,
From hearts that ne'er knew pity; dark and vengeful;
Who quaff the tears of orphans, bathe in blood,
And know no muſic but the groans of Sweden.
Yet, not for that my ſiſter's early innocence,
And mother's age now grind beneath captivity:
Nor that one bloody, one remorſeleſs hour
Swept my great ſire, and kindred from my ſide;
For them Guſtavus weeps not, though my eyes
Were far leſs dear, for them I will not weep.
But, Oh, great parent, when I think on thee!
Thy numberleſs, thy nameleſs, ſhameful infamies,
My widow'd country! Sweden! when I think
Upon thy deſolation, ſpite of rage——
And vengeance that would choak them—tears will flow.
  And. Oh, they are villains, ev'ry Dane of them,
Practis'd to ſtab and ſmile; to ſtab the babe
That ſmiles upon them.
  Arn. What accurſed hours
Roll o'er thoſe wretches, who to fiends like theſe
In their dear liberty, have barter'd more
Than worlds will rate for?
  Guſ. Oh, liberty, Heav'n's choice prerogative!
True bond of law, thou ſocial ſoul of property,
Thou breath of reaſon, life of life itſelf!
For thee the valiant bleed. Oh, ſacred liberty!
Wing'd from the ſummer's ſnare, from flatt'ring ruin,
Like the bold ſtork you ſeek the wint'ry ſhore,
Leave courts, and pomps, and palaces to ſlaves,
Cleave to the cold, and reſt upon the ſtorm.
Upborn by thee, my ſoul diſdain'd the terms
Of empire——offer'd at the hands of tyrants.
With thee, I ſought this fav'rite ſoil; with thee,
Theſe fav'rite ſons I ſought; thy ſons, Oh, Liberty:

For

For ev'n amid the wilds of life you lead them,
Lift their low rafted cottage to the clouds,
Smile o'er their heaths, and from their mountain tops
Beam glory to the nations.

    All. Liberty! Liberty!

    Guſt. Are ye not mark'd, ye men of Dalecarlia,
Are ye not mark'd by all the circling world
As the great ſtake, the laſt effort for liberty?
Say, is it not your wealth, the thirſt, the food,
The ſcope and bright ambition of your ſouls?
Why elſe have you, and your renown'd forefathers,
From the proud ſummit of their glitt'ring thrones,
Caſt down the mightieſt of your lawful kings
That dar'd the bold infringement? What, but liberty,
Through the fam'd courſe of thirteen hundred years,
Aloof hath held invaſion from your hills,
And ſanctify'd their ſhade?—And will ye, will ye
Shrink from the hopes of the expecting world;
Bid your high honours ſtoop to foreign inſult,
And in one hour give up to infamy
The harveſt of a thouſand years of glory?

    1ſt Dale. No.

    2d Dale. Never, never.

    3d Dale. Periſh all firſt.

    4th Dale. Die all!

    Guſ. Yes, die by piecemeal!
Leave not a limb o'er which a Dane may triumph!
Now from my ſoul I joy, I joy, my friends,
To ſee ye fear'd; to ſee that ev'n your foes
Do juſtice to your valours!—There they be,
The pow'rs of kingdoms, ſumm'd in yonder hoſt,
Yet kept aloof, yet trembling to aſſail ye.
And, Oh, when I look round and ſee you here,
Of number ſhort, but prevalent in virtue,
My heart ſwells high and burns for the encounter.
True courage but from oppoſition grows;
And what are fifty, what a thouſand ſlaves,
Match'd to the ſinew of a ſingle arm
That ſtrikes for liberty? That ſtrikes to ſave
His fields from fire, his infants from the ſword,
His couch from luſt, his daughters from pollution;
And his large honours from eternal infamy?

What

What, doubt we then ? Shall we, shall we stand here
'Till motives that might warm an ague's frost,
And nerve the coward's arm, shall poorly serve
To wake us to resistance ?—Let us on !
Oh, yes, I read your lovely fierce impatience ;
You shall not be withheld ; we will rush on them—
This is indeed to triumph, where we hold
Three kingdoms in our toil ! Is it not glorious,
Thus to appal the bold, meet force with fury,
And push yon torrent back, 'till ev'ry wave
Flee to its fountain ?

 3d Dale. On, lead us on, Gustavus ; one word more
Is but delay of conquest.

 Guf. Take your wish.
He, who wants arms, may grapple with the foe,
And so be furnish'd.   You, most noble Anderson,
Divide our pow'rs, and with the fam'd Olaus
Take the left rout—You, Eric, great in arms !
With the renown'd Nederbi, hold the right,
And skirt the forest down : then wheel at once,
Confess'd to view, and close upon the vale ;
Myself, and my most valiant cousin here,
Th' invincible Arvida, gallant Sivard,
Arnoldus, and these hundred hardy vet'rans,
Will pour directly on, and lead the onset.
Joy, joy, I see confess'd from ev'ry eye,
Your limbs tread vigorous, and your breasts beat high !
Thin though our ranks, though scanty be our bands,
Bold are our hearts, and nervous are our hands.
With us, truth, justice, fame, and freedom close,
Each, singly equal to an host of foes,
I feel, I feel them fill me out for fight,
They lift my limbs as feather'd Hermes' light !
Or like the bird of glory, tow'ring high,
Thunder within his grasp, and light'ning in his eye !

END of the THIRD ACT.

A C T

A C T   IV.

SCENE *before the Camp.*

Enter Cristiern, Trollio, *and Attendants.*

CRISTIERN.

YOUR obfervation's juft, I fee it, Trollio :
   Men are machines, with all their boafted freedom,
Their movements turn upon fome fav'rite paffion ;
Let art but find the latent foible out,
We touch the fpring, and wind them at our pleafure.
  Trol. Let Heav'n fpy out for virtue, and then ftarve it ;
But vice and frailty are the ftatefman's quarry,
The objects of our fearch, and of our fcience,
Mark'd by our fmiles, and cherifh'd by our bounty ;
'Tis hence you lord it o'er your fervile fenates ;
How low the flaves will ftoop to gorge their lufts
When aptly baited : ev'n the tongues of patriots,
(Thofe fons of clamour) oft relax the nerve
Within the warmth of favour.
  Crift. How elfe fhould kings fubfift ? For what is pow'r,
But the nice conduct of another's weaknefs ?
That thing call'd Virtue, is the bane of government,
A libel on the ftate, that afks fuppreffion ;
It has a hateful and unbending quality ;
It ferves no end, ftill reftive to the rein,
And to the fpur unfpeedy : they who boaft it
Are traitors, rivals of their king, my Trollio ;
And, wanting other fubjects, greatly dare
To lord it o'er themfelves.   Such is Guftavus,
If yet he be——
And fuch Arvida was ; though now, I truft,
He is too far advanc'd in our defigns
To think of a retreat.
  Trol. Impoffible !
Already has he leap'd the guilty mound
That might appal his virtue ; for the world
He dare not now look back ; where fhame purfues,
And cuts off all retreat.

Enter

Enter Gentleman Usher and Peterson, *who kneels.*
Gent. My liege, Lord Peterson.
Crist. Rise to our trust, most worthy Peterson;
Rise to our friendship: by my head, I swear,
Bar but our Trollio here, there's not a Swede,
Who holds thy valued level in our heart!
For thou'rt unshaken, though thy nation swerve;
Faithful among the faithless.
Peter. What I am,
Let this inform your majesty.   [*Gives a pacquet.*
Trol. A pacquet!
Whence had you that, my friend?
Peter. Even from the hands
Of the once great Gustavus.
Crist. Then you have seen him. Tell me, tell me,
            Peterson,
What said he? Eh! How look'd the mighty rebel?
His means, his scope, the pride of his presumption,
Give me the whole!
Peter. Last night, my gracious Lord,
While yet I held your messenger in conference;
Arriv'd, who brought a letter from Gustavus,
Wherein, digesting many flagrant terms
Of mutinous import against the state
Of your high dignity; by morning light
He pray'd me to attend him; boasting much
Of plenteous hopes, and means of boldest enterprize.
Of this I gave you notice; and ere dawn
Set out for fresh intelligence—I came;
I saw him shrunk, that glory of the north,
Soil'd with the vileness of a slave's attire;
Where in the depth and darkness of the mines,
For six long months he hath not seen the sun;
Colleagu'd with circling horrors; hourly toil
Hath been his watch, and penury his earning;
But like the lion, newly broke from bonds,
The mingling passions from his eyes dart glory;
Pride lifts his stature, and his opening front
Still looks dominion.
Crist. Who were his adherents?
Peter. The traitor Anderson, and a few friends,
To whom, ere I set out, he stood reveal'd.
And when I seem'd to question on his pow'rs

Of rivalſhip, the props whereon he meant
To lift contention to the princely front
Of ſuch high oppoſition; he reply'd,
His powers were near your perſon.
   Criſt. How! what's here?   [*Looks on the pacquet.*
To Laurens, Aland, Haquin, and Roderic,
Confuſion! Treaſon's in our camp! Who's there?
   Gent. My liege!
   Criſt. Bear this to Norbi——Bid him ſeize
                          [*Gives a ſignet.*
The Swediſh captains.
   Trol. Might I but preſume—
   Criſt. I will not be controul'd—bid him ſeize all,
Soldiers and chiefs! By hell, there's not a Swede,
But lurks an inſtrument to prompt rebellion,
And plots upon my life! Look there, 'tis evident:
                   [*Gives* Trollio *a letter.*
They are all leagu'd, confed'rate with Guſtavus,
Th' abettors of his treaſon.
   Trol. It ſhould ſeem ſo:
And yet it ſhould not—Tell me, Peterſon,
Art thou aſſur'd thy credit with Guſtavus
Will anſwer to a truſt like this?—Ha! Say.
   Peter. Yes, well aſſur'd: my zeal appear'd too warm
To give the leaſt cold colour for ſuſpicion.
   Trol. I fear, my friend, I fear he has o'er-reach'd you.
Divide and conquer, is the ſum of politics.
Beyond the dreaded circle of his ſword,
Guſtavus triumphs in an ample genius;
He walks at large, ſees clear and wide around him;
Calm in the ſtorm and turbulence of action;
He ponders on the laſt event of things,
And makes each cauſe ſubſervient to the conſequence.
   Criſt. You over-rate his craft; they're falſe, my Trol-
Falſe ev'ry Swede of them; I read their ſouls.   [lio,
        Enter Criſtina *and* Mariana.
   Criſtina. I heard it was your royal pleaſure, Sir,
I ſhould attend your highneſs.
   Criſt. Yes, Criſtina,
But buſineſs interferes.   [*Exeunt* Chriſtina *and* Mar.
          Enter an Officer.
   Off. My ſovereign liege!
Wide o'er the weſtern ſhelving of yon hill,

We think, tho' indistinctly, we can spy,
Like men in motion must'ring on the heath;
And there is one who saith he can discern
A few of martial gesture, and bright arms,
Who this way bend their action.

Crist. Friends, perhaps:
For foes it were too daring——Haste thee, Trollio,
Detach a thousand of our Danish horse,
To rule their motions.   We will out ourself,
And hold our pow'rs in readiness.   Lead on.   [*Exeunt.*
             Enter Cristina *and* Mariana.

Mar. Ha! did you mark, my Princess, did you mark?
Should some reverse, some wond'rous whirl of fate,
Once more return Gustavus to the battle,
New nerve his arm, and wreathe his brow with conquest,
Say, would you not repent that e'er you sav'd
This dreadful man, the foe of your great race,
Who pours impetuous in his country's cause,
To spoil you of a kingdom?

Cristina. No, my friend;
Had I to death or bondage sold my fire,
Or had Gustavus on our native realms
Made hostile inroad, then, my Mariana,
Had I then sav'd him from the stroke of justice,
I should not cease my suit to Heav'n for pardon.
But if, tho' in a foe, to rev'rence virtue,
Withstand oppression, rescue injur'd innocence,
Step boldly in betwixt my fire and guilt,
And save my king, my father from dishonour;
If this be sin, I have shook hands with penitence.
First, perish crowns, dominion, all the shine
And transience of this world, ere guilt shall serve,
To buy the vain incumbrance.

Mar. Do not think
I meant, my Princess, to arraign your virtues,
Howe'er I seem'd to question on the consequence.

Cristina. The consequence of virtue must be good;
It must.   Tho' it should prove my father's lot,
In being rescu'd from one act of guilt,
To lose the whole of all his wide dominions,
He were a gainer.   Blasted be that royalty,
Which murder must make sure, and crimes inglorious!
                          E   The

The bulk of kingdoms, nay, the world is light,
When guilt weighs oppofite.   Oh, would to Heav'n,
The lofs of empire would reftore his innocence,
Reftore the fortunes, and the precious lives
Of thoufands, fall'n the victims of ambition !
                    Enter Laertes.
Ha, Laertes ! moft welcome—Well, and have you ? Say,
    Laer. O, royal maid !——   [Laertes——
    Criftina. Thy looks are doubtful.   Speak——
Why art thou filent ? Does he live ?
    Laer. He does:
But death, ere night, muft fill a long account.
The camp, the country's in confufion ; war
And changes ride upon the hour that haftes
To intercept my tongue——I elfe could tell
Of virtues hitherto beyond my ken ;
Courage, to which the lion ftoops his creft,
Yet grafted upon qualities as foft
As a rock'd infant's meeknefs ; fuch as tempts
Againft my faith, my country, and allegiance,
To wifh thee fpeed, Guftavus.
    Criftina. Then you found him.
    Laer. I did ; and warn'd him ; but in vain ; for death
To him appear'd more grateful than to find
His friend's difhonour.   [Laertes !
    Criftina. Give me the manner—quick——foft, good

        Enter Criftiern, Trollio, Peterfon, Danes, &c.

    Crift. Damn'd, double traitor! Oh, curs'd, falfe Arvida !
Guard well the Swedifh pris'ners; bind them hard.
Stand to your arms.   Bring forth the captives there:
            Enter Augufta *and* Guftava *guarded.*
    Trol. My liege————
    Crift. Away! I'll hear no more of politics.
Fortune ! we will not truft the changeling more,
But wear her girt upon our armed loins,
Or pointed in our grafp.
                Enter an Officer.
    Off. The foe's at hand.
With gallant fhew your thoufand Danes rode forth,
But fhall return no more.   I mark'd the action ;
A band of defp'rate refolutes rufh'd on them,
                                        Scarce

Scarce numb'ring to a tenth, and in mid way
They clos'd ; the fhock was dreadful, nor your Danes
Could bear the madding charge ; a while they ftood,
Then fhrunk, and broke, and turn'd ; when, lo, behind,
Faft wheeling from the right and left there pour'd,
Who intercepted their return, and, caught
Within the toil, they perifh'd.
 Crift. 'Tis Guftavus !
No mortal elfe, not Ammon's boafted fon,
Not Cæfar would have dar'd it.   Tell me, fay,
What numbers in the whole may they amount to ?
 Off. About five thoufand.
 Crift. And no more ?
 Off. No more,
That yet appear.
 Crift. We count fix times their fum.
Hafte, foldier, take a trumpet ; tell Guftavus,
We have of terms to offer, and would treat
Touching his mother's ranfom ; fay, her death,
Sufpended by our grace, but waits his anfwer.   [*Exit Off.*
Madam, it fhould well fuit with your authority   [*To Aguf.*
To check this frenzy in your fon.   Look to it,
Or, by the faints, this hour's your laft of life.
 Auguf. Come, my Guftava ; comé, my little captive ;
We fhall be free ; our tyrant is grown kind ;
And for thefe chains that bind thy pretty arms,
The golden cherubim fhall lend thee wings,
And thou fhalt mount amid the fmiling choir
Of little heav'nly fongfters, like thyfelf,
All rob'd in innocence.
 Guftava. Will you go, mother ?
 Auguf. So help me, mercy ! Yes, I'll go, my child ;
And I will give thee to thy father's fondnefs,
And to the arms of all thy royal race
In heav'n, who fit on thrones, with loves, and joys,
And pleafures fmiling round.
 Crift. Is this my anfwer ?
Come forth, ye minifters of death, come forth.

  Enter Ruffians, who feize Augufta *and* Guftava.

Pluck them afunder.   We fhall prove you, lady.
'Tis my damn'd lot, thus ever to be crofs'd
With rank blown pride, and infolence eternal.
    E 2   *Guftava.*

Guflava. Oh, mother, take me, take me from thefe
They fright me with their looks.   [men!
   Auguf. Alas, my child, I cannot take thee from them!
   Guflava. Oh, they will hurt me! Can't you take me,
        mother?
   Auguf. They can't, they cannot hurt you, my Guftava.
Fear not, my little one; your name fhould be
A charm o'er cowardice; for you are call'd
After your valiant brother.   He'll difown you;
He will not love you, if you fear, Guftava.
   Criflina. Ah, I can hold no longer! Royal Sir,
Thus on my knees, and lower, lower ftill——
   Crifl. My child! What mean you?
   Criflina. Oh, my gracious father!
Kill, kill me, rather; let me perifh firft;
But do not ftain the fanctity of kings
With the fweet blood of helplefs innocence;
Do not, my father; fpare the little orphans,
And let the lambs go free.
   Auguf. Ha! who art thou,
That look'ft fo like the 'habitants of heav'n?
Like mercy, fent upon the morning's blufh,
To glad the heart, and cheer a gloomy world
With light till now unknown?
   Crifl. Away! they come.
I'll hear no more of your ill-tim'd petitions.
   Criflina. Oh, yet, for pity!
   Crifl. I will none on't.   Leave me.
Pity! it is the infant fool of nature.
Tear off her hold, and bear her to her tent.
             [*Exeunt* Criflina, Mar. Laer. *and Attendants.*
                Enter an Officer.
   Off. My liege, Guftavus, tho' with much reluctance,
Confents to one hour's truce.   His foldiers reft
Upon their arms, and, follow'd by a few,
He comes to know your terms.
   Crifl. I fee; fall back.
Stand firm.   Be ready, flaves, and, on the word,
Plunge deep your daggers in their bofoms. [*Points to* Aug.

Enter Guftavus, Arvida, Anderfon, Arnoldus, Sivard, &c.

Hold!
   Guf. Ha! 'tis, it is my mother!   *Crifl.*

Crift. Tell me, Guftavus, tell me, why is this,
That, as a ftream diverted from the banks
Of fmooth obedience, thou haft drawn thofe men
Upon a dry unchannell'd enterprize,
To turn their inundation ? Are the lives
Of my mifguided people held fo light,
That thus thou'dft pufh them on the keen rebuke
Of guarded majefty ; wheie juftice waits,
All awful, and refiftlefs, to affert
Th' impervious rights, the fanctitude of kings,
And blaft rebellion ?

 Guf. Juftice, fanctitude,
And rights ! Oh, patience ! Rights ! What rights, thou
Yes, if perdition be the rule of power,   [tyrant ?
If wrongs give right, Oh, then, fupreme in mifchief,
Thou wert the lord, the monarch of the world !
Too narrow for thy claim, But if thou think'ft .
That crowns are vilely propertied, like coin,
To be the means, the fpecialty of luft,
And fenfual attribution ; if thou think'ft
That empire is of titled birth or blood ; .
That nature, in the proud behalf of one,
Shall difenfranchife all her lordly race,
And bow her gen'ral iffue to the yoke
Of private domination ; then, thou proud one,
Here know me for thy king. Howe'er, be told,
Not claim hereditary, not the truft
Of frank election,
Not ev'n the high anointing hand of Heav'n,
Can authorife oppreffion, give a law
For lawlefs power, wed faith to violation,
On reafon build mifrule, or juftly bind
Allegiance to injuftice. Tyranny
Abfolves all faith ; and who invades our rights,
Howe'er his own commence, can never be
But an ufurper. But for thee, for thee
There is no name. Thou haft abjur'd mankind,
Dafh'd fafety from thy bleak, unfocial fide,
And wag'd wild war with univerfal nature.

 Crift. Licentious traitor ! thou canft talk it largely.
Who made thee umpire of the rights of kings,
And pow'r, prime attribute ? As on thy tongue

The poife of battle lay, and arms, of force,
To throw defiance in the front of duty.
Look round, unruly boy ! thy battle comes
Like raw, disjointed muft'ring, feeble wrath,
A war of waters, borne againft the rock
Of our firm continent, to fume, and chafe,
And fhiver in the toil.
   Guf. Miftaken man !
I come impower'd, and ftrengthen'd in thy weaknefs ;
For tho' the ftructure of a tyrant's throne
Rife on the necks of half the fuff'ring world,
Fear trembles in the cement ; prayers, and tears,
And fecret curfes fap its mould'ring bafe,
And fteal the pillars of allegiance from it :
Then let a fingle arm but dare the fway,
Headlong it turns, and drives upon deftruction.
   Trol. Profane, and alien to the love of Heav'n !
Art thou ftill harden'd to the wrath divine,
That hangs o'er thy rebellion ? Know'ft thou not
Thou art at enmity with grace, caft out,
Made an anathema, a curfe enroll'd
Among the faithful, thou and thy adherents
Shorn from our holy church, and offer'd up,
As facred to damnation ?
   Guf. Yes, I know,
When fuch as thou, with facrilegious hand,
Seize on the apoftolic key of heav'n,
It then becomes a tool for crafty knaves
To fhut out virtue, and unfold thofe gates,
That Heav'n itfelf had barr'd againft the lufts
Of avarice and ambition.   Soft and fweet,
As looks of charity, or voice of lambs
That bleat upon the morning, are the words
Of chriftian meeknefs ! miffion all divine !
The law of love fole mandate.   But your gall,
Ye Swedifh prelacy, your gall hath turn'd
The words of fweet, but indigefted peace,
To wrath and bitternefs.   Ye hallow'd men,
In whom vice fanctifies, whofe precepts teach
Zeal without truth, religion without virtue ;
Who ne'er preach heav'n, but with a downward eye,
That turns your fouls to drofs ; who, fhouting, loofe

                      The

The dogs of hell upon us.   Thefts and rapes,
Sack'd towns, and midnight howlings thro' the realm,
Receive your sanction.   Oh, 'tis glorious mischief!
When vice turns holy, puts religion on,
Affumes the robe pontifical, the eye
Of faintly elevation, bleffeth fin,
And makes the feal of fweet offended Heav'n
A fign of blood, a label for decrees,
That hell would fhrink to own.
   Crift. No more of this.
Guftavus, wouldft thou yet return to grace,
And hold thy motions in the fphere of duty,
Acceptance might be found.
   Guf. Imperial fpoiler!
Give me my father, give me back my kindred,
Give me the fathers of ten thoufand orphans,
Give me the fons in whom thy ruthlefs fword
Has left our widows childlefs.   Mine they were,
Both mine, and ev'ry Swede's, whofe patriot breaft
Bleeds in his country's woundings.   Oh, thou canft not!
Thou haft outfinn'd all reck'ning! Give me then
My all that's left, my gentle mother there,
And fpare yon little trembler.
   Crift. Yes, on terms
Of compact and fubmiffion.
   Guf. Ha! with thee?
Compact with thee! and mean'ft thou for my country,
For Sweden? No, fo hold my heart but firm,
Altho' it wring for't, tho' blood drop for tears,
And at the fight my ftraining eyes ftart forth——
They both fhall perifh firft.
   Crift. Slaves, do your office.
   Guf. Hold yet——Thou canft not be fo damn'd? My
I dare not afk thy bleffing.   Where's Arvida? [mother!
Where art thou? Come, my friend, thou'ft known temp-
And therefore beft canft pity, or fupport me.   [tation,
   Arv. Alas! I fhall but ferve to weigh thee downward,
To pull thee from the dazzling, fightlefs height,
At which thy virtue foars.   For, O, Guftavus!
My foul is dark, difconfolate and dark;
Sick to the world, and hateful to myfelf.
I have no country now; I've nought but thee;

And·

And fhould yield up the int'reft of mankind,
Where thine's in queftion.
    Augufta. See, my fon relents.
Behold, O King! yet fpare us but a moment;
His little fifter fhall embrace his knees,
And thefe fond arms around his duteous neck,
Shall join to bend him to us.
    Crift. Could I truft ye————
    Arv. I'll be your hoftage.
    Crift. Granted.
    Guf. Hold, my friend————
    [*Here* Arvida *breaks from* Guftavus, *and paffes to* Cri-
        ftern's *party, while* Augufta *and* Guftava *go over to*
        Guftavus.
    Augufta. Is it then giv'n, yet giv'n me, ere I die,
To fee thy face, Guftavus? Thus to gaze,
To touch, to fold thee thus?——My fon, my fon!
And have I liv'd to this? It is enough.
All arm'd, and in thy country's precious caufe
Terribly beauteous; to behold thee thus!
Why, 'twas my only, hourly fuit to Heav'n,
And now 'tis granted. Oh, my glorious child!
Blefs'd were the throes I felt for thee, Guftavus;
For from the breaft, from out your fwathing bands,
You ftepp'd the child of honour.
    Guf. Oh, my mother!
    Augufta. Why ftands that water trembling in thy eye?
Why heaves thy bofom? Turn not thus away;
'Tis the laft time that we muft meet, my child,
And I will have thee whole. Why, why, Guftavus,
Why is this form of heavinefs? For me,
I truft, it is not meant; you cannot think
So poorly of me. I grow old, my fon,
And to the utmoft period of mortality,
I ne'er fhould find a death's hour like to this
Whereby to do thee honour.
    Guf. Roman patriots!
Ye, Decii, felf-devoted to your country,
You gave no mothers up! Will annals yield
No precedent for this, no elder boaft,
Whereby to match my trial?
    Augufta. No, Guftavus;
    I   **For**

For Heav'n ftill fquares our trial to our ftrength,
And thine is of the foremoft.   Noble youth!
Ev'n I, thy parent, with a confcious pride,
Have often bow'd to thy fuperior virtues.
Oh, there is but one bitternefs in death!
One only fting——
  Guf. Speak, fpeak!
  Auguft. 'Tis felt for thee.
Too well I know thy gentlenefs of foul,
Melting as babes; ev'n now the preffure's on thee,
And bends thy lovelinefs to earth.   O, child!
The dear, but fad foretafte of thy affliction
Already kills thy mother.   But, behold,
Behold thy valiant followers, who to thee,
And to the faith of thy protecting arm,
Have giv'n ten thoufand mothers, daughters too,
Who in thy virtue yet may learn to bear
Millions of free-born fons to blefs thy name,
And pray for their deliverer.   Oh, farewel!
This, and but this, the very laft, adieu!
Heav'n fit victorious on thy arm, my fon,
And give thee to thy merits.
  Crift. Ah, thou trait'refs!
  Guftava. O, brother! an't you ftronger than that man?
Don't let him take my mother.
  Augufta. See, Guftavus;
My little captive waits for one embrace.
  Guf. Come to my arms, thou lamb-like facrifice;
Oh, that they were of force to hold thee ever,
To let thee to my heart, there lock thee clofe,
And circle thee with life! But 'twill not be.
  Guftava. I'll ftay with you, my brother.
  Guf. Killing innocence!
That I was born to fee this hour!
The pains of hell are on me! Take her, mother.
  Guftava. I will not part with you; indeed I will not.
  Guf. Take her—Diftraction! Hafte, my deareft mother;
Oh!—elfe I fhall run mad —quite mad—and fave ye.
  Arv. Hold, Madam—Hear me, thou moft dear Gufta-
Thus low I bend my pray'r; reject me not: [vus!
If once, if ever thou didft love Arvida,
Oh, leave me here to anfwer to the wrath

                                                    Of

Of this fell tyrant! Save thy honour'd mother,
And that sweet lamb from slaughter.

    Gus. Cruel friendship!

    Crist. And, by my life, I'd take thee at thy word,
Thou doubly damn'd! but that I know 'twould please thee.

    Augusta. No, gen'rous Prince; thy blood shall never be
The price of our dishonour. Come, my child;   [thee.
Weep not, sweet babe; there shall no harm come nigh

    Crist. 'Tis well, proud dame; you are return'd, I see.
Each to his charge.   Here break we off, Gustavus;
For to the very teeth of thy rebellion
We dash defiance back.

    Gus. Alas, my mother!
Grief choaks up utt'rance; else I have to say
What never tongue unfolded——Yet return,
Come back, and I will give up all to save thee:
For on the cov'ring of thy sacred head
My heart drops blood.   Thou fountain of my life!
Dearer than mercy is to kneeling penitence,
My early blessing, first and latest joy,
Return, return, and save thy lost Gustavus!

    Crist. No more, thou trifler!

    Augusta. Oh, farewel for ever!
    [*Exeunt* Cristiern *and his party.* Gustavus *and his par-*
        ty remain.

    Gust. Then she is gone——Arvida! Anderson!
For ever gone——Arnoldus, friends, where are ye?
Help here! heave, heave this mountain from me—Oh!—
Heav'n keep my senses!——So—We will to battle:
But let no banners wave—Be still, thou trump,
And ev'ry martial sound that gives the war
To pomp or levity; for vengeance now
Is clad with heavy arms, sedately stern,
Resolv'd, but silent as the slaughter'd heaps
O'er which my soul is brooding.

    Arn. Oh, Gustavus!
Is there a Swede of us, whose sword and soul
Grapples not to thee, as to all they hold
Of earthly estimation? Said I more,
It were but half my thought.

    And. On thee we gaze,
As one unknown till this important hour;
Pre-eminent of men!

Siv. Accurs'd be he,
Who, in thy leading, will not fight, and strive,
And bleed, and gasp with pleasure!
   And. We are thine,
All, all, both we and ours; whom thou this day
Hast dearly purchas'd.
   Arn. Tho', to yield us up,
Had scarce been less than virtue.
   Guf. Oh, my friends!
I see 'tis not for man to boast his strength
Before the trial comes.   This very hour,
Had I a thousand parents, all seem'd light,
When weigh'd against my country; and, but now,
One mother seem'd of weight to poize the world,
Tho' conscious truth and reason were against her.
For, Oh, howe'er the partial passions sway,
High Heav'n assigns but one unbiass'd way;
Direct thro' ev'ry opposition leads,
Where shelves decline, and many a steep impedes.
Here hold we on, tho' thwarting fiends alarm,
Here hold we on, tho' devious syrens charm;
In Heav'n's disposing pow'r events unite,
Nor aught can happen wrong to him who acts aright.
                                        [*Exeunt.*

END of the FOURTH ACT.

A C T   V.

S C E N E, *the Royal Tent.*

Enter Cristina *and* Mariana.

CRISTINA.

HARK, Mariana! list—No, all is silent——
   It was not fancy, sure—Didst thou hear aught?
   Mar. Too plain, the voice of terror seiz'd my ear,
And my heart sinks within me.
   Cristina. Oh, I fear
The war is now at work!—As winds, methought,
Long borne thro' hollow vaults, the sound approach'd;
                                        One

One found, yet laden with a thousand notes
Of fearful variation; then it swell'd
To diſtant ſhouts, now coming on the gale;
Again. borne backward with a parting groan,
All ſunk to horrid ſtillneſs.
    Mar. Look, my Princeſs;
Ah, no! withhold thy eyes! the place grows dark,
A ſudden cloud of ſorrow ſtains the day,
And throws its gloom around.

Enter four ſlaves as bearing the bodies of Auguſta *and* Guſta-
    va *on a bier covered; four women, in chains, follow
    weeping.*

    Criſtina. Whence are you, ſay, you daughters of afflic-
Their ſpeech is in their tears—Avert, ye ſaints,   [tion?
Avert that thought!—Soft—hold ye! I've a tear
For ev'ry mourner—Ah!   [*Looks under the covering.*
    Mar. What mean you, Madam?
    Criſtina. Reflection, come not there----See it not, eyes!
How art thou ſplit, thou blood of royalty!
Cloſe at the paleneſs of its parent-breaſt
The babe lies ſlaughter'd.   Tell me, who did this?
No, hold ye—Say not that my father did it;
For duty then turns rebel.   Cruel father!
Oh, that ſome villager, whoſe early toil
Lifts the penurious morſel to his mouth,
Had claim'd my birth! Ambition had not then
Thus ſtepp'd 'twixt me and heav'n.
    Mar. Go, bear it hence————
Turn, turn, my royal miſtreſs.
    Criſtina. Ah, Auguſta!
Among thy foes thou'rt fall'n; thou'rt fall'n in virtue.
Exalt thyſelf, O Guilt! for here the good
Have none who may lament them.   Sit we down;
For I grow weary of the world; let Death
Within his vaulty durance, dark and ſtill,
Receive me too; and where th' afflicted reſt,
There fold me in for ever.
                    Enter Laertes.
    Laer. Ariſe, Criſtina; fly, thou royal virgin!
This morn beheld thee miſtreſs of the North,
Bright heir of Scandinavia; and this hour

                                        Has

Has left thee not, throughout thy wide dominions,
Whereon to reſt thy foot.

   Criſtina. Now, praiſe to Heav'n !
Say but my father lives———

   Laer. At your command
I went; and, from a neighb'ring ſummit, view'd
Where either hoſt ſtood adverſe, ſternly wedg'd,
Reflecting on each other's gloomy front
Fell hate and fix'd defiance. When at once
The foe mov'd on, attendant to the ſteps
Of their Guſtavus—He, with mournful pace,
Came ſlow and ſilent ; till two hapleſs Danes
Prick'd forth, and on his helm diſcharg'd their fury:
Then rouz'd the lion—To my wond'ring ſight
His ſtature grew twofold; before his eye
All force ſeem'd wither'd, and his horrid plume
Shook wild diſmay around; as Heav'n's dread bolt
He ſhot; he pierc'd our legions ; in his ſtrength
His ſhouting ſquadron gloried, ruſhing on
Where'er he led the battle. Full five times,
Hemm'd by our mightier hoſt, the foe ſeem'd loſt,
And ſwallow'd from my ſight ; five times again
Like flame they iſſued to the light ; and thrice
Theſe eyes beheld him ; they beheld Guſtavus
Unhors'd, and by a hoſt girt ſingly in,
And thrice he broke through all.

   Criſtina. My blood runs chill.

   Laer. With ſuch a ſtrenuous, ſuch a labour'd conflict,
Sure never field was fought ! until Guſtavus
Aloud cry'd, Victory ! and on his ſpear
Rear'd high th' imperial diadem of Denmark.
Then ſlack'd the battle, then recoil'd our hoſt ;
His echo'd, victory ! and now would know
No bounds ; rout follow'd, and the face of fight———
She heeds me not.

   Criſtina. Oh, ill-ſtarr'd royalty !
My father ! cruel, dear, unhappy father !
Summon'd ſo ſudden ! fearful, fearful thought !
Step in, ſweet mercy ! for thy time was——Ha !

F

Enter

Enter Criſtiern, *flying, without his helmet, in diſorder,
his ſword broken, and his garments bloody ; he throws
away his ſword, and ſpeaks.*

    Criſt. Give us new arms of proof ; freſh horſes, quick !
A watch without there—Set a ſtandard up,
To guide our ſcatter'd powers—Haſte, my friends, haſte !
We muſt begone——Oh, for ſome cooling ſtream,
To ſlake a monarch's thirſt !
    Laer. A poſt, my liege,
A ſecond poſt from Denmark ſays———
    Criſt. All's loſt.
Is it not ſo ? Begone ! Perdition choak thee———
Give me a moment's ſolitude—Thought, thought,
Where wouldſt thou lead ?
    Criſtina. He ſees me not—Alas, alas, my father !
Oh, what a war there lives within his eye !
Where greatneſs ſtruggles to ſurvive itſelf.
I tremble to approach him ; yet I fain
Would bring peace to him—Don't you know me, Sir ?
My father ! look upon me : look, my father !
Why ſtrains your lip, and why that doubtful eye,
Thro' fury melting o'er me ? Turn, ah, turn !
I cannot bear its ſoftneſs——How ! nay, then,
There is a falling dagger in that tear,
To kill thy child. to murder thy Criſtina.
    Criſt. Then thou'rt Criſtina.
    Criſtina. Yes.
    Criſt. My child ?
    Criſtina. I am.
    Criſt. Curſe me, then, curſe me ! join with heav'n, and
And hell, to curſe !   [earth,
    Criſtina. Alas ! on me, my father,
Thy curſes be on me ; but on thy head
Fall bleſſings from that Heav'n which has this day
Preſerv'd thy life in battle.
    Criſt. What have I
To do with Heav'n ? Damnation ! What am I ?
All frail and tranſient as my laps'd dominions !
Ev'n now the ſolid earth prepares to ſlide
From underneath me.   Nature's pow'r cries out,
Leave him, thou univerſe !—No—Hold me, Heav'n !

Hold me, thou heav'n whom I've forſaken—hold
Thy creature, tho' accurs'd!
   Criſtina. Patience and peace
Poſſeſs thy mind! Not all thy pride of empire
E'er gavē ſuch bleſs'd ſenſation, as one hour
Of penitence, tho' painful—Let us hence—
Far from the blood and buſtle of ambition.
Be it my taſk to watch thy riſing wiſh,
To ſmooth thy brow, find comfort for thy cares;
And for thy will, obedience; ſtill to cheer
The day with ſmiles, and lay the nightly down
Beneath thy ſlumbers.
   Criſt. O thou all that's left me!
Ev'n in the riot, in the rage of fight,
Thy guardian virtues watch'd around my head,
When elſe no arm could aid—for thro' my ranks,
My circling troops, the fell Guſtavus ruſh'd;
Vengeance! He cry'd, and with one eager hand
Grip'd faſt my diadem—his other arm,
High rear'd the deathful ſteel—ſuſpended yet;
For in his eye, and thro' his varying face,
Confliคting paſſions fought—he look'd——he ſtood
In wrath reluctant—Then, with gentler voice;
Criſtina, thou haſt conquer'd! Go, he cry'd,
I yield thee to her virtues.
     Enter Trollio *and Guards, ſwords drawn.*
  Troll. Haſte, O King!
The foe hath hem'd us round; O haſte to ſave
Thyſelf and us!
   Criſt. Thy ſword. [*Takes a ſword from one of the Guards.*
  Troll. What means my—
  Criſt. Villain!
Well thought, by hell! Ha! Yes,—thou art our miniſter,
The rev'rend monitor of vice—the ſoil,
Baneful and rank with ev'ry principle,
Whence grow the crimes of Kings. Firſt periſh thou!
                 [*Stabs him.*
Who taught the throne of pow'r to fix on fear,
And raiſe its ſafety, from the public ruin;
Fall thou into the gulph thyſelf haſt fix'd
Between the Prince and people; cutting off
Communion from the ear of royalty,

F 2

And

And mercy from complaint—away, away,
Thy death, old man, be on thy monarch's head;
On thine, the blood of all thy countrymen,
Who fell beneath thy counsels.   [*Exeunt.*
             Trollio *attempts to rise and then speaks.*
   Troll. Thou bloody tyrant! late, too late I find,
Nor faith, nor gratitude, nor friendly trust,
No force of obligations can subsist
Between the guilty—Oh, let none aspire
To be a King's convenience! Has he virtues,
Those are his own; his vices are his minister's.
Who dares to step 'twixt envy and the throne,
Alike to feel the caprice of his Prince,
As public detestation.—Ha! I'm going
But whither? No one near! to feel! to catch!
The world but for an instant! for one ray
To guide my soul! Her way grows wond'rous dark,
And down, down, down!   [*Dies.*

   Enter Gustavus, Anderson, Arnoldus, Sivard, *&c. in tri-*
     umph.   Gustavus *advances, and the rest range themselves*
     on each side of the stage.

   Guf. That we have conquer'd, first we bend to heav'n!
   And. And next to thee!
   All. To thee, to thee, Gustavus!
   Guf. No, matchless men; my brothers of the war!
Be it my greatest glory to have mix'd
My arms with yours, and to have fought for once
Like to a Dalecarlian; like to you,
The fires of honour, of a new-born fame,
To be transmitted, from your great memorial,
To climes unknown, to age succeeding age,
'Till time shall verge upon eternity,
And patriots be no more—
   Arn. Behold, my Lord,
The Danish pris'ners, and the traitor Peterson,
Attend their fate.
   Guf. Send home the Danes with honour,
And let them better learn, from our example,
To treat whom next they conquer, with humanity.
   And. But then for Peterson!
                                                    Guf.

Guf. His crimes are great:
A single death were a reward for treason:
Let him still languish—Let him be exil'd.
No more to see the land of liberty,
The hills of Sweden, nor the native fields
Of known, endear'd idea.

And. Royal Sir,
This is to pardon, to encourage villains;
And hourly to expose that sacred life,
Where all our safety centers.

Guf. Fear them not.
The fence of virtue is a chief's best caution;
And the firm surety of my people's hearts
Is all the guard that e'er shall wait Gustavus.
I am a soldier from my youth; yet, Anderson,
These wars, where man must wound himself in man,
Have somewhat shocking in them: trust me, friend,
Except in such a cause as this day's quarrel,
I wou'd not shed a single wretch's blood
For the world's empire!

Arn. O exalted Sweden!
Bless'd people! Heav'n! wherein have we deserv'd
A man like this to rule us?

Enter Arvida *leading in* Cristina. *He runs to* Gustavus.

Guf. My Arvida!
Arv. My King! O hail! Thus let me pay my ho-
mage.   [*Kneels.*
Guf. Rise, rise, nor shame our friendship.   [*raising.*
Arv. See, Gustavus! Behold, nor longer wonder at my
Guf. Be faithful, eyes! Ha! Yes, it must be so.
'Tis she—For Heav'n would chuse no other form
Wherein to treasure every mental virtue.

Cristina. Renown'd Gustavus! mightiest among men!
If such a wretch, the captive of thy arms,
Trembling and aw'd in thy superior presence,
May find the grace that ev'ry other finds,
For thou art said to be of wond'rous goodness!
Then hear, and O excuse a foe's presumption!
While low, thus low you see a suppliant child,
Now pleading for a father, for a dear,
Much lov'd; if cruel, yet unhappy father.

O, let

O, let him 'scape; who ne'er can wrong thee more!
If he with circling nations could not stand
Against thee single; singly, what can he,
When thou art fenc'd with nations?
   Guf. Ha! that posture!
O rise—surpriz'd, my eye perceiv'd it not.
Cristina! thou all form'd for excellence!
I've much to say, but that my tongue, my thoughts
Are troubled; warr'd on by unusual passions.
'Twas hence thou had'st it in thy power to ask,
'Ere I could offer—Come, my friend, assist,
Instruct me to be grateful. O Cristina!
I fought for freedom, not for crowns, thou fair one,
They shall sit brighter on that beauteous head,
Whose eye might awe the monarchs of the earth,
And light the world to virtue—My Arvida!
   Arv. O great and good, and glorious to the last!
I read thy soul, I see the gen'rous conflict,
And come to fix, not trouble thy repose.
Cou'd you but know with what an eager haste
I sprung to execute thy late commands;
To shield this lovely object of thy cares,
And give her thus, all beauteous to thy eyes!
For I've no bliss but thine, have lost the form
Of ev'ry wish that's foreign to thy happiness.
But, O, my King! my conqu'rer! my Gustavus!
It grieves me much that thou must shortly mourn,
Ev'n on the day in which thy country's freed.
That crowns thy arms with conquest and Cristina.
   Guf. Alas! your cheek is pale—You bleed, my bro-
   Arv. I do indeed—to death.   [ther!
   Guf. You have undone me:
Rash, headstrong man! O was this well, Arvida?
                              [*Turns from him.*
   Arv. Pardon, Gustavus! mine's the common lot,
The fate of thousands fall'n this day in battle.
I had resolv'd on life, to see you bless'd;
To see my King and his Cristina happy.
Turn, thou beloved, thou honour'd next to heav'n!
And to thy arms receive a penitent,
Who never more shall wrong thee.
                                        Guf.

Guf. O Arvida !
Friend ! Friend !   [*Turns and embraces him.*

  Arv. Thy heart beats comfort to me ! in this breaft,
Let thy Arvida, let thy friend furvive.
O, ftrip his once lov'd image of its frailties,
And ftrip it too of ev'ry fonder thought,
That may give thee affliction————Do, Guftavus;
It is my laft requeft; for heav'n and thou
Art all the care and bufinefs—of Arvida.   [*Dies.*

  Guf. Friend ! brother ! fpeak—He's gone—and here
That's left of him who was my life's beft treafure. [is all
How art thou fall'n, thou greatly valiant man !
In ruin graceful, like the warrior fpear
Tho' fhiver'd in the duft—fo fall Guftavus—
But thou art fped, haft reach'd the goal before me ;
And one light lapfe throughout thy courfe in virtue
Shews only thou wert man, ordain'd to ftrive,
But not attain perfection.—
Doft thou too weep ? tranfcendent, lovelieft maid !
Pardon a heart o'ercharg'd with fwelling grief,
That in thy prefence will not be exil'd,
Tho' ev'ry joy dwells round thee.

  Crif. O Guftavus !
A bofom pure like thine muft foon regain
The heart-felt happinefs that dwells with virtue;
And heav'n on all exterior circumftance
Shall pour the balm of peace, fhall pay thee back
The blifs of nations, breathing on thy head
The fweets that live within the pray'rs of foes
Subdued unto thy merits—fare, farewel !

  Guf. Thou fhalt not part, Criftina.

  Criftina. O—I muft—

  Guf. No, thou art all that's left to fweeten life,
And reconcile the wearied to the world.

  Criftina. It will not be————I dare not hear———

  Guf. You muft.
I am thy fuppliant in my turn—but O
My fuit is more, much more than life or empire,
Than man can merit, or worlds give without thee.

  Criftina. Now aid me, aid me, all ye chafter pow'rs
That guard a woman's weaknefs !—'tis refolv'd—
Thy own example charms thy fuit to filence.

Nor

Nor think alone to bear the palm of virtue,
Thou, who haſt taught the world, when duty calls,
To throw the bar of ev'ry wiſh behind them.
Exalted in that thought, like thee I riſe,
While ev'ry leſs'ning paſſion ſinks beneath me.
Adieu, adieu, moſt honour'd, firſt of men,
I go, I part, I fly, but to deſerve thee.
   Guſ. Yet ſtay—a moment—till my utt'ring heart
Pour forth in love, in wonder pour before thee.
Thou cruel excellence——Wou'dſt thou too leave me?
Not if the heart, the arms of thy Guſtavus
Have force to hold thee.
   Criſtina. O delightful notes !
That I do love thee, yes, 'tis true, my Lord,
The bond of virtue, friendſhip's ſacred tie,
The lover's pains, and all the ſiſter's fondneſs,
Mine has the flame of ev'ry love within it :
But I have a father, guilty if he be,
Yet is he old ; if cruel, yet a father.
Abandon'd now by ev'ry ſupple wretch
That fed his years with flattery.   I am all
That's left to calm, to ſooth his troubled ſoul,
To penitence, to virtue ; and perhaps
Reſtore the better empire o'er his mind,
True ſeat of all dominion—Yet, Guſtavus,
Yet there are mightier reaſons—O farewel !
Had I ne'er lov'd I might have ſtay'd with honour.
                              [*Exit.*

Guſtavus *looks after* Criſtina, *then turns and looks on* Arvida,
     ——Anderſon, Arnoldus, *&c. advance.*

   And. Behold, my Lord, behold the ſons of war,
Of triumph, turn'd to tears ; while from that eye
All Sweden takes her fate ; and ſmiles around,
Or weeps with her Guſtavus.
   Arn. Wilt thou not cheer them, ſay, thou great de-
Siv. O General !   [liv'rer ?
1ſt Dale. King !
2d Dale. Brother !
3d Dale. Father !
All. Friend !
                              Guſ.

Guſ. Come, come, my brothers all, yes I will ſtriye
To be the fum of every title to you ;
And you ſhall be my fire, my friend reviv'd,
My ſiſter, mother, all that's kind and dear,
For fo Guſtavus holds ye —— O I will
Of private paſſions all my foul diveſt,
And take my dearer country to my breaſt.
To publick good transfer each fond defire,
And claſp my Sweden with a lover's fire.
Well pleas'd, the weight of all her burdens bear;
Diſpenſe all pleaſure, but engrofs all care.
Still quick to find, to feel my people's woes,
And wake that millions may enjoy repofe.

A Tragi.

[70]

A TRAGI-COMIC
EPILOGUE,

By Way of ENTERTAINMENT.

By Mr. OGLE.

Intended for *Mr. Wright, Mrs. Giffard,* and *Mrs. Clive.*

Mr. WRIGHT.

WELL, Ladies, to the court your plea submit,
 Box, Upper-Region, Gallery, and Pit.
Our poet, trembling for his first essay,
Fear'd to dismiss you, tho' you sav'd his play.
 Cry'd Nell (in pity for the bashful rogue)
‘ *Give 'em a joke! a joke was once in vogue!*
‘ *Thus authors us'd, in less judicious times,*
‘ *When merry epilogues were thought no crimes.*
 ‘ *That (said Cristina) wou'd his ruin crown;*
‘ *Nothing, but virtue, takes this virtuous town.*
‘ *No! let his epilogue be clean and chaste.*
‘ *This is the sense of ev'ry man of taste!*——’
 High rose the conflict in our room of state,
Where tragic Kings and Queens maintain debate;
When, lo! we heard, " your powers began to rise,"
Whose horrid cat-call is our worst excise!
Our inmost palace felt the loud dissention;
Where each new tragedy's a new convention.
Whence we determin'd without further pother,
To give you, of the one, and of the other.

Mrs. GIFFARD.

 Our author on the brave and chaste relies;
He thinks, the virtuous are the only wise.
And, if his muse, with voice exalted, sings,
Of camps and courts, of ministers and kings,

Yet,

Yet, be not, to the great, his rules confin'd !
His moral is a leſſon to mankind.
If virtue, beauteous ; vice, deform'd, be draws ;
You, that applaud him, found your own applauſe.
Where vice, diſtaſte, where virtue, gives delight,
Alike, who judge or paint, are juſt and right.

* Virtue, like vice, eſcapes the public eye,*
In humble life, yet blazes in the high.
Hence, tragedy, that owns no vulgar flight,
Shines, with the King, in a mild ſphere of light,
Or vagrant, with the tyrant, ſtrains to run,
A burning comet—not a cheering ſun !
That worth is worth, be by Guſtavus known :
More glorious in a mine, than on a throne !
And, for Criſtina, might I hope a ſmile,
Leſs great was ſhe in empire than exile !

* Some worth it ſhows, to aim at worthy praiſe.—*
Then, wither not the plant that you may raiſe !
Cruſh not his youth ? No !---give him age to ſpread !
For we have heard you rumbling o'er his head.
Fell a few flaſhes, with portentous blaze,
To blaſt th' ambitious branches of his bays ;
Yet, if ſoft ſorrows ſtream'd from virtuous eyes,
If roſe, from gen'rous breaſts, regaling ſighs :
Refreſh'd by the attack, the laurel ſtands,
And dares the loudeſt thunder---of your hands.

Mrs. CLIVE.

* Great the deſign !---I grant—the moral, good !*
But, 'tis my weakneſs, I am fleſh and blood.
What virgin, here, ſo tender and ſo kind,
Wou'd not her love, with her own hands, unbind ?
Preliminaries ſettle in the dark,
And, tho' ſhe loſt her father, fix her ſpark ?
Or, when ſhe bade th' attendant, ' Save him ! Fly !'
Wou'd ſhe not ſend, a billet, by-the-by ?
Not article ? 'Tis nonſenſe to ſay, Not !
Had ſhe no feel, no gueſs, of what-is-what ?

* At her expence, the great Guſtavus ſhines ;*
My lover, he !-- I'd ſend him to the mines.-- ----
Arvida falls !---Guſtavus wails his end !
And many a ſpouſe careſſes ſuch a friend.

Well

Well, let him wail his death; then, rife to life:
Clasp the fond maid, too strict to be his wife!
He held her in his camp; might hold, alone:
Compulsion some humanity had shown.
Thy countrymen---will damn thee---thy third day---
This is not, sure, the true Hibernian way?

But, I forgive him. He's a young beginner!
Not quite a proftitute! And yet, a finner!
Forward, to please! Yet awkward, to delight!
He wants a kindly hand to guide him right!
A novice yet---Inftruct him---He will mend---
Full many a widow wishes such a friend?
Ev'n marry'd dames may think a greater curfe
The flow performer, that grows worse-and-worse!
This. with a blush, I say, behind my fan---
Cherish the boy, you'll raise him to a man!

Mr. WRIGHT.

The cause is heard. Ye gentle, and ye brave,
'Tis yours to damn him---But, you join to fave---
Then, hail Guftavus, who his country freed!
Ye fons of Britain, praise, the glorious Swede!
Who, bravely ra's'd, and generoufly releas'd,
From blood-ftain'd tyrant, and perfidious prieft;
The ftate and church expiring, at a breath!
Who held a life of flav'ry worfe than death!
Reform'd religion! re-eftablifh'd law!
---And, that you dare to praise him, hail Naffau!---

M.rs HUNTER in the Character of PENELO.

And see! the shade of my much injured ___

BELL'S EDITION.

U L Y S S E S.

A TRAGEDY.

As written by N. ROWE, *Esq.*

AND PERFORMED AT THE

Theatre-Royal in Drury-Lane.

Stultorum regum & populorum continet æstus---
Rursus quid virtus, & quid sapientia possit
Utile proposuit nobis exemplar Ulyssem.
HORAT. Epist. Lib. 1. Epist. 2.

LONDON:
Printed for JOHN BELL, near *Exeter-Exchange*, in the *Strand.*

MDCCLXXVIII.

SIDNEY Lord GODOLPHIN,

Lord High-Treasurer of England, and Knight of the most Noble Order of the Garter.

My Lord,

IF those cares in which the service of a great Queen, and the love of your country, have so justly engaged your Lordship, would allow any leisure to run back and remember those arts and studies, which were once the grace and entertainment of your Lordship's youth; I have presumption enough to hope, that this tragedy may, some time or other, find an hour to divert your Lordship. Poetry, which was so venerable to former ages, as in many places to make a part of their religious worship, and every where to be had in the highest honour and esteem, has miserably languished and been despised, for want of that favour and protection which it found in the famous Augustan age. Since then, it may be asserted without any partiality to the present time, it never had a fairer prospect of lifting up its head, and returning to its former reputation than now : and the best reason can be given for it, is, that it seems to have a particular hope from, and dependence upon your Lordship, and to expect all just encouragement, when those great men, who have the power to protect it, have so delicate and polite a taste and understanding of its true value. The restoring and preserving any part of learning, is so generous an action in itself, that it naturally falls into your Lordship's

A 2

pro-

province, fince every thing that may ferve to improve the mind, has a right to the patronage of fo great and univerfal a genius for knowledge as your Lordfhip's. It is indeed a piece of good fortune, upon which I cannot help congratulating the prefent age, that there is fo great a man, at a time when there is fo great an occafion for him. The divifions which your Lordfhip has healed, the temper which you have reftored to our councils, and that indefatigable care and diligence which you have ufed in preferving our peace at home, are benefits fo virtuoufly and fo feafonably conferred upon your country, as fhall draw the praifes of all wife men, and the bleffings of all good men upon your Lordfhip's name. And when thofe unreafonable feuds and animofities, which keep faction alive, fhall be buried in filence and forgotten, that great public good fhall be univerfally acknowledged, as the happy effect of your Lordfhip's moft equal temper and right underftanding. That this glorious end may very fuddenly fucceed to your Lordfhip's candor and gerous endeavours after it, muft be the wifh of every good Englifhman. I am,

My Lord,

Your Lordfhip's moft obedient

Humble fervant,

N. ROWE.

PRO-

PROLOGUE.

TO-night, in honour of the marry'd life,
 Our author treats you with a virtuous wife;
A lady, who, for twenty years, withstood
The preſſing inſtances of fleſh and blood;
Her huſband, ſtill a man of ſenſe reputed,
(Unleſs this tale his wiſdom have confuted,)
Left her at ripe eighteen, to ſeek renown,
And battle for a harlot at Troy town;
To fill his place, freſh lovers came in ſhoals,
Much ſuch as now-a-days are Cupid's tools, }
Some men of wit, but the moſt part were fools.
They ſent her billets-doux, and preſents many,
Of ancient tea and Thericlean china;
Rail'd at the gods, toaſted her o'er and o'er,
Dreſs'd at her, danc'd and fought, and ſigh'd, and ſwore;
In ſhort, did all that men could do to have her,
And damn'd themſelves to get into her favour;
But all in vain, the virtuous dame ſtood buff,
And let them know that ſhe was coxcomb proof:
Meſſieurs the beaux, what think you of the matter?
Don't you believe old Homer given to flatter?
When you approach, and preſſing the ſoft hand.
Favours, with well-bred impudence, demand, }
Is it in woman's weakneſs to withſtand?
Ceaſe to be vain, and give the ſex their due;
Our Engliſh wives ſhall prove this ſtory true:
We have our chaſte Penelope's, who mourn
Their widow'd beds, and wait their lord's return;
We have our heroes too, who bravely bear,
Far from their home, the dangers of the war;
Who careleſs of the winter ſeaſon's rage,
New toils explore, and in new cares engage;
From realm to realm their chief unweary'd goes,
And reſtleſs journies on, to give the world repoſe.
Such are the conſtant labours of the ſun,
Whoſe active, glorious courſe is never done;
And though, when hence he parts, with us 'tis night,
Still he goes on, and lends to other worlds his light.
Ye beauteous nymphs, with open arms prepare
To meet the warriors, and reward their care;
May you for ever kind and faithful prove,
And pay their days of toil with nights of love.

A 3

DRA.

DRAMATIS PERSONÆ.

MEN.

Ulysses, king of Ithaca, concealed for some time under the name of *Æthon*.

Eurymachus, king of *Samos*.

Polydamas,
Thoon, } Neighbouring princes,
Agenor, } pretenders to the Queen.
Ephialtes,

Telemachus, son to *Ulysses* and *Penelope*.

Antinous, a nobleman of Ithaca, secretly in love with the Queen.

Cleon, } Friends to *Antinous*.
Arcas, }

Mentor, tutor to *Telemachus*.

Eumæus, an old servant, and faithful to *Ulysses*.

Ceraunus, a *Samian* officer belonging to *Eurymachus*.

WOMEN.

Penelope, queen of *Ithaca*,   Mrs. Hunter.
Semanthe, daughter to *Eurymachus*.

Several *Samian* and *Ithacan* Officers and Soldiers, with other Attendants, Men and Women.

SCENE, ITHACA.

ULYSES.

ULYSSES.

ACT I.

SCENE, *a Palace.*

Enter Telemachus *and* Mentor.

TELEMACHUS.

OH, Mentor! urge no more my royal birth,
Urge not the honours of my race divine,
Call not to my remembrance what I am,
Born of Ulyſſes, and deriv'd from Jove;
For 'tis the curſe of mighty minds oppreſs'd,
To think what their ſtate is, and what it ſhould be;
Impatient of their lot, they reaſon fiercely,
And call the laws of Providence unequal.

Men. And therefore wert thou bred to virtuous know-
And wiſdom early planted in thy ſoul;   [ledge,
That thou might'ſt know to rule thy fiery paſſions,
To bind their rage, and ſtay their headlong courſe,
To bear with accidents, and ev'ry change
Of various life, to ſtruggle with adverſity,
To wait the leiſure of the righteous gods,
Till they, in their own good appointed hour,
Shall bid thy better days come forth at once,
A long and ſhining train; till thou, well-pleas'd,
Shalt bow, and bleſs thy fate, and own the gods are juſt.

Tel. Thou prudent guide and father of my youth,
Forgive my tranſports, if I ſeem to loſe
The rev'rence to thy ſacred precepts due:
'Tis a juſt rage, and honeſt indignation.
Ten years ran round e'er Troy was doom'd to fall;
Ten tedious ſummers, and ten winters more,
By turns have chang'd the ſeaſons ſince it fell;
And yet we mourn my godlike father's abſence,
As if the Grecian arms had ne'er prevail'd,
But Jove and Hector ſtill maintain'd the war.

Men.

Men. Tho' abfent, yet if oracles are true,
He lives, and fhall return.   Where'er he wanders,
Purfu'd by hoftile Trojan gods, in peril
Of the wafte defart, or the foamy deep,
Or nations wild as both, yet courage, wifdom,
And Pallas, guardian of his arms, is with him.

Tel. And, Oh, to what does the god's care referve him ?
Where is the triumph fhall go forth to meet him ?
What Pæan fhall be fung to blefs his labours ?
What voice of joy fhall cry, Hail King of Ithaca ?
Riot, and wrong, and woful defolation,
Spread o'er the wretched land, fhall blaft his eyes,
And make him curfe the day of his return.

Men. Your gueft, the ftranger, Æthon.

Enter Æthon.

Tel. By my life,
And by the great Ulyffes, truly welcome.
Oh, thou moft worthy Æthon ! thou that wert,
In youth, companion of my father's arms,
And partner of his heart, does it not grieve thee,
To fee the honour of his royal name
Defpis'd and fet at nought, his ftate o'er-run,
Devour'd and parcell'd out by flaves fo vile,
That if oppos'd to him, 'twould make comparifon
Abfurd and monftrous feem, as if to mate
A mole-hill with Olympus ?

Æth. He was my friend ;
I think I knew him ; and, to do him right,
He was a man indeed.   Not as thefe are,
A rioter, or doer of foul wrongs ;
But boldly juft, and more like what man fhould be.

Tel. From morn till noon, from noon till the fhades dar-
From evening till the morning dawns again,   [ken
Lewdnefs, confufion, infolence, and uproar,
Are all the bus'nefs of their guilty hours ;
The cries of maids enforc'd, the roar of drunkards,
Mix'd with the braying of the minftrels' noife,
Who minifters to mirth, ring thro' the palace,
And echo to the arch of heav'n their crimes.
Behold, ye gods, who judge betwixt your creatures,
Behold the rivals of the great Ulyffes !

Men. Doubt not but all their crimes, and all thy wrongs

I   Are

Are judg'd by Nemefis and equal Jove.
Suffer the fools to laugh and loll fecure;
This is their day; but there is one behind
For vengeance and Ulyffes.
    Æth. Till that day,
That day of recompence and righteous juftice,
Learn thou, my fon, the cruel arts of courts;
Learn to diffemble wrongs, to fmile at injuries,
And fuffer crimes thou want'ft the power to punifh;
Be eafy, affable, familiar, friendly, ·
Search, and know all mankind's myfterious ways;
But truft the fecret of thy foul to none.
Believe me, feventy years, and all the forrows
That feventy years bring with them, thus have taught me,
Thus only, to be fafe in fuch a world as this is.
Enter Antinous.
    Ant. Hail to thee, Prince! thou fon of great Ulyffes,
Offspring of gods, moft worthy of thy race;
May ev'ry day like this be happy to thee,
Fruition and fuccefs attend thy wifhes,
And everlafting glory crown thy youth,
    Tel. Thou greet'ft me like a friend. Come near, An-
May I believe that omen of my happinefs,   [tinous;
That joy which dances in thy chearful eyes?
Or doft thou, for thou know'ft my fond, fond heart,
Doft thou betray me to deceitful hopes,
And footh me, like an infant, with a tale
Of fome felicity, fome dear delight, ·
Which thou didft never purpofe to beftow?
    Ant. By Cytherea's altar, and her doves,
By all the gentle fires that burn before her,
I have the kindeft founds to blefs your ear with,
Nay, and the trueft too, I'll fwear, I think,
That ever love and innocence infpir'd.
    Tel. Ha! from Semanthe?
    Ant. From the fair Semanthe,
The gentle, the forgiving————
    Tel. Soft, my Antinous,
Keep the dear fecret fafe; wifdom and age
Reafon perverfely when they judge of love.
A bus'nefs of a moment calls me hence,   [*To* Mentor.
That ended, I'll attend the Queen; till then,
Mentor,

Mentor, the noble stranger is thy care——
Fly with me to some safe, some sacred privacy,   [*To* Ant.
There charm my senses with Semanthe's accents,
There pour thy balm into my love-sick soul,
And heal my cares for ever.   [*Exeunt* Tel. *and* Ant.

Æth. This smooth speaker,
This supple courtier, is in favour with you.
Mark'd you the Prince, how at this man's approach
The fierceness, rage, and pride of youth declin'd,
His changing visage wore a form more gentle,
And ev'ry feature took a softer turn ;
As if his soul, bent on some new employment,
Of different purpose from the thought before,
Had summon'd other counsels, other passions,
And dress'd her in a gay, fantastic garb,
Fit for th' adventure which she meant to prove ?
By Jove, I lik'd it not——

Men. The Prince, whose temper
Is open as the day, and unsuspecting,
Esteems him as devoted to his service,
Wise, brave, and just ; and since his late return
From Nestor's court at Pyle, he still has held him
In more especial nearness to his heart.

Æth. 'Tis rash, and savours of unwary youth.
Tell him, he trusts too far.   If I mistook not,
You said he was a wooer.

Men. True, he was ;
Noble by birth, and mighty in his wealth,
Proud of the patriot's name and people's praise,
By gifts, by friendly offices, and eloquence,
He won the herd of Ithacans to think him
Ev'n worthy to supply his master's place.

Æth. Unthinking, changeable, ungrateful Ithaca!
But, Mentor, say, the Queen, could she forget
The difference 'twixt Ulysses and his slave ?
Did not her soul resent the violation,
And, spite of all the wrongs she labour'd under,
Dash his ambition and presumptuous love ?

Men. Still great and royal in the worst of fortunes,
With native power and majesty array'd,
She aw'd this rash Ixion with her frown,
Taught him to bend his abject head to earth,

And

And own his humbler lot. He ſtood rebuk'd,
And full of guilty ſorrow for the paſt,
Vow'd to repeat the daring crime no more,
But with humility and loyal ſervice
To purge his fame, and waſh the ſtains away.
    Æth. Deceit and artifice ! the turn's too ſudden ;
Habitual evils ſeldom change ſo ſoon,
But many days muſt paſs, and many ſorrows,
Conſcious remorſe and anguiſh muſt be felt,
To curb deſire, to break the ſtubborn will,
And work a ſecond nature in the ſoul,
Ere Virtue can reſume the place ſhe loſt ;
'Tis elſe diffimulation. But no more ;
The ruffling train of ſuitors are at hand,
Thoſe mighty candidates for love and empire !
'Tis well the gods arc mild, when theſe dare hope
To merit their beſt gifts by riot and injuſtice.

        Enter Polydamas, Agenor, Thoon, Ephialtes, *and*
                Attendants.

    Pol. Our ſouls are out of tune, we languiſh all,
Nor does the ſweet returning of the dawn
Cheer with its uſual mirth our drouſy ſpirits,
That droop'd beneath the lazy leaden night.
    Agen. Can we, who ſwear we love, ſmile or be gay,
When our fair queen, the goddeſs of our vows,
She that adorns our mirth, and gilds our day,
Withholds the beams that only can revive us ?
    Tho. Night muſt involve the world till ſhe appear,
The flowers in painted meadows hang their heads,
The birds awake not to their morning ſongs,
Nor early hinds renew their conſtant labour ;
Ev'n nature ſeems to ſlumber till her call,
Regardleſs of th' approach of any other day.
    Eph. Why is ſhe then withheld, this public good ?
Why does ſhe give thoſe hours that ſhould rejoice us,
To tears, perverſeneſs, and to ſullen privacy,
While vainly here we waſte our luſty youth,
In expectation of the uncertain bleſſing ?
    Pol. For twice two years this coy, this cruel beauty
Has mock'd our hopes, and croſs'd them with delays ;
At length the female artifice is plain,

                                            The

The riddle of her myftic web is known,
Which ere her fecond choice fhe fwore to weave;
While ftill the fecret malice of the night
Undid the labours of the former day.

Agen. Hard are the laws of love's defpotic rule,
And ev'ry joy is trebly bought with pain;
Crown we the goblet then, and call on Bacchus,
Bacchus, the jolly god of laughing pleafures,
Bid ev'ry voice of harmony awake,
Apollo's lyre, and Hermes' tuneful fhell;
Let wine and mufic join to fwell the triumph,
To footh uneafy thought, and lull defire.

Æth. Is this the rev'rence due to facred beauty,
Or thefe the rights the Cyprian goddefs claims?
Thefe rude licentious orgies are for Satyrs,
And fuch the drunken homage which they pay
To old Silenus nodding on his afs.
But be it as it may, it fpeaks you well.

Eph. What fays the flave?

Tho. Oh, 'tis the fnarler, Æthon!
A privileg'd talker.   Give him leave to rail;
Or fend for Irus forth, his fellow droll,
And let them play a match of mirth before us,
And laughter be the prize to crown the victor.

Æth. And doft thou anfwer to reproof with laughter?
But do fo ftill, and be what thou wert born;
Stick to thy native fenfe, and fcorn inftruction.
Oh, Folly! what an empire haft thou here!
What temples fhall be rais'd to thee! what crowds,
Of flav'ring, hooting, fenfelefs, fhameful ideots:
Shall worfhip at thy ignominious altars,
While princes are thy priefts!

Pol. Why fhouldft thou think,
O'erweening, infolent, unmanner'd flave,
That wifdom does forfake the wealth, the honours,
And full profperity of princes' courts,
To dwell with rags and wretchednefs like thine?
Why doft thou call him fool?

Æth. Speech is moft free;
It is Jove's gift to all mankind in common.
Why doft thou call me poor, and think me wretched?

Pol. Becaufe thou art fo.

Æth.

Æth. Anſwer to thyſelf,
And let it ſerve for thee, and for thy friend.
    Agen. He talks like oracles, obſcure and ſhort.
    Æth. I would be underſtood ; but apprehenſion
Is not thy talent——Midnight ſurfeits, wine,
And painful undigeſted morning fumes,
Have marr'd thy underſtanding.
    Eph. Hence, thou miſcreant !
My Lords, this railer is not to be borne.
    Æth. And wherefore art thou borne, thou public grie-
Thou tyrant, born to be a nation's puniſhment ;   [vance,
To ſcourge thy guilty ſubjects for their crimes,
And prove Heaven's ſharpeſt vengeance ?·
    Eph. Spurn him hence,
And tear the rude unhallow'd railer's tongue
Forth from his throat.
    Æth. If brutal violence,
And luſt of foul revenge, ſhould urge thee on,
Spite of the Queen and hoſpitable Jove,
T' oppreſs a ſtranger, ſingle, and unarm'd,
Yet, mark me well, I was not born thy vaſſal ;
And wert thou ten times greater than thou art,
And ten times more a king, thus would I meet thee,
Thus naked as I am, I would oppoſe thee,
And fight a woman's battle with my hands,
Ere thou ſhouldſt do me wrong, and go unpuniſh'd.
    Eph. Ha ! doſt thou brave me, dog ? [*Coming up to* Æth.
    Tho. Avaunt !
    Pol. Begone !
                Enter Eurymachus.
    Eur. What daughter of old Chaos and the Night,
What fury loiters yet behind the ſhades,
To vex the peaceful morn with rage and uproar ?
Each frowning viſage doubly dy'd with wrath,
Your voices in tumultuous clamours rais'd,
Venting reproach, and ſtirring ſtrong contention.
Say, have you been at variance ?—Speak, ye Princes,
Whence grew th' occaſion ?
    Æth. King of Samos, hear me.
To thee, as to a king, worthy the name,
The majeſty and right divine of pow'r,
Boldly I dare appeal. This King of Seriphos,
                                [*Pointing to* Eph.
            B   This

'This ifland lord, this monarch of a rock,
He, and his fellow-princes there, yon band
Of eating, drinking lovers, have in fcorn
Of the gods' laws, and ftrangers' facred privilege,
Offer'd me foul offence, and moft unmanly injuries.

    Eur. Away! It is too much——You wrong your
      honours,   [*To the wooers.*
And ftain the luftre of your royal names,
To brawl and wrangle with a thing beneath you.
Are we not chief on earth, and plac'd aloft?
And when we poorly ftoop to mean revenge,
We ftand debas'd, and level with the flave
Who fondly dares us with his vain defiance.

    Eph. Henceforward let the ribald railer learn
To curb the lawlefs licence of his fpeech;
Let him be dumb; we wo' not brook his prating.

    Eur. Go to! you are too bitter. But no more. [*To Æth.*
Let ev'ry jarring found of difcord ceafe,
Tune all your thoughts and words to beauty's praife,
To beauty, that, with fweet and pleafant influence,
Breaks like the day-ftar from the chearful eaft;
For fee, where, circled with a crowd of fair-ones,
Frefh as the fpring, and fragrant as its flowers,
Your queen appears, your goddefs, your Penelope.

    Enter the Queen, with Ladies, and other Attendants.

Diana thus on Cynthus' fhady top,
Or by Eurota's ftream, leads to the chafe
Her virgin train, a thoufand lovely nymphs,
Of form celeftial all, troop by her fide;
Amidft a thoufand nymphs the goddefs ftands confefs'd,
In beauty, majefty, and port divine,
Supreme and eminent.

    Qu. If thefe fweet founds,
This humble fawning phrafe, this faithlefs flattery,
If thefe known arts could heal my wounded foul,
Could recompenfe the forrows of my days,
Or footh the fighings of my lonely nights,
Well might you hope to wooe me to your wifhes,
And win my heart with your fond tales of love.
But fince whate'er I've fuffer'd for my lord,
From Troy, the winds and feas, the gods, and you,

Is deeply writ within my fad remembrance,
Know, Princes, all your eloquence is vain.
Agen. If thofe bright eyes, that wafte their lights with
Would kindly fhine upon Agenor's hopes,   [weeping,
Behold he offers to his charming Queen
His crown, his life, his ever-faithful vows,
What joys foe'er or love or empire yield,
To blefs her future days, and make 'em happy all.
    Pol. Accept my crown, and reign with me in Delos.
    Tho. Mine, and the homage of my people wait you.
    Eph. I cannot court you with a filken tale,
With eafy ambling fpeeches, fram'd on purpofe,
Made to be fpoke in tune——But be my queen,
And leave my plain-fpoke love to prove its merit.
    Qu. And am I yet to learn your love, your faith?
Are not my wrongs gone up to heav'n againft you?
Do they not ftand before the throne of Jove,
And call inceffant on his tardy vengeance?
What fun has fhone that has not feen your infolence,
Your wafteful riot, and your impious mirth,
Your fcorn of old Laertes' feeble age,
Of my fon's youth, and of my woman's weaknefs?
Ev'n in my palace here, my lateft refuge,
(For you are lords of all befide in Ithaca)
With ruffian vio'ence and murd'rous rage,
You menace the defencelefs and the ftranger,
And from th' unhofpitable dwelling drive
Safety and friendly peace.
    Æth. For me it matters not;
Wrong is the portion ftill of feeble age.
My toilfome length of days full oft has taught me
What 'tis to ftruggle with the proud and powerful:
But 'tis for thy unhappy fate, fair Queen,
'Tis to behold thy beauty and thy virtue,
Tranfcendant both, worthy the gods who gave them,
And worthy of their care, to fee them left,
Abandon'd and forfaken, to rude outrage,
And made a prize for drunkards; 'tis for this
My foul takes fire within, and vainly urges
My cold enervate hand to affert thy caufe.
    Qu. Alas! they fcorn the weaknefs of thy age,
As of my fex——But mark me well, ye Princes!

Whoe'er amongst you dares to lift his hand
Against the hoary head of this old man,
This good old man, this friend of my Ulysses,
Him will I hold my worst, my deadliest foe,
Him shall my curses and revenge pursue,
And mark him from the rest with most distinguish'd hatred.
   Eph. That you are weak, defenceless, and opprefs'd,
Impute not to the gods, they have befriended you,
With lavish hands they spread their gifts before you;
What pride, revenge, what wanton love of change,
Or woman's wish can afk, behold, we offer you.
Curse the perverfenefs of your stubborn will then,
That has delay'd your choice, and in that choice your
      happinefs.
   Qu. And muft I hear this ftill, and ftill endure it?
Oh, rage! dishonour! wretched, helplefs Queen!
Return, return, my hero, my Ulysses;
Bring him again, you cruel feas and winds;
Troy and adult'rous Paris are no more;
Reftore him then, you righteous gods of Greece,
T' avenge himfelf and me upon thefe tyrants,
And do a fecond juftice here at home.
   Eur. Amongft the mighty manes of the Greeks,
Great names, and fam'd for higheft deeds in war,
His honour'd fhade refts from the toils of life,
In everlafting indolence and eafe,
Carelefs of all your pray'rs and vain complainings, [nefs.
Which the winds bear away, and fcatter in their wanton-
Turn thofe bright eyes then from defpair and death,
And fix your better hopes among the living;
Fix them on one who dares, who can defend you,
One worthy of your choice.
   Qu. If my free foul
Muft ftoop to this unequal hard condition,
If I muft make this fecond hated choice,
Yet by connubial Juno, here I fwear,
None fhall fucceed my lord, but that brave man
That dares avenge me well upon the reft.
Then let whoever dares to love be bold,
Be, like my former hero, made for war,
Able to bend the bow, and tofs the fpear;

For

For ev'ry wrong his injur'd Queen has found,
Let him revenge and pay it with a wound;
Fierce from the flaughter let the victor come,
And tell me that my foes have met their doom;
Then plight his faith upon his bloody fword,
And be, what my Ulyffes was, my beft, my deareft lord.

[Exeunt all but Æthon.

Æth. Oh, matchlefs proof of faith and love unchang'd!
Left in the pride, the wifhing warmth of youth,
For ten long years, and ten long years to that,
And yet fo true! Befet with ftrong allurements,
With youth, proud pomp, and foft bewitching pleafure,
'Tis wonderful! and wives in later times
Shall think it all the forgery of wit,
A fable curioufly contriv'd t' upbraid
Their fickle eafy faith and mock them for their lightnefs.
But fee, the Samian King returns.

Enter Eurymachus.

Eur. I fought you
Amidft the crowd of princes who attend
The Queen to Juno's temple.

Æth. When I worfhip,
And bow myfelf before the awful gods,
I mingle not with thofe who fcorn their laws,
With raging, brutal, loofe, voluptuous crowds,
Who take the gods for gluttons like themfelves.

Eur. This fullen garb, this moody difcontent,
Sits on thee well, and I applaud thy anger,
Thy juft difdain of this licentious rout:
Yet all are not like thefe; nor ought thy quarrel
Be carry'd on to all mankind in common.

Æth. Perhaps the untaught plainnefs of my words
May make you think my manners rude and favage;
But know, my country is the land of liberty;
Phæacia's happy ifle, that gave me birth,
Forbids not any to fpeak plain and truly;
Sincere and open are we, roughly honeft,
Upright in deed, tho' fimple in our fpeech,
As meaning not to flatter or offend;
The ufe of words we have, but not the art;
And ev'n as nature dictates, fo we fpeak.

Eur. Now, by great Juno, guardian of our Samos,

In

In ftrong defcription haft thou well exprefs'd
That manly virtue I would make a friend of.
Nor thou, brave Æthon, fhalt difdain our amity,
Our proffer'd love; for know, that kings, like gods,
With all things good adorn their own creation,
And where their favour fixes, there is happinefs.

 Æth. Yes, Sir, you are a king, a great one too;
My humbler birth has caft me far beneath you,
And made me for the proffer'd grace unfit:
Friendfhip delights in equal fellowfhip,
Where parity of rank and mutual offices
Engage both fides alike, and keep the balance even.
'Tis irkfome to a gen'rous, grateful foul,
To be opprefs'd beneath a load of favours,
Still to receive, and run in debt to friendfhip,
Without the pow'r of paying fomething back.

 Eur. I know thee grateful; juft and gen'rous minds
Are always fo; nor is thy pow'r fo fcanty,
But that it may vie with a king's munificence,
May make me large amends for all my bounty,
May blefs me with a benefit I want,
And give me that which my foul moft defires:
The Queen————

 Æth. How, Sir, the Queen!

 Eur. The beauteous Queen,
That fummer-fun in full meridian glory,
Brighter than the faint promife of the fpring,
With bleffings ripen'd to the gath'rer's hand,
Mature for joy, and in perfection lovely;
Ev'n fhe!
The pride of Greece, the wifh of youthful princes,
Severe, and cold, and rigid as fhe is,
Looks gently on thee, Æthon, fhe beholds thee
With kind regard, and liftens to thy counfels. [go on.

 Æth. Be ftill, thou beating heart! [*Afide.*] Well, Sir,

 Eur. No more, there needs no more; thy piercing wit,
I read it in thy eyes, hath found my purpofe.
Be favourable then, be friendly to me;
Nay, I'll conjure thee, by my hopes, by thine,
Whether they follow wealth, or power, or fame,
Or what defires foe'er warm thy old breaft,
Counfel me, aid me, teach me, be my friend.

                Æth.

Æth. Suppofe me fuch, what fhould my friendfhip
    profit you ?

Eur. Oh, by ten thoufand ways! Has not that age
That turn'd thy rev'rend locks fo filver white,
Has it not giv'n thee fkill in woman-kind,
Sagacious wifdom to explore their fubtleties,
Their coy averfions, and their eager appetites,
Their falfe denials, and their fecret yieldings?
Yet more, thy friendfhip with her former lord
Gives thee a right to fpeak, and be believ'd.

Æth. Then you would have me wooe her for you, win
This queen, this wife of him that was my friend? ['n [her,

Eur. Thou fpeak'ft me well; of him that was my friend.
His death has broke thofe bonds of love and friendfhip,
And left me free and worthy to fucceed
Both in her heart and thine.

Æth. Excufe me, Sir,
Nor think I meant to queftion your high worth.
I am but ill at praifing, or my tongue
Had fpoke the great things that my heart thinks of you:
Suppofe me wholly yours——Yet do you hold
This fov'reign beauty made of fuch light ftuff,
So like the common changelings of her fex,
That he that flatter'd, figh'd, and fpoke her fair,
Could win her from her ftubborn refolution,
And chafte refervednefs, with his fweet perfuafion?

Eur. No, were fhe form'd like them, fhe were a conqueft
Beneath a monarch's love, or Æthon's wit.
Not but I think fhe has her warmer wifhes,
'Twere monftrous elfe, and nature had deny'd
Her choiceft bleffing to her faireft creature,
Her foft defires, that fteal abroad unfeen,
Like filver Cynthia fliding from her orb,
At dead of night, to young Endymion's arms.

Æth. How! think you fo?—But fo 'tis true it may be;
The beft of all the fex is but a woman ;
And why fhould Nature break her rule for one,
To make one true, when all the reft are falfe ?
To find thofe wifhes then, thofe fond defires,
To trace the fulfome haunts of wanton appetite,
She muft be try'd.

Eur.

Eur. That to thy care, my Æthon,
Thy wit, and watchful friendſhip, I commend.

Æth. Yes, Sir, be certain on't, ſhe ſhall be try'd;
Thro' all the winding mazes of her thoughts,
Thro' all her joys, her ſorrows, and her fears,
Thro' all her truth and falſhood, I'll purſue her;
She ſhall be ſubtler than deceit itſelf,
And proſperouſly wicked, if ſhe 'ſcape me.

Eur. Thou art my genius, and my happier hours
Depend upon thy providence and rule.
This day, at her return from Juno's altar,
I have obtain'd an hour of private conference.

Æth. What! private, ſaid you? 'Twas a mark of fa-
Diſtinguiſhingly kind.   [vour,

Eur. Somewhat I urg'd
That much concern'd her honour and her ſafety;
Nay, ev'n the life of her belov'd Telemachus,
Which to her ear alone I would diſcloſe.
Thou ſhalt be preſent——How I mean to prove her,
Which way to ſhake the temper of her ſoul,
And where thy aid may ſtand me moſt in ſtead,
I will inſtruct thee as we paſs along.

Æth. I wait you, Sir.

Eur. Nor doubt of the ſucceſs.
This ſtubborn beauty ſhall be taught compliance.
Fair daughter of the ocean, ſmiling Venus,
Thou joy of gods and men, aſſiſt my purpoſe!
Thy Cyprus and Cythera leave a while,
Thy Paphian groves and ſweet Idalian hill,
To fix thy empire in this rugged iſle;
Bring all thy fires from ev'ry lover there,
To warm this coy, this cruel frozen fair;
Let her no more from nature's laws be free,
But learn obedience to thy great decree,
Since gods themſelves ſubmit to Fate, and thee.

                                                    [*Exeunt.*

             END of the FIRST ACT.

                                              ACT

A C T II.

Enter Antinous, Cleon, *and* Arcas.

ANTINOUS.

'TIS thus, my fellow-citizens and friends,
  'Tis thus unhappy Ithaca muſt groan
Beneath the bondage of a foreign lord ;
A needy upſtart race of hungry ſtrangers
Shall ſwarm upon the land, eat its increaſe,
Devour the labours of the toiling hind,
And gather all the wealth and honours of our iſle.
  Cle. The ſilken minions of the Samian court,
To lord it o'er the province ſhall be ſent,
To rule the ſtate, to be the chiefs in war,
And lead our hardy Ithacans to battle.
Freedom and right ſhall ceaſe, our corn, wine, oil,
The fatneſs of the year, ſhall all be theirs ;
Our modeſt matrons, and our virgin daughters,
Ev'n all we hold moſt dear, ſhall be the ſpoil,
The prey of our imperious haughty maſters.
  Arc. Would I could ſay I did not fear theſe evils !
  Ant. Oh, honeſt Arcas ! 'tis too plain a danger.
The Queen, requir'd by public voice to wed,
To end at once the hopes and riotous concourſe
Of princely gueſts, contending for her love.
O'er-paſſing all the nobleſt of our iſle,
Inclines to fix her choice on proud Eurymachus.
  Cle. Why rides the Samian fleet within our harbour,
But to ſupport their tyrant's title here ?
With cauſes feign'd they linger long, pretending
Rude winter ſeas, with omens that forbid
The frighted mariner to leave the ſhore ;
While Neptune ſmooths his waters for their paſſage,
And gently whiſtling winds invite their ſails,
As if they wiſh'd to waft them back to Samos.
  Arc. Ulyſſes is no more ; the partial gods,
Who favour'd Priam and his hapleſs race,
Have pour'd their wrath on his devoted head,
And now, in ſome far diſtant realm, expos'd,
To glut the vulture's and the lion's maw,
Or in the oozy bottom of the deep,

Full

Full many a fathom down, the hero lies,
And never shall return——What then remains,
But that our country fly to thee for succour,   [*To* Ant.
To thee, the noblest of the lords of Ithaca ?
And since, so fate ordains, our Queen must wed,
Be thou her second choice, be thou our ruler,
And save our nation from a foreign yoke.

  Ant. You are my friends, and over-rate my worth:
But witness for me, for you still have known me,
Whene'er my country's service calls me on,
No enterprise so doubtful, or so dangerous,
But I will boldly prove it, to preserve thee,
Oh, Ithaca ! from bondage.

  Cle. Wherefore urge you not
Your suit among the rest ?

  Ant. The cruel Queen
Rejects my humble vows with angry scorn ?
And when I once presum'd to speak my passion,
She call'd it insolence——Since then I've strove
To hide th' unlucky folly from all eyes
But yours, my friends, who view my naked soul.

  Arc. Avow your flame in public, tell the world,
Antinous is worthy of a queen :
So many valiant hands shall own your cause,
So shall the voice in Ithaca be for you,
The Queen shall own your love has made her great,
And giv'n her back an empire she had lost.

  Ant. Think not I dream the hours of life away,
Supine, and negligent of love and glory ;
No, Arcas, no ; my active mind is busy,
And still has labour'd with a vast design ;
Ere long the beauteous birth will be disclos'd,
Then shall your pow'rs come forth, your swords and coun—
And manifest the love you bear Antinous.   [*fels.*
'Till then be still——To favour my design,
With low submissions, with obsequious duty,
And vows of friendship fit to flatter boys with,
I've wound myself into the Prince's heart.

  Cle. 'Tis said the love-sick youth doats ev'n to death
Upon the Samian Princess, fair Semanthe.

  Ant. Let it go on ; 'tis a convenient dotage,
And suits my purpose well—The youth by nature

Is active, fiery, bold, and great of foul;
Love is the bane of all thefe noble qualities,
The fickly fit that palls ambition's appetite;
And therefore have I nurs'd the fond difeafe,
Infpiring lazy wifhes, fighs, and languifhings,
Unactive dreaming floth, and womanifh foftnefs,
To freeze his veins, and quench his manly fires.
The froward God of Love, to boaft his pow'r,
Has bred of late fome little jars between them;
But 'twas my care to reconcile their follies,
And, if my augury deceives me not,
This day a prieft in private makes them one,
Unknown or to the Queen or to Eurymachus.
But fee! they come——Retire.

Enter Telemachus and Semanthe.

Do, figh, and fmile,
And print thy lips upon the foft white hand;
Sceptres and crowns are trifles none regard,
That can be blefs'd with fuch a joy as this is.

[Exeunt Ant. Cle. and Arc.

Tel. Yes, my Semanthe, ftill I will complain,
Still I will murmur at thee, cruel maid,
For all that pain thou gav'ft my heart but now.
What god, averfe to innocence and love,
Could fhake thy gentle foul with fuch a ftorm?
Juft at that happy moment, when the prieft   [thee,
Had join'd our hands, thou ftart'dft as death had ftruck
And, fighing, cry'd, Ah, no!—it is impoffible!

Sem. And yet, Oh, my lov'd lord! yet I am yours;
This hand has giv'n me to you, and this heart,
This heart, that achs with tendernefs, confirm'd it.

Tel. And yet thou art not mine; elfe why this forrow?
Why art thou wet with weeping, as the earth,
When vernal Jove defcends in gentle fhow'rs,
To caufe increafe, and blefs the infant year,
When ev'ry fpiry grafs, and painted flow'r,
Is hung with pearly drops of heav'nly rain?

Sem. Ye woods and plains, and all ye virgin dryads,
Happy companions of thofe woods and plains,
Why was I forc'd to leave your chearful fellowfhip,
To come and lofe my peace of mind at Ithaca?
And, Oh, Semanthe! wherefore didft thou liften

2

To

To that dear voice ? Why didſt thou break thy vow,
Made to the huntreſs, Cynthia, and her train ?
Ah, ſay, fond maid ! ſay, wherefore didſt thou love ? .
    Tel. Alas, my gentle love ! how have I wrong'd thee ?
By what unwilling crime have I offended,
That thus with ſtreaming eyes thou ſhouldſt complain,
Thus daſh my joys, and quench thoſe holy fires,
By yellow Hymen's torch ſo lately lighted,
Thus ſtain this bleſſed day, our bridal day,
With the deteſted omen of thy ſorrows.
    Sem. Of what ſhould I accuſe thee ? Thou art noble,
Thy heart is ſoft, is pitiful, and tender;
And thou wilt never wrong the poor Semanthe.
And yet ———
    Tel. What mean'ſt thou ?
    Sem. What have we been doing ?
    Tel. A deed of happineſs.
    Sem. Are we not marry'd ?
    Tel. We are; and like the careful, thrifty hind,
Who, provident of winter, fills his ſtores
With all the various plenty of the autumn,
We've hoarded up a mighty maſs of joy,
To laſt for all our years that are to come,
And ſweeten ev'ry bitter hour of life.
    Sem. Fain would I ſooth my ſoul with theſe ſweet hopes,
Forget the anguiſh of my waking cares,
And all thoſe boding dreams that haunt my ſlumbers.
Laſt night, when after many a heavy ſigh,
And many a painful thought, the god of ſleep,
Inſenſible and ſoft, had ſtole upon me;
Methought I found me by a murm'ring brook,
Reclin'd at eaſe upon the flow'ry margin,
And thou, thou firſt and laſt of all my thoughts,
Thou dear, eternal object of my wiſhes,
Cloſe by my ſide wert laid ———
    Tel Delightful viſion !
And, Oh, Oh, pity that it was not real !
    Sem. Awhile on many a pleaſing theme we talk'd,
And mingled ſweet diſcourſe; when on the ſudden,
The cry of hounds, the jolly huntſman's horn,
With all the chearful muſic of the chaſe,
Surpris'd my ear, and ſtraight a troop of nymphs,
Once the dear partners of my virgin heart,

Flew

Flew lightly by us, eager of the fport;
Laft came the goddefs, great Latona's daughter,
With more than mortal grace fhe ftood confeft,
I faw the golden quiver at her back,
And heard the founding of her filver bow;
Abafh'd I rofe, and lowly made obeyfance;
But fhe, not fweet, nor affable, nor fmiling,
As once fhe wont, with ftern regard beheld me;
And wherefore doft thou loiter here, fhe faid,
Of me, thy fellows, and our fports unmindful?
Return, thou fugitive; nor vainly hope
To drefs thy bridal bed, and wafte thy youth
In wanton pleafures, and inglorious love!
A virgin at my altar wert thou vow'd,
'Tis fix'd by fate, and thou art mine for ever.
With that fhe fnatch'd a chaplet from my hand,
Which for thy head in fondnefs I had wove,
And bore me fwiftly with her.—In my flight,
Backwards, methought, I turn'd my eyes to thee,
But found thee not, for thou wert vanifh'd from me,
And in thy place my father lay extended
Upon the earth, a bloody lifelefs corfe;
Struck to the very heart, I fhriek'd aloud,
And waking, found my tears upon my pillow.
   Tel. Vex not thy peaceful foul, my fair Semanthe,
Nor dread the anger of the awful gods,
Safe in thy native unoffending innocence.
Still when the golden fun withdraws his beams,
And drowzy night invades the weary world,
Forth flies the god of dreams, fantaftic Morpheus,
Ten thoufand mimic phantoms fleet around him,
Subtle as air, and various in their natures,
Each has ten thoufand, thoufand diff'rent forms,
In which they dance confus'd before the fleeper,
While the vain god laughs to behold what pain
Imaginary evils give mankind.
   Sem. Not happy omens that approve our wifhes,
When bright with flames the chearful altar fhines,
And the good gods are gracious to our offerings,
Not oracles themfelves, that fpeak us happy,
Could charm my fears, and lull my froward forrows,
Like the dear voice of him whom my foul loves.
Ev'n while thou fpok'ft my breaft begun to glow,

I felt sweet hopes, and joy, and peace returning,
And all the fires of life were kindled up anew.

Tel. Hence then, thou meager care, ill-boding me-
Anxious disquiet, and heart-breaking grief,   [lancholy,
Fly to your native seats, where deep below
Old night and horror with the furies dwell,
Love and the joyful genial bed disclaim you;
To-night a thousand little laughing Cupids
Shall be our guard, and wakeful watch around us;
No found, no thought shall enter to disturb us,
But sacred silence reign; unless, sometimes,
We sigh and murmur with excess of happiness.

   Sem. Alas, my Lord!

   Tel. Again that mournful found!

   Sem. What other pain is this? What other fear,
So diff'rent quite from what I felt before?
Alternate heat and cold shoot through my veins;
Now a chill dew hangs faintly on my brow,
And now with gentle warmth I glow all o'er;
Short are my sighs, and nimbly beats my heart,
I gaze on thee with joy, and yet I tremble;
'Tis pain and pleasure blended, both at once,
'Tis life and death, or something more than either.

   Tel. Thus untry'd soldiers, when the trumpet sounds,
Expect the combat with uncertain passions;
Thus Nature speaks in unexperienc'd maids,
And thus they blush, and thus like thee they tremble.
At even, when the queen retires to rest,
I'll meet thee here, and take thee to my arms,
Thy best, thy surest refuge.——
But see! the stranger Æthon comes; retire;
I would not have his watchful eye observe us.

Enter Æthon.

I charge thee loiter not, but haste to bless me,
Haste, at th' appointed hour——
Think with what eager hopes, what rage I burn,
For ev'ry tedious minute how I mourn;
Think how I call thee cruel for thy stay,
And break my heart with grief, for thy unkind delay.

[*Exeunt* Telemachus *and* Sem.

   Æth. Ha! what, so close! How cautious to avoid me!
As who should say, old man, you are too wife,

What

What has my youth to do with your inſtructions,
While folly is ſo pleaſant to my taſte,
And damn'd deſtruction wears a face ſo fair?
This Samian king is happy in his arts;
His daughter, vow'd a virgin to Diana,
Is brought to play the wanton here at Ithaca:
No matter for religion; let the gods
Look to their rites themſelves: the youth grows fond,
Juſt to their wiſh! and ſwears himſelf their vaſſal.
His mother follows next——But ſoft——They come;
Now to put on the pander—That's my officc.

Enter the Queen and Eurymachus.

  Queen. Have I not anſwer'd oft, it is in vain,
In vain to urge me with this hateful ſubject?
As thou art noble, pity me, Eurymachus,
Add not new weight of ſorrows to my days,
That drag too ſlow, too heavily along;
Compel me not to curſe my life, my being,
To curſe each morn, each chearful morn, that dawns
With healing comfort on its balmy wings,
To ev'ry wretched creature but myſelf;
To me it brings more pain, and iterated woes.

  Eur. Oh, god of eloquence, bright Maia's ſon!
Teach me what more than mortal grace of ſpeech,
What ſounds can move this fierce relentleſs fair,
This cruel Queen, that pityleſs beholds
My heart that bleeds for her, my humble knee,
In abject low ſubmiſſion bent to earth,
To deprecate her ſcorn, and beg in vain,
One gracious word, one favourable look.

  Queen. Count back the tedious years, ſince firſt my hero
Forſook theſe faithful arms to war with Troy;
And yet in all that long, long tract of time,
Witneſs, ye chaſter powers, if e'er my thoughts
Have harbour'd any other gueſt but him;
Remember, king of Samos, what I have been,
Then think if I can change——Æthon, come near.

[Æthon comes forward.

Good honeſt man! how rare is truth like thine!
Thou great example of a loyal friend!

  Æth. Oh, lady, ſparc that praiſe; if few like me
Are friends, yet none have ever lov'd like you;

C 2   Why

Why what a mighty fpace is twenty years !
'Tis irkfome to remembrance, to look back
Upon your youth, that happier part of life,
Like fome fair field, of rich and fertile foil,
That might have bleft the owner with abundance,
But left unheeded, like a barren moor,
Lies fencelefs, wild, uncultivate, and wafte.

   Queen. Alas!

   Eur. Were youth and beauty giv'n in vain ?
Why were the gods fo lavifh of their gifts
To one whofe fullen pride neglects to ufe them,
As if fhe fcorn'd the care heav'n took to make her happy ?

   Æth. More than enough of forrow have you known ;
Give eafe at length to your afflicted foul,
Be comforted, and now while time is yours,
'Tafte the good things of life, yet e'er they perifh,
Yet e'er the happy feafon pafs away.

   Queen. What fov'reign balm, what heav'nly healing
Can cure a heart fo torn with grief as mine,   [fair,
Can ftay this never-ceafing ftream of tears,
And once more make my fenfes know delight ?

   Eur. What god can work that miracle but Love ?
Love, who difpenfes joy to heav'n itfelf,
And cheats his fellow-gods more than their nectar,
'Till wrapt with vaft, unutterable pleafures,
Such as immortal natures only know,
Each owns his pow'r, and blefles the fweet boy.

   Queen. Now, Æthon, by thy friendfhip to my Lord,
Anfwer, I charge thee, to this cruel king ;
Demand if it be noble to prophane
My virtue thus, with loofe difhoneft courtfhip.

   Æth. Are love and virtue then fuch mortal foes,
That they muft never meet ?

   Queen. Never with me,
Unlefs my Lord return.

   Æth. Vain expectation !

   Queen. Ha ! Surely I miftook !——What faid'ft thou,
      Æthon ?

   Æth. That you have waited long for that return,
Wafted too much of life, and caft away
Thofe precious hours, that might have been employ'd
'To better ufe than weeping.

                              Queen.

Queen. This from thee !
Oh, faithlefs ! Truth is vanifh'd then indeed.
Oh, Æthon !—art thou too become my enemy !
    Æth. If, to reward your faith to loft Ulyffes,
I pray the gods to heap their bleffings on you,
To make you miftrefs of a mighty nation,
An empire greater, nobler than your own,
And crown you with this valiant monarch's love,
If this be enmity, you may accufe me.
    Queen. Doft thou folicit for him ? Doft thou dare
Invade my peace, my virtue ?
    Æth. Not for him,
But for the common happinefs of both.
    Queen. Traitor ! no more—at length thy wicked arts,
Thy falfe diffembled friendfhip for my Lord,
Thy pious journey hither for his fake,
Thy care of me, my fon, and of the ftate,
Thy praife, thy counfels, and thy fhew of virtue,
So holy, fo adorn'd with rev'rend age,
All are reveal'd, and thou confeft a villain ;
Hire, and the fordid love of gain have caught thee ;
Gold has prevail'd upon thee to betray me,
And bargain for my honour with this prince.
                    [*Pointing to* Eurymachus.
    Æth. It grieves me I offend you—fure I am,
I meant it as a friend.
    Queen. Hence from my fight !
    Eur. Æthon, no more—Since love and willing friend-
Employ their pious offices in vain,   [fhip
Learn we, henceforth, from this imperious beauty,
Learn we, from her example, to be cruel ;
And though our fofter paffions reft unfatisfy'd,
Yet the more fierce, the manly, and the rough,
Shall be indulg'd and riot to excefs.
Up then, Revenge, and arm thee, thou fell fury,
Up then, and fhake thy hundred iron whips ;
To-day I vow to facrifice to thee,
And flake thy horrid thirft with draughts of royal gore.
    Queen. What fays the tyrant ? [*Afide.*] Oh, Euryma-
What fatal purpofe has thy heart conceiv'd ?   [chus !
What means that rage that lightens in thy eyes,
That fwells fo fierce, and menaces deftruction ?
    Eur. The lambent fire of love prevails no more,
                    C 3   And

And now another mightier flame fucceeds ;
Vaunt not too foon, nor triumph in thy fcorn ;
For know, proud Queen, in fpite of thy difdain,
There is a way ev'n yet to reach thy heart.
Thou haft a fon, the darling of thy eyes—
   Queen. Oh, fatal thought !
Fear, like the hand of death, hath feiz'd my heart,
Cold, chilling cold——my fon ! Oh, my Telemachus !
   Æth. That ftroke was home---now, Virtue, hold thy
      own.   [*Afide.*
   Eur. Know then, that fon is in my pow'r, and holds
His frail uncertain being at my pleafure ;
And when I frown, death and deftruction, greedy,
Watchful, intent like tygers on their prey,
Start fudden forth, and feize the helplefs boy.
'Three hundred chofen warriors from my fleet,
Who undifcern'd, in parties, and by ftealth,
Late came a-fhore, now wait for my commands ;
'Think on them as the minifters of fate,
For when I bid them execute, 'tis done.
   Queen. If, as my foul prefages from thofe terrors
Which gather on thy ftern, tempeftuous brow,
Thou art feverely bent on death and vengeance,
Yet hear me, hear a wretch's only pray'r,
Oh, fpare the innocent, fpare my Telemachus,
Let not the ruffian's fword nor murd'rous violence
Cut off the noble promife of his youth,
Oh, fpare him, and let all thy rage fall here ;
Remember, 'twas this haughty, ftubborn queen
Refus'd thy love, and let her feel thy hate.
   Eur. A fecret joy glides through my fullen heart,
To fee fo fair a fuitor kneel before me.
But what have I to do with thoughts like thefe ?
Æthon, go bear this ring to bold Cerauuus,
The valiant leader of our Samian band ;
My laft of orders, which this morn I gave him,
Bid him perform ; hafte thou, and fee it done.
   Queen. Stay I conjure thee, Æthon——Cruel king !
Speak, anfwer me, unfold this dreadful fecret ;
Where points this fudden, dark, myfterious mifchief ?
Say, at the head of what devoted wretch

This winged thunder aims—Say, while my fears
Have left me yet a little life to hear thee.
  Eur. Already doft thou dread the gath'ring ftorm,
That grumbles in the air, preluding ruin?
But mark the ftroke, keep all thy tears for that,
Too foon it fhall be told thee—Æthon, hence.
  Queen. [*Holding Æthon.*] Not for thy life---No, not
        till thou haft heard me.   [*To* Eurymachus.
Too well, alas! I underftand my fate.
How have I been, among the happy mothers,
Call'd the moft happy, now the moft miferable:
Then barren, comfortlefs fate down and wept,
When they compar'd their marriage-beds with mine;
The fruitful, when they boafted of their numbers,
With envy and unwilling praife, confeft
That I had all their bleffings in my one.
Our virgins, when they met him, figh'd and blufh'd,
Matrons and wives beheld him as a wonder,
And gazing crouds purfu'd and bleft him as he pafs'd.
But then his youth! his tendernefs! his piety!
Oh, my Telemachus! my fon! my fon!
  Eur. And what are all thefe tears and helplefs wailings,
What poor amends to injur'd love and me?
How have I mourn'd thy fcorn, unkind and cruel?
How have I melted in unmanly weeping?,
How have I taught the ftubborn rocks of Ithaca,
And all the founding fhore to echo my complainings?
And haft thou e'er relented? Now mourn thou,
And murmur not, nor think thy lot too hard,
Since equal juftice pays thee but thy own.
  Queen. Oh, didft thou know what agonies I feel,
Hard as thou art, thou wouldft have pity on me:
Death is too poor a name, for that means reft,
But 'tis defpair—'tis mad—tormenting rage,
'Tis terrible—'tis bitter pain—it is
A mother's mourning for her only fon.
  Æth. Now, now her labouring heart is rent with an-
Oh, nature, how affecting are thy forrows!   [guifh!
How moving, melting in a mother's eyes!
So filver Thetis, on the Phrygian fhore,
Wept for her fon, fore-knowing of his fate,
The fea-nymphs fate around, and join'd their tears,
                                    While

While from his lowest deep old father ocean
Was heard to groan, in pity of their pain.   [*Aside.*

   Eur. Fair mourner, rise—Thus far thou hast prevail'd.
                       [*Offering to raise her.*

If, to atone for all I have endur'd,
For all thy cold neglect, thy arts, delays,
For all my years of anxious expectation,
This night thou give thy beauties to my arms ;
This night ! for love, impatient of my wrongs,
Allows not ev'n a moment's space beyond it ;
The prince, thy lov'd Telemachus, shall live,
And danger and distress shall never know thee more.

   Queen. Oh, shame ! Oh, modesty ! connubial truth
And spotless purity ! Ye heav'nly train !
Have I preserv'd you in my secret soul,
To give you up at last, then plunge in guilt,
Abandon'd to dishonour and pollution !
Oh, never ! never ! let me first be rack'd,
Torn, scatter'd by the winds, plung'd in the deep,
Or bound amidst the flames——Oh, friendly earth
Open thy bosom——And thou, Proserpine,
Infernal Juno, mighty queen of shades,
Receive me to thy dark, thy dreadful empire,
And hide me, save me from this tyrant's fury.

   Æth. Oh, racking, racking pain of secret thought !
                       [*Aside.*

   Eur. Hence ! hence, thou trifler, love ! fond, vain de-
I cast, I tear thee out——Æthon, begone !   [ceiver !
   Queen. Then drag me too !—Yet hear me once, once
For I will speak to thee of love !—of rage !   [more,
Of death ! of madness ! and eternal chaos !

   Eur. Away, thou loiterer !   [*To Æthon.*
   Æth. Then I must go?
   Queen. Eurymachus !   [*Holding out her hand to him.*
   Eur. Speak———
   Queen. Mercy !
   Eur. Love !
   Queen. Telemachus.
   Eur. My queen ! My goddess ! Art thou kind at last !
Oh, softly, softly breathe the charming sound,
And let it gently steal upon my soul,
Gently as falls the balmy dew from heav'n,
                           Or

Or let thy kind confenting eyes fpeak for thee,
And bring me the fweet tidings from thy heart;
She yields! Immortal gods, fhe yields!
   Queen. Where is he?
Where is my fon? Oh, tell me, is he fafe,
Swear to me fome moft facred folemn oath,
Swear my Telemachus is free from danger.
   Eur. Hear me, great Jove, father of gods and men,
And thou, blue Neptune, and thou, Stygian Pluto,
Hear, all ye greater and ye leffer powers,
That rule in heav'n, in earth, in feas, and hell,
While to my queen, on this fair hand I fwear,
That royal youth, that beft-lov'd fon is fafe,
Nor dies, unlefs his mother urge his fate.
At night, a prieft, by faithful Æthon's care,
In private fhall attend at thy apartment,
There while rich gums we burn, and fpicy odours,
The gods of marriage and of love invoking,
I will renew my vows, and at thy feet,
Devote ev'n all my pow'rs to thy command.
   Queen. 'Till then be kind, and leave me to myfelf;
Leave me to vent the fulnefs of my breaft,
Pour out the forrows of my foul alone,
And figh myfelf, if poffible, to peace.
Oh, thou dear youth, for whom I feel again
My throes, and twice endure a mother's pain;
Well had I dy'd to fave thee, Oh, my fon!
Well, to preferve thy life, had giv'n my own;
But when the thoughts of former days return,
When my loft virtue, fame, and peace I mourn,
The joys which ftill thou gav'ft me I forget,
And own I bought thee at a price too great.   [*Exit.*
   Eur. At length we have prevail'd: fear, doubt and
Thofe peevifh female virtues, fly before us,   [fhame,
And the difputed field at laft is ours.
   Æth. Yes, you have conquer'd, have approv'd yourfelf
A mafter in the knowledge of the fex.
What then remains, but to prepare for triumph,
To rifle all the fpoils of captive beauty,
And reap the fweet reward of your paft labours?
What of the prince?
   Eur. He lives, but muft be mine,

And

And my Semanthe's love the band to hold him;
But to to-morrow's dawn leave we that care:
The prefent day, for deep, for vaft defigns,
And hardy execution is decreed.
This night, according to their wonted riot,
The rival princes mean to hold a feaft.

   Æth. I mark'd but now the mighty preparation,
When to the hall the fweating flaves paft in,
Bending beneath the maffie goblets' weight,
Whofe each capacious womb, fraught with rich juice
Drawn from the Chian and the Lefbian grape,
Portended witlefs mirth, vain laughter, boafting,
Contentious brawling, madnefs, mifchief, and foul mur-
While to appeafe the glutton's greedy maw   {der;
Whole herds are flain, more than fuffice for hecatombs,
Ev'n more than zeal, with pious prodigality,
Beftows upon the gods to feed their priefts with.

   Eur. Then mark me well, or e'er the rowling night
Hath finifh'd half her courfe, the fumy vapours
And mounting fpirits of the deep-drunk bowl,
Shall feize the brains of thefe caroufing lovers;
Then fhalt thou, Æthon, with my valiant Samians,
Arm'd and appointed all at thy command,
Surround the hall, and on our common foes
At once revenge my queen, thyfelf, and me.

   Æth. Ha! At a blow!—'tis juft—'tis greatly thought!
By Jove th'avenger, 'twill be noble flaughter;
Nor doubt the event.   I anfwer for them all,
Ev'n to a man.

   Eur. Thine then be all the care,
While I with fofter pleafures crown my hours,
And revel in delight.

   Æth How! At that hour!   [*Starting.*
Ha!——— In enjoyment! Can that be?

   Eur. It muft.
Fierce for the joy, in fecret, and alone
I'll fteal upon my love.

   Æth. Stay! that were well!
Alone you muft———

   Eur. None but the confcious prieft———
That too muft be thy care, to chufe one faithful,
One for the purpofe fit.

                                 Æth.

Æth. Moſt worthy office !   [*Aſide.*
One to your wiſh, try'd in theſe pious ſecrets,
My friend of ancient date, is now in Ithaca;
Him ſworn to ſecrecy, and well prepar'd,
I will inſtruct to wait you with the Queen.
   Eur. Then be propitious, Love !
   Æth. And thou, Revenge,
Shoot all thy fires, and wake my ſlumb'ring rage,
Let my paſt wrongs, let indignation raiſe
My age to emulate my youthful praiſe ;
Let the ſtern purpoſe of my heart ſucceed,
Let riot, luſt, and proud injuſtice bleed :
Grant me but this, ye gods, who favour right,
I aſk no other bliſs nor fond delight,
Nor envy thee, Oh, king, thy bridal night. [*Exeunt.*

'END of the Second Act.

A C T   III.

Enter Æthon, Mentor, *and* Eumæus.

Æthon.

IF virtue be abandon'd, loſt and gone,
   No matter for the means that wrought the ruin;
Whether the pomp of pleaſure danc'd before her,
Alluring to the ſenſe, or dreadful danger
Came arm'd with all its terrors to the onſet,
She ſhould have held the battle to the laſt,
Undaunted, yieldleſs, firm, and dy'd or conquer'd.
   Men. Think on what hard, on what unequal terms
Virtue, betray'd within by woman's weakneſs,
Beſet without with mighty fears and flatteries,
Maintains the doubtful conflict---Sure if any
Have kept the holy marriage-bed inviolate,
If all our Grecian wives are not like Helen,
That praiſe the Queen, my royal miſtreſs, merits.
   Eum. And, Oh, impute not one unheeded word,
Forc'd from her in the bittereſt pangs of ſorrow,
When fierce conflicting paſſions ſtrove within,
Like all the winds at once let looſe upon the main,
When wild diſtraction rul'd——Oh, urge not that,

I   A blemiſh

A blemish on her fair, her matchless fame.

Æth. Oh, Mentor, and Eumæus, faithful pair!
To whom my life, my honour, all I truſt,
Theſe eyes beheld her yielding----Curſed object!
Beheld her in the Samian king's embrace;
The ſight of hell, of baleful Acheron
That rolls his livid waves around the damn'd,
Roaring and yelling on the farther ſhore,
Was not ſo terrible, ſo irkſome to me,
As when I ſaw his arms infold Penelope.
I heard the fatal compact for to-night,
The joys which he propos'd, nor ſhe deny'd————
But ſee ſhe comes————

Men. How much unlike a bride!

Enter the Queen.

Behold her tears, ſee comfortleſs affliction,
Anguiſh, and helpleſs, deſolate misfortune
Writ in her face. -

Æth. Retire; I would obſerve her.

    [Men. *and* Eum. *retire to the back part of the ſtage.*

Queen. And doſt thou only weep? Shall that put off
Th' approaching hour of ſhame, or ſave thy ſon?
Thou weep'ſt, and yet the ſetting ſun deſcends
Swift to the weſtern waves; and guilty night,
Haſty to ſpread her horrors o'er the world,
Rides on the duſky air————And now it comes,
The fatal moment comes, ev'n that dread time
When witches meet to gather herbs on graves,
When diſcontented ghoſts forſake their tombs,
And ghaſtly roam about, and doleful groan;
And hark! the ſcreech-owl ſcreams, and beats the window,
With deadly wings---And hark!---More dreadful yet,
Like Thracian Tereus to unhappy Philomel,
The furious bridegroom comes,---the tyrant raviſher!
And ſee! the ſhade of my much-injur'd Lord
Starts up to blaſt me!---Hence!---Begone, you horrors,
For I will hide me in the arms of death,
And think on you no more---That traitor here!

                            [*Seeing* Æthon.

Æth. Hail, beauteous Queen! The god of love ſalutes
And thus by great Eurymachus he ſpeaks: [thee,
Be ſorrow and misfortune on thy foes;

                                     But

But let thy days be crown'd with smiling peace,
Content and everlasting joy dwell with thee.
   Queen. Com'st thou to greet me with the sounds of joy,
Thou messenger of fate ?—So the hoarse raven
Croaks o'er the mansion of the dying man,
And often warns him with this dismal note,
To think upon his tomb.
   Æth. Or I mistook,
Or I was bid to treat of gentler matters,
Kindly to ask at what auspicious hour,
Your royal bridegroom and the priest should wait you.
   Queen. Too well my boding heart foretold thy tidings.
Now what reply ?—There is no room for choice,
'Tis one degree of infamy to doubt :
What must be must be—Let me then resolve,
'Tis only thus—no more----and I am free.   [*Aside.*
Say to the Samian king, thy master, thus ;
When Menelaus and the fate of Greece
Summon'd my Lord to Troy, he left behind him
None worthy of his place in love or empire.
   Æth. How, lady!—Whither points her meaning now ?
                              [*Aside.*
   Queen. Say too, I've held his merit in the balance,
But find the price of honour so much greater,
That 'twere an ideot's bargain to exchange them ;
Yet tell him too, I have my sex's weakness,
I have a mother's fondness in my eyes,
And all her tender passions in my heart.
   Æth. Ay, there ! 'tis there she's lost !   [*Aside.*
   Queen. Nor can I bear
To see what more, far more than life I joy in,
My only pledge of love, my Lord's dear image,
My son by bloody hands mangled and murder'd ;
(Oh, terrible to nature!) Therefore one,
One remedy alone is left to save me,
To shield me from a sight of so much horror,
And tell Eurymachus, I find it——here.
     [*She offers to stab herself; Æthon catches hold of her
             arm, and prevents her.*
   Æth. Forbid it, gods ! Perish the tyrant rather,
Let Samos be no more.
   Queen. Off ! Off, thou traitor !
              D   Give

Give way to my juſt rage!——Oh, tardy hand!
To what haſt thou betray'd me! Let me go,
Oh, let me, let me die, or I will curſe thee,
'Till hell ſhall tremble at my imprecations,
'Till Heav'n ſhall blaſt thee—loſt!—undone for ever!
   Æth. Oh, trifler that I am! Mentor, Eumæus,
                      [*They come forward.*

Come to my aid!——Be calm but for a moment,
And wait to ſee what wonders it will ſhew thee.
Guard her upon your lives, remember that,
Guard her from ev'ry inſtrument of death,
Sooth and aſſuage her grief, till my return;
Unfold the mighty ſecret of her fate,
And once more reconcile her ſoul to peace.
                      [*Exit Æthon.*
   Queen. And are you too my foes? Have you conſpir'd
And join'd with that falſe Æthon to betray me?
Here ſit thee down then, humbly in the duſt,
Here ſit, a poor, forlorn, abandon'd woman;
Caſt not thy eyes up to yon' azure firmament,
Nor hope relief from thence, the gods are pitileſs,
Or buſy in their heav'n, and thou not worth their care;
And, Oh! Oh! caſt them not on earth, to ſeek
For ſuccour from the faithleſs race of man;
But as thou art forſaken and alone,
Hope not for help, where there is none to help thee,
But think——'tis deſolation all about thee.
   Men. Far be that thought, to think you are forſaken;
Gods and good men ſhall make you ſtill their care.
And, Oh! far be it from your faithful ſervants,
For all thoſe honours mad ambition toils for,
For all the wealth that bribes the world to wickedneſs,
For hopes or fears, for pleaſures or for pains,
To leave our royal miſtreſs in diſtreſs.
   Eum. At length time's fulneſs comes, and that great
For which ſo many tedious years roll'd round;   [period,
At length the white, the ſmiling minute comes,
To wipe the tears from thoſe fair eyes for ever;
That good we daily pray'd for, but pray'd hopeleſs,
That good, which ev'n the preſcience of the gods
(So doubtfully was it ſet down in fate,)
Uncertainly foreſaw, and darkly promis'd,
   I

                                  That

That good, one day, the happiest of our lives,
Freely and fortunately brings to pass.
    Men. And hark! vindictive Jove prepares his thunder.
                                    [*Thunders.*

Let the wrong-doer and the tyrant tremble;
The gods are present with us——And behold!
The folid gloom of night is rent afunder,
While floods of dazzling, pure ætherial light,
Break in upon the fhades—She comes, fhe comes!
Pallas, the fautrefs of my mafter's arms.
And fee where terrible in arms, majeftic,.
Celeftial, and ineffably effulgent,
She fhakes her dreadful Ægis from the clouds!
Bend, bend to earth, and own the prefent deity.
                                    [*It thunders again.*

The SCENE *opens above, and difcovers* Pallas *in the Clouds.
                They kneel.*

    Eum. Daughter of mighty Jove, Tritonian Pallas,
Be favourable! Oh!——Oh! be propitious,
And fave the finking houfe of thy Ulyffes.
    Men. Goddefs of arts and arms, thou blue-ey'd maid,
Be favourable! Oh!—Oh! be propitious,
And glad thy fuppliants with fome chearful omen.
    Queen. Virgin, begot and born of Jove alone,
Chafte, wife, victorious, if by thy affiftance
The Greeks were well aveng'd on perjur'd Troy,
If by thy aid, my Lord from Thracian Rhefus
Obtain'd his fnowy fteeds, and brought fuccefsful
Thy fatal image to the tents of Greece;
Once more be favourable——be propitious,
Reftore my Lord——Or, if that be deny'd,
Grant me to fhare his fate, and die with honour.
            [*Thunder again—The Scene clofes above—They rife.*
    Men. The goddefs fmiles—Moft happy be the omen!
And to the left aufpicious rolls the thunder.

Enter Æthon, *or* Ulyffes, *without his difguife, magnifi-
            cently arm'd and habited.*

    Queen. What other god art thou?—Oh, facred form!
I dream, I rave!—Why put'ft thou on this femblance?,
                    D 2   What

What shall I call thee?——Say, speak, answer me.
   [*She advances two or three steps looking amazedly.*
Son of Laertes! King! My Lord!——Ulysses! ·
 Ulyss. Why dost thou gaze?—Am I so dreadful still?
Is there so much of Æthon still about me?
Or hast thou——is it possible——forgot me?
Does not thy heart acknowledge something here?
 Queen. Nay, 'tis, 'tis most impossible to reason.
But what have I to do with thought or reason?
Thus mad, distracted, raging with my joy,
I'll rush upon thee, clasp thee to my bosom,
And if it be delusion, let me die,
Here let me sink to everlasting rest,
Just here, and never never think again.
 Ulyss. No, live, thou great example of thy sex,
Live for the world, for me, and for thyself;
Unnumber'd blessings, honours, years of happiness,
Crowns from the gods, enrich'd with brightest stars,
All heav'n and earth united in applause,
Wait, with officious duty, to reward thee.
Live to enjoy ev'n all thou hast deserv'd,
That fulness of delight, of which these arms
And this transporting moment gives thee earnest.
 Queen. I gaze upon thy face, and see thee here.
The sullen pow'rs below, who rule the dead,
Have listen'd to my weeping, and relented,
Have sent thee from Elysium back to me;
Or from the deep, from sea-green Neptune's seats,
Thou'rt risen like the day-star; or from heav'n
Some god has brought thee on the wings of winds;
Oh, ecstasy!- -But all that I can know,
Is that I wake and live, and thou art here.
 Ulyss. Troy, I forgive thee now! Ye toils and perils
Of my past life, well are you paid at once.
For this the faithless Syrens sung in vain;
For this I 'scap'd the den of monstrous Polypheme,
Fled from Calypso's bonds and Circe's charms;
For this, seven days, and seven long winter nights,
Shipwreck'd I floated on a driving mast;
'Tost by the surge, pierc'd by the bitter blasts
Of bleak north-winds, and drench'd in the chill wave,
I strove with all the terrors of the deep.

          Queen.

Queen. Yes, thou haft borne it all, I know thou haft,
Thefe wars, winds, magic, monfters, all for me.
Bleft be the gracious gods that gave thee to me!
Say then! Oh, how fhall I reward thy labours?
But I will fit and liften to thy ftory,
While thou recount'ft it o'er; and when thou fpeak'ft
Of difficulties hard and near to death,
I'll pity thee, and anfwer with my tears;
But when thou com'ft to fay how the gods fav'd thee,
And how thy virtue ftruggled through the danger,
For joy, I'll fold thee thus with foft endearments,
And crown thy conqueft with ten thoufand kifles.

Ulyff. It is a heavy and a rueful tale,
But thou wilt kindly fhare with me in all things;
It fhall be told thee then, whate'er I fuffer'd,
Since, in a lucklefs hour, I firft fet out,
Ev'n to that time, when fcarce twice ten days paft,
As from Phæacia homeward bound to Ithaca,
A ftorm o'ertook and wreck'd me on the coaft;
Alone and naked was I caft a-fhore.
And only to thefe faithful two made known,
'Till Jove fhould point me out fome opportunity,
Once more to feize my right in thee and empire.

Men. 'Tis hard, injurious, an offence to virtue,
To interrupt your joys, ye royal pair;
But, Oh, forgive your faithful fervant's caution,
Think where you are, what eyes malicious chance
May bring to pry into the happy fecret,
Untimely to difclofe the fatal birth,
And rafhly bring it immature to light.

Ulyff. Mentor, thou warn'ft us well — Retire, my love.

Queen. What muft we part already?

Ulyff. For a moment,
Like waves divided by the gliding bark,
That meet again, and mingle as before.

Queen. Be fure it be not longer.

Ulyff. Sweet, it fha' not.
I'll meet thee foon, and bring our mutual blefling,
Our fon, t' increafe the joy.

Queen. I muft obey you.
Remember well how long thou haft been abfent,
And what a poor amends this fhort enjoyment makes me.

D 3

Oh,

Oh, I shall die with strong desire to thee,
Shall think this one impatient minute more,
Than all thy long, long twenty years before.   [*Exit.*

Enter at the other door Telemachus.

Tel. The Queen my mother, past she not this way?
Men. She did, my Lord, ev'n now.
Tel. Saw you not too
The Samian princess, fair Semanthe, with her?
Say; went they not together?
Ulyss. Might I speak,
I think it is not fit they were together;
For wherefore should the queen of Ithaca
Hold commerce with the daughter of Eurymachus?
Pardon me, Sir, I fear you are offended,
And think this boldness does not fit a stranger.
Tel. 'Tis true, thou art a stranger to my eyes;
And yet, methought, thou spok'st with Æthon's voice,
Save, that th'untoward purpose of thy words
Seem'd harsh, ungentle, and not like my friend.
Ulyss. Whate'er I seem, believe me, princely youth,
Thou hast not one, one dear selected mate,
That ought to stand before me in thy heart;
Though from your tender infancy till now,
He dwelt within thy bosom, thou in his,
Though every year has knit the band more close,
Though variance never knew you, but complying
Each ever yielded to the other's wishes,
Though you have toil'd and rested, laugh'd and mourn'd,
And ran through every part of life together,
Though he was all thy joy, and thou all his,
Yet sure he never lov'd thee more than I do.
Tel. Whoe'er thou art (for though thou still art Æthon,
Thou art not he, but something more and greater)
I feel the force of every word thou speak'st,
My soul is aw'd with reverential fear,
A fear not irksome, for 'tis mix'd with love,
Ev'n such a fear as that we worship Heav'n with;
Oh, pardon if I err, for if thou art not
Æthon, my father's friend, thou art some god.
Ulyss. If barely to have been thy father's friend
Could move thee to such tender, just regards,

Thus,

Thus, let me thus indulge thy filial virtue,
[Embracing him.
Thus prefs thee in my arms, my pious fon,
And while my fwelling heart runs o'er with joy,
Thus tell thee that I am, I am thy father.
 Tel. Oh, moft amazing!——
 Men. Yes, my royal charge,
At length behold thy god-like fire, Ulyffes.
Bleft be my age, with all its cares and forrows,
Since it is lengthen'd out to fee this day,
To give thee back, thou dear entrufted pledge,
Thus worthy as thou art, to thy great father's arms.
 Tel. Oh, 'tis moft certain fo, my heart confeffes him,
My blood and fpirits, all the pow'rs of life,
Acknowledge here the fpring from whence they came.
Then let me bow me, caft me at his feet,
There pay the humble homage of my duty,
There wet the earth before him with my tears,
The faithful witneffes of love and joy:
And when my tongue for rapture can no more,
Silent, with lifted eyes, I'll praife the gods,
Who gave me back my King, my Lord, my father.
 Ulyff. Oh, rife, thou offspring of my nuptial joys,
Son of my youth, and glory of my ftrength,
Rob not thy father's arms of fo much treafure,
But let us meet, as Jove and Nature meant us,
Thus, like a pair of very faithful friends;
And though I made harfh mention of thy love,
(Oh, droop not at the name) by blue-ey'd Pallas
I meant it not in angry, chiding mood;
But with a tender and a fond concern,
Reminded thee of what thou ow'ft to honour.
 Tel. When I forget it, may the worft afflictions,
Your fcorn, your hate, and infamy o'ertake me;
Be that th'important bus'nefs of my life,
Let me be tafk'd to hunt for it through danger,
Through all the roar of the tumultuous battle,
And dreadful din of arms; there, if I fail,
May cowards fay I'm not Ulyffes' fon,
And the great author of our race difclaim me.
 Ulyff. Oh, noblenefs innate! Oh, worth divine!
Æthereal fparks! that fpeak the hero's lineage,

How

How are you pleasing to me ?——So the eagle,
That bears the thunder of our grandsire Jove,
With joy beholds his hardy youthful offspring
Forsake the nest, to try his tender pinions,
In the wide untract air ; till bolder grown,
Now, like a whirlwind, on the shepherd's fold
He darts precipitate, and gripes the prey ;
Or fixing on some dragon's scaly hide,
Eager of combat, and his future feast,
Bears him aloft, reluctant, and in vain
Writhing his spiry tail.
   Tel. I would be active,
Get me a name distinguish'd from the herd
Of common men, a name worthy my birth.
   Ulyss. Nor shalt thou want th'occasion ; now it courts
Stands ready, and demands thy courage now.   ·[thee,
Were I indeed as other fathers are ;
Did I but listen to soft Nature's voice,
I should not urge thee to this high exploit,
For though it brings thee fame, it brings thee danger.
   Tel. Now by the god of war, so much the better :
Let there be honour for your son to win,
And be the danger ne'er so rude and deadly,
No matter, 'twill enhance the prize the more,
And make it lovely in a brave man's eye ;
So Hydra's and Chimera's form'd in gold,
Sit graceful underneath the nodding plume,
And terribly adorn the soldier's helm.
   Ulyss. Know then, on this important night depends
The very crisis of our fate ; to-night
That sleeping vengeance of the gods shall wake,
And speak confusion to our foes in thunder :
Justice entrusts her sword to this right hand,
And I will see it faithfully employ'd.
   Tel. By virtue and by arms 'tis noble work !
I burn impatient for it——Oh, my father,
Give me my portion of the glorious labour.
   Ulyss. Once more immediate danger threats thy mother,
That to avert, must be thy pious care.
While Mentor, with Eumæus and ourself,
Back'd by a chosen band, (whom how prepar'd,
How gather'd to our aid, the pressing hour

Allows

Allows not now tell) invade yon drunkards,
Immerſt in riot, careleſs, and defying
The gods as fables, ſtart upon them ſudden,
And ſend their guilty ſouls to howl below,
Upon the banks of Styx : while this is doing,
Dar'ſt thou defend thy mother?

 Tel. Oh! to death,
Againſt united nations would I ſtand
Her ſoldier, her defence, my ſingle breaſt
Oppos'd againſt the rage of their whole war;
She is ſo good, ſo worthy to be fought for,
The ſacred cauſe would make my ſword ſucceſsful,
And gain my youth a mighty name in arms.

 Ulyſſ. Then prove the peril, and enjoy the fame.
Ere the mid-hour of rolling night approach,
Remember well to plant thee at that door,
Thou know'ſt it opens to the Queen's apartment.
To bind thee yet more firm ; for, Oh, my ſon !
           [Drawing his ſword.
With powerful oppoſition ſhalt thou ſtrive,
Swear on my ſword, by thy own filial piety,
By all our race, by Pallas and by Jove,
If any of theſe curſed foreign tyrants,
Thoſe rivels of thy father's love and honour,
Shall dare to paſs through that forbidden entrance,
To take his forfeit life for the intruſion.

 Tel. I ſwear——And may my lot in future fame
     [Telemachus kneels and kiſſes the ſword.
Be good or evil but as I perform it.

 Ulyſſ. Enough——I do believe thee.

 Men. Hark ! my Lord !
       [A confuſed noiſe is heard within.
How loud the tempeſt roars ! The bellowing voice
Of wild, enthuſiaſtic, raging mirth,
With peals of clamour ſhakes the vaulted roof.

 Tel. Such ſurely is the ſound of mighty armies
In battle join'd, of cities ſack'd at midnight,
Of many waters, and united thunders ;
My gen'rous ſoul takes fire, and half repines,
To think ſhe muſt not ſhare the glorious danger,
Where numbers wait you, worthy of your ſwords.

 Ulyſſ. No more, thou haſt thy charge, look well to that ;
               For

For thefe, thefe riotous fons of noife and uproar,
I know their force, and know I am Ulyffes.
So Jove look'd down upon the war of atoms,
And rude tumultuous chaos, when as yet
Fair nature, form, and order had not being,
But difcord and confufion troubled all ;
Calm and ferene upon his throne he fate,
Fix'd there by the eternal law of fate,
Safe in himfelf, becaufe he knew his pow'r ;
And knowing what he was, he knew he was fecure.
                                            [*Exeunt.*

END of the THIRD ACT.

A C T   IV.

Enter Telemachus *and* Atinous.

ANTINOUS.

THE king return'd ? So long conceal'd in Ithaca ?
    Æthon the king ? What words can fpeak my won-
Tel. Yes, my Antinous, 'tis moft amazing,   [der ?
'Tis all the mighty working of the gods ;
Unfearchable and dark to human eyes :
But, Oh, let me conjure thee by our friendfhip,
Since to thy faithful breaft alone I've trufted
The fatal fecret, to preferve it fafe,
As thou wouldft do the life of thy Telemachus.
    Ant. Wrong not the truth of your devoted flave,
To think he would betray you for whole worlds.
Have you not faid it, that your own dear life,
And all your royal race, depends upon it ?
Far from my lips, within my breaft I'll keep it ;
Nor breathe it foftly to myfelf alone,
Left fome officious murmuring wind fhould tell it,
And babbling echoes catch the feeble found.
    Tel. No, thou art true, fuch have I ever found thee ;
But hafte, my friend, and fummon to thy aid
What force the fhortnefs of the time allows thee ;
Then with thy fwifteft diligence return,
Since as I urg'd to thee before, it may
Import the fafety of my royal parents.

                                            Some

Some black defign is by thefe ftranger-princes
Contriv'd againft the honour of the Queen.

Ant. Ere night a bufy rumour ran around,
Of armed parties fecretly difpos'd
Between the palace-gardens and the fea ;
Bold Cleon ftraight, and Arcas I difpatch'd
To fearch the truth, that known, with hafte to raife
And arm our citizens for your defence :
Ere this they have obey'd me ; when I've join'd
The pow'r their diligence has drawn together,
I'll wait you here again upon the inftant.   [*Exit.*

Tel. Oh, love ! how are thy precious fweeteft minutes
Thus ever crofs'd, thus vex'd with difappointments !
Now pride, now ficklenefs, fantaftic quarrels,
And fudden coldnefs, give us pain by turns ;
Malicious meddling chance is ever bufy
To bring us fears, difquiet, and delays ;
And ev'n at laft, when after all our waiting,
Eager, we think to fnatch the dear-bought blifs,
Ambition calls us to its fullen cares,
And honour ftern, impatient of neglect,
Commands us to forget our eafe and pleafures,
As if we had been made for nought but toil,
And love were not the bus'nefs of our lives.

Enter Eurymachus.

Eur. The Prince yet here ! Twice have I fought, fince
To pafs in private to the Queen's apartment,   [night,
But found him ftill attending at the door.
What can it mean ?

Tel. It is Semanthe's father !
Ha !—Sure the gods, in pity of our loves,
Have deftin'd him to 'fcape Ulyffes' vengeance.

Eur. How comes it, gentle youth when wine and mirth
Cheer ev'ry heart to-night, and banifh care,
I find thee penfively alone, avoiding
The pleafures and companions of thy youth,
And, like the fighing flave of forrow, wafting
The tedious time in melancholy thought ?

Tel. Behold the ruins of my royal houfe,
My father's abfence, and my mother's grief,
Then tell me if I have not caufe too great
To mourn, to pine away my youth in fadnefs ?

Eur.

Eur. Our daughter once was wont to fhare your
Believe me, fhe has reafon to complain, [thoughts;
If you prefer your folitude to her.
While here you ftay, difconfolate and mufing,
Lonely fhe fits, the tender-hearted maid,
And kindly thinks of you, and mourns your abfence.

 Tel. The conftant, faithful fervice of my life,
My days and nights devoted all to her,
Poorly repay the fair Semanthe's goodnefs: -
Yet they are hers, ev'n all my years are hers,
My prefent youth, my future age, is hers, .
All but this night, which here I've fworn to pafs,
Revolving many a fad and heavy thought, .
And ruminating on my wretched fortunes.

 Eur. How, here!—to pafs it here!

 Tel. Ev'n here, my Lord.

 Eur. Fantaftic accident!—Whence could this come?
[*Afide.*

Well, Sir, purfue your thoughts. I have fome matters
Of great and high import, which, on the inftant,
I muft deliver to the Queen, your mother.

 Tel. Whate'er it be, you muft of force delay it
Till morning.

 Eur. How, delay it!—'Tis impoffible.
But wherefore?——Say.

 Tel. The Queen is gone to reft,
Opprefs'd and wafted with the toil of forrows,
Weary as miferable painful hinds,
That labour all the day to get them food,
She feeks fome eafe, fome interval of cares,
From the kind god of fleep, and fweet repofe.
Ere fhe retir'd fhe left moft ftrict command,
None fhould approach her till the morning's dawn.

 Eur. Whate'er thofe orders were, I have my reafons
To think myfelf excepted. And whoe'er
Brought you the meffage, thro' officious hafte,
Miftook the Queen, and has inform'd you wrong.

 Tel. Not fo, my Lord; for, as I honour truth,
Ev'n from herfelf did I receive the charge.

 Eur. Vexation and delay!—Then 'tis thy own,
Thy error, and thou heard'ft not what fhe faid.
I tell thee, Prince, 'tis at her own requeft,

Her

Her bidding, that at this appointed hour
I wait her here.   Detain me then no more
With tedious vain replies : for I muſt paſs.
  Tel. Were it to any but Semanthe's father,
That miſtreſs of my reaſon and my paſſions,
Who, charming both, makes both ſubmit alike,
Perhaps I ſhould in rougher terms have anſwer'd ;
But here imperious love demands reſpect,
Conſtrains my temper, to my ſpeech gives law,
And I muſt only ſay, You cannot paſs.
  Eur. Ha !—Who ſhall bar me ?
  Tel. With the gentleſt words
Which reverence and duty can invent,
I will intreat you not to do a violence,
Where nought is meant to you but worthieſt honour.
  Eur. Oh, trifling, idle talker !—Know, my purpoſe
Is not of ſuch a light, fantaſtic nature,
That I ſhould quit it for a boy's intreaty.
More than my life or empire it imports,
All that good fortune or the gods can do for me,
Depends upon it, and I will have entrance.
  Tel. Nay, then 'tis time to ſpeak like what I am,
And tell you, Sir, you muſt not, nor you ſha' not.
  Eur. 'Twere ſafer for thy raſh, unthinking youth
To ſtand the mark of thunder, than to thwart me.
Beware, leſt I forget thy mother's tears,
The merit of her ſoft complying ſorrows,
Dreadful in fury leſt I ruſh upon thee,
Graſp thy frail life, and break it like a bubble,
To be diſſolv'd, and mix'd with common air.
  Tel. Oh, 'tis long ſince that I have learnt to hold
My life from none, but from the gods who gave it ;
Nor mean to render it on any terms,
Unleſs thoſe heav'nly donors aſk it back.
  Eur. Know'ſt thou what 'tis to tempt a rage like mine ?
But liſten to me, and repent thy folly,
This night, this night, ordain'd of old for bliſs,
Mark'd from the reſt of the revolving year,
And ſet apart for happineſs by fate,
The charming Queen, thy mother, is my bride.
  Tel. Confuſion ! Curſes on the tongue that ſpoke it !
  Eur. To-night ſhe yields, ev'n for thy ſake ſhe yields :
E

To-night

The bulk of kingdoms, nay, the world is light,
When guilt weighs oppofite.   Oh, would to Heav'n,
The lofs of empire would reftore his innocence,
Reftore the fortunes, and the precious lives
Of thoufands, fall'n the victims of ambition !

     Enter Laertes.

Ha, Laertes ! moft welcome—Well, and have you ? Say,
 Laer. O, royal maid !——   [Laertes——
 Criftina. Thy looks are doubtful.   Speak——
Why art thou filent ? Does he live ?
 Laer. He does:
But death, ere night, muft fill a long account.
The camp, the country's in confufion ; war
And changes ride upon the hour that haftes
To intercept my tongue——I elfe could tell
Of virtues hitherto beyond my ken ;
Courage, to which the lion ftoops his creft,
Yet grafted upon qualities as foft
As a rock'd infant's meeknefs ; fuch as tempts
Againft my faith, my country, and allegiance,
To wifh thee fpeed, Guftavus.
 Criftina. Then you found him.
 Laer. I did ; and warn'd him ; but in vain ; for death
To him appear'd more grateful than to find
His friend's difhonour.   [Laertes !
 Criftina. Give me the manner—quick——foft, good

  Enter Criftiern, Trollio, Peterfon, Danes, &c.

 Crift. Damn'd, double traitor! Oh, curs'd, falfe Arvida!
Guard well the Swedifh pris'ners; bind them hard.
Stand to your arms.   Bring forth the captives there.
   Enter Augufta *and* Guftava *guarded.*
 Trol. My liege————
 Crift. Away ! I'll hear no more of politics.
Fortune ! we will not truft the changeling more,
But wear her girt upon our armed loins,
Or pointed in our grafp.
    Enter an Officer.
 Off. The foe's at hand.
With gallant fhew your thoufand Danes rode forth,
But fhall return no more.   I mark'd the action ;
A band of defp'rate refolutes rufh'd on them,

          Scarce

Scarce numb'ring to a tenth, and in mid way
They clos'd; the fhock was dreadful, nor your Danes
Could bear the madding charge; a while they ftood,
Then fhrunk, and broke, and turn'd; when, lo, behind,
Faft wheeling from the right and left there pour'd,
Who intercepted their return, and, caught
Within the toil, they perifh'd.
    Crift. 'Tis Guftavus!
No mortal elfe, not Ammon's boafted fon,
Not Cæfar would have dar'd it.   Tell me, fay,
What numbers in the whole may they amount to?
    Off. About five thoufand.
    Crift. And no more?
    Off. No more,
That yet appear.
    Crift. We count fix times their fum.
Hafte, foldier, take a trumpet; tell Guftavus,
We have of terms to offer, and would treat
Touching his mother's ranfom; fay, her death,
Sufpended by our grace, but waits his anfwer.   [*Exit Off.*
Madam, it fhould well fuit with your authority [*To Aguf.*
To check this frenzy in your fon.   Look to it,
Or, by the faints, this hour's your laft of life.
    Auguf. Come, my Guftava; comé, my little captive;
We fhall be free; our tyrant is grown kind;
And for thefe chains that bind thy pretty arms,
The golden cherubim fhall lend thee wings,
And thou fhalt mount amid the fmiling choir
Of little heav'nly fongfters, like thyfelf,
All rob'd in innocence.
    Guftava. Will you go, mother?
    Auguf. So help me, mercy! Yes, I'll go, my child;
And I will give thee to thy father's fondnefs,
And to the arms of all thy royal race
In heav'n, who fit on thrones, with loves, and joys,
And pleafures fmiling round.
    Crift. Is this my anfwer?
Come forth, ye minifters of death, come forth.

    Enter Ruffians, who feize Augufta *and* Guftava.

Pluck them afunder.   We fhall prove you, lady.
'Tis my damn'd lot, thus ever to be crofs'd
With rank blown pride, and infolence eternal.
E 2

Guftava.

Sem. What says my father?—No—it is impossible!
He could not, would not—for Semanthe's sake.

Enter Telemachus.

Tel. Alas! there is none near; no help—Semanthe!
                                        [*Crying out.*

Eur. And see, he bears the trophy of his conquest;
Behold his sword yet reeking with my blood;
Then doubt no more, nor ask whom thou shouldst curse;
It is Telemachus; on whom revenge me,
But on Telemachus?—Why do I leave thee
A helpless orphan in a foreign land,
But for Telemachus?——Who tears thee from me?
Telemachus.   Why is thy king and father
Stretch'd on the earth a cold and lifeless corse,
Inglorious and forgotten?—Oh, Telemachus!   [*Dies.*

Sem. Cruel!—unkind and cruel!——

      [*She faints, and falls upon the body of* Eurymachus.

Tel. She faints!
Her cheeks are cold, and the last leaden sleep
Hangs heavy on her lids——Wake, wake, Semanthe!
Oh, let me raise thee from this seat of death!

          [*Raising her up, and supporting her in his arms.*

Lift up thy eyes.   Wilt thou not speak to me?

Sem. Let me forget the use of ev'ry sense,
Let me not see, nor hear, nor speak again,
After that sight, and those most dreadful sounds.
Where am I now? What, lodg'd within thy arms!
Stand off, and let me fly from thee for ever,
Swifter than lightning, winds, or winged time;
Fly from thee till there be whole worlds to part us,
Till Nature fix her barriers to divide us,
Her frozen regions, and her burning zones,
Till danger, death and hell do stand betwixt us,
And make it fate that we shall never meet.

Tel. 'Tis just, I own thy rage is just, Semanthe;
Each fatal circumstance is strong against me.
Then if thy heart severely is resolv'd
Never to listen when I plead for mercy,
Tho' piety and honour join with love,
And humbly at thy feet make intercession,
If thou art deaf to all, then this alone
Is left me, to receive my doom, and die.

                                        Sem.

Sem. Are love, are piety, and honour, parricides?
Are they like thee? Do they delight in blood?
Oh, no! celeſtial ſweetneſs dwells with them,
Friendly forgiveneſs, gentleneſs and peace,
Mercy and joy; but thou haſt violated
The ſacred train, brought murder in amongſt them;
And ſee, diſpleas'd, to heav'n they take their flight,
And have abandon'd thee and me for ever.

Tel. If ſudden fury have not chang'd thee quite,
If there be any of Semanthe left,
One tender thought of that dear maid remaining,
Yet, I conjure thee, hear me.

Sem. 'Tis in vain;
And that known voice can never charm me more.

Tel. Be witneſs for me, Heav'n, with what reluctance
My hand was lifted for this fatal ſtroke.
With injuries which manhood could not brook,
With violence, with proud inſulting ſcorn,
And ignominious threat'nings, was I urg'd;
Long, long I ſtrove with riſing indignation,
And long repreſs'd my ſwelling, youthful rage;
I groan'd, and felt an agony within:
'Twas hard indeed; but to myſelf I ſaid,
It is Semanthe's father, and I'll bear it.   [ſufferings?

Sem. And couldſt thou do no more? Call'ſt thou theſe
Theſe ſhort, tumultuous, momentary paſſions?
What would not I have borne for thee, thou cruel one?
For thee; ſo fondly was my heart ſet on thee,
Forgetful of my tender, helpleſs ſex,
I would have wander'd over the wide world,
Known all calamities and all diſtreſſes,
Sickneſs and hunger, cold and bitter want;
For thee retir'd within ſome gloomy cave,
I would have waſted all my days in weeping,
And liv'd and dy'd a wretch, to make thee happy;
'Till I had been a ſtory to poſterity,
Till maids, in after-times, had ſaid, behold
How much ſhe ſuffer'd for the man ſhe lov'd.

Tel. And is there any one, the moſt afflicting
Of all thoſe miſeries mankind is born to,
Which for thy ſake I would refuſe?——But, Oh,
Mine was a harder, a ſeverer taſk!

E 3

The

The Queen, my mother, trufted to my charge,
My royal father's honour, and my own,
The pledges of eternal fame, or infamy,
United urg'd, and call'd upon my fword.
  Sem. What is this vain, fantaftic pageant, honour,
This bufy, angry thing, that fcatters difcord
Amongft the mighty princes of the earth,
And fets the madding nations in an uproar?
But let it be the worfhip of the great;
Well haft thou warn'd me, and I'll make it mine:
Yes, Prince, its dread command fhall be obey'd;
Our Samian arms fhall pour deftruction on you,
Your yellow harvefts and your towns fhall blaze,
The fword fhall rage, and univerfal wailings
Be heard amongft the mothers of your Ithaca,
Till war itfelf grow weary, and relent,
And that poor bleeding King be well reveng'd.
  Tel. Hafte then, and let the trumpet found to arms,
Semanthe's vengeance fhall not be delay'd;
Prepare for flaughter and wide-wafting ruin,
Prepare to feel her wrath, ye wretched Ithacans!
Lift not a fword, nor bend a bow againft her,
But all, like me, with low fubmiffion meet her,
And let us yield up our devoted lives,
Nor once implore her mercy; for, alas!
Cruel Semanthe has forgot to pardon:
For blood, deftruction, and revenge fhe calls,
And gentlenefs and love are ftrangers to her.   [thought!
  Sem. Love! didft thou fpeak of love?—Oh, ill-tim'd
Behold it there! behold the love thou bear'ft me!
                    [*Pointing to the body of* Eurymachus.
Behold that, that!—more dreadful than Medufa;
It drives my foul back to her inmoft feats,
And freezes ev'ry ftiff'ning limb to marble.
Seeft thou that gaping wound, and that black blood
Congealing on that pale, that afhy breaft?
Then mark the face—how pain and rage, with all
The agonies of death, fit frefh upon it.
This was my father——Was there none on earth,
No hand but thine?————
  Tel. Within my own fad heart
I felt the fteel, before it reach'd to his.

How

How much more happy is his lot ? The sleep
Of death is on him, and he is in peace ;
While I, condemn'd to live, must mourn for him,
Mourn for myself, and, to compleat my woes,
Feel all thy pains redoubled on Telemachus.
  Sem. I know thou hat'st me, and that deadly blow
Was meant to do a murder on Semanthe.
But, Oh, it needed not ! for thy unkindness
Had been as fatal to me as thy sword.
If one cold look, one angry word, had told me
That thou wert chang'd, and I was grown a burthen to
I should have understood thy cruel purpose,   [thee,
Sat down to weep, and broke my heart, and dy'd.
  Tel. It is too much, and I will bear no more.
Oh, thou unjust, thou lovely false accuser !
How hast thou wrong'd my tender, faithful love !
In spite of all these horrors of my guilt,
And that malignant fate that doom'd me to it,
In spite of all, I will appeal to thee,
Ev'n to thyself, inhuman as thou art,
If ever maid was yet belov'd before thee,
With such heart-aching, eager, anxious fondness,
As that with which my soul desires my dear Semanthe ?
  Sem. Detested be the name of love for ever !
Henceforth let easy maids be warn'd by me,
No more to trust your breasts that heave with sighing,
Your moving accents, and your melting eyes ;
Whene'er you boast your truth, then let them fly you,
Then scorn you, for 'tis then you mean deceiving :
If yet there should some fond believer be,
Let the false man betray the wretch, like thee;
Like thee, the lost, repenting fool disclaim,
For crowns, ambition, and your idol, fame ;
When warm, when languishing with sweet delight, }
Wishing she meets him, may he blast her sight   }
With such a murder, on her bridal night.   [*Exit.*]
  Tel. Now arm thee for the conflict, Oh, my soul !
And see how thou canst bear Semanthe's loss ;
For she is lost—most certain—gone irrevocable.
Mentor nor Æthon now, my king, my father,
Shall need t' upbraid me with th' unhappy passion——
Ha ! that has wak'd a thought——'Tis certain so ;

And this is all the work of cruel policy.
The danger of the Queen was from Eurymachus,
Therefore my fword was chofen to oppofe it,
That it might cut the bands of love afunder.
Oh, dreamer that I was!

Enter Antinous, Cleon, *and* Arcas *with Soldiers.*

Ant. My Lord, where are you?
Thus to his fon, our King, the great Ulyffes,
By me commands! Your royal mother's danger
Is now no more, fince all the rival princes
Are in the hall befet, and ev'n this moment
Revenge and flaughter are let loofe among them:
Hafte then to join your godlike father's arms,
To bring your pious valour to his aid,
And fhare the conqueft and the glory with him.
Tel. Ha! com'ft thou from the hall, Antinous?
Ant. Ev'n now, my Lord. As I was hafting hither,
It was my chance to meet my royal mafter;
Eager with joy, I threw me at his feet,
With wond'rous grace he rais'd me and embrac'd me,
Then bid me fly to bear his orders to you.
By the loud cries, the fhouts, and clafh of arms,
Which, juft as I had left him, ftruck my ear,
I guefs ere this the combat is begun.
Tel. Yes, yes, my friend, that danger of the Queen
Is now no more. However, be thou near,
To guard her, to fupport her, left the terrors
Of this tumultuous, this moft dreadful night,
May fhake her foul. I will obey the King,
And gladly lofe the life he gave me, for him.
And fince the pleafure of my days is loft,
Since my youth's deareft, only hopes are crofs'd,
Carelefs of all, I'll rufh into the war,
Provoke the lifted fword, and pointed fpear,
Till, all o'er wounds, I fink amidft the flain,
And blefs the friendly hand that rids me of my pain.
[*Exit* Tel.

Cleon. Behold, my Lord, and wonder here with us;
The Samian King——
Ant. Eurymachus!——'Tis he.
Surprifing accident!—Whence came this blow?

But

But 'tis no matter, fince it makes for us,
Nor have we time to wafte in vain enquiry ;
Let it fuffice that we have loft au enemy.
Hafte to the Queen, my Cleon, and perfuade her
To feek her fafety with us in the city :
If fhe refufe, bear her away by force.
Do you attend him.   [*To the Soldiers.*

   Arc. Had you ta'en my counfel,
The Prince fhould not have 'fcap'd us.
   Ant. Arcas, no !
A life like his is but a fingle ftake,
Unworthy the contention it might coft.
Gaining the Queen, I have whate'er I wifh.
Fear of the Samians and the fubtle King,
Forbade my coming with a ftronger power,
Left they had ta'en th' alarm, and turn'd upon us :
Therefore I held it fafer by a wile
To work upon the youth, and fend him hence,
And that way gain admittance to his mother.
   Arc. Our Ithacans, who give the King for loft,
Shall deem this tale of his return a fable ;
Or tho' they fhould believe it, yet will join us,
And with united arms affift our caufe.
Why do we linger then ?—Heard you that cry ?
                     [*Cry of women within.*
Succefsful Cleon, of his prey poffefs'd,
Leads us the way, and haftens to the city.
   Ant. Come on, and let the crafty fam'd Ulyffes
Repine and rage, by happier frauds excell'd.
Let the forfaken hufband vainly mourn
His tedious labours, and his late return ;
In vain to Pallas and to Jove complain,
That Troy and Hector are reviv'd again.
Poffefs'd, like happy Paris, of the fair,
I'll lengthen out my joys with ten years war, }
And think the reft of life beneath a lover's care. }
                     [*Exeunt.*

END of the FOURTH ACT.

ACT

A C T V.

SCENE, *the City.*

Enter severally Mentor *and* Eumæus.

EUMÆUS.

WHERE is the joy, the boast of conquest now ?
    In vain we triumph o'er our foreign tyrants,
So soon to perish by domestic foes.
Why shone the great Ulysses dreadful, fierce
As Mars, and mighty as Phlegræan Jove ?
Why reeks yon marble pavement with the slaughter
Of rival kings, that fell beneath his sword,
Victims to injur'd honour and revenge,
Since, by the fatal error of Telemachus,
The prize for which we fought, the Queen, is lost,
Is yielded up a prey to false Antinous ?

   Men. He trusted in the holy name of friendship,
And, conscious of his own uprightness, thought
The man whom he had plac'd so near his heart
Had shar'd as well his virtues as his love.

   Eum. How bears the Prince this chance ?

   Men. Alas, Eumæus !
His griefs have rent my aged heart asunder.
Stretch'd on the damp unwholsome earth he lies,
Nor had my pray'rs or tears the power to raise him ;
Now motionless as death his eyes are fix'd,
And then anon he starts and casts them upwards,
And groaning, cries, I am th' accurs'd of Heav'n.
My mother ! my Semanthe, and my mother !

   Eum. The King, whose equal temper, like the gods,
Was ever calm and constant to itself,
Struck with the sudden, unexpected evil,
Was mov'd to rage, and chid him from his sight.
But now returning to the father's fondness,
He bade me seek him out, speak comfort to him,
And bring him to his arms.

   Men. Where have you left
Our royal master ?

   Eum. Near the palace gate,
Attended by those few, those faithful few,

Who

Who dare be loyal at a time like this,
When ev'n their utmoſt hope is but to die for him.
  Men. That laſt relief, that refuge of deſpair,
Is all I fear is left us——From the city,
Each moment brings the growing danger nearer;
There's not a man in Ithaca but arms;
A thouſand blazing fires make bright the ſtreets,
Huge gabbling crowds gather, and roll along,
Like roaring ſeas that enter at a breach;
The neighb'ring rocks, the woods, the hills, the dales,
Ring with the deaf'ning ſound, while bold rebellion
With impious peals of acclamation greets
Her trait'rous chief, Antinous——Where is then
One glimpſe of ſafety, when we hardly number
Our friends a twentieth part of this fierce multitude?
  Eum. Yet more, the Samians, by whoſe arms aſſiſted
We late prevail'd againſt the riotous wooers,
By ſome ſiniſter chance have learnt the fate
Of their dead monarch, and call loud for vengeance:
With cloudy brows the ſullen captains gather
In murm'ring crowds around their weeping princeſs,
As if they waited from her mournful lips
The ſignal for deſtruction; from her ſorrows
Catching new matter to encreaſe their rage,
And vowing to repay her tears with blood.
But ſee, ſhe comes, attended with her guard.
  Men. Retire, and let us haſte to ſeek the Prince;
This danger threatens him.   If he ſhould meet them,
His piety would be repaid with death,
Nor could his youth or godlike courage ſave him,
Unequally oppreſs'd, and cruſh'd by numbers.
                          [*Exeunt* Mentor *and* Eumæus.

*Enter two Samian Captains and Soldiers, ſome bearing the
    body of* Eurymachus; Semanthe *following with Officers
    and Attendants.*

  Sem. Ye valiant Samian chiefs, ye faithful followers
Of your unhappy king, juſtly perform
Your pious office to his ſacred relics;
Bear to your fleet his pale, his bloody corſe,
Nor let his diſcontented ghoſt repine,

To think his injur'd afhes fhall be mix'd
With the detefted earth of cruel Ithaca.   [thee,
     1 *Capt.* Oh, royal maid ! whofe tears look lovely on
Whofe cares the gods fhall favour and reward,
Queen of our Samos now, to whom we offer
Our humble homage, to whofe juft command
We vow obedience, fuffer not the feaman
T' unfurl his fails, or call the winds to fwell them,
Till the fierce foldier have indulg'd his rage,
Till from the curled darlings of their youth,
And from the faireft of their virgin daughters,
We've chofe a thoufand victims for a facrifice,
T' appeafe the manes of our murder'd lord.   [d'rer ?
     Sem. Now, now, Semanthe, wilt thou name the mur-
Wilt thou direct their vengeance where to ftrike ? [*Afide.*
Oh, my fad heart !——Hafte to difpofe in fafety
Your venerable load ; and if you lov'd him,
If you remember what he once was to you,
How great, how good and gracious, yield this proof
Of early faith and duty to his daughter,
Reftrain the foldiers' fury, till I name
The wretch by whom my royal father fell.
Let fome attend the body to the fhore,
The reft be near and wait me.
     [*Exeunt fome with the body ; the reft retire within the
       fcene, and wait as at a diftance.*

          Enter at the other door Telemachus.

     Tel. Why was I born ? Why fent into the world,
Ordain'd for mifchievous mifdeeds, and fated
To be the curfe of them that gave me being ?
Why was this mafs ta'en from the heap of matter,
Where innocent and fenfelefs it had refted,
To be indu'd with form, and vex'd with motion ?
How happy had it been for all that know me,
If barrennefs had blefs'd my mother's bed !
Nor had fhe been difhonour'd then, nor loft,
Nor curs'd the fatal hour in which fhe bore me :
Love had not been offended for Semanthe,
Nor had that fair-one known a father's lofs.
     Sem. What kind companion of Semanthe's woes
Is that, who, wand'ring in this dreadful night,

                        I   Sighs

Sighs out her name with such a mournful accent ?
Ha !——but thou art Telemachus——Let darkness
Still spread her gloomy mantle o'er thy visage,
And hide thee from these weeping eyes for ever.

   Tel. Yes, veil thy eyes, or turn them far from me;
For who can take delight to gaze on misery ?
Fly from the moan, the cry of the afflicted,
From the complaining of a wounded spirit,
Lest my contagious griefs take hold on thee,
And ev'ry groan I utter pierce thy heart.

   Sem. Oh, soft enchanting sorrows ! Never was
The voice of mourning half so sweet—Oh, who
Can listen to the sound, and not be mov'd,
Nor bear a part, like me, and share in all his pain? [*Aside.*

   Tel. But if perhaps thy fellow-creature's sufferings
Are grown a pleasure to thee, (for, alas !
Much art thou alter'd) then in me behold
More than enough to satisfy thy cruelty ;
Behold me here the scorn, the easy prize,
Of a protesting, faithless, villain friend.
I have betray'd my mother, I betray'd her,
Ev'n I, her son, whom with so many cares
She nurs'd and fondled in her tender bosom.
Would I had dy'd before I saw this day !
I left her, I forsook her in distress,
And gave her to the mercy of a ravisher.

   Sem. Yes, I have heard, with grief of mind redoubled,
The too hard fortune of the pious Queen ;
For her my eyes enlarge and swell their streams,
Tho' well thou know'st what cause they had before
To lavish all their tears.   I pity her,
I mourn her injur'd virtue : but for thee,
Whate'er the righteous gods have made thee suffer,
Just is the doom, and equal to thy crimes.

   Tel. 'Tis justice all, and see I bow me down
With patience and submission to the blow ;
Nor is it fit that such a wretch as I am
Should walk with face erect upon the earth,
And hold society with man — Oh, therefore
Let me conjure thee by those tender ties
Which held us once, when I was dear to thee,
And thou to me, as life to living creatures,

F

Or

Or light and heat to univerſal nature,
The comfort and condition of its being,
Complete th' imperfect vengeance of the gods,
Call forth the valiant Samians to thy aid,
Bid them ſtrike here, and here revenge——
　　Sem. Oh, hold!
Stay thy raſh tongue, nor let it ſpeak of horrors
'That may be fatal to——
　　Tel. What mean'ſt thou?
　　Sem. Something
For which I want a name——Is there none near?
No conſcious ear to catch the guilty ſound?
None to upbraid my weakneſs, call me parricide,
And charge me as conſenting to the murder?
For, Oh, my ſhame, my ſhame! I muſt confeſs it,
Tho' piety and honour urg'd me on,
Tho' rage and grief had wrought me to diſtraction,
I durſt not, could not, would not once accuſe thee.
　　Tel. And wherefore art thou merciful in vain?
Oh, do not load me with that burthen, life,
Unleſs thou give me love, to cheer my labours.
Tell me, Semanthe, is it, is it thus　　　　　　[ing,
The bride and bridegroom meet? Are tears and mourn-
This bitterneſs of grief, and theſe lamentings,
Are theſe the portion of our nuptial night?
　　Sem. But thou, thou only didſt prevent the joy,
'Tis thou haſt turn'd the bleſſing to a curſe:
Live, therefore, live, and be, if it be poſſible,
As great a wretch as thou haſt made Semanthe.
　　Tel. It ſhall be ſo; I will be faithful to thee,
For days, for months, for years, I will be miſerable,
Protract my ſuff'rings ev'n to hoary age,
And linger out a tedious life in pain;
In ſpite of ſickneſs and a broken heart,
I will endure for ages to obey thee.
　　Sem. Oh, never ſhalt thou know ſorrows like mine!
Never deſpair, never be curs'd as I am.
Yes, I will open my afflicted breaſt,
And ſadly ſhew thee ev'ry ſecret pain,
Tho' hell and darkneſs with new monſters teem,
Tho' furies, hideous to behold, aſcend,
Toſs their infernal flames, and yell around me;

Tho'

Tho' my offended father's angry ghoft
Should rife all pale and bloody juft before me,
Till my hair ftarted up, my fight were blafted,
And ev'ry trembling fibre fhook with horror;
Yet—yet—Oh, yet, I muft confefs I love thee!

Tel. Then let our envious ftars oppofe in vain
Their baleful influence, to thwart our joys;
My love fhall get the better of our fate,
Prevent the malice of that hard decree,
That feem'd to doom us to eternal forrows;
And yet in fpite of all we will be happy.

Sem. Let not that vain, that faithlefs hope deceive thee,
For 'tis refolv'd, 'tis certainly decreed,
Fix'd as that law by which imperial Jove,
According to his prefcience and his pow'r,
Ordains the fons of men to good or evil;
'Tis certain, ev'n our love, and all the mis'ries
Which muft attend that love, are not more certain,
Than that this moment we muft part for ever.

Tel. How! Part for ever? That's a way indeed
To make us miferable. Is there none,
No other fad alternative of grief,
No other choice but this?—What, muft we part for ever?

Sem. Oh, figh not, nor complain! Is not thy hand
Stain'd with my father's blood? Juftice and nature,
The gods demand it, and we muft obey:
Yes, I muft go, the preffing minutes call me,
Where thefe fond eyes fhall never fee thee more,
No more with languifhing delight gaze on thee,
Feed on thy face, and fill my heart with pleafure,
Where day and night fhall follow one another,
Tedious alike and irkfome, and alike
Wafted in weary lonelinefs and weeping.

Tel. Here then, my foul, take thy farewel of happinefs;
That and Semanthe fly together from thee:
Henceforth renounce all commerce with the world,
Nor hear, nor fee, nor once regard what paffes.
Let mighty kings contend, ambitious youth
Arm for the battle, feafons come and go,
Spring, fummer, autumn, with their fruitful pleafures,
And winter with its filver froft, let Nature
Difplay in vain her various pomp before thee,

'Tis

'Tis wretched all, 'tis all not worth thy care,
'Tis all a wildernefs, without Semanthe.

 Sem. One laft, one guilty proof, how much I love thee;
(Forgive it, gods!) Ceraunus and the Samians
Shall bring thee from me, ere I part from Ithaca,
That done, I'll hafte, I'll fly, as I have fworn,
For thy lov'd fake, far from the fight of man,
Fly to the pathlefs wilds, and facred fhades,
Where Dryads and the mountain-nymphs refort,
There beg the rural deities to pity me,
To end my woes, and let me on their hills,
Like Cypariffus, grow a mournful tree,
Or melt, like weeping Byblis, to a fountain.

 Tel. Since fate divides us then, fince I muft lofe thee,
For pity's fake, for love's, Oh, fuffer me,
Thus languifhing, thus dying, to approach thee,
And figh my laft adieu upon thy bofom!
Permit me, thus, to fold thee in my arms,
To prefs thee to my heart, to tafte thy fweets,
Thus pant, and thus grow giddy with delight.
Thus for my laft of moments gaze upon thee,
Thou beft, thou only joy—thou loft Semanthe!

 Sem. For ever I could liften; but the gods,
The cruel gods, forbid, and thus they part us.
Remember, Oh, remember me, Telemachus!
Perhaps thou wilt forget me; but no matter;
I will be true to thee, preferve thee ever
The fad companion of this faithful breaft,
While life and thought remain; and when at laft
I feel the icy hand of death prevail,
My heart-ftrings break, and all my fenfes fail,
I'll fix thy image in my clofing eye,
Sigh thy dear name, then lay me down and die. [*Exit.*

 Tel. And whither wilt thou wander, thou forlorn,
Abandon'd wretch?—The King thy father comes;
Fly from his angry frown, no matter whither;
Seek for the darkeft covert of the night,
Seek out for death, and fee if that can hide thee,
If there be any refuge thou canft prove,
Safe from purfuing forrow, fhame, and anxious love.
           [*Exit.*

           Enter

Enter Ulysses, Eumæus, *and Attendants.*

Ulyss. To doubt if there be juſtice with the gods,
Or if they care for aught below, were impious.
Oft have I try'd, and ever found them faithful ;
In all the various perils of my life,
In battles, in the midſt of flaming Troy,
In ſtormy ſeas, in thoſe dread regions where
Swarthy Cimmerians have their dark abode,
Divided from this world, and borderers on hell,
Ev'n there the providence of Jove was with me,
Defended, cheer'd, and bore me thro' the danger :
Nor is his pow'r, nor is my virtue leſs,
That I ſhould fear this rude, tumultuous herd.

Eum. So feeble is our band, ſo few our friends,
We hope not ſafety from ourſelves, but thee ;
In thee, our king, we truſt, in thee, our hero,
Favour'd of Heav'n, in all thy wars victorious.
But ſee where proud rebellion comes againſt thee, [*Shout.*
Securely fierce, and breathing bold defiance.
Now let our courage and our faith be try'd,
And if, unequal to thy great example,
We cannot conquer like thee, yet we can die for thee.

Shout, drums, and trumpets ; then enter Antinous, Cleon,
and Soldiers.

Ant. What bold invader of our laws and freedom,
Uſurps the ſacred name of king in Ithaca ?
Who dares to play the tyrant in our ſtate,
And in deſpite of hoſpitable Jove,
Defames our iſland with the blood of ſtrangers ?
Ulyss. Have you forgot me then, you men of Ithaca ?
Did I for this, amongſt the Grecian heroes,
Go forth to battle in my country's cauſe ?
Have I by arms and by ſucceſsful counſels
Deſerv'd a name from Aſia's wealthy ſhores
Ev'n to the weſtern ocean, to thoſe bounds
That mark the great Alcides' utmoſt labours,
And am I yet a ſtranger here——at home ?   [tions,
Ant. And wherefore didſt thou leave thoſe diſtant na-
Thro' which thy name and mighty deeds were ſpread ?
We never ſought to know thee, and now known,

Regard thee not, unlefs it be to punifh,
Thy violation of our public peace.

Ulyff. And doft thou dare, doft thou, audacious flave!
Thou rafh mifleader of this giddy crowd,
Doft thou prefume to match thyfelf with me,
To judge between a monarch and his people?
If Heav'n had not appointed me thy-mafter,
Yet it had made me fomething more than thou art,
Then when it made me what I am—Ulyffes!

Ant. Then be Ulyffes! echo it again,
And fee what homage thefe will pay the found:

[Pointing to the Soldiers.

Tell them the ftory of your Trojan wars,
How Hector drove you headlong to the fhore,
And threw his hoftile fires amidft your fleet;
Then mark with what applaufe they will receive thee.
Say, countrymen, will you revenge the princes
This wanderer has flain, and join with me?

Omnes. Antinous! Antinous!

Ant. What of your monarch?

Omnes. Drive him out to banifhment.   [carelefs,

Ulyff. Were there no gods in heav'n, or were they
And Jove had long forgot to wield his thunder,
And dart deftruction down on crimes like thine;
Yet, traitor, hope not thou to 'fcape from juftice,
Nor let rebellious numbers fwell thy pride;
For know, Ulyffes is alone fufficient
To punifh thee, and on thy perjur'd head
Revenge the wrongs of love and injur'd majefty.

Ant. And fee, I ftand prepar'd to meet thy vengeance;
Exert thy kingly pow'r, and fummon all
Thy ufeful arts and courage to thy aid:
And fince thy faithful Diomede is abfent,
Since valiant Ajax, with his feven-fold fhield,
No more fhall interpofe 'twixt thee and danger,
Invoke thofe friendly gods, whofe care thou art,
And let them fave thee, now affert thy caufe,
And render back to thy defpairing arms
The beauteous Queen, whom, in defpite of them
And thee, this happy night I made my prize.

Ulyff. Hear this, ye gods! he triumphs in the rape.
Moft glorious villain!——But we paufe too long.

On

On then, and tempt our fate, my gallant friends,
From this defier of the gods, this monster;
Let us redeem my Queen, or die together;
And, equal to our great forefathers' fame,
Defcend and join thofe demi-gods of Greece,
Who with their blood enrich'd the Dardan plains,
To vindicate a hufband's facred right.   [Shout.

Enter Arcas *wounded.*

Ant. What means that fudden thunder-clap of tumult?
Art thou not Arcas?—Thou art faint and bloody.

Arc. I have paid you the laft office of my friendfhip;
Scarce have I breath enough to fpeak your danger:
The furious Samians, led by young Telemachus,
Refiftlefs, fierce, and bearing all before them,
Have from the caftle forc'd the captive Queen;
Fir'd with fuccefs, they drive our fainting troops,
And hither urge their way with threat'ning cries,
Loudly demanding your devoted head,
A juft atonement for their murder'd lord.

Ulyff. Celeftial pow'rs! ye guardians of the juft!
This wond'rous work is yours, and yours be all the praife.

Ant. Confufion!—Wherefore didft thou not proclaim
My innocence, and warn them of their error?

Arc. Behold thefe wounds, through which my parting
Is hafting forth, and judge my truth by them.   [foul
Whate'er I could, I urg'd in thy defence;
But all was vain: with clamorous impatience,
They broke upon my fpeech, and fwore 'twas falfe;
Their Queen, the fair Semanthe, had accus'd thee,
And fix'd her royal father's death on thee.
If any way be left yet, hafte and fly;
Th' inconftant, faithlefs Ithacans join with them,
And all is loft——What dearer pledge than life
Can friendfhip afk? Behold I give it for thee.   [Dies.
                                                     [Shout.

Ulyff. They come! Succefs and happinefs attend us!
Pallas, and my victorious fon, fight for us!

Ant. Thou and thy gods at laft have got the better.
                                                [To Ulyffes.
Yet know, I fcorn to fly; that great ambition
That bid me firft afpire to love and empire,
Still brightly burns, and animates my foul.

                                                        Be

Be true, my fword, and let me fall reveng'd,
And I'll forgive ill fortune all befides.
          [Ulyffes, Antinous, *and their parties, fight.*

Enter Telemachus, *.* Ceraunus, *and Samian foldiers; they
    join* Ulyffes, *and drive* Antinous, Cleon, *and the reft
    off the ftage. Then enter at one door* Ulyffes, *at the
    other the Queen,* Mentor, *and Attendants.*

Ulyff. My Queen! my love!   [*Embracing.*
Qu. My hero! my Ulyffes!
Once more thou art reftor'd, once more I hold thee!
At length the gods have prov'd us to the utmoft,
Are fatisfy'd with what we have endur'd,
And never will afflict nor part us more.
'Tis not in words to tell thee what I've felt,
The forrows and the fears; ev'n yet I tremble,
Ev'n yet the fierce ideas fhock my foul,
And hardly yield to wonder and to joy.
    Men. A turn fo happy, and fo unexpected,
None but thofe over-ruling pow'rs who caus'd it
Could have forefeen. The beauteous Samian Princefs,
Within whofe gentle breaft revenge and tendernefs
Long ftrove, and long maintain'd a doubtful conflict,
At length was vanquifh'd by prevailing love,
And, happily, to fave the Prince, imputed
To falfe Antinous her father's death.
Heav'n has approv'd the fraud of fond affection,
The juft deceit, a falfhood fair as truth,
Since 'tis to that alone we owe our fafety.
          Enter Telemachus.
    Tel. Here let me kneel, and with my tears atone
                              [*Kneeling.*
The rafh offences of my heedlefs youth;   [*Ul. raifes him.*
Here offer the firft trophies of my fword,
And once more hail my father King of Ithaca.
Antinous, the rebel faction's chief,
Is now no more, and your repenting people
Wait with united homage to receive you;
The ftrangers too, to whom we owe our conqueft,
Hafte to embark, and fet their fwelling fails,
To bear the fad Semanthe back to Samos.

                              Joy!

Joy, like the cheerful morning, dawns on all,
And none but your unhappy fon fhall mourn.

Ulyſſ. Like thee, the pangs of parting love I've known,
My heart like thine has bled——But, Oh, my fon !
Sigh not, nor of the common lot complain ;
Thou, that art born a man, art born to pain :
For proof, behold my tedious twenty years,
All fpent in toil, and exercis'd in cares.
'Tis true, the gracious gods are kind at laft,
And well reward me here for all my forrows paft.

[*Exeunt.*

End of the Fifth Act.

EPILOGUE.

Spoken by SEMANTHE.

*JUST going to take water, at the stairs
I stopp'd, and came again to beg your pray'rs;
You see how ill my love has been repaid,
That I am like to live and die a maid;
Poetic rules and justice to maintain,
I to the woods am order'd back again,
To Madam Cynthia and her virgin train.
'Tis an uncomfortable life they lead;
Instead of quilts and down, the sylvan bed,
With skins of beasts, with leaves and moss, is spread;
No morning toilets do their chambers grace,
Where famous pearl cosmetics find a place,
With powder for the teeth, and plaister for the face.
But in defiance of complexion, they,
Like arrant housewives, rise by break of day,
Cut a brown crust, saddle their nags, and mounting,
In scorn of the green-sickness, ride a hunting.
Your sal, and hartshorn drops, they deal not in;
They have no vapours, nor no witty spleen.
No coffee to be had; and I am told,
As to the tea they drink, 'tis mostly cold.
For conversation, nothing can be worse,
'Tis all amongst themselves, and that's the curse;
One topic there, as here, does seldom fail,
We women rarely want a theme to rail;
But, bating that one pleasure of backbiting,
There is no earthly thing they can delight in.
There are no Indian houses to drop in,
And fancy stuffs, and chuse a pretty screen,
To while away an hour or so——I swear
These cups are pretty, but they're deadly dear;
And if some unexpected friend appear,
The dev'l!—Who could have thought to meet you here?
We should but very badly entertain
You that delight in toasting and champagne.
But keep your tender persons safe at home;
We know you hate hard riding: but if some
Tough, honest country fox-hunter would come,
Visit our goddess, and her maiden court,
'Tis ten to one, but we may shew him sport.*